# FIRES OF THE HEART

**DAWN PUT HER HANDS ON HIS SHOULDERS.**

"As Madam Ching says, Jack, you are a special kind of man."

"Do I detect a hint of jealousy?"

Dawn felt her cheeks flaming. "That's absurd!"

"Is it?" He pulled her against him and bent his face to hers. Stunned, Dawn offered no resistance.

Jack's mouth closed over hers tenderly. She shut her eyes and went limp in his embrace. Then, as the ardor of the kiss heightened, and the blood pumped faster in her veins, Dawn stirred to life. A spark glowed at the very core of her being. Desire obliterated all sense of conscience or commitment to her husband.

They separated then, and Jack held her at arm's length. "All the rules have changed out here, Dawn. Back in the civilized world we were snatched from, I would have cut off my hand before I touched you, even though I've been aching for you since the first day we met. But this is a different world, and you and I are different from who we were before this happened."

"Dearest," sighed Dawn. "I want you now."

D1010417

# FIRES
## OF THE
# HEART

## STEPHANIE BLAKE

PLAYBOY
PAPERBACKS

FIRES OF THE HEART

Copyright © 1982 by Stephanie Blake

Cover illustration copyright © 1982 by PEI Books, Inc.

Published simultaneously in the United States and Canada by Playboy Paperbacks, New York, New York. Printed in the United States
of America. Library of Congress Catalog Card Number: 81-84140.
First edition.

Books are available at quantity discounts for promotional and industrial use. For further information, write to Premium Sales, Playboy
Paperbacks, 1633 Broadway, New York, New York 10019.

ISBN: 0-867-21059-1

First printing May 1982.

# BOOK ONE

# CHAPTER ONE

*"Beans are on the table, daylight's in the swamp.*
*You lazy lumberjacks, ain't you ever gettin' up?"*

The popular ballad of the lumber camps was sung every morning by the cook's helper, an apple-cheeked boy of fourteen, when he came out on the back steps of the cookhouse with an iron stove poker and beat out reveille on the big gut hammer that hung from an eave on a length of bailing wire.

Wielding the poker with both hands, he swung it around inside the steel triangle until the clanging echoed across the silent forest like a firehouse klaxon. The ice and snow crusted on the rusty metal shattered in a needle spray that stung his face and hands.

"Day-ay-light in the swamp!" he bellowed. "Day-ay-light in the swamp!"

Overhead the stars were brilliant in a black velvet

sky, and the crescent moon dipped low above the frozen Tittabawassee River. It was 4:30 A.M. on a cold January morning in the year 1880, the beginning of a new day for thousands of loggers in the Michigan woods.

In the large, rambling hilltop home of Walter Roberts, founder and owner of the Roberts Lumber Company, lights shone in two of the upstairs bedroom windows as Roberts and his daughter Dawn got out of bed and lit their oil lamps. Shivering from the cold, the tall girl, in her sixteenth year, pulled the voluminous Mother Hubbard nightgown over her head and tossed it onto the bed. She appraised herself in the long mirror hanging over her dresser. Her naked body had a wraithlike cast in the pale illumination of the lamp. She was a big, strong girl, a woman really. Broad of shoulder and hip, slender through the waist, with long shapely limbs, she was unquestionably feminine. Her green eyes were luminous in the looking glass.

Hurriedly she dressed in long woolen underwear, a heavy lumberjack's shirt, and two pullover sweaters —bulky garb that camouflaged her pear-shaped breasts. Her heavy wool trousers were lined with two additional layers of wool, and she had on two pairs of heavy wool socks inside her hobnailed boots, which laced up to the knee.

She braided her long, straight red hair, standing back from the mirror so that her breath wouldn't fog up the glass. Ready for breakfast, she clomped through the upper hall and down the stairs.

Her mother, Tess, clad in a fleece-lined robe, was stoking the wood cookstove, preparing to make breakfast. Dawn would have preferred to eat in the cookhouse with the camp's loggers, but her mother was adamant on that score.

"It's bad enough you look like those jacks and walk like them, but you're not about to talk like them. I know what kind of language they bandy around when they're eating!"

Dawn grinned. "What do you think they talk like when they're working? English drawing-room chit-chat?"

Her father came in from the back porch, carrying a load of firewood. He smiled and put an arm around Dawn's shoulders.

"Feeling fit and sassy? We got a long day ahead of us."

"Can't wait to get an ax in my hand," she responded.

"That's my—" He caught himself before he almost said the wrong word. "—girl," he finished.

Walter had fathered three girls and not one son to work shoulder to shoulder with him in the swamp and to take over the family business one day. Although he would have cut out his tongue before he would ever betray his secret disappointment to his beloved daughters or to his wife, Dawn shared a special empathy with her father, and she sensed the void in his life. And from the time she sat on his knee as a child, she had made a dedicated effort to replace the son that fate had deprived him of. A tomboy, she cultivated the friendship of her male schoolmates, competing with them in athletic events and holding her own against the muscular competitors. At the age of twelve, she had decked the eighth-grade bully with an overhand right that had broken his nose.

Dawn's favorite pastime, though, was to accompany her father on his daily chores in the swamp—a forest of white pine that ran from the western tip of Lake Erie to the western tip of Lake Superior and contained more timber than could be cut in a thousand years. Early in the 1850s, because its gold reserves were low, the U.S. government had put up for public sale, at $1.25 an acre, its vast timberlands by the shores of the Great Lakes. At bargain rates like these, it was no time at all before the lake states had replaced Maine as the world's lumber capital; the quality of the pine was better as well.

During the ensuing years, the Erie Canal was swamped by the heaviest traffic in its history, conveying billions of feet of lumber to the East and thousands of migrating lumberjacks westward. It was a roistering, ribald era for the settlements along the waterway. The hard-fighting, hard-drinking redshirts swept through them like an invading army, leaving a trail of broken bottles and broken heads in their wake. The wise barkeepers quickly learned to take down their mirrors and stow excess glassware and bric-à-brac under the counter as soon as the loggers' theme song came echoing down the "Big Ditch."

*I've got a mule and her name is Sal,*
*Fifteen miles on the Erie Canal*
*She's a good worker and a good old pal,*
*Fifteen miles on the Erie Canal.*

The loggers settled Saginaw and Bay City, blazed a trail up the Saginaw River, and fanned out up the Flint, Shiawassee, Cass, and Tittabawassee rivers throughout all of Michigan. The majority of them lived as if there were no tomorrow, content to fell their allotment of pine, draw their paychecks, eat three square meals a day, and blow their money on liquor and women in Saginaw or Bay City.

A few of the more ambitious ones—like Walter Roberts, a young Canadian from Montreal—realized that there was more to be gained in the lumber business than shouldering an ax. Roberts saved every cent he earned for two years and invested it in a tract of timber along the Saginaw River. The eastern marketplace was insatiable, and the Roberts Lumber Company doubled, tripled, and quadrupled its holdings in successive years.

Walter married the daughter of an Irish pub keeper, Tess O'Hara, built a large house on a hill overlooking the main camp and fathered three daughters. But not the son he wanted so badly. "Dawn is the next best thing," he consoled himself. And, to the despair of his wife and his other two daughters, he encouraged Dawn's masculine endeavors.

She became the darling of all the lumberjacks who worked the Roberts timberlands, an engaging figure walking along at the side of big Walt Roberts, matching him stride for stride, with her gorgeous red hair gathered up under her red wool logger's cap. Seeing her for the first time, new hands almost always mistook her for a slender youth until they were enlightened by older crewmen.

Only the best axmen qualified for duty as sawyers, felling the trees. By the time she was sixteen, Dawn rated the highest accolade that one sawyer could bestow on another: "The scarf of her undercut is as smooth as the cut of a saw."

Since she didn't possess the physique or the physical strength to work at this laborious job for very long, Dawn concentrated her efforts on limbing and bucking the trees after they were felled—lopping off the branches and cutting them into logs of manageable length, then stacking them in cold decks.

Working with the high riggers up in the treetops, Dawn was as surefooted as a cat. Certain trees were left standing to be limbed and topped so that blocks and tackles could be strung up on them for loading the massive logs onto sleds. Every night during the winter a watering detail would spray down the roads leading to the river, and by morning they would be glazed over with ice so that the horse-drawn sleds could be dragged over the slick paths with a minimum of effort. Hills were hazardous, and lengths of heavy chain were wrapped around the sleds' runners to brake the descent. Even so, an occasional sled would get out of control and skate off the road, crushing the horses and very often the driver. A teamster who sluiced his rig in this manner and survived was blackballed all over the swamp.

At the river, the logs were unloaded and yarded into stacks near long wooden chutes that ran down the bluffs to the water's edge. When the ice broke in the spring, they would be sent down the rollways into the river and floated downriver to the mills.

On this morning, like every other morning, Dawn and her father ate a hearty breakfast of flapjacks, thick-sliced bacon, eggs, and homemade bread and butter topped off by pie or cake and steaming coffee.

"It's a wonder you don't get fat as a horse," Tess commented as she watched her daughter help herself to a second helping of eggs and pancakes.

"Haven't got an ounce of blubber on my body," Dawn boasted. It was true. Standing naked in the bathtub, she would regularly pinch her midriff; she could barely grasp a fold of skin between her fingers.

"What's our schedule for today, Dad?" she asked.

"We're high-rigging up at the north fork. Got to get the logs they've been cutting all week to the river before the thaw sets in."

"That means you'll be late," Tess said. "The girls and I will eat by ourselves, and I'll save you and Dawn hot plates."

"You do that. We could be out there as long as fourteen hours."

A short day for the loggers of Michigan was ten to twelve hours, as long as there was daylight. During a typical stint in the swamp, the men were afforded two breaks to gather around the Mary Anne, the horse-drawn chow wagon. The cookie, the cook's teenage helper, would ladle hot coffee or tea into huge mugs and pass out enormous sandwiches, usually fatty slabs of pork between two-inch slices of bread. This was one aspect of logging life that Dawn declined to partake of. She preferred to bring along meat and cheese sandwiches from home.

When father and daughter stepped out of the house into the icy blue dawn, the moisture on their lips froze instantly. Dawn took a small jar of petroleum jelly out of her knapsack, and they greased up their mouths and around their eyelids.

"This is one for the record books," Walt observed as he looked at the thermometer alongside the back door, whose mercury hovered just below the minus-20 marker.

They pulled on their fleece-lined leather gloves, wound their long woolen mufflers a few extra times around their throats, and turned up the high collars of their sheepskin coats. Then they walked down the hill to the compound.

The cookhouse squatted in the center of the camp, a five-acre clearing hacked out of thick pine forest. Flanking it were two bunkhouses—long, narrow rectangular buildings that sheltered a hundred men each under tar-paper roofs. Inside, triple-decker wooden bunks were built flush against the side walls. The only other appointments were the deacon seats, two rough split-log benches that ran along the bottom tier of bunks on both sides of the bunkhouse.

Despite the hard wooden bunks and spruce-bough mattresses, the men slept soundly; after swinging an ax twelve hours a day at sub-zero temperatures, a logger could curl up on a tree stump and fall asleep instantly.

Although the bunkhouses provided protection against snow and rain, the wind whistled freely through the uncaulked log walls, and frequently it was just as cold inside as outside. But when the air was still, the body heat of the men and the wood fire blazing in a shallow pit in the middle of the earth floor combined to maintain a relatively comfortable temperature.

Before the last jarring echoes of the gut hammer had faded away, the loggers were rolling out of their bunks, grunting, coughing, spitting, cursing as they bumped into one another in the pitch darkness. A crew boss threw a pile of fresh logs on the glowing embers in the fire pit. The flames licked up the dry bark, and a spiral of smoke and sparks rose lazily toward the round hole in the roof.

"Come on, you lice. Rise and shine," he growled. "We gotta let some daylight into this swamp before sunup."

By the time Roberts and Dawn arrived on the scene,

the loggers were crowded into the cookhouse, sitting hip to hip on benches at long, rough pine tables. The cookies were serving them tin platters heaped with salt pork and great slabs of bread covered with molasses and beans.

At the back end of the room, Lars Swensen, the cook, worked stripped to the waist over a huge open-pit fire. Sweat glistened in the thick hair that covered his muscular shoulders. Swensen was an angry-looking Swede with a handsome handlebar mustache. Like most lumber-camp cooks he ran a strict cookhouse. Horseplay and idle conversation were forbidden. You wolfed down your food and got out as fast as you could to make room for those who were lined up outside waiting to eat.

The men on line greeted the boss and his daughter affably. They all respected Walt Roberts; he was a man's man, a true logger like them. His hands still bore the badge of honor of the profession—calluses as hard as armadillo shells. He was not afraid to wield an ax with the sawyers and high riggers, and when there was a logjam, he was the first man to grab a peavey hook and leap into the thick of it.

They respected Dawn as well, and as soon as she approached the line, all blasphemous or salacious language ceased.

"We'll be over at the office," Roberts informed them. "Call us when you're ready to move out."

The office was a long rectangular building like the bunkhouses, only smaller. One of the cookies had stoked the iron potbelly stove in the center of the room, and when they entered, the metal sides were cherry red.

"Brrr . . . that feels good." Dawn went to it and held

out her hands to receive the warmth it radiated. Two walls of the room were covered with file cabinets. On either side of the stove was a large rolltop desk. They removed their jackets and gloves and sat down at the desks. Roberts took a stack of orders out of the incoming box on one side of the green blotter.

"Feel up to a little dictation, honey?" he inquired.

"Fire away." Dawn had devised her own brand of shorthand, and took dictation faster than her father's former secretary and assistant, who had graduated from a Chicago secretarial school.

She was halfway through the third letter when the crew chief knocked on the door.

"We're set to move," he called out.

They put on their winter gear and left the office.

"There's quite a backup on those acknowledgment letters," Roberts said to Dawn. "Tell you what—suppose you come back with the Mary Anne at lunch break and process as many orders as you can. Dennis Price will be here at three to bring the company books up to date. You can give him a hand."

Dawn's heart did a little flip-flop. Dennis Price was a good-looking young accountant from the East who worked for a half dozen of the biggest lumber camps in the swamp.

"Anything you say, Dad," she said casually, thinking that she would be back in time to take a bath and wash her hair before Dennis arrived.

Dawn had had a crush on the young man since the age of twelve. He had always regarded her as a kid sister and used to call her pet names such as "honey" and "kitten." But with her accelerating pubescence he avoided such endearments. She sensed that now he was very much aware of her as a woman. At Christmastime she had kissed him underneath the mistletoe she had hung up from an office beam, and he had blushed to the roots of his hair. He was always careful to avoid unnecessary physical contact with her.

As they walked toward the sleigh that would take them up the Saginaw to the north fork, Dawn cast a sideways glance at her father and smiled. Little did he guess that dwelling within his rugged, roughshod tomboy was a rather substantial woman—a female capable of demonstrating demureness, tenderness, femininity, and ardent passion. Dawn was still a virgin, but an extremely impatient one.

Sitting cross-legged among the loggers in the back of the lead sled, Dawn joined in with great enthusiasm as they sang their lusty woodsmen's ballads.

*"My lover was a logger,*
*There's none like him today.*
*If you'd pour whiskey on it,*
*He would eat a bale of hay.*

*And so I lost my lover,*
*And to this café I come,*
*And here I wait till someone*
*Stirs coffee with his thumb."*

A lover. Yes, Dawn mused, with determination. It was time she found herself a lover.

# CHAPTER TWO

The Mary Anne arrived back at the Roberts camp shortly before two. Dawn raced up the hill to the house and burst into the kitchen, where her two sisters were canning tomatoes that had arrived from southern California that same morning by freight train.

"Where's Mama?" she demanded breathlessly.

"Down in the root cellar fetching more jars," Peg informed her.

Peg, at eighteen, was the oldest of the Roberts girls. She was statuesque, with strong features and gray eyes. Immaculately groomed and coiffured, she wore a frilly princess gown. Her brown hair was rolled up in two fancy curls at the back of her head that were held in place by mother-of-pearl combs.

"I have to hurry and bathe. Would you ask her please to iron my green tunic skirt and the petticoat with the wide ruffles at the hem."

Lucy, the youngest at twelve, gaped at her incredulously. "I don't believe it! A bath at two o'clock in the afternoon and wearing Sunday-go-to-meeting clothes! Did you hear her, Peg?"

Lucy was the prettiest and most delicate of the sisters, with fragile porcelain features, wide-set violet eyes, and hair like fine, spun gold. In her dress of Swiss cotton batiste trimmed with ruffles and frills and dusty-pink lace, she looked like a china doll.

Peg put a hand on Dawn's forehead. "She's delirious. It must be the flu."

"Maybe she's got a beau?" Lucy's eyes flashed mischievously.

"Leave me alone!"

She stormed out of the kitchen, but not before Peg observed, "What are you blushing for, Sis?"

The Roberts house had the distinction, rare even in big cities like Chicago, of having a kerosene-powered hot-water heater in the bathroom. Dawn filled the tub half full and got in. She lay back, luxuriating in the soothing caress of the hot water on her aching muscles. Lazily she soaped her neck, shoulders, and breasts. Her nipples tingled and stiffened against her palms. The perfumed soap, the steam, and the buoyancy of her body in the water created a highly sensual environment. Her breath caught in her throat as she lathered her pubic hair and between her thighs. Her loins throbbed with hot blood. Time and time again she had vowed to abstain from what the girls at school called "diddling" herself. But she almost always succumbed, and now she floated with her eyes closed as her mind conjured up lewd images of Dennis entering the bathroom, undressing, and climbing into the tub with her. The ecstasy was too much to bear any longer, and the waves of fulfillment commenced.

When she emerged from the bathroom, she found the dress and petticoat she had requested laid out neatly on her bed. At the back of her bottom bureau drawer, hidden underneath a pile of work pants, was a lace-trimmed camisole and French panties of knitted organdy silk that she had purchased surreptitiously the last time the family had visited Chicago.

Feeling as wicked as original sin, she donned them and put on the petticoat and dress. Then she brushed out her auburn hair until it lay across her back like a glistening fan. Last of all she put on a pair of silk stockings held up by scarlet garters and a pair of flat satin slippers to minimize her height. In her everyday boots she was as tall as Dennis.

Bracing herself for her sisters' reactions, she left her room and went down the stairs, treading very softly. If she was lucky, she might be able to get her coat and boots out of the hall closet without attracting attention. But her heart fell when she reached the first landing. Awaiting her were her mother and two sisters, all wearing knowing smirks on their faces.

"Dawn's got a boyfriend!" Lucy jeered.

"Who is it?" Peg asked.

"I have a pretty good idea," Tess said. "Daddy has mentioned him several times. Says Dawn makes goo-goo eyes at him whenever he's working down at the office. That young accountant."

"Dennis Price!" Lucy exclaimed.

"That's a joke," Peg snapped with a tinge of irritation in her voice. "Why would an older man like Dennis Price be interested in a child like Dawn?"

"I am *not* a child, Margaret, and Dennis is *not* an older man. He's twenty-six."

Peg drew herself up haughtily. "He's even too old for me."

"You know, Margaret, age has nothing to do with maturity. In many ways *I* am far more a woman of the world than you are."

Tess Roberts was laughing so hard she almost doubled over. "Woman of the world! Oh, wait until your father hears about this."

Dawn opened the hall closet and removed her snow boots and long winter dress coat. "I don't have time to stand here and make childish chatter. I must get down to the office and get Father's books ready for Dennis. And I have a deluge of orders to process and acknowledge."

"All right, woman of the world," Peg gibed. "Why is it you go out of your way constantly to behave like a man? Spending most of your time in man's clothing. Talking like a man. Walking like a man. Associating with those crude, uncouth loggers."

Dawn's eyes lit up with anger. She opened her mouth to speak, thought better of it, and compressed her lips. As she exited, Peg flung a parting taunt after her:

"Bye-bye, Daddy's big tough boy."

Tears dimmed Dawn's vision as she hurried down the snowy path to the road.

When Dennis Price arrived at the office at ten minutes past three, Dawn was typing a letter to a New York lumber firm. It was she who had persuaded her father to purchase Remington's new and revolutionary mechanical writing machine.

"It sure lends class to our letters," Roberts conceded after inspecting the first samples she produced.

"Do you think you can learn to write on the contraption?"

In less than two weeks Dawn could type in five minutes a letter that would have required fifteen minutes in painstaking hand lettering.

She looked up from the typewriter and smiled. "Hello, Dennis. Dad said you were going to bring the books up to date. I've laid them out for you on that table in the corner. If you want, you can move closer to the stove."

"No, that will be fine, Dawn. I've got on two sweaters under my coat." He removed his topcoat and fur cap and hung them on a clothes tree by the door. "I didn't expect to find you here this early."

"Dad asked me to come back with the chow wagon and clear up some of the back work."

Dennis Price was a sturdy, medium-sized man with broad shoulders and slim hips. He had a strong jaw and a snub nose. His ruddy complexion and Irish blue eyes gave him a rough, sexy look. Dawn ached to have him touch her with his long, slender, sensitive fingers.

He sat down on a corner of her desk and rubbed his hands together. "Got to thaw out before I start work. An accountant's no good with frozen fingers." He was regarding Dawn in a way that made her feel very special.

Summoning up her courage, she held out her hands to him. "Here, I'll warm them up for you, Dennis. My hands are like two hot-water bottles."

"Oh, that won't be necessary, Dawn. Thanks just the same." He laughed self-consciously.

"No, I mean it, Dennis. Just look at your fingers. They're blue from cold."

"I forgot my gloves."

He coughed nervously as she stood up and came around the desk to where he was sitting. Before he knew what was happening, Dawn had lifted his hands, placed them together, and clasped them between her own.

"There now. How does that feel?"

"Warm. Oh yes, very warm indeed."

"I'm very warm-blooded."

He flushed and averted his eyes.

"Do you like my dress?"

"Yes, you look very pretty today. Is it some special occasion?"

"Not really. Mother and my sisters are always tormenting me because I wear pants and work shirts." She giggled. "Maybe they have a point. You know, sometimes I forget I'm a girl."

"I could never forget you're a girl. An extremely lovely girl." His eyes met her eyes. "It's amazing. It seems only yesterday that you were a little squirt in pigtails. And here you are now, a grown woman."

"Yes, I am. And it's about time you started treating me like a woman." She moved closer to him, throwing back her shoulders to emphasize her breasts. She pressed her thigh against his knee. Even through the layers of their clothing, the sensation sent shivers along her spine.

"I don't understand," he said, badly flustered. He tried to slide off the corner of the desk, but that only resulted in even more intimate contact. His knee slid between her thighs and her breasts brushed against him.

"I say, I'm dreadfully sorry, Dawn."

"Sorry for what?" She placed her hands on his shoulders and bent her head so that their lips were only inches apart.

"Good Lord! This is madness!" he said tersely. "But I can't help myself." He put his arms around her waist and drew her to him. Their mouths touched—tenderly at first, then with mounting ardor and urgency. Dawn pressed herself against his hard muscular thigh, delighting in the surging thrust of his masculinity against her quivering belly.

Abruptly, he regained control of himself and pushed her away to arm's length.

"I must be out of my mind. You, too. Your father would have me tarred and feathered if he knew what we were doing."

"He's not about to know."

"I'm a lecherous child molester." He stood up, covering the embarrassing bulge in his trousers with a manila folder.

"I'm not a child." She grabbed one of his hands and pressed it to her breasts. "Do I feel like a child, Dennis?" She snatched the folder from him and pressed against him, undulating her hips against his erection. "Tell the truth. Do I feel like a child?"

"No, you don't. But this has to stop. If you keep it up I'll go out of my mind with lust and rape you right here on the floor."

"I won't resist. I want you just as desperately as you want me. Will you make love to me, Dennis? I've dreamed so many times that you and I were together." She laughed. "Just before, in my bath, I fantasized that you were in the tub with me."

"What a wanton wench you are. And here I've been thinking you were made of sugar and spice and everything nice."

"I am a hot-blooded female in desperate need of a mate."

"Let's forget about the books and go someplace where we can be alone," he said.

"Where?"

"My place."

Dennis was renting a small cottage on the outskirts of the village five miles from the camp.

At that moment they heard heavy boots stomping on the steps outside. Dawn flew around the desk and sat down while Dennis rushed over to the bookkeeping table. When Tess Roberts entered the office they were working industriously over papers and ledgers.

"I just baked an apple pie and I thought you and Dennis might enjoy some with hot coffee, dear." She put a wicker hamper on the desk. "How are you, Mr. Price? It's been a month since you were here last."

"Very well, Mrs. Roberts. And you?"

"Holding my own."

He stood up and made a stiff bow.

"You look as if you might have a fever?" she said with concern.

"No, no, it's wind chap. I have delicate skin."

Dawn's laughter startled her mother. "Whatever are you laughing at, Dawn? Chapped skin is no laughing matter."

"I'm sorry, Mother. It reminded me of something one of the girls at school used to say."

"Well, never mind. Serve Mr. Price his pie and coffee before it gets cold." She opened the hamper and removed an urn of coffee and a platter containing two huge slabs of flaky apple pie. "There are small plates and forks, too. Now I have to get back to the house and prepare for supper. Would you care to join us, Mr. Price?"

"That's awfully kind of you, ma'am, but I already have an engagement tonight."

"Well, the offer is an open invitation, anytime you are in the neighborhood."

"Thank you. I'll remember."

After her mother had departed, Dawn sat down at the desk and buried her face in her hands. Her body shook with mirth.

"No, it's wind chap," she mimicked Dennis. "I have delicate skin."

He blushed again. "It's the truth. Look, let's have the pie and coffee and get down to work. It's too late now to go to my place in any case."

"Suppose I ride over there tomorrow afternoon?"

"That's wonderful. I'll work at home."

"The waiting will be sheer torture."

"Will it? You are a virgin, I assume?"

"I am, as you will discover for yourself."

"Then you've been waiting sixteen years. Another day shouldn't make any difference."

"When one is on the threshold of a new experience, the suspense and anticipation can be agonizing," she said teasingly.

She served him pie and a mug of coffee and resumed typing the company letters.

That evening at the dinner table, Dawn endured a sound roasting at the hands of her sisters.

"I wonder how much work was accomplished this afternoon at the office?" Peg speculated.

"I wonder what else was accomplished?" Lucy taunted.

"Don't tease your sister," Tess reprimanded them.

"When I arrived there with the pie and coffee, Mr. Price and Dawn were deeply engrossed in their work."

"But were they working just before you walked in?" Peg wondered.

Dawn was furious at herself for blushing, but Peg's random thrust had been right on the mark. She threw down her napkin and stood up, striving to maintain her dignity.

"I think I'll retire to my room, if you will please excuse me. I'm really very weary."

"Sweet dreams of Dennis," Lucy called after her.

Upstairs, Dawn lit the oil lamp and turned it up full. She undressed and stood before the mirror, admiring herself. Dawn Roberts had no false modesty. She had a fine body and she knew it. She cupped her breasts in her hands and lifted them, gently stroking the nipples with her thumbs. *Tomorrow Dennis will be caressing me.*

She ran her hands down her sides, along the indentation of her waist and the curve of her hips, across the soft swell of her abdomen and down into the gleaming red pubic hair.

Flaming desire engulfed her. Gooseflesh spread over her bosom, her belly, her buttocks. She shut her eyes and emitted a long, shuddering moan. *Take me, Dennis, take me! If you don't take me soon, I'll go mad.*

# CHAPTER THREE

The next morning, when the summons of the gut hammer echoed across the camp, Dawn rolled over and went back to sleep. Some time later, her father knocked on her bedroom door.

"Dawn, are you up?"

"Come in, Dad," she called out. She sat up, yawning and stretching.

"You're still in bed?" he said with surprise.

"Yes, I don't think I'll go out with the crew today. I think I may be coming down with a cold."

"Sure, honey. We'll have to get along without you. You stay in bed and rest."

She lay back on the pillow and stared out the window. In the pre-dawn obsidian sky, the Milky Way cut a luminous swath across the heavens like a river of diamonds. She remembered what today was, and a sensation of warm, pleasurable lassitude invaded her limbs.

She slept until nine, when Lucy came into her room. "What are you doing home? Are you sick?"

"Slight case of sniffles."

"That never stopped you before. Yesterday, primping up in all your best finery. Now in bed until nine. Something is definitely amiss with you, Sister."

"Leave me alone. I've got to dress."

Dawn spent the morning at the company office, processing orders and typing letters to customers. She went back to the house at lunchtime.

"What are your plans for this afternoon?" her mother inquired. "More office work?"

"No, I thought I'd get some fresh air. Dusty hasn't had much exercise lately."

Dusty was the palomino gelding Dawn's father had given her on her twelfth birthday.

"That's a good idea. Don't overdo it, though, in this bitter cold."

"I won't."

Peg and Lucy were in the sewing room making new gowns. On her way down the hall, Dawn poked her head into the room.

"Tut, tut, don't you two look domestic."

Peg stuck out her tongue. "And don't you look remarkably tidy for horseback riding. I believe that's the first time you've worn that chic riding habit since Mother made it for you."

Dawn felt her cheeks burn. She responded carefully. "I know, and I've been feeling guilty about it. Mama worked so hard on it." She did a pirouette. "Do you like it?"

"Ravishing." Lucy looked too innocent. "I'm sure Dennis will love it."

Dawn swallowed her mounting anger. "Dennis? I'm riding alone. I don't think that eastern tenderfoot has ever been on a horse in his life."

She strode down the hall to the door. Before she put on her heavy mackinaw, she appraised herself in the full-length mirror on the closet door.

The matching tweed riding jacket and breeches might have been molded to her figure. Under the jacket she wore a white satin blouse with a black string tie at the throat. Her riding boots were polished to mirror brightness. She decided against wearing a hat. She had worked too hard on her hair, which was rolled up in back and held in place by small barrettes.

She went back to the barn, where the handyman was pitching hay out of the loft. He tipped his cap.

"Do anything for you, Miss Roberts?"

"No, thanks. I'm going riding, but I can saddle up Dusty myself."

The big horse whinnied and slapped his tail against the stall when he saw his mistress.

"Hello, baby. Are you glad to see me? Of course you are." She stroked the horse's nose and kissed him on the snout. "Come along."

Ten minutes later they were galloping over the trail that led to the village.

Dennis must have been watching for her at the window, because as soon as she rode into the yard, he came out the door.

"Here, I'll put Dusty back in the shed. There's plenty of feed there for him. Dobbin and Chet will enjoy the company."

After Dusty was settled in, they went into the house. It was small but extremely cozy with an abundance of overstuffed furniture and pillows. There was a fireplace on one wall ablaze with aromatic pine logs. The hearth was covered by a large bear-skin rug.

"Sit down," he invited her, shifting nervously from one foot to the other and rubbing the back of his neck.

Dawn felt a bit awkward herself. After all, this would be her very first time with a man. Actually, she had never even been alone with a man in his house before. She sat down gingerly on the edge of the sofa.

"You look smashing in that outfit," he told her.

"Thank you."

"Can I get you some refreshments? I have some wine in the kitchen. Or would you prefer apple brandy?"

"The wine will be fine, thank you."

While he was in the kitchen, Dawn wandered around the room, picking up knickknacks and looking at the pictures on the wall, most of which had a western motif. She stood before the fire warming her icy hands, which were cold from anxiety rather than because of the frigid weather.

Dennis returned with a tray, two wine glasses, and a bottle of wine.

"What shall we drink to?" he asked.

She hesitated. "I can't think of anything very original. What about 'To us'?"

"All right. And to this very special day as well."

They touched glasses and sipped the wine.

"I love your bear rug."

"It's comfortable and warm."

They sat down on the rug, Dennis with his legs

crossed and Dawn with her knees drawn up under her chin and her arms clasped around her legs.

"This is cozy," she said.

They finished the first glass of wine and Dennis poured them a second. By then Dawn was feeling relaxed, flushed, and excited. She put down the empty glass on the floor next to the rug and turned to him.

"Dennis . . . kiss me."

She lay back in his arms and lifted her mouth to his as he bent over her. His tongue explored the sensitive membrane underneath her tongue, triggering a rush of blood through her body that inflamed her breasts and her loins. She was consumed with desire.

Dawn sat up briefly and removed her jacket. She opened the buttons down the front of her blouse, then lay back in Dennis's embrace again. She took one of his hands and guided it inside her satin blouse, under which she wore no undergarment. The touch of his hand on her breast caused Dawn to writhe in delight. Her taut nipple was like a small transmitter. Every time his fingers brushed it, waves of pleasure were sent coursing through her body.

"Take off your trousers," she whispered to Dennis.

While he was obliging her, she lay back on the rug and lifted her hips so that she could slip off her breeches. She removed her blouse but left on her French panties. She had heard from older girls that a man becomes more excited when a girl leaves something to his imagination.

Dennis stripped down to his drawers. Then once more he took her in his arms. The crescendo of their lovemaking built like a Beethoven symphony. His hands seemed to be everywhere on her body. Her breasts and her throat. Teasing the fine down on her belly and buttocks. Causing her to cry out as he stroked her clitoris.

Her fingers were barely able to encircle his tumescent penis. She stroked him lovingly and caressed his hard, tight testicles.

"Oh, my darling," she gasped. "How fiercely I want you inside me. Don't wait another moment."

They tore off their underwear and Dawn lay back on the rug, opening her thighs to receive him. Suddenly she felt reverent, mystical. There was a decidedly religious magic to the sexual ritual, particularly when it was her initiation to womanhood.

She met his rhythmic thrusts with an eagerness equal to his own. Despite the pain from his assault on her maidenhead, she had the strange sensation that she had been doing this all her life. It was that natural, that comfortable. Her climax was like nothing she had felt in her private explorations of herself. It seemed that her brain was temporarily displaced from her flesh, observing the writhing bodies on the rug with vicarious delight. Each surge of passion crested higher than the previous one, like crashing waves in a storm at sea. The final height cast her into nirvana.

"Why does it have to end?" She sighed as they lay limp, side by side, hand in hand.

Dennis chuckled. "So that we can renew ourselves for the next time."

"Time after time after time, through all eternity," she whispered.

Dennis braced himself on an elbow and looked down into her dreamy eyes. "Through all eternity. Yes, that is exactly the point of what I am about to say. Dawn, this is not what the loggers call a roll in the hay. I've been in love with you for some time now, and have wanted you so badly. And I will want you forever, through all eternity. In other words, darling, I want you to become my wife."

"Your wife?" Dawn was stunned.

"Don't you care enough about me to consider marriage?"

She reached out and stroked his cheek. "My dear love, it's not that. I love you, too. I'd be honored to become your wife. It's just that . . ."

"Your family won't approve of me, is that it?"

"No, no, darling. Both Mother and Father think you are a fine, upstanding young man. My sisters like you, too."

"Then what is the obstacle?"

"I don't have to tell you that I am my father's favorite."

"Favorite daughter, I know that. He dotes on you."

"Favorite daughter . . ." An enigmatic smile spread over her lovely face. "There is something funny, ironic really . . . Dad doesn't suspect that I know, but I have since I was a child. His big disappointment in life is that he never fathered a son. Not that he doesn't love us, his daughters, but he will never get over not having a son. A son to work beside him in the swamp. A son to inherit the Roberts business."

"Of course! You're his substitute son. All these years the tomboy act. That's all it was—an act! He thinks of you as a son."

"I've done my best to please him." She laughed. "And it wasn't all acting. I've become a damn good logger. Ask any of the redshirts."

"I don't have to ask. I've heard them. They're in awe of you. But what has this to do with our getting married? Certainly you can't be at your dad's side for the rest of your life. You have a private life to pursue. Marriage. Motherhood."

"Yes, I want those things, and I intend to have them. But I need time. Next year I'm going to enroll in business college in Chicago. When Dad dies, someone is going to know how to manage the business, of that I'm determined. And I am the only reasonable candidate. The only aspirations Peg and Lucy have are to sew, cook, play the piano, and manage a drawing room. Both proper young ladies waiting for Mr. Right to come along and keep them comfortable for life. I intend to be the best damned lumberwoman in the lake states."

Dennis shook his head and laughed. "You are one girl in a million, Dawn Roberts. Now, let me remind you of something. I am a damn good accountant. Outside of you and your father, I know more about the business affairs of the Roberts Lumber Company than anyone else. I've been doing your books for five years. Think what a boon it would be for everyone concerned if I became your husband. God forbid anything premature should happen to Walt, but if fate should frown on him, I will be at your side to help you make the transition to power."

"That's a comforting thought, Dennis. And, yes, I will marry you, but not for two years. I still have too much to learn about big business to let marriage and homemaking get in the way for the present."

She put her arms around his neck and drew his face down to hers. "That doesn't mean that we can't enjoy this highly satisfying relationship. Now, enough shop talk. I'd like to have a second helping before I go back home."

He pressed his lips to hers and placed a hand tenderly on her heaving breast.

# CHAPTER FOUR

The next four months were idyllic for Dawn Roberts. She and Dennis Price met twice a week at his cottage, and, as Dawn said, "We're as good as married, darling. I don't need a piece of paper to make me feel any more a wife to you than I am now."

"I feel that way too, sweetheart," he acknowledged. "But I don't like to sneak around. And it troubles me greatly that we're deceiving your mother and father."

"It isn't truly a deception. It would hurt them so much if they knew their daughter was a scarlet woman. Besides, when I come back from school we will be married."

In 1881 the lake states were blessed with an early spring. One evening in April, Walt Roberts announced at supper: "The ice is breaking up much sooner than we anticipated, and I've never seen the river running so high. Almost time for the spring drive."

This was the high point of the loggers' year. When the snow melted in the highlands, a thousand torrents gushed down the mountainsides to swell the Saginaw, the Tittabawassee, and the other rivers in the swamp. Soon the air would be alive with the thunder of timber rumbling down the rollways. The days were getting progressively longer, and the redshirts took advantage of every minute of light to get the logs to the booms downriver while the water was running high.

"I've added another dozen river hogs to the company roster," Walt said. And, snapping his red suspenders with his thumbs, he beamed at his family. "Now listen to this. Ever hear of Silver Jack McHugh?"

"Silver Jack McHugh!" Dawn was aghast. "You mean Silver Jack is for real?"

"You better believe it, honey. And next week he's coming to work for the Roberts Lumber Company. Cost me a bundle to lure him away from Sam Tucker, but he's worth double what I paid."

Dawn's fork clattered to the floor, her eyes big as saucers. "I don't believe you, Dad. Silver Jack McHugh *here?*"

"All the kids at school sing about Silver Jack," Lucy chimed in:

*"I was on the drive in '80 working under Silver Jack.*
*Which the same is now in Jackson Pen and ain't*
*soon expected back."*

"That's terrible, Lucy," her mother scolded. "That is not a proper ditty for a young lady to recite. I never want to hear it again in this house."

Dawn laughed. "You ought to hear the rest of it, Mama. Your hair would curl."

"I don't want to hear another word about this Silver Jack McHugh. Now eat your supper, all of you."

The exploits of Silver Jack McHugh were extolled in countless bawdy ballads and anecdotes throughout the swamp. His reputation was second only to that of Paul Bunyan. McHugh's odyssey was spotty because he had been in and out of prison on assorted raps of assault, mayhem, and attempted murder. But in between jail time, the Bull of the Woods, as he was called, had become a legend from Saginaw to Duluth.

Silver Jack McHugh tossed an armful of logs on the fire in the bunkhouse and walked back to his bunk. His closest buddy, Pig Iron Sam Malone, was sitting on the deacon seat lacing up his heavy steel-caulked boots.

"Move your ass, Pig," Jack said. "We gonna get an early start. Want to get to the Roberts spread before dark."

Pig grunted and took a hefty chaw of tobacco.

Jack put on his red wool shirt, trousers, and boots, tucking the pants cuffs well down inside the high boots. Last of all he put on his mackinaw and stocking cap. Then he reached under his mattress and pulled out a bottle which bore the label BEEF TONIC—BUILD UP YOUR BLOOD. The bottle contained a unique blend of beef tonic and alcohol spiced with liniment and vanilla extract, which Jack mixed with great care. He drained an inch off the bottle and passed it to Pig Iron Sam.

Silver Jack stood six feet four inches and had the physique of a minotaur: a massive chest and shoulders and a leonine head capped by platinum-blond hair. Wherever he worked, and he had worked almost every lumber camp in the swamp, he was hired as crew foreman by virtue of his ability to outwork and outfight any man in his crew. Legend had it that when a logger walked through the woods, the trees trembled. And when Silver Jack McHugh walked among them, the trees just gave up and toppled over.

The close friendship between Jack and Pig Iron Sam was a most unusual relationship. Pig was a big powerful man, six feet tall and 220 pounds of bone and muscle, but he was dwarfed by Silver Jack McHugh. He had matted steel-wool hair, and his face was a fascinating study in ugliness, with its scars, knobs, craters, and other mementos of innumerable no-quarter battles. Under a short, bristling beard his skin had the texture of a steel file. His front teeth, top and bottom, had all been knocked out. One ear was badly mangled and his other was a shapeless, putty-like stump of flesh, a souvenir of his first encounter with Silver Jack.

In a short barroom brawl, Jack had completely chewed off Pig's ear. After Jack had put the boots to him—it was traditional to trample on a defeated foe with one's hobnail boots—Pig had pledged undying friendship to his conqueror.

"Fightingest man in the Saginaw Valley," he would say in genuine awe.

"And you're the worst tasting man in the Saginaw Valley," Jack would retort and cuff Pig playfully on the head.

Aside from a flattened nose, Silver Jack McHugh carried few battle scars. His body was almost completely free of loggers' smallpox—the blemishes that all men who worked in tall timber bore from having the boots put to them persistently.

At breakfast on his last day at Sam Tucker's lumber camp, Silver Jack indulged his favorite pastime, antagonizing the French-Canadian cook. Flaunting the cookhouse rules of no frivolity at mealtimes, Jack burst into song halfway through breakfast:

*"There was a young lady from Bangor,*
*Who slept while the ship lay at anchor,*
*She rose in dismay when she heard the mate say,*
*Lift up the top-sheet and spanker!"*

The other loggers guffawed over their platters while the cook glowered at Jack from over the fire pit. Grinning broadly, Jack took a dead roach from his pocket and held it up, loudly pronouncing, "Hey, Frenchie, I see you're putting meat in the beans now."

The cook turned beet red and screamed: *"Sacre bleu!* You one big liar, McHugh! I run clean cookhouse here."

Jack shook his head sadly. "Never did see such a hardtack outfit as this." He picked up a slab of pork. "Remember the horse what broke his leg last week on that rollway? This here pork smells just like him."

Taking his cue from Jack, Pig called out, "Damn it, Frenchie, did you dig up that old hayburner?"

One of the cookies began to titter too close to the cook. A clout on the side of the head sent him flying across the room. Then, moving with the false calm and deliberation of cold fury, the cook picked up a meat cleaver and stalked to the head of the table where Silver Jack held court. A tense hush settled over the assembly; even the clatter of forks and knives was stilled.

Jack rolled and lit a cigarette with seeming unconcern, pretending not to notice that the irate cook was hovering over him. A chorus of gasps erupted from those at the table as the cleaver slashed down inches from Jack's nose, slicing the lit tip off the cigarette, cutting the pork and tin plate in two, and burying itself a half inch into the table.

"You see, McHugh, the meat she is not tough at all," the cook said mildly and walked back to the stove.

The loggers stared expectantly at Silver Jack, who was staring cross-eyed at the half cigarette in his mouth.

"You gonna let him get away with that, Jack?" Pig whispered.

Jack favored his audience with a weak grin. "I'm not gonna mess with a crazy Frenchman with a cleaver in his hand. No, siree." He stood up. "Come on, Pig. It's time we was on our way. Got to stop first at the commissary and settle up our wangan charges."

The company store, known throughout the swamp as the wangan box, supplied tobacco, matches, clothing, axes, and other essentials to the lumberjacks. The charges were recorded and deducted from their wages at the end of the spring drive. But inasmuch as Jack and Pig were leaving prematurely, they would settle up now,

"How much do I owe the company, Mr. Inkslinger?" Jack asked the bespectacled clerk.

"Wangan charges are eighteen seventy-five, Jack," was the reply.

Pig whistled in shock. "Jee-sus Christ! You better go easy, Jack!"

Loggers were notoriously parsimonious during the working season. Then they would blow an entire year's wages in one wild binge in Saginaw or Bay City.

"Never you mind, Pig. Just so long as I save enough to get my ashes hauled a few times, I'll make out."
"Gimmee a package of Daniel Scotten's Hiawatha and add it up," he said to the clerk.

That accomplished, they climbed aboard the mail wagon on its way to the railway depot.

"Roberts Lumber Company, here we come. Watch out!"

Silver Jack and Pig Iron Sam arrived on the night before the big birling contest at the Roberts camp. It was good sport and it helped the loggers sharpen up their skills for the spring drive.

Birling was derived from a form of horseplay engaged in by the men while on the drive. When there was nothing better to do, two river hogs would take a stance on opposite ends of a floating log and attempt to shake each other off into the river. Over the years, birling had developed into a contest with many subtle refinements. Each practitioner had his own pet twists, turns, and stops. Before a birling match, the contestants would spend hours studying a log and learning its idiosyncrasies. Pine logs rolled faster than spruce. Cedar logs rode exceptionally high in the water. And a log with the bark peeled was as elusive as a greased pig.

Silver Jack McHugh was proclaimed by fellow loggers as the champion birler of the swamp. He had weight, tremendous leg power, and the ability of a cat.

The week before the spring drive was an idle period for the loggers. They loafed about the camp, sleeping, gambling, drinking, and telling tall tales around the bunkhouse fire. And they practiced birling daily in the small cove in the river below the camp.

The morning after their arrival at the Roberts compound, Silver Jack and Pig Iron Sam were invited to participate in the birling contests.

"Reckon we'll show up after the preliminaries are

over," Jack said airily. "After the men have been separated from the boys."

He and Pig sat on the steps of the bunkhouse and swilled beef tonic and regaled the cookies with lurid stories of past barroom brawls, logjams, and whorehouses. At about eleven o'clock, boisterous cheering and applauding could be heard from the river.

"Guess it's about time we moseyed on down there," Jack said, corking his bottle. On the way, he rolled a cigarette and passed the sack to Pig.

"Here comes Silver Jack!" the enthusiastic onlookers yelled.

"And just in time to challenge the new champ."

Jack smiled condescendingly. "Which one is he?"

A slim figure standing with a group of loggers on the far side of the cove was pointed out to him.

"That's the champ—the little one."

Jack's jaw dropped, and he looked at Pig in utter disbelief. "I don't believe my eyes. Why, that little punk looks like a sapling in a forest of oaks."

"Shee-it!" Pig laughed. "You can blow 'im off the log, Jack!"

The other loggers around them joined in the laughter, but there was a conspiratorial quality to their hilarity that escaped Jack and Pig.

"Go get 'im, Silver Jack!" they encouraged.

When Jack and the kid, as Jack condescendingly called his opponent, faced each other from either end of the cedar log, Jack's incredulity mounted. The kid stood no more than five-eight or five-nine, and though it was difficult to judge his physique because of the logger's bulky shirt and trousers, he could tell the kid had slender arms and legs. He looked downright effeminate, with his smooth skin and rather sensitive features.

"He's a real purty one. Ain't he, Jack?" Pig jeered.

"All right, you river hogs," the referee shouted. "Git ready, git set, and *go!*"

The kid was smirking at Jack, who glowered back at him. "You won't be smiling long, kid," he growled.

Jack took charge right off, as expected. Pedaling slowly at first, he moved his feet faster and faster until the log was a spinning blur beneath them. It seemed inevitable that Jack's lightweight opponent would fly off sooner or later through sheer centrifugal force. But a murmur of admiration went up as the slight figure jogged along effortlessly with the spinning log, fingers hooked casually under his suspender straps.

After about ten minutes of this, Jack braked the log abruptly with his spikes. His foe hung on like a fly. He turned his insolent grin on Jack again and began jumping up and down.

Jack scowled and took a deep breath. Now he tried different tactics. Standing with his feet somewhat apart, his spikes dug deep into the bark, he rolled the log hard to the right, then jerked it back sharply to the left—back and forth, back and forth, kicking up little waves that broke over the feet of the onlookers around the perimeter of the cove. The infuriating kid never once unhooked his thumbs from his suspenders.

Jack employed every trick he had mastered over the years in the swamp. Propelled and controlled by his nimble feet and powerful legs, the log behaved as if it were alive, but the kid took the best he could muster, and the insolent smile never left his sissy face.

Finally, Jack had to resort to a strategy that he usually reserved for championship matches with hundreds of dollars riding on the outcome. He put the log into a high-speed spin, as fast as his legs could drive it. Then, with an astonishing display of balance and coordination, he threw the log into reverse and succeeded in ruffling his opponent's composure for the first time. The kid threw up his hands and teetered briefly, but regained his balance quickly. Jack kept it barreling in the opposite direction, and the kid had no chance to shift around so that he could jog into the spin. Both contestants were back-pedaling, one of the most difficult maneuvers in birling. The spectators watched the unbelievable performance, speechless and transfixed.

Neither Jack nor the kid were looking at each other any longer. Their eyes were fixed downward at the wet bark, sparkling in the sunlight as it flashed beneath their boots.

At last the other loggers could no longer endure the suspense. There were cries of "Call it a draw!" and "A draw! A draw!"

The humiliation of having this punk kid force him into a draw stung Silver Jack into one final desperate attempt to upset his opponent. But to his horror and disbelief, Jack suddenly found himself treading thin air! Water closed over his head.

When he came up, he was greeted by the mortifying applause and cheers for his conqueror. And to add insult to injury, the kid was standing on the shore, holding out a hand to him.

"Let me help you, Jack."

That did it. Silver Jack McHugh had never been so mad in his life.

"Go to hell, you little bastard!" he shouted, and waded out of the water prepared to commit murder. He got within striking distance of this little menace when the youth snatched his stocking cap off his head.

To the amazement of Jack and the Pig, a cascade of rich auburn hair fell down the kid's back.

"Jesus Christ!" he exclaimed, and his hands fell loosely to his sides. "It's a girl!"

And a damned pretty girl, he thought, with the most beautiful green eyes he'd ever looked into. Gaped at was more like it.

The girl stepped up to him and held out her right hand.

"Welcome to the Roberts spread, Jack. It's a distinct pleasure to meet you. A genuine honor. I'm Dawn Roberts, Walt Roberts's daughter."

Jack held out a limp hand to her. He tried to speak, but his tongue got all twisted up like a pretzel.

The green eyes flashed mischievously and cut briefly to the log in the cove. "About that, just bad luck on your part. Besides, you didn't have a chance to study the drift of the log. It could never happen again. Everybody knows that Silver Jack McHugh is the best river hog in the swamp."

Jack grinned sheepishly and found his voice. "Yeah, sure. Just bad luck. But lemme tell you, kid—I mean, Miss Roberts—you are one helluva birler. Up there with the best."

"That makes my day, Jack. Come up to the house and meet my mother and sisters. You like apple pie? My maw bakes the best."

"Mighty kind of you, ma'am. This here is my pal Pig Iron Sam Malone."

She shook Pig's hairy paw. "Nice to meet you too, Pig. You're pretty famous here in the swamp yourself. I can't wait to listen to you two spinning yarns."

Jack shifted from one leg to the other. "Not much

of what Pig and me have got to say is fit for ladies' ears."

Dawn laughed. "I'm sure you can clean up your act for my benefit."

Her eyes hypnotized Jack. What a remarkable woman! Beauty, brains, and she could birl like a whirling dervish. He fell in love with Dawn Roberts on the spot.

# CHAPTER FIVE

On the first day of each spring drive, a school holiday was declared, and all the boys and girls from miles around flocked to the big rivers throughout the lake states to watch the spectacle. The arrival of the stars of the show, the red-shirted river hogs, was heralded hours ahead by booming echoes carrying down the river valleys like distant thunder.

Upstream a constant procession of logs sluiced down the rollways into the rivers. Soon the water was so thick with timber that a person could walk from bank to bank without getting his feet wet.

The loggers had to be as quick and surefooted as antelope, for anyone who fell into this grinding, churning maelstrom was a dead man.

Silver Jack, the chief gang boss of the Roberts Lumber Company, liked to boast, "I kin throw a bar of soap in the water and ride the bubbles to shore."

The peavey hook was to the river hog what the ax was to the sawyer. A long staff with a spike on one end and a steel cant hook that moved up and down on a metal collar, it worked on the same principle as an iceman's tongs and was used to drag and roll the logs about in the water. It also served as a balancing pole for the loggers. Any river hog who lost his peavey in the river was disgraced, and the cost of it was deducted from his pay.

The spring drive was planned with the care and precision of a battle campaign. Men were stationed at critical points along the banks for miles downstream to "tend out." Their job was to pole snagged logs off the banks and prevent jams. The whole camp moved with the drive. Tents, pots, food, equipment, and supplies were hauled to designated campsites in the wangan wagons. The big, colorfully painted wagons were each drawn by ten horses, and when they rolled through a town, they created as much excitement as the arrival of the circus train.

"They'll be rounding the bend any minute," a small boy shouted downstream near the Roberts compound.

The older boys, who were more experienced with the habits of the spring drive, remained silent, ears attuned to the subtle nuances of the clamor echoing down the valley. Certain locations on the river, like the nearby bend, spelled trouble for the river hogs. Rocks, shallows, and other snags could jam up the drive. And it turned out to be one of those days.

The first indication was the harsh, steady drone of the logs floating free with the current. There was a series of violent explosions, followed by grinding, squealing, and creaking as the pileup intensified. The water level dropped with astonishing swiftness as the river backed up against a dam of logs.

Ten miles upriver, the logs were flung like jackstraws across a sharp, narrow bend in the waterway. The creaking and groaning built to an ear-splitting cacophony as the pressure of the water built up behind the mass. Fat timbers snapped in two like dowel sticks. One cluster of logs upended like giant fingers pointing to the sky.

Above the clamor, Silver Jack shouted at his crew: "River hogs you call yourselves? Shee-it! The lot of you ain't fit to be gandy dancers. If I had the time I'd whup your asses good!"

He grabbed a peavey hook and struck out across the jam with the grace of a high-wire artist. "Come on you bums, let's go find that king log."

The king log was like the keystone of an arch; remove it and all the rest of the logs would come tumbling free. Cursing and muttering, the loggers scampered across the logs, peaveys clanking as they tested suspicious-looking logs.

After half an hour of futile searching, Jack wiped the sweat from his brow and complained: "Damn! This one is a real bitch. Ain't it, Pig?"

Pig grunted. "Sure could use a little swallow of your beef tonic, Jack."

"You find me that king log and I'll buy you a case."

At that moment there was a commotion from the middle of the river, where a crowd of loggers was forming around a familiar slim figure. Jack and Pig made their way across the bridge of logs.

"Goddamn!" Jack cursed as he recognized Dawn at the center of attention. "What in hell is she doing out here?"

Dawn grinned as he came up. "Don't look so grim, Jack. I think I've found the king log."

Jack was unpacified. "I don't care if you *are* the boss's daughter, Miss Roberts. You ain't got no business being out here. It's too dangerous. I'm responsible for the safety of all these people, and I'm in charge. Now git back to shore where you belong."

The smile vanished from her face, and her green eyes flashed with anger. "Back where you belong," she mimicked him. "Where do you think that is, Mr. McHugh? Back home acting the good little girl, helping Mama with the cooking, cleaning, and sewing? You think a woman's place is in the home? Well, let me tell you something, big man. A woman's place is wherever she wants to be, not where some oafish male tells her to be. And right now I want to be here with the rest of the crew!" She advanced at him, wagging a finger under his nose. "And don't you ever forget it, Silver Jack!"

It was the only time in his life that Silver Jack McHugh ever backed away from anyone, man or woman.

"Now stop the nonsense and take a look at that log." She jabbed at a half-submerged log with her peavey. "The one with the crotch."

Jack knelt down for a closer look. "By Christ! I told them thickheads to split them schoolmarms before they sent them down the rollways." He rubbed his stubbled jaw, deep in thought. "Looks like she's snagged on something. And it's gonna take some doing to free her."

Pig spat tobacco juice. "And once she hauls, it's a long run to shore."

"Tell you what, Pig. You, Flint, Peters, and me will have a go at it. The rest of you go back to shore."

Dawn started to protest but thought better of it. This was a task for brute strength. And the fewer red-shirts there were on the jam when it hauled, the better the chances that Silver Jack and the others would make it safely back to the bank.

Pig, Flint, and Peters fixed their peavey hooks at strategic locations on the king log as Jack instructed.

"Now!" he said, and they all put their weight against the monster. It gave about an inch.

"Git hold of it again, boys. She's giving to the right."

They heaved to. There was a long, excruciating squeal as the log slid free and bobbed to the surface. Upriver, as far as the eye could see, the mountainous jam of timber began to quiver as if in the grip of an earthquake. There was a curious medley of sounds, like the popping of a thousand champagne corks, followed by a thunderous crash as the jam hauled.

"Let 'er go!" Silver Jack shouted and streaked for the nearest bank.

The logs were shifting and moving about like ice breaking up in the spring thaw. Jack pulled up short and almost lost his balance as a tangle of smaller logs broke away from the mass, opening up a six-foot gap of water.

Three-quarters of the way to the bank, Jack saw they would never make it. She was hauling too fast.

"Grab yourself a fat perch!" he shouted to the others. "We'll have to ride it out!"

With a gigantic roar, the dammed-up river broke through in a tidal wave. Jack dug his cleats into a large log and crouched low to ride the crest of the boiling front.

Flint shot into the milltail just behind and to one side of him. Suddenly the wave broke and he was flung high into the air. He landed in the water, arms and legs flailing, screaming in terror. Then the murderous mass engulfed him and he was gone.

A quarter of a mile downstream, when the drive was flowing normally again, Jack and the other two survivors clambered back on shore. After a bit, they managed to recover Flint's body from the water, and they buried it on the bank. They hung his steel-caulked boots from a tree branch above his grave, according to logging tradition, a sign to other redshirts that "another river hog had rode 'em through the milltail of hell."

They had just finished burying Flint when Dawn came riding down a path through the forest. At the sight of Silver Jack, her face was illuminated by enormous relief. She dismounted from Dusty and ran to Jack.

"Thank God, you're all right." To the surprise of the onlooking loggers, and to Jack's dismay, she put her arms around him and hugged him. "When the jam hauled so quickly, I thought you were all goners."

Her attention was caught by the grave and the boots. She bit her lip and cursed: "Damn! Who is it?"

"Flint," Jack told her. "He'd been a logger too long. Sooner or later your luck runs out."

"One of the original old-timers," she said, fighting back tears. "I used to call him Uncle Pete." She walked to the grave and knelt down, clasping her hands in prayer.

Silver Jack's narrow escape marked a new phase in his relationship with Dawn Roberts. He visited the Roberts homestead on the hill at least twice a week to confer with the company's owner. Walt Roberts's respect for his chief foreman continued to grow.

"What a shame a man with his abilities never got an

education," Roberts said to his wife one day after one of Silver Jack's visits. "He's as smart as a pistol, you know. He's got an intuitive grasp of everything about the lumber business except for the bookkeeping. Do you know what he came up with last week? He wants to replant saplings in all the areas we've stripped. I said to him, 'Hell, Jack, what's the point? It'll take a hundred years before they'd be fit to cut. Who'll reap the benefit?' And he says to me, 'Your great-grandchildren, their children, and their grandchildren's children.' Now, there's a man with a far-reaching perspective on life and the future."

One day when Silver Jack visited the house, Dawn took him into her father's well-stocked library. His eyes shone at the sight of the book-lined walls.

"Never seen so many books in my life."

"Never *saw*," she corrected him deliberately.

He felt belittled. "Sorry I don't speak proper, but I never had much education. Just past the fifth grade, and then I had to go to work. My paw was dead and my maw was sick."

"It's no disgrace to be uneducated. But with an intelligent mind like yours, it's a shame not to put it to use."

"How do you mean?"

"Many men and women are self-educated. My dad is one of them. He learned by reading all these books. That's how he derived his education."

"Derived?" he asked.

"To receive or get."

He laughed sheepishly. "Always did like big words."

"Then you shall learn them. Jack, can you read and write?"

"Oh, sure. I always did love reading. In the school I went to, the teacher used to lend me books."

Dawn clapped her hands together. "Then you shall resume your reading. You can borrow any of the books here. Let's see, what shall we begin with?"

She went to a shelf and removed a fat volume from its niche. "I know you'll like this one. It's called *Tom Jones*. It's about a poor lad, born a bastard, thrown out by his foster father, who becomes a wandering wastrel. But in the end he attains respectability and wealth."

Jack accepted the book and grinned. "Sounds a little like me," he joked. "Except for the part about becoming respectable and rich. Not much chance of that. It only happens in books."

"Don't be too sure. Anyway, you take it with you and read it whenever you have the time."

"Thanks a lot, Miss Roberts. I truly appreciate it. Now, I really have to be gettin' back."

"Get*ting* back," she reminded him. "A good place to start learning is not to forget to pronounce the whole word. Stop dropping your *g*'s."

"I'll try and remember." At the door he turned and addressed Dawn with a lopsided smile: "I *derive* great pleasure from speak*ing* with you, Miss Roberts."

"Bravo!" She was delighted. "Another thing, Jack. I wish you'd call me by my Christian name. Dawn."

"Dawn. It's a purty name." Before she could say it, he amended, *"Pretty* name."

Dawn stared after him thoughtfully as he closed the front door.

For the next year, Silver Jack McHugh borrowed three or four books from the Roberts's library every week. Although the volumes covered a broad spectrum of fiction and nonfiction, Jack favored subjects related to business, law, and forestry. His diction improved so markedly that Pig Iron Sam complained to his fellow loggers: "The man is turning into a complete stranger. You hear the phony way he talks? Other night he was reciting poetry to me. It's that danged Roberts gal. She put some kind of spell on him."

A burly man cast a log on the bunkhouse fire and snorted: "It's her tits and ass that put a spell on old Jack. That and his hots to get into her pussy."

"Shut up, Fournier," Pig warned him.

Too late. Jack McHugh was standing in the doorway, legs spread wide, muscles bunching tensely under his red shirt. His face was a mask of fury.

Joe Fournier was a great big hairy fellow with a flat simian face and prodigious strength. Behind his back, fellow loggers whispered that he was a throwback to prehistoric man. For some years an unofficial rivalry had existed between Jack and Fournier. Both men had large followings throughout the swamp, and both factions frequently engaged in battle to defend the prowess of their respective champions. Jack and Fournier had managed to stay aloof from the petty squabbling. Like all strong and self-confident men, they did not go out of their way to seek trouble.

"I don't have to look for a fight," Jack liked to say. "Fights are always looking for me."

Until the spring drive in '81 the paths of the two men had crossed only infrequently. But from the day that both signed on with the Roberts camp, excitement and speculation had been growing among their co-workers. Now at long last the showdown was at hand.

Silence settled over the bunkhouse as Jack walked toward Fournier. The other loggers backed up against the bunks on either side, giving the adversaries a wide berth. Fournier hooked his thumbs inside his belt and stood his ground, feet spread wide apart.

When he was within spitting distance, Jack stopped and spoke in an ominously quiet voice. "I must have heard wrong, Frenchie. Would you care to repeat it to relieve my doubts?"

Fournier grinned, baring his fanglike teeth. "Sure, McHugh. I said you were hot for her tits and her ass and her pussy. That Roberts wench."

In a lightning movement, Jack jammed both his thumbs into Fournier's eye sockets. While Joe was hopping about, screaming in pain, with his hands plastered over his eyes, Jack lectured him.

"In the future show a little respect for decent ladies, you damned barbarian. If I ever hear you mention Miss Roberts's name again, I'll whup you good."

Fournier wiped away the tears streaming down his cheeks and glared at Jack through bloodshot eyes.

"You filthy peeg!" he growled and rushed at Jack, a veritable human juggernaut. Both men fell to the sawdust-covered floor of the bunkhouse and rolled around, grappling like two bears. Although Fournier was shorter than Jack, he outweighed him by thirty or forty pounds. In close-quarter combat he was able to put his weight to good advantage. Jack was getting the worst of it until he managed to tear free from Fournier and get up on his knees. He was setting himself to throw a punch when the Frenchman lashed out with a boot and caught Jack hard on the chest. Jack toppled backward, and Fournier was on top of him again like a wild animal.

A groan went up from Jack's supporters as Fournier clamped his enormous hands around Jack's throat. Jack bucked and twisted and pounded the Frenchman's head with both hands, but his best blows bounced harmlessly off the granite skull.

As the powerful fingers contracted evermore tightly on Jack's windpipe, his color went from crimson to purple. Through the fog that was enveloping him, he noticed that in order to maintain his leverage over his opponent, Fournier had planted one thick boot against the deacon bench behind him. Mustering the last reserves of his waning strength, Jack drove a foot hard against Fournier's instep. He felt the long steel caulks bite through leather and grind against bone.

Fournier lost his grip and reared up in the air like a cat whose tail has been stepped on. Jack rolled away from him, gasping for breath. He bounced to his feet and dodged to one side as Fournier charged at him, trying to stay away until oxygen renewed his strength.

Fournier attacked him now with his secret weapon, his head. It was bull against matador. Jack sidestepped nimbly, and Fournier crashed into one of the triple-decker bunks. It collapsed like a house of cards. Shaking the splinters out of his hair, he whirled and charged again. Jack avoided him, and as Fournier flew past, he hooked a hard right to the pit of his stomach.

The air rushed out of Fournier's lungs with a sound like a blacksmith's bellows. He staggered back and grasped at another bunk for support. Before he could recover, Jack stepped in and pounded his gut with a left and a right. Fournier's legs gave way and he collapsed onto the floor.

Jack turned him over on his back and straddled his body. Grabbing a handful of sawdust, he stuffed it into the beaten man's open mouth.

"Fournier," he said easily. "You are going to eat

macaroni until you apologize for what you said about Miss Roberts. You understand?"

The gagging Fournier nodded his head frantically.

"Okay." Jack got up and stood over him.

Fournier sat up and spat out the sawdust. When he could breathe normally again, he looked up at Silver Jack, holding his sore belly with both hands.

"By gar, McHugh! A mule she keek me once in the belly and break her leg. I never been hit so hard in all my life."

Jack went to his bunk and took a bottle of beef tonic out from under his mattress. He went back to Fournier and handed it to him.

"Take a swig of this, Frenchie, and you'll feel better."

Fournier took a long swallow and gasped. "Thees poison is even stronger than you!" He wiped his mouth and got up.

"And now for the apology," Jack said.

Fournier hung his head. "I am sorry I said such untruths about you and Miss Roberts. I am *damned* sorry!"

Several days later, Dawn visited Dennis Price at his cottage. After a strenuous session of lovemaking, they were lying in bed when Dennis said, "Say, have you heard about the big fight between Silver Jack and Joe Fournier?"

"No, should I have?"

"Seems only fitting. After all, it was over you."

"Over me?" She was incredulous. "I don't believe it."

"Oh, it's true, all right. Seems Fournier said some randy things about you, and Jack came close to killing him."

"Well, I never! I wonder what Fournier said?"

"He intimated that Silver Jack had lecherous intentions toward you."

Dawn burst out laughing. "That's the funniest thing I've ever heard. Lecherous intentions, indeed. Why the poor man has never laid a finger on me."

"I'm not surprised, though. After all, you are creating a new Silver Jack McHugh out of a block of solid, insensitive pine. Men have always worshiped their creators."

Later, when Dennis and she were indulging in foreplay, she found herself fantasizing that it was Silver Jack McHugh making love to her. That his hands were caressing her breasts and her buttocks. His mouth was nuzzling her navel and the inferno between her thighs. It was Jack whom she straddled. His hardness expanded her eager flesh as he entered her. Her ecstatic contractions commenced, pumping the vital juices out of Silver Jack McHugh.

# CHAPTER SIX

In the late 1870s and early 1880s the plains and forests
of Wisconsin, Iowa, Minnesota, Illinois, Indiana, Michigan, and the Dakotas were plagued by drought. Fires
were a daily occurrence, most of them contained by
diligent fire watchers, or spotters, and enthusiastic fire-
fighting crews, predominantly volunteer loggers. What
was even more menacing was the continual production
of methane gas in the water-deprived swamps. It was
not unusual when a fire broke out in a swampy area
for balls of gaseous fire to be flung high into the atmosphere and to drop out of the sky like fiery meteors
on hapless settlements twenty or thirty miles away.

In early October of 1882, Silver Jack was in charge
of a high-rigging team limbing and topping trees
around the proposed winter felling sites. Just before
the lunch break, Dawn rode up on Dusty.

"Jack, Dad has a report from Joe McKenna's camp

that one of his riggers to the northwest has spotted smoke. We're a lot closer and on high ground."

Jack started to call up to the men in the treetops, then thought better of it. "I'd better have a look for myself."

He proceeded to climb the big fir while Dawn watched him anxiously. "Please, God, don't let it be smoke," she murmured.

Jack climbed to the best vantage point he could find and peered out across the crown of the forest to the northwest, shading his squinting eyes with one hand.

"I dunno," he said finally. "Peterson, what do you think?" he called to a rigger working just below him. "Come on up here."

The logger obeyed and followed the direction of Jack's extended arm. After scanning the distant scene, he rubbed his jaw. "Dunno, Jack. Looks to me like shimmering heat waves."

"Maybe, but we can't take chances. You men finish up here. I'll go back and roust out some of the boys who are off today and take a trip up there."

He descended and told Dawn of his decision. She approved and patted the saddle behind her. "Hop aboard and I'll take you back to camp. It's a lot faster than the wangan wagon."

"Right you are." He swung up behind her easily. "Lucky this gelding is a big, strong fellow. Never even bent an inch when I mounted."

Dawn slapped Dusty's side and they galloped off down the trail that led to the camp. As soon as they arrived, they conferred with Walt Roberts in his office.

"You're right, Jack, we can't risk having a fire get out of hand no matter how slight the odds. Jack, you round up a crew. We'll need every man we can get if it turns out to be a fire. Dawn, you pick some men and load up the wagon."

Dennis Price, who was working on the company books in the corner, got up. "I'd like to volunteer."

Walt, Dawn, and Jack looked at one another uncertainly.

Dennis flushed and said in an acerbic tone, "What's wrong, don't you think I'm man enough to be on your team, McHugh?"

Silver Jack's steely blue eyes bored into Price's eyes. "You heard what Walt said—every man we can get."

Within fifteen minutes a horse-drawn wagon carrying ten fire fighters, including Dennis, and a battery of fire-fighting equipment was rumbling back up the trail to the northwest. Dawn and her father rode alongside on their saddle horses. Piled in the back of the wagon with the men were long-handled shovels, burlap sacks, fire swatters, grub hoes, axes, and Pulaski tools—a combination ax and grub hoe.

They had covered about ten miles when Walt Roberts said to Dawn: "Come on. You and I will reconnoiter ahead." They galloped off in a cloud of heavy dust kicked up from the parched trail.

Five miles along the trail they reached the site and discovered a modest blaze covering perhaps a quarter of an acre and spreading slowly in the still, Indian summer air.

Dawn was perplexed. "It's positively eerie. It's burning soundlessly. No snapping or crackling."

Walt nodded grimly. "Bad sign. Shows how dry the brush is. No moisture to make sound when it's burning. We shouldn't have too much trouble containing it if the wind stays like it is." He frowned in the direction of a lone, stark dead tree in the center of the burning area, pointing toward the sky like a dark finger. Smoke poured out of its rotting trunk as if it were a smokestack.

"No, sir, don't like that at all," he said grimly.

They could hear the clatter of the wagon approaching when it happened. Without warning, the top of the blackened tree exploded, sending a shower of large sparks streaming into the air, where they were caught by high wind currents, carried along, and dumped into timber almost a mile away.

"Now we're in for it," Walt said.

When the fire fighters arrived in the wagon a short time later, Walt told them the bad news. "I'm going to take three of the men and check out the secondary fire. Maybe we'll get lucky." He picked three redshirts and told them to bring along a full complement of fire-fighting equipment.

Jack gathered the others around him and outlined the battle plan. "First thing, we have to build a fire line across the head of the fire. I'd say fifteen feet will be about right."

"The head of the fire is determined by the direction in which it's spreading the fastest," Dawn explained to Dennis, who appeared to be bewildered by all the commotion. "All fires have a circular shape at the onset, but depending upon the air currents, the shape of the terrain, and available fuel, they soon take on direction and assume an elliptical shape. Sort of like an egg, with the fat part representing the head. You have to attack the head first, and when the advance has been stopped, you work down the flanks to the rear."

Silver Jack described the strategy they would pursue. "Our fire line will be about a hundred feet long—a trench two feet wide, clearing away all the duff and dry litter, down to mineral soil."

With a stick, he traced the route of the fire line, a serpentine line that detoured around bushes too large to be uprooted and low-hanging tree limbs.

Two redshirts worked the advance, breaking ground with their hoes and clearing away loose litter, shoving it into the path of the advancing flames.

Silver Jack and Pig followed them with Pulaski tools, hacking out stubborn roots and small shrubs and cutting deeper into the forest floor.

Bringing up the rear were Dawn and Dennis, who were using shovels to scoop up loose matter out of the ditch and sluicing a light layer of soil across the ground in front of the line. Everyone worked intently, speaking only when necessary in order to conserve their wind, and the line expanded rapidly. Still, the fire was within two feet of the barrier when Dawn sent the final shovel of soil rattling into the flames.

The heat was searing, and their lobster-red faces streamed with perspiration. Wet clothing was plastered to their bodies, and they were caked with mud. Dawn and Dennis staggered back from the line and collapsed on the ground.

Silver Jack came over and passed a canteen to Dawn. "Better enjoy your breather. The worst is yet to come." He took a long swig from his own canteen and emptied the remainder over his head.

After a five-minute break, Jack gave Dawn and Dennis long-handled beaters. He and the other loggers were armed with water-soaked burlap bags.

"The thing now is to patrol the line and keep a sharp watch for embers that fly over it."

They spread out at twenty-five-foot intervals, with

Pig and Jack each holding down an end of the line. The flames reached the edge and leaned hungrily across it.

Dawn slapped the flat of her rubber beater down on a spark that was smoldering on her side of the line.

Dennis stared at the licking tendrils of fire in fascination. "It's almost as if it were a living thing, the way it reaches out for you."

At his end of the line, Jack cast aside his smoking burlap sack and grabbed a shovel. With horror Dawn saw a thin trail of fire race around the end of the ditch and blaze up in a patch of grass around Jack's legs. She ran down to him, and together they extinguished the flames and the long fuse of burning grass that had ignited it.

For another half hour they battled the tenacious foe with fierce determination, and at last the fire surrendered. Its efforts to leap the barrier waned and finally died out altogether.

"Looks like we got her," Jack said with satisfaction. The rest of them sent up a cheer.

But their victory was short-lived. In their determination to hold the fire line, they had ignored the dead tree in the center of the burned-out area, now a solid pillar of fire reaching high into the air. It stood a safe distance from the other trees, and Jack reckoned the chief hazard it posed was the occasional explosion of sparks emitted from its hollow trunk. Then disaster struck.

Crumbling from decay and the ravages of termites, and further weakened by the flames, the towering snag suddenly gave way at the base. As the fire fighters stared in speechless horror, it began to topple in slow motion in the direction of a thick cluster of pines on the left flank of the fire. It crashed into the grove, engulfing the thick, dry foliage with fiery sparks. Instantly the crowns of the trees erupted in a huge balloon of flame with an explosion that shook the earth. The surface fire had heated the foliage to the point of combustion; it was the same as touching a match to a gas jet.

A blast of red-hot air singed Dawn's eyelashes and eyebrows and the hair poking out from beneath her cap. She screamed and stumbled back, protecting her face with her arms. Jack grabbed a bucket of water and sloshed it over her head.

They craned their necks upward as the trees all around them began to rustle as if a giant, invisible hand were shaking them.

"What the hell's that?" Dennis asked. "It can't be wind."

"It's wind, all right," Jack told him. "Once these forest fires get going, they make their own wind."

"It's as if you were standing by a big bonfire," Dawn explained to the greenhorn. "You must have noticed how the updraft of hot air creates a vacuum around the fire that sucks in leaves and other small particles."

"What do we do now, Jack?" Pig wondered.

Jack shook his head in despair and pointed to the flames raging out of control across the crown of the forest. "Only one thing to do—get out of here. We don't want to get caught in here when she really takes off. There's a firebreak, an ox path about a half mile back. We'll go there and wait for reinforcements."

"Reinforcements?" Dennis said, on the verge of hysteria. "My God! There's only the ten of us!"

"Not for long," Dawn assured him. "By now the lookouts from all the lumber camps have verified that there's a bona fide forest fire burning in this sector. Help is on the way, you can depend on it."

They took off for the ox path double-time, and as they ran, Dawn explained to Dennis the tactics employed to fight a major fire. "All over the swamp there are various kinds of firebreaks, some of them natural —rivers and streams, for instance—others man-made, like railroad right-of-ways, existing roads and trails, and lines like the little one we made."

As Dawn had predicted, by the time they reached the firebreak, men were piling out of wagons that were arriving from all over the area. To her relief, Dawn saw her father holding a council of war with the crew chiefs.

"To those of you who have never fought forest fires before, here's a briefing." He smiled ruefully. "Believe me, it will be brief. The idea is to light our backfires on the edge of the fire line, so that they'll be drawn into the advancing fire by back drafts. The air currents created by a big blaze tend to suck in the smaller backfires. Ideally, the two fires will meet head-on and die because all the fuel in advance of the main fire has been exhausted."

"That's under ideal conditions," Jack chimed in. "Don't count on it."

"Silver Jack is right. A forest fire is even more unpredictable than a woman."

Dawn marched up to him and stomped a foot, glowering at him indignantly as the gaggle of men around them roared with laughter.

"Can I quote you to Mother and Peg and Lucy?" she demanded. "I think life may be hard on you around the house if I do, dear father."

Walt Roberts held up his hands and backed off.

"Dawn, honey, you wouldn't visit a fate like that on your old dad!"

"Well, I'll give you one more chance." She grinned broadly. "Guess you guys didn't have any more luck than we did."

He embraced her warmly. "No, she's out of hand, but good. This is going to be a monster, honey. Maybe you ought to go back to camp."

Her smile vanished. "I'm every bit as capable of swinging my weight as you or Jack. Remember, we need every available hand to fight this one. You said so. Well, I'm here and I'm available."

Off to the side, Silver Jack shook his head in admiration. "I've said it before, and I'm saying it again. When they made that little gal, they threw the mold away."

"Yeah, so I've heard," Pig said with irony. And in a lower voice to himself, "God! How many times I've heard it!"

In back of the line, a wooden table had been set up in a small clearing, and Walt Roberts and the other crew chiefs were gathered around it, studying a map that the local forest ranger had spread out on the counter.

Ranger Adams indicated a section of the map shaded in red pencil. "This represents the burned-out area as it stands now. The front is roughly twenty-five hundred feet across, and it's spreading fast."

Silver Jack whistled. "I don't figure it was more than a hundred feet when we pulled out."

"It wasn't," Walt Roberts said. "But since then it joined up with the secondary fire that we tackled."

Ranger Adams continued: "The way I see it, we've

got to give her plenty of room. If we can hold her down to two hundred acres, I'll be plenty satisfied."

He ran his finger along a ridge that ran off diagonally to the road in a northeast direction on the right flank of the fire. Then he penciled an $X$ at the foot of the ridge directly in line with the head of the fire.

"Our best chance is to start backfiring here about a half mile due east. That ridge is a natural firebreak because it's mostly rock with only scrubby vegetation. It won't take more than a skeleton crew to work that side. Walt, you and Silver Jack take ten men and start setting things up on the south line. A three-thousand-foot line should do it."

From the foot of the ridge he drew another line, extending in a southeast direction. "We'll backfire for another three thousand feet on this line. The rest of you gang chiefs will round up your men and get to work on that right off."

He put a hand on Dawn's arm. "You and Price can help out on the ridge as fire scouts. Walt, I think maybe you'd better stay here and help me get things organized. Pig, you go with Jack instead."

As the fire fighters formed into groups, Dawn and Dennis walked to the wangan wagons, ten of them all lined up like a wagon train. The cooks from the different camps were doling out steaming-hot suppers to the fire fighters: beans, pork, and thick slabs of bread.

"Eat hearty, darling," Dawn advised Dennis. "We've got a long night ahead of us.

"I can't believe it's getting dark already," he said with some surprise. "Look at that golden cloud hanging over the forest. What a beautiful halo."

"Deadly beauty," Dawn said grimly. "That's the effect of the rays of the setting sun slanting from below the horizon onto the screen of smoke hovering over the burned-out area."

"How in hell can anyone work in these woods at night?" Dennis wondered.

"It's not easy. Normally, Ranger Adams would wait until morning, but conditions being what they are, he wants to keep on top of it every minute. Besides, the rate of spread declines sharply through the night because the winds die down, and that's a big edge for us."

They carried their heaping tin plates and canteen cups over to a grassy knoll and sat down cross-legged.

"What do we do as scouts?" he asked.

"Run messages up and down the line so that the HQ here can keep in touch with the progress in all sectors at all times. We're going to be plenty leg-weary before this night is over."

After they finished eating, they went over and dropped their plates and cups into a huge tub of steaming water beside one of the wagons. It was dark now, but the reflected light of the forest fire on the ceiling of smoke that hung over them cast an eerie, rosy twilight glow over the area.

Dawn and Dennis were assigned to accompany the first wagons moving out through the woods toward the foot of the pivotal ridge where the fire line would be anchored. Just before they reached their destination, the caravan had to stop, while sawyers hacked a path through dense foliage. They were followed up by horse-drawn plows that cleared an area large enough so that the wagons and equipment could assemble.

In less than half an hour they were ready to go to work. The fire fighters were split up into two teams, striking out to the northeast and southwest. They were preceded by the plows, which cleared a strip through the trees twenty-five feet wide, rooting up the thick duff on the forest floor. Men armed with shovels followed the plows, piling up soil and sand in a high bank against the advancing flames. Behind them came the high riggers, who lopped off low branches that hung across the firebreak.

"You're Dawn Roberts, aren't you?" the crew boss asked the girl. "Walt Roberts's kid?"

"Yes, and you're Joe Eastman from the Tibbits camp. I met you once at a barn dance."

"You've grown some since then. You and your buddy can work the top of the ridge. Find the gang bosses and see how things are shaping up in their sectors."

"We're on our way, Joe."

Dawn and Dennis climbed a steep rocky ravine at the right of the clearing. From the crest, which was forty feet higher than the surrounding terrain, they had an unrestricted view along the length of the ridge.

There was a blood-red full moon balanced on the fiery crown of the forest. It was obvious to Dawn why the ranger had chosen this site to construct the fire line. It was a natural barrier running straight as an arrow to the northwest, at least a mile long from tip to tip. Its rocky slopes, barren except for grass and stunted shrubs, swept down about a hundred feet on each side to the edge of the woods. The ridge was a great scar in the rich Michigan earth left by a passing glacier aeons past.

When Dawn and Dennis reached the midpoint of the ridge, they saw the work gang—dim, hunched silhouettes as they scurried back and forth across the crest. A beefy man, leaning on a shovel as he shouted orders to the other fire fighters, greeted them.

"You the fire scouts?"

"Yes, I'm Dawn Roberts and this is Dennis Price."

The man did a double take. "Dawn Roberts? Say, I almost mistook you for a boy. You're Walt's gal. Pleased to meet you, Miss. I'm Alan Sloan, the gang boss. What the devil is a little lady like you doing up here? This is dangerous work."

"No more dangerous for me than it is for you," she said lightly. "You got a report for headquarters?"

"You tell 'em everything looks pretty good from here. We're clearing a strip about ten feet wide just below the crest on the far side. We'll start our back-fires down there in the tall grass running back to the woods. For good measure, we'll light another one along the top of the ridge."

Suddenly he frowned and turned his nose up in the air like a scenting hound. "Hey, you feel that?" He wet his finger in his mouth and held it up.

Dawn was aware of a cool, gentle breeze on the left side of her face.

When he spoke again, his voice was as taut as a bowstring. "Wind's picking up, and it appears to be swinging to the southwest. That means the fire will veer smack into this ridge. You better get that news back to headquarters pronto."

Dawn and Dennis raced back along the ridge and stumbled down the ravine. Joe Eastman listened grave-ly as Dawn told him about the change in the wind's direction.

"I dunno," he said. "We just got a report from the south line. They report it's hell on wheels down there. Of course, it would be too early to notice any effect on the head of the fire. We'll have to play it by ear. I don't want to risk giving HQ any false alarms just yet." He gazed skyward. "Keep your fingers crossed it doesn't blow up real strong. She'd probably crown again, and that could mean spot fires all over the swamp. There'd be no stopping her then. Not to mention the danger it would pose to all of us here. If fires begin to spread far to the rear of the line, we might find ourselves surrounded by fire and cut off."

A runner came into the camp. "It's confirmed. The wind's shifting and they're decided to hold off setting the backfires down south."

"All right." Eastman turned to Dawn. "Go back up the ridge and tell Sloan he can start backfiring anytime."

After they had reported to Sloan, they dragged their feet back to the campsite. Eastman put his arms around their shoulders.

"You two look as if you could use a break. Go sack out in one of the wagons. I'll call you if anything new develops."

They chose a wagon on the perimeter of the clearing where there wasn't so much noise and commotion, climbed in the back, and lay down, covering themselves with surplus sacks.

Dennis sighed. "I never thought I'd be too tired to make love, but tonight's the night."

"My sentiments exactly," Dawn said with a yawn.

Seconds later they were fast asleep.

It seemed to Dawn only moments later that Eastman roused them. Actually, three hours had elapsed.

"All hands are on alert. There's a real southwester blowing up!"

The sight that greeted them as they leaped out of the wagon was frightening. To the east, as far as the eye could see, the canopy of the forest was one mas-

sive inferno of raging, writhing flame. Geysers of fire
spewed high into the air, whipped fiercely by the strong
wind blowing from the southwest. The head of the
fire had veered off sharply and was attacking the ridge
along its entire length.

Eastman handed Dawn a handwritten report and
said, "Take this back to Sloan up on the ridge. Tell
him to relay it to every gang boss on the ridge. If she
breaches the line, they're to pull out everyone and
withdraw to the road. If this wind keeps up, we might
not be able to hold her there."

As Dawn and Dennis were leaving, another scout
came in and reported breathlessly, "Everyone is pulling out of the south line before we're cut off."

Dawn and Dennis started up the ravine, but East-
man called them back. "It'll be hot as Hades up there.
Better circle around the far side of the ridge. . . . Jesus!
Look at that, will you!"

Small brush fires were creeping toward the clearing
on the flank of the main fire.

"I guess we better get set to move out ourselves."

Dawn and Dennis made their trip on the back side
of the ridge. The thorny crest was vividly outlined
against a crimson curtain. There was turmoil on the
protected slope: It was teeming with men, horses and
wagons, and two newly arrived tank wagons equipped
with water pumps and hoses.

"If we had had those tank wagons sooner, we might
have stopped the fire where it started," Dawn said.
"Now their main purpose is to give us time to
evacuate."

The tank wagons rumbled back and forth at the
foot of the slope, dousing trees and shrubs with water.
Other fire fighters were lined up just below the crest

with water-soaked bags and fire swatters, extinguishing the steady flow of flaming debris that blew over the top. They were dwarfed by the towering flames that were beginning to arch over the crest, seeking a hold on this side of the ridge.

"The fire almost seems to have a malevolent intelligence," Dawn observed with awe. "Those fingers of flame are actually reaching out for the men."

Even as she was speaking, a tendril of fire snaked around a redshirt's waist. He screamed and rolled on the ground as his buddies beat out the flames with wet bags.

Dawn and Dennis traveled the full length of the ridge, passing the word to all the fire bosses along the way. At the end of the ridge, the last crew was laboring frantically to build a hasty fire line at right angles to the ridge to stop the ground fires racing down the edge of the forest.

"No damned use!" the gang boss said wearily and tossed his shovel aside. "Nothing short of a miracle will stop her now."

# CHAPTER SEVEN

Indeed, it seemed that Armageddon was descending on the swamp. Throughout the lake states, forest fires raged everywhere, one feeding upon the other. Gale-force winds, created by the fires themselves, carried hurricanes of flame hurtling through the sky like giant meteors over vast distances to ignite still other fires when they exploded into the earth. Towns and villages were encircled by fire before the inhabitants had a chance to flee. Peat bogs exploded into raging infernos, without even being touched by flame, when the rising methane gas reached the incendiary point in the scorching winds.

In the village where Dennis Price lived, panic-stricken citizens dumped their precious possessions into wells and cisterns before rushing to the nearby river. The heat became so intense that houses exploded from spontaneous combustion. Those who reached the river had renewed hope, but their reprieve was short. Grotesque sheets of flame swept up and down the river, darting here and there to claim a victim. Eventually the air itself became so hot that breathing it instantly scorched one's lungs. Most of the victims chose the more merciful death by deliberately drowning their children and themselves.

By four o'clock in the morning, the main fire was burning on a 175-mile front and a call for volunteers was put out in ten states. Hundreds answered the summons, and the battle swelled to epic proportions. Walt Roberts arrived with Ranger Adams and embraced Dawn. "Baby, you've had a rough night, I've heard. Are you all right?"

"I'm fine, Dad. And everyone has had a rough night, not just me. Do you think we can stop it here?"

"Not a chance, unless the wind lets up." He consulted his pocket watch. "Come on, morning, where are you?"

There was not an idle hand on the line. Shovels, axes, Pulaski tools beat out a terse crescendo that echoed up and down the line.

"Reminds me of when we wuz bracing for the Rebs' first attack at the battle of Bull Run," one old-timer commented.

Water wagons rumbled up and down the road, saturating the foliage and underbrush on both sides of the line.

"Hey, turn those hoses on us for a while!" Dawn shouted to one of the drivers.

Cheers went up from the other smoke eaters, and the driver obliged. Nothing she had ever experienced in her life—sex excepted—had ever felt as good as the cool water flowing over her mud-encrusted body. Dawn shivered with ecstasy and opened her mouth to lave her swollen tongue and parched throat.

The line was completed in record time, and none too soon. The head of the fire was no more than two hundred yards away when Ranger Adams gave the order to backfire. Funereal silence settled over the throng as they watched the backfires flare up strong in the dry brush. Their progress was more rapid than anyone had anticipated.

"Look at 'em go!"

The two fires met, and there was an agonizing instant of indecision before Adams yelled, "It stopped her dead!"

A mighty roar of relief and joy swept up and down the line. Time and time again, the stalled fire ejected long streamers of flame at the trees across the line, but each time the dripping boughs repulsed them.

Then, miracle of miracles, the wind ceased, as if someone had turned off a fan.

Dawn smiled. "God! Look at the horizon."

A widening band of silver was visible in the east.

"It's dawn!" she shouted. "With the onset of daylight the wind always dies."

"We did it!" Dennis shouted and leaped up and down, seizing Dawn in a bear hug and swinging her around.

A gruff voice intruded from the shadows. "Better hold the hugging and kissing and celebrating for a time, friend. There's still plenty of life in that old she-devil yet. And there's still plenty of back-breaking work to be done before we get this front nailed down solid. Grab your picks and shovels and let's get to work."

Silver Jack McHugh turned away brusquely from

Dawn and Dennis. He couldn't bear the sight of her in the other man's arms.

By the time the sun nudged over the horizon, they had stopped the fire on this line cold. Dawn ran a hand over the ash-encrusted bark of one of the trees on their side of the road.

"These trees that were so badly burned—will they survive?" she asked Ranger Adams.

"Good chance they will," he answered. "A tree is sort of like a human being. It can survive bad burns, although it will be scarred for life. I figure these old fellows have a good chance to make it."

"I hope so." Dawn scratched her arm. "I have never been so filthy in my life. I wish I could wash up and change my clothes."

Adams grinned. "I've got a spare shirt and work pants in my wagon. You're welcome to borrow them."

She brightened. "Thanks, Mr. Adams. I sure would appreciate it." Her face fell. "Only thing, it would be a waste to put clean clothes on my dirty body."

"There's a spring about a half mile down the hill. You can wash up there."

"Can you spare us for an hour or so?"

"Sure thing. Take two, and grab a catnap. I'll be back in a while with your duds."

"I hope it's a big spring," she mused. "Big enough to take a full bath."

Dennis smiled and put an arm around her waist. "Big enough for two, *I* hope."

Adams returned and handed her a pair of neatly folded trousers and a checkered shirt. "May be a trifle long in the pants and a baggy shirt, but you'll make out."

"You bet I will. Thanks a million, Mr. Adams. Come on, Dennis."

Hand in hand, they walked downhill along a well-used trail until they came to the spring. To Dawn's delight it was actually a brook with a basin about fifteen feet in diameter that had been scooped out by local hunters years before.

Dennis looked around nervously as Dawn began to undress. "Suppose someone comes along and sees us?"

"We'll invite him in to join us," she teased, as she began to discard her grimy shirt and trousers, and then her underclothes. She stretched her arms high over her head, knowing full well that Dennis was hypnotized by the upthrusting of her breasts.

"You're so beautiful," he said in a hoarse voice. "Every time I see you with your clothes off, it affects me like the first time."

He was enraptured by the saucy flexing of her buttocks as she waded into the water.

"Brrrr . . . it's cold," she said. She stopped, knee-deep, knees locked together and slightly bent, her hands clamped coyly between her legs.

"You look like a painting I saw in a museum in New York. *September Morn,* it was called."

Dawn held her breath and plunged head first into the icy pool. She surfaced, spewing water from her mouth. "Oh, it's wonderful once you get used to it. Come on, sissy."

Watching her undress had excited Dennis so that he was fully erect as he approached the water. He dove under and came up beside her. They frolicked about in the cold pool, teasing and touching each other, the tension of the previous hours momentarily forgotten.

Dennis put his arms around Dawn and pulled her

against him. His manhood pushed against her belly, and Dennis felt her taut nipples dig into his chest.

"That little pine grove over there looks very private," said Dawn.

She took his hand and they waded onto the bank. They walked to the cluster of baby pines some twenty yards from the pool and pushed through the thick-needled branches to the very center, where there was a small clearing heavily covered with fine, soft needles.

"Almost as soft as a feather bed," she said as she sat down. Dennis knelt beside her and took her in his arms. He kissed her eyelids, her lips, her throat. His hands caressed her breasts. He stroked her belly, his fingers moving slowly, teasingly, into her rich auburn nest.

Dawn threw back her head and moaned with desire. She lay back on the soft forest duff and drew him down on top of her, her thighs trembling as he penetrated her. She gazed blindly into the bright blue sky overhead and felt the tide of their passion rise higher and higher. Abruptly, the universe dissolved in a kaleidoscope of brilliant colors as he thrust deeply into her, and then she was aware of nothing but the exquisite response of her body to his pounding manhood.

The heat of the rising sun was rapidly dissipating the pockets of cool air left over from the past night in the forest. When they had satisfied their hunger for each other, they stretched out on the soft pine bed, and sleep instantly claimed their weary bodies and minds.

Dawn awake to the klaxon sound of the gut hammer echoing downhill from the fire line. Dennis sat up instantly, his eyes as wild as a spooked horse's.

"What the hell is that?"

She gripped his arm tensely. "Out here when they sound the gut hammer it means it's an emergency. The fire must have gotten out of hand again. Come on, we'd better get up there!"

She ran to the pond, where the ranger's clothing was folded on the bank, and dressed quickly.

Dennis had rinsed his clothes as best as he could and draped them over a tree branch to dry. His pants and shirt were damp, but at least they were moderately clean.

Overhead the wind was rustling the crowns of the pines. "It must be the stiff blow that revived the fire," Dawn said. "Hurry!"

They ran up the winding path through the woods. Dawn stopped suddenly as she reached the top of a small knoll.

"Dennis! Look at that!"

Directly ahead of them was a thick wall of smoke, and behind it they could hear the crackling of fire.

"I can't believe it's come so far," she gasped. "They must have evacuated the road. No chance of joining up with them now. Come on, we'd better get out of here fast!"

They ran back down the path, past the brook, and through the woods to the south. When they reached the top of a rise and paused to reconnoiter, a chilling sight greeted their eyes. Not only had the fire jumped the line, but on the flanks, where the dry brush and thickets were in heavy abundance, its advance was accelerating faster than in the center. To the east and west, flames raced at breakneck speed in the same direction as they were retreating.

"We've got to outdistance the fire before it cuts us off. Hurry, Dennis, or we'll never make it."

They sprinted down the trail, dodging rocks, branches, and other impediments. Around a twist in the path they encountered a fallen tree. Dennis vaulted over it, with Dawn right behind. When he landed on the far side, he lost his balance and almost fell. Striving to regain his footing, he twisted his ankle and dropped to his hands and knees. Dawn stopped short. "Are you all right?"

He tried to stand up and fell to one side. Dawn caught him by the arm as he got up gingerly. He put his weight on his left foot, his face contorting with pain.

"What's the matter?"

"I think I sprained my ankle. Maybe broke it."

"Oh, dear God!" She gazed around wildly, feeling the terror and fear of a trapped animal. Can't you walk at all?" She spied a knotted stick lying at the side of the trail and picked it up. "Here, use it like a cane."

It afforded him some comfort, but it could not increase the pace of his gait.

"What are we going to do?" she asked, panic in her voice.

"You go on, and don't worry about me," Dennis said calmly.

"I can't leave you here like this. You'll be killed!"

"That's no reason why the two of us should be killed. Go on, Dawn, I don't want any more arguments."

Dawn hesitated, looking ahead down the path, then back at Dennis. Suddenly she grabbed him by both arms.

"Dennis! There's one chance. I overheard my dad and Ranger Adams talking last night about one of the local landmarks in these parts, Meteorite Hill."

"I've heard of it, but I don't know where it is."

"Well, I've seen it plenty of times. And I think it's not far from where we are now. We always came in from the south canyon, but I remember noticing that a path just like this one runs right to the foot of it. You come along as fast as you can while I run up ahead and try to find the hill."

She raced down the path and had covered no more than half a mile when she emerged into a clearing. And there it was, directly ahead—Meteorite Hill.

It rose up like an oversized muffin with steep grassy slopes. At the top was a deep crater where a meteor had plowed into the earth thousands of years earlier. After heavy rains, the crater was usually filled with water, but because of the drought it was bone dry now.

Dawn ran back to Dennis, who was making surrisingly rapid progress.

"The fear is worse than the pain," he said wryly.

"Get rid of that stick and put an arm around my shoulders; we can make better time. The hill isn't very much farther."

It was an awkward performance, but it got them to the foot of Meteorite Hill. They started up the steep, grassy slope that ran up to the summit, two hundred feet above ground level.

From an aerial view, the top of the hill would have resembled a large archery target, with the meteorite crater at the bull's-eye, surrounded by concentric circles of red and yellow gravel, and an outer ring of grass that ran around the perimeter of the hilltop.

At this height they had to crouch on hands and knees to keep from being blown away. The fire reached the base of the hill and burned its way around through the tall grass only minutes after they had scrambled their way to the top. From their high vantage point they had a panoramic view of the forest fire ravaging the countryside on all sides. A quarter of a mile to the south, the two flank fires had finally united. Dawn and Dennis were now isolated on an island in the midst of a sea of flame. The constantly shifting wind currents sent a hail of hot coals and blazing twigs raining down on the hill.

"Come on, we've got to get inside the crater," Dawn urged, and helped Dennis over to the lip of the crater.

"Christ! How do we get down there? It must be thirty or forty feet deep. And how will we ever get out?"

"No problem. See, over on the other side, there's a ladder for tourists who want to explore the bottom of the crater."

They skirted the rim until they arrived at the place where the ladder was braced against the almost vertical wall of the big hole.

"I'll go first," Dawn said. "Take it nice and easy, there's no hurry."

She descended the ladder quickly and nimbly. Dennis climbed more slowly. He paused occasionally with his good foot on a rung to rest. Dawn breathed a sigh of relief when he reached the hard crust of the floor, made of glittering obsidian formed by the intense heat of the ancient meteor.

Dawn inspected the crater, which was at least thirty feet in diameter. At one point she came upon a niche in the smooth sides of the crater that ran back some eight feet into the earth around it—a small cave of sorts.

"Come here, Dennis," she called out. "See what I've discovered."

The little grotto's ceiling was quite low, and they had to crawl in on hands and knees. Dawn sat with her back braced against the rear wall and her knees drawn up. Dennis lay back against her legs with his legs stretched out in front of him.

"How's your ankle?" she asked.

"I think I'm too scared to feel the pain."

"It looks badly swollen."

He shrugged. "I'll live." Then with a dry laugh. "On second thought, I'll reserve judgment on that statement."

They both recoiled as a shower of fiery particles came tumbling down into the crater. The hill was now under direct attack on all sides from the fire. The shower of sparks continued unabated for ten minutes. Fortunately, there was no fuel in the rocky crater to feed them, and they quickly burned out.

Dawn's main concern was oxygen. As their breathing became more and more labored, their heartbeats grew rapid and thready.

"Hold on, darling," she comforted Dennis. "It can't continue much longer."

The sparse grass at the base of the hill and on the slopes was soon consumed by the fire, which then raced on to the south, driven by the high tail winds.

Dawn and Dennis were almost unconscious when the first cool draft of fresh air stirred up the ashes in the crater.

"Breathe deeply," she told Dennis, and gulped in the lifesaving oxygen. "We've made it. We're safe at last."

When they had recovered their wind, they crawled out of the cave, then quickly retreated as Dennis burned his hands on the hot lava crust of the pit.

"We'll have to wait until it cools," Dawn said, and they settled back to wait. It was a half hour before they were able to walk on the ground outside the cave, and even then the heat made their feet uncomfortably warm through the thick soles of their boots.

"I'll go up the ladder first. You take your time," Dawn said.

An awesome sight greeted her as she climbed out of the crater and stood on the summit of the hill. Acre upon acre of once heavily wooded countryside around Meteorite Hill had been totally annihilated except for the stark, blackened, smoldering skeletons of the trees that had not been felled. The earth was black as well and littered with glowing embers, smoke rising from it like vapors from a swamp.

"It looks like the beginning of time," she mused, reminded of sketches she had seen in books depicting artists' conceptions of prehistoric times.

While she was contemplating the devastation, Dennis crawled out of the crater and lay exhausted on the ground.

Dawn went over to him and knelt down. "How are you feeling?"

"Rapturous. I'll never again take life and all its joys for granted."

She bent over him and kissed him on the mouth. "Just imagine, never to experience again the wonder and joy of love." Her shirttails were hanging out of her trousers, and Dennis slipped a hand up inside the shirt and caressed her breasts.

They lay in each other's arms, kissing and fondling each other, not out of a sexual need, but more in tender appreciation of what each meant to the other.

They were still cuddled in each other's arms, sleeping as peacefully as children, when a rescue party discovered them.

# CHAPTER EIGHT

Although the most devastating forest fire in the history of the lake states destroyed thousands of acres of timberland, it did not seriously affect the lumber industry, so abundant were the big trees in the swamp.

Not long after the disaster, Dawn enrolled in a business school in Chicago, There she lived in a rooming house with two other female students. By the time she returned home early the following summer, she had considerably improved her typing skills and had acquired a wealth of knowledge about big business and commerce.

She was surprised and pleased to find that her father had appointed Silver Jack McHugh his special administrative assistant in the field and had even enlarged the company's offices to provide accommodations for the new administrator. Dennis Price was now working exclusively for the Roberts Lumber Company —with the titles chief accountant and vice-president.

"I can't get over how much has changed in the short time I've been away," Dawn marveled.

"Progress, my darling," her father explained. "In less than a year, our government contracts alone have doubled. This country is really opening up. The Arizona Territory, the New Mexico Territory, Oklahoma, clear cross the country to California. Immigration is on the increase from Europe. No telling where the boom will end. All I know is that we're working night and day to keep up with the demand for lumber.

"There's an eastern syndicate of multimillionaires that wants to buy me out. They're offering ten million."

"You're not seriously considering it, are you?" Dawn inquired anxiously.

"All of us think Daddy should accept it," Lucy said. "Mama and Peg and me. Maybe you can convince him, Sis."

Peg clapped her hands. "Just think of it. We could travel through Europe, around the whole world. Daddy could even buy his own yacht."

Lucy chimed in, "Peg and I could attend the most fashionable schools in England and France."

"Shop in Paris."

"Vacation in Rome."

Walt Roberts wore a long-suffering expression as he ate without relish. He smiled when Dawn said: "I'm on Daddy's side. That kind of fancy living might be all right for those who were born to it, but we're of hardier stock. Besides, I love it here in the woods. Big cities give me claustrophobia."

"Good for you, honey," her father said gratefully.

Tess, Peg, and Lucy looked as if they had all bitten into unripe persimmons.

Walt tried to pacify them. "You tell 'em, Dawn. Anyway, in another few years the Roberts Lumber Company will be netting ten million a year. Look, Tess, we've got all the money we'll ever need right now. If you and Lucy and Peg want to travel abroad, hell, go ahead. This summer if you want."

Peg and Lucy were ecstatic. "Oh, Mama, let's do it!" Peg begged.

Lucy was jumping up and down in her chair. "Goody! And Peg and I can get new wardrobes in Paris for when we attend Vassar College next fall."

Dawn snorted. "You're not old enough to go to college."

Lucy stuck out her tongue at her sister. "There's a finishing school associated with Vassar which I can go to until I'm ready for college. Please, Mother, say you'll take us."

Tess sighed and threw up her hands. "I don't have much choice, do I? It's evident your father and sister want to get rid of us anyway."

Walt reached over and took her hand. "I'll miss the three of you every minute of the day."

"And so will I," Dawn added.

That matter settled, her sisters ganged up on Dawn. "Have you and Dennis decided when you're getting married?" Lucy asked.

"Not for another year. I want to finish two years at the business school."

"And what a job they do at that college," Walt said proudly. "You should read the business letters she writes for me. And the contracts." He shook his head.

"Dawn, Dennis, and Jack could run the whole shebang by themselves. I'm beginning to feel like a fifth wheel."

He knew it was a fatal error as soon as he had said it.

There was a gleam in his wife's eyes. "Since you are so dispensable, my dear Walter, you can accompany the girls and me to Europe."

"*Yes*, Papa!" Lucy and Peg chorused.

Walt looked at Dawn for help, but she merely shrugged and smiled. "It wouldn't hurt you to take a little vacation, Dad. You're not getting any younger."

"Thanks a lot," he said with sarcasm. "Believe me, I don't have to be reminded."

"Your arthritis and bursitis were never so bad as they were last winter," Tess reminded him. "You could go to one of those health spas while we're over in Europe. They say they perform miracles."

"All right," he said. "I'll go. Come to think of it, I'm really interested in the state of the lumber industry in Europe. Maybe I can drum up some overseas sales. Though God knows we can hardly satisfy our domestic market."

After dinner, Dawn followed her father into the study, where he took his brandy and coffee. "Dad, I was thinking about those eastern tycoons. It might not be a bad idea to let them have a piece of the action."

Walt blinked uncomprehendingly. "A piece of the action?"

The girl laughed. "A term employed by the business community. It means the Roberts Lumber Company could go public. I'll bet those millionaires would gobble up all the stock we'd care to sell them. That way, you could invest their money instead of yours in a radical expansion without risk and without tying up your personal capital."

Walter was impressed. "You learn that at the business college?"

"That and considerably more. Warrants, debentures, notes, mergers, trusts . . ." For the next hour, Dawn regaled her admiring father with a gold mine of information about the world of big business and high finance.

When she finished, he smiled ruefully and massaged the back of his neck. "And I thought I was making a joke before—I *am* a fifth wheel!"

In addition to expanding the company offices while Dawn was in Chicago, Walt Roberts had built two small bungalows up the hill near the big house for his new executive officers, Silver Jack McHugh and Dennis Price.

Several months before Dawn's return from Chicago, Jack moved out of the bunkhouse into his new diggings. That day he took an unmerciful ribbing from his fellow redshirts.

"That's what comes of all that reading he's been doing," Pig Iron Sam lamented. "My old man used to say nothing poisons a man's mind worse than education."

"By gar, Jack," Joe Fournier crowed, "next time we fight, you gonna be like leetle baby in my hands. All that soft livin' eet gonna ruin you, man."

Jack tossed a caulked boot in his direction, but Fournier ducked. Jack waved a fist at the circle of grinning faces.

"Listen here, all you swamp rats, come a time when I can't kick all of your asses around this barrack or all over the swamp, I'll hang my boots on a tree, dig a hole for myself, climb in, and pull the top down."

"Let's hear it for Silver Jack!" someone shouted.

A loud cheer went up and bottles were produced and passed around as they drank one toast after another to their departing foreman.

"To the camp's new administrator!" Pig swallowed a mouthful of beef tonic and passed it to Jack.

When the party ended, Jack swung his knapsack over his shoulder and picked up his bulging duffel bag. At the door, he paused and advised the assembly: "Just remember, I may live up on the hill, but from dawn to dusk I'll be down here riding your butts in the old swamp. See you at supper."

On Dawn's second morning home, she and Silver Jack met in front of the Roberts house as the family was preparing to drive to church in their carriage. Jack was bringing Walt Roberts a report he had worked on until the wee hours of the morning. He removed his cap and made a stiff little bow from the waist. "Good morning, ladies. You look very lovely today."

He addressed them all, but his attention was directed at Dawn. She was wearing a white dress that had a soft blouson bodice and wide sleeves swathed in lace from shoulder to wrist. Her long auburn hair hung loose down her back, investing her with a quality of innocence and purity that wrenched at Jack's heart. Perched on her head was a wide-brimmed straw hat festooned with flowers. He gazed into her luminous green eyes, which swirled with flecks of gold like the still water of a pond with sun full upon it.

"Good to see you back home, Miss Roberts."

"It's good to be home, Jack. And congratulations on your promotion." She offered him her hand, and he took it hesitantly. The mere touch of her velvety fingers set him aflame with excitement.

She gazed in the direction of the two cottages standing side by side on the hillside about a quarter mile off. "What adorable little bungalows! I can't wait to see the interiors."

He shifted uncomfortably from one foot to the other and kicked at a stone with the toe of a boot. "Well, I'd be much obliged if you'd stop by after church and I'll give you a tour. A tour, that's funny. You can stand in the middle and swing a cat around by the tail, and he's had the tour."

They both laughed as Tess Roberts called from the carriage, "Come along, Dawn, or we'll be late. And you know how the Reverend Peters dislikes tardiness."

"I'll see you later," Dawn promised and climbed into the elegant carriage, which held four in the tonneau and a buckboard seat for the driver up front.

"While the cat's away, the mice will play," Peg teased her sister, referring to the fact that Dennis was away attending his uncle's funeral.

Dawn regarded her haughtily. "For a young lady who is going to go to Vassar, you certainly behave in a callow and adolescent manner."

"Girls, girls!" their mother cautioned. "No fighting. Remember it's the Sabbath."

Peggy sniffed. "Well, I don't think it's proper for a respectable young woman to visit a strange man's house without a chaperone. Especially a man like Silver Jack McHugh."

"What's wrong with Silver Jack?" Dawn bridled.

"You can't be serious? Those bawdy ballads the loggers sing around their fires all over the swamp—they're mostly about *his* exploits!"

From the driver's seat Walt called back, "Folk heroes like Silver Jack McHugh frequently receive a lot more notoriety than they earn. The stories grow as the word is passed around from one mouth to another. Fact is, Jack is settling down. He told me the other day that he's not going to Saginaw or Bay City this summer for the annual loggers' wingding. He's going to stay here and help me with the books and catch up on his own reading. Would you believe it, Dawn? Since you exposed him to books, he's become a voracious reader. I imagine he's just about exhausted our poor library."

"Then I'll talk to Sara Wetson. Her aunt is head librarian of a big library in Saginaw. Maybe we can make some arrangement so Jack can borrow books from there."

"For a girl who's engaged to be married, you take an unusual interest in Silver Jack," Lucy offered.

Dawn smiled. "Right from the start, when I recognized that he had a good mind and a desire to learn and improve himself, I had this idea that I could make a totally new man out of him."

Her sisters hooted and guffawed, and Tess Roberts shook her head. "Listen to the girl, Walter. Ever since she was a toddler, she always thought she could do anything she set her mind to. And now she wants to play God." She lapsed into pensive silence.

"Penny for your thoughts, Mama," Lucy said.

Tess looked hard at Dawn. "I hope Dennis comes back soon."

When Dawn returned from church, she changed into a new riding habit she had purchased in Chicago. It had a tight jacket bodice and a slightly caught up double skirt that fell to just below the knee, trimmed with sad-

dle stitching in flat braid. She tied back her hair with a
black velvet ribbon and wore her riding cap at a jaunty
angle.

She gave Dusty a good workout, riding him at full
gallop along the bridle path that ran beside the bank
of the Saginaw River for two miles and then let him
cool down, making the return trip at a slow pace.

Later, she walked the quarter mile to Silver Jack's
bungalow. He was smoking a cigar on the front porch,
with his feet propped up on the railing. When he saw
Dawn coming, he snuffed out the cigar and put his
feet down.

"Don't stop smoking on my account," she said as
she climbed the steps. "I like an occasional cigarette
myself."

"Do your folks approve of smoking?"

"It's not their right to approve or disapprove. I'm
a responsible adult. Of course, I don't smoke in the
house, because that is Mother's province and she makes
the house rules. And they apply to my father as well,
except for his study."

His smile was perplexed. "You sure are some kind
of girl—I mean a woman. Say, you look very pretty
in that outfit."

"Thank you. And you look very handsome, I might
say." She had never seen Jack out of his loggers' uni-
form. Today he was wearing gray striped suit trousers
and a white shirt and tie. "You've had a haircut," she
observed.

He flushed. "Yes, I did, when I was last in Saginaw.
Bought a suit, too. And some other things, but that's
a surprise."

"Good, I love surprises. Well, do I get the tour now?"

"Sure thing." He held open the front door for her.

"It's small, but it's a lot more space than I had in the bunkhouse."

"Do you miss the camaraderie of the bunkhouse?"

"Cama-what?" He blinked. "No, don't tell me. I'd rather look it up in the dictionary myself. That way I won't forget it."

"All right." She stifled the urge to laugh. The process of transition from crude, uneducated redshirt to country gentleman would continue to be difficult until he felt more comfortable in his new role.

The living room was fifteen feet square and boasted a small fireplace with a brick hearth. She recognized the sofa and two easy chairs and the pictures on the wall as castoffs that her parents had stored in the attic for years. There was a small kitchen off the living room and a bedroom next to it.

He went to the bedroom door and opened it. "The surprise is in here."

She could not contain her laughter this time. "I've heard lines similar to that before from certain gentlemen, but I must say your delivery is unique."

His mouth flew open and he blushed furiously. "Miss Roberts! I didn't mean . . . Oh, my God, I sure do put my foot in my mouth!"

She put a hand on his arm. "Oh, Jack, I'm only joking. You've got to develop a sense of humor with all your new knowledge. It's an essential quality in a gentleman or a lady—the ability to laugh at oneself as well as at others." She walked past him into the bedroom.

Jack's surprise hit her the second she crossed the threshold. There was a spare bed and a single chair with a washbasin in the corner, but bookcases completely dominated the room—they covered three walls from floor to ceiling, and the shelves were at least half full.

"Surprise indeed!" she exclaimed. "I am overwhelmed. Where on earth did all this come from?"

"Well, I built the bookcases, and the books I bought in Saginaw. Secondhand, of course. Got 'em cheap."

Dawn walked to the nearest bookcase and took down a leather-bound volume with frayed edges: *The Collected Comedies of William Shakespeare.*

"Got the tragedies, too."

She put the book back and ran her eyes along the titles on the shelf. "Homer . . . Horace . . . Julius Caesar . . . Dickens. I must say you have highfalutin tastes."

"Highfalutin . . . that reminds me." He pulled a large dictionary down from a shelf and opened it. "Let's see. Ca-ma-ra-de-rie—comradeship. Yes, I like that one. And high-fa-lu-tin—here we are." He frowned, and his voice had an injured tone. "Pompous. Is that what you think I am?"

It was Dawn's turn to flush. "No, most certainly not. I used the word mistakenly. You see, I don't know everything, either. I apologize, Jack. One thing you are not is pompous."

He smiled. "All right then. Would you like some fresh lemonade? I've got it in the cooler with a chunk of ice I got from the company icehouse."

"I'd love some lemonade, Jack."

They sat in the living room on the couch and ate cookies along with the tangy cold drink.

"I'm very proud of you, Jack," she confessed. "It's amazing how your education has progressed in so short a time."

He was pleased. "Real credit goes to you, Miss Roberts. You got me started."

She reached over and put a hand on top of his big hand resting on one knee. "That isn't so. I may have encouraged you, but *you* did it by yourself. And it required courage, hard work, diligence."

His eyes met hers, and beneath the surface of the pale blue ice of his eyes there were pools of passion and warmth.

"Miss Roberts . . ."

"Dawn."

"Dawn. It wasn't hard at all. Because I had something worth working for."

"And what was that, Jack?"

"You."

"Me?" Dawn was mildly disconcerted, and she withdrew her hand from his.

"You are very special to me, Dawn. You must have guessed that before this."

"I—I'm not sure what you mean."

"You're the first real lady I ever met. You and your mother and sisters. Oh, don't get me wrong. I'm not fool enough to imagine that you would want to live your life with a roughneck like me, no matter how much reading and education I get. My maw used to say, 'Can't make a silk purse out of a sow's ear.' That's me, a sow's ear. The thing is that I don't fool myself about it. It's enough that I can—what did that Shakespeare say about his love in one sonnet? 'I worship you from afar.' That's how it is for me, Dawn. All of my life I will worship you from a distance." He tapped his temple. "I carry your picture up here in my mind, and I always will."

Tears dimmed Dawn's vision.

Jack looked alarmed. "I'm sorry, I didn't mean to cause you any pain."

She shook her head. "No, it isn't that. No one has ever said anything more beautiful to me in all of my life." Dawn was troubled. "Jack, Dennis and I are engaged to be married, you know that."

"Of course, and I wish the two of you all the luck in the world. He's a good man. He earned my respect when we were fighting that awful fire. He worked shoulder to shoulder with the rest of us and never flinched once, even though he holds down an office job and doesn't keep in shape. He is one lucky man to have a woman like you in love with him."

"Jack, one day you'll find a woman who will love you as much as I love Dennis. I know it's none of my affair, Jack, but how old are you?"

"Twenty-six."

She was surprised. She had guessed he was at least thirty.

He read her mind. "I look older from all the brawls and hard work and hard drinking. Do you know, I've been working the swamp since I was thirteen. But that's behind me, the wastrel's life. I've sworn off booze and brawls and——" He hesitated.

Dawn laughed. "And wild, wild women."

He grinned sheepishly.

Tactfully she changed the subject. "Dad was telling me about your idea of expanding overseas. He's going to mix some business with pleasure when he and Mother vacation in Europe."

"I wasn't thinking of Europe. Malaya and India were what I had in mind."

Her eyes widened. "Malaya and India? Are you serious?"

"You know what teakwood is?"

"I've heard of it."

"Teak is superior to every other wood when it comes to construction. Especially floors and exterior shingles. When combined with iron, it contains oils that prevent the iron from rusting. And most important of all, it is the ideal wood for shipbuilding. It resists rot, termites, you name it. Teak beats all other woods hands down."

"But is there a demand for teakwood?"

"There would be if it were easily available. The thing is, the poor countries where it grows, like India and Malaya, don't have the know-how or the equipment to mass-produce teak lumber for export. If Roberts Lumber were to buy up land where the teak forests flourish—and we could buy it dirt cheap—we could field a team over there to organize a logging industry the same as we've done in the lake states. What do you think?"

"I'm overcome by the scope of your imagination. I suppose the idea is viable."

"It can't miss. Cheap land, cheap labor. The Roberts Lumber Company could buy its own fleet of freighters—fast clippers. Two or three shuttling back and forth from Asia to the west coast of the United States. We could build mills right there outside of San Francisco, which would cut out cross-country shipping charges. Another thing, growing and felling teak, there's no sweating out the winter thaw so you can start the spring drive. Over there it's drive time twelve months a year, with some slow spells only during the monsoon season."

Dawn was impressed. "The more you talk about it, the more logical it sounds. Obviously you have researched the subject thoroughly."

"You bet. I've got five books in my library about the lumber industry in the Far East. Now that I've tried out my pitch on you, I'll discuss it with your dad. I didn't mention teak explicitly when I suggested overseas expansion. Now I'm ready."

Dawn's smile was secretive.

"You look like the cat that swallowed the canary," Jack told her.

"You know, Jack, you are a marvel. You soak up knowledge like a sponge. And your vocabulary! Why, it wasn't too far back that you didn't know what words like 'explicitly' and 'expansion' meant. Now they trip off your tongue as naturally as if you had been using them all your life. You are some kind of man, Jack McHugh. Let me tell you, the girl who gets you will be one lucky woman. Now I must leave."

Jack walked Dawn to the front door.

"Thank you for the lemonade and for an enjoyable afternoon. I really love your little house. Would you like me to make curtains for the windows?"

He was flustered. "Oh, I couldn't impose on you like that. Next time I'm in Saginaw, I'll get some store-bought ones."

"No, you won't," she said firmly. "I want to give them to you as a housewarming gift."

"I'm mighty obliged, ma'am." He saw her frown of disapproval. "I mean, Dawn."

"That's settled."

On the porch she turned to face him. Rising up on tiptoe, she kissed him on the cheek.

"That's for my very, very dear friend, Silver Jack McHugh, the notorious Bull of the Woods." She looked at him quizzically. "Only now the Bull is becoming domesticated."

He grinned shyly. "I reckon his horns have been clipped a trifle."

He watched her walk down the path and across the field to the Roberts house. Rather wistfully he touched his hand to the place on his cheek where she had kissed him.

# CHAPTER NINE

The wedding of Dawn Roberts to Dennis Price in Chicago in June of 1884 was a big social event. Dawn wore her mother's wedding gown—white taffeta, the voluminous skirt worn over a crinoline petticoat. The trim bodice was festooned with tiny seed pearls and trimmed with imported Valenciennes lace. The bridal veil was a waterfall of Lyons silk falling from an ivory tiara. Mellowed by age, both gown and veil had the off-white texture of rich cream.

Peg, Dawn's maid of honor, wore a pastel pink gown of patterned chiffon with a matching picture hat. Lucy and the other two bridesmaids, Dawn's favorite high-school chums, wore lemon yellow gowns of silk taffeta and matching picture hats. The maid of honor and bridesmaids carried small bouquets of red tea roses. Dawn's bridal bouquet was made up of white roses bound together with white satin ribbons. Her mother wore a heavy slipper satin skirt with a satin bodice and a flaring collar to frame the V-neckline.

The bridegroom and the bride's father looked uncomfortable in their black tuxedoes and celluloid collars, but not nearly as uncomfortable as Silver Jack McHugh and a score of other loggers who had been invited to the wedding, all of them wearing store-bought suits that none of them would ever wear again, except maybe at their own funerals.

Silver Jack and Pig Iron had acquired their duds in a most unconventional manner. While walking along Genesee Street in Saginaw, they were attracted by the sounds of a brass band around which a crowd was forming. They moseyed over and Jack asked a stranger, "What's this, a medicine show?"

"Naw, it's Jake Levy's weekly giveaway party. Pretty soon he'll be coming out on that little balcony overhead with a bag of vests. He heaves the vests into the air and all the fellers battle to get holt of one. Anybody gets a vest, he goes into Jake's dry-goods store and Jake gives him the suit that goes with it."

"I'll be damned!" Pig exclaimed. "Want to give it a try, Jack? Maybe we won't have to pay for our wedding clothes."

Jack already had a perfectly good suit, but he'd had a few drinks in a saloon when they got off the train and was in a reckless mood. "What the hell! Why not?"

Jake Levy presently appeared on the balcony, and, after a brief spiel about the high quality of Levy clothing, he cast a dozen vests of multicolored hues and gaudy designs high into the air above the crowd. The pandemonium that followed was terrible to witness. A score of hands clutched at each fluttering vest. The redshirts fought for the cheap garments with the zeal and ferocity of Roman gladiators.

Jack singled out a group of brawlers who were competing for two of the vests and motioned for Pig to follow him. Jack picked a man off the top of the pile by the scruff of his neck and his belt and sent him flying through the air to land facedown in the dusty street. Pig similarly dispatched another one. They systematically disposed of the contestants until all that remained were the tattered remnants of the two vests.

"Here you go." Pig handed one of the relics to Jack, who held it distastefully at arm's length.

"I reckon I'll pass up my free suit. I'd look like a circus clown in this."

"I don't give a damn what them suits is like," Pig said stoutly. "I earned this, and I'm gonna get what's mine. Come on."

Pig marched into Jake Levy's store with Jack right behind him.

A short, wiry, bald-headed man in his late fifties, Jake beamed at his customers when Pig presented his trophy. He grabbed Pig's hand and shook it heartily.

"Congratulations, my boy. You just won a Levy custom-fitted special."

He undraped the tape measure from around his neck and strapped it around Pig's chest.

"*Himmel!* A fifty chest, no less. You are a big, big lad."

He stepped back and studied Pig, head cocked to one side, a finger scratching his chin. "Let's see, my friend, what type are you? Mmmmm . . . I'd say the outdoor sportsman—pipe and tweeds. I have just the thing. Excuse me." He went into the back of the shop.

Jack was convulsed with laughter. "Outdoor sportsman! Pipe and tweeds! Lordy!"

"Woman in Bay City told me I looked distinguished," Pig said, bridling. "So button your lip!"

Levy returned with a suit cut from loosely woven cloth that looked like unadulterated burlap. Silver Jack's eyes popped at the pattern—enormous red and yellow checks set off by vertical blue stripes.

Pig was ecstatic. "Damn! You ever seen anything like that before, Jack?"

"Can't say as I have. Try it on."

Levy helped him into the jacket, which fit so snugly across his back that the bristles growing on his shoulders poked through the weave.

"Seems a mite tight," he complained.

"That's how they're wearing them in New York and London this year," the merchant assured him. "You want to be in style, don't you? Believe me, this suit was made for you." He turned to Jack. "What do you think, my friend?"

"It takes my breath away."

Pig was jubilant. "Wait till those gals on Water Street see me comin' down the block."

"They'll think it's a wangan wagon," Jack said.

Pig glared at him. "What do you know, you old river hog? Jake here says it's the style; I'll take his word over yourn." He removed the jacket carefully and gave it back to Levy. "Pack it up and we'll be on our way."

Levy held up the tattered vest that Pig had presented. "There's one thing bad, my friend. This vest ain't no good. It's ruined."

"The hell with the vest."

"My dear boy. No gentleman with good taste and breeding would be caught dead out in public without his vest. It breaks my heart to see anyone leave my premises who ain't dressed in the height of fashion."

Pig was crestfallen. "Yeah. . . . Well, how about you give me another vest?"

"I only wish I could oblige, but I'd have to break up another suit, and that would reduce its value."

Pig rubbed his jaw thoughtfully. "I'd be willing to make up what you lose. How much?"

Levy sighed and laid a hand on Pig's shoulder. "I hate to disappoint a customer, so I'll do it. And you can have the vest wholesale. Ten dollars—no more, no less. I'm losing money, but I don't care. The customer is always right."

On the way out, they passed a line of fellow winners who were waiting to collect their free suits. Pig recognized one logger and grinned at him.

"Hey there, Lobo, wait till you see the flashy suit I got. Ain't another one like it in the store, I'll bet." He opened the bag and showed off his acquisition.

Lobo whistled and shaded his eyes. "Flashy is right. I wouldn't look at that suit too long, Pig. You might go blind."

A stranger, leaning against the doorjamb, commented, "Won me a suit like that last year, but I gave it to a cookie back at camp."

Pig blinked. "A cookie? A little kid? Why, man, no cookie I ever seen was near as big as you."

The man grinned. "That's right. Only first time I wore it, I got caught in the rain."

The other men doubled up with laughter, while the irate Pig stormed out of the store, cursing and vowing, "Next man says anything about this suit, I'm gonna put the boots to him!"

\*　　\*　　\*

The church was packed with relatives and friends of the bride and groom, but the only person Dawn noticed when she marched down the aisle was Pig Iron Sam Malone in his eye-catching suit.

At the wedding reception, Dawn and Dennis waltzed once around the dance floor before the other guests joined them, and the orchestra on the dais of the grand ballroom played Strauss's "The Blue Danube."

"Happy, darling?" Dennis whispered in her ear.

"It's the happiest day of my life, sweetheart, though I do feel a bit of an imposter."

"How is that?"

"Wearing white, the symbol of the chaste virgin bride."

Dennis laughed and held her tighter. "There's no one knows except thee and me, and I promise not to tell."

"Excuse me, may I have this dance, Mrs. Price?" Walt Roberts tapped Dennis on the shoulder. "Mind if I cut in?"

"She's all yours, sir, but just on temporary loan." Dennis blew his bride a kiss and left the floor.

"Still can't believe it—my little girl a grown married woman. I sure am going to miss you, Dawn. All of us will. Mama, Peg, Lucy, and especially Silver Jack and all your logger buddies. No more working with them in the swamp."

"Don't be too sure, Dad. You don't really think I'm going to join the ranks of the fat matron ladies who fritter away their time playing whist and gossiping, do you? I'll be back in the office bright and early the day after we get home from our honeymoon."

"Maybe not. I want to propose something to you and Dennis when you return from New York."

"Oh?"

"You know that the Roberts Lumber Company has purchased the first of three clipper ships for our new Far Eastern trade?"

"Yes, Silver Jack's idea to add teakwood to our lumber line."

"Inasmuch as it was his idea, I intend to send him to India to organize a branch office. He'll be looking over some teak forest land along the Malabar Coast that we have an option on through some of our London contacts. His responsibilities will be monumental. He will quite literally be introducing native laborers to the logging trade, teaching them everything they need to know about forestry. I don't envy him, I can tell you. Pig Iron Sam is going along as his assistant, but Jack's time will be taken up with his duties in the field. What we need are responsible people to organize the office work, which will be considerable at first. I was hoping I could induce you and Dennis to represent Roberts Lumber in India."

Dawn was flabbergasted. "The very idea takes my breath away. I've always been intrigued by the Far East. Do you think we're capable enough to accomplish such a formidable task?"

"Eminently capable. I wouldn't trust the job to anyone else. You and Dennis and Silver Jack McHugh— the three of you constitute an unbeatable team."

*"You and Dennis and Silver Jack McHugh . . . an unbeatable team."*

"Of course I must discuss it with Dennis before we give you a definite answer."

"Certainly. In fact, I should have broached the subject to you jointly. I apologize, it was thoughtless of me. It's not every day a father marries off a daughter, and I must confess I'm a bit tipsy, particularly after all those champagne toasts."

She laughed and kissed his cheek. "I'm sure Dennis will sympathize. I have a feeling he's had at least as much champagne as you. And my head is fairly whirling in the clouds."

The loggers looked uncomfortably at the reception, keeping to themselves in a corner of the reception hall. They drank surprisingly little of the liquors and wines that were dispensed by rolling bars. Their sobriety was largely due to the influence of Silver Jack McHugh.

"This isn't Tillie's barroom," he had warned them before the wedding. "Any man steps out of line, I'll put the boots to him but good. Understand?"

They understood and acted accordingly.

Shortly before she and Dennis left the festivities to begin their honeymoon, Dawn approached the loggers, who lapsed into strained silence.

She smiled when she addressed them. "I just want to tell you how grateful my husband and I are to you for attending our wedding. And thank you for the lovely silver tea service that you gave us as a gift. I will treasure it all my life." Then she looked squarely at Silver Jack. "Jack, I'd consider it an honor if you would dance with me before we leave."

Silver Jack seemed unable to move, and his face turned beet red. Behind him the redshirts were as quiet as church mice, no man daring to meet the eyes of the other for fear that eye contact would precipitate the laughter that would incite the terrible ire of Silver Jack McHugh.

"Ma'am?" he finally managed to say in a weak voice. "Me dance with you? Miss Roberts . . . I've never set foot on a proper dance floor in my entire life."

Her eyes twinkled with mischief. "Then it's time you took the plunge. Part of your continuing education. Besides, I've heard tales that you cut a mean figure in the dance halls of Saginaw and Bay City."

He stared at her dumbly. How could he explain to a lady that hoofing with whores in dime-a-dance saloons had nothing to do with the fancy dancing taking place in this ballroom?

She guessed what was on his mind and added: "There has been a request to the orchestra to play a set of Irish jigs. I imagine that you will comport yourself extremely well." She offered him her arm, and there was nothing he could do but take the invitation. Dawn led him into the center of the floor, where other couples were forming sets.

Jack took a deep breath as the music began, and Dawn smiled at him reassuringly. Stiff at first, he resembled a stick figure as he jigged around the polished dance floor with the bride, but gradually the lively spirit of the tune overcame his awkwardness, and Silver Jack danced as he had never danced before. He and Dawn were by far the most animated couple on the floor, and near the end of the set the other couples stopped to form a circle around them, clapping and tapping with their feet to the tempo of the Irish jig.

Dawn was exhilarated as Jack whirled her about so fast that the faces around them were meaningless blurs. When the final chord had sounded, she was far too dizzy to stand unsupported, and she sagged against Jack.

"That was marvelous, the best time I've had all night," she gasped.

Dennis came over to them solicitously. "You two put on quite a show. Are you all right, darling?"

"Marvelous." She linked her arms in theirs, and together the three of them walked off the floor.

"Here we are, the Three Musketeers," she said gaily. "At least we will be when we set sail for India."

Dennis smiled, somewhat ruefully. "You look surprised, Jack. Hasn't Mr. Roberts advised you that Dawn and I will accompany you and Pig to the Far East to do the book work for our new branch office?"

Jack recovered from the initial shock. "As a matter of fact, he hasn't mentioned it to me yet."

"You don't sound very enthusiastic about it," Dawn said.

"That's not it at all, Miss Roberts. I just reckoned that you and your husband would want to settle down to housekeeping when you get back from your honeymoon. I mean, from what I've heard and read, India is not exactly Chicago, U.S.A. It's got snakes and bugs and wild animals, and it's either beastly hot or swamped with rainfall."

"We'll survive very well, thank you. Now, Dennis and I must be off." She shook hands with him. "We'll be back in a month. Until then, *auf Wiedersehen*. Look that one up in your German dictionary."

"I don't have to, Miss—" He stopped and looked mortified.

Dawn laughed. "You called me that before. Is it that hard to get used to?"

"I mean, Mrs. Price," he said humbly.

Dennis clapped him on the shoulder. "I can't get used to it either, old man."

Dawn pursued it. "You were about to say that you didn't have to—what?"

"Look up *auf Wiedersehen*. It means 'Till we meet again.' "

He looked after them as they walked off the dance floor and out the door of the ballroom.

Pig came up behind him. "You did mighty well by yourself, old buddy."

"Yeah . . ." Jack said absently. Then his face took on a determined expression. "Pig, let's you and me get out of here and head for River Street and do some serious drinking and wenching."

" 'Bout time!" Pig said enthusiastically. "Iffen I don't get out of this starched collar and tie, I'll plumb garrote myself to death!"

# BOOK TWO

# CHAPTER ONE

The clipper *Golden Cloud* was long and slender as an arrow: Though she measured 245 feet from stem to stern, she was only 35 feet wide. Her hull was painted black with a line of gold trim just below the rail running the length of the ship. Her decks had been holystoned to chalk white, as they were before each new voyage, and one could see one's reflection in the metalwork. Adorning her bowsprit was a figurehead—the nude upper torso of a woman carved out of polished teak. At the stern, the Stars and Stripes whipped smartly in the breeze blowing off San Francisco Harbor.

Flying from the top of the *Golden Cloud*'s tallest mast was the guidon of the owner, the Roberts Lumber Company, a pennant embossed with a crossed lumberman's ax and a peavey hook.

As the Prices walked down the quay, Dawn marveled, "Isn't she the most beautiful ship you've ever seen, Dennis?"

"Magnificent. Truly a queen of the seas. She has speed written all over her, and speed means money. Clippers deliver cargo halfway around the world in half the time a lumbering cargo vessel can make the run, and where produce is involved, it's delivered fresh."

When they reached the foot of the gangplank, Dennis called to two officers at its top: "We're the Prices. I do believe we're expected."

The men straightened up. They were tall, erect young men wearing neatly pressed dark uniforms, white shirts with black ties, and black patent-leather shoes.

"Please come aboard, Mr. and Mrs. Price," the shorter of the two said. From the number of gold stripes on his arm, Dawn guessed he was the first mate. Her hunch was confirmed when they reached the deck.

Both men saluted, and the shorter one introduced himself. "I am First Officer Delano. This is Mr. Lassiter, the second mate. Mr. Roberts is with the captain and Mrs. Gresham in their quarters. Please come this way."

"Did you hear what he said? 'Mrs. Gresham'?" Dennis said in a tone of surprise.

"From what I understand, a clipper captain is a special man and rates special privileges."

Dawn realized that "special privileges" was an understatement as soon as they set foot in the captain's quarters. The suite and its appointments were positively luxurious. The living accommodations of the master and his wife consisted of a large combination bedroom and sitting room paneled in rosewood and mahogany. There were padded benches built into two walls of the room and a variety of easy chairs, along with a couch. What most astounded Dawn was the elaborately carved baby-grand piano in one corner of the room.

Captain Grant Gresham was a ruggedly handsome young man with a brush mustache and an athletic physique; he was dark of hair, eyes, and complexion. His wife, Teresa, a sweet-faced brunette with merry blue eyes, was well along "in the family way" as her husband delicately phrased it.

Dawn sat down beside her on the couch while Dennis and her father accepted Captain Gresham's invitation to step over to the small but well-stocked serving bar near the piano.

"I'm expecting my baby in another two months," Teresa confided.

Dawn did some rapid reckoning. "That means you'll give birth while we're at sea."

The girl smiled. "It's commonplace, Mrs. Price. Stone, our ship's physician, is highly competent. Ours will not be the first baby he has delivered at sea."

"Your first?"

"Yes, Grant and I have been married for three years, but this is our first."

"How remarkable. And in those three years have you always accompanied him on these voyages?"

"Oh, to be sure. We're quite inseparable. When Grant was still a first officer, he served under a captain who had quite literally raised a family of three children aboard his command ships."

"I can't help but observe how youthful your husband is; his officers, too. I've always envisioned all sea captains as bearded, grizzled, godlike men—all ancient mariners."

Teresa laughed and said with a note of pride: "Clipper captains are a special breed of men. From the instant they set foot on board a ship as youths, they share one consuming ambition: that one day they will be the master of a clipper. They must be strong, aggressive, and stern. Many of them tend to be merciless." She smiled. "That is where Grant is in a class by himself. He is the unqualified master of every ship over which he assumes command, but his mastery is tempered by the quality of mercy.

"And the clipper crewmen, from master down to the lowest deckhand, are special, superior seamen. Most clipper captains are worshiped by their crewmen, but seldom loved. Grant's men love him. They know he's a driver, obsessed with speed and more speed, and that he will spare nothing to strengthen the rig and extend more canvas. And they, in turn, are bulldogs who hang on grimly until the spars are splintering and the head knees are splitting." Two pink spots appeared in her white cheeks. "I'm sorry, Mrs. Price. I have a bad habit of running off at the mouth about my husband."

"And you have every right to. He's a fine figure of a man."

She'd had no idea that a ship's captain might be such a dandy. Gresham's blue swallowtail coat was expertly tailored, contrasting with skin-tight light-gray trousers. A heavy gold watch chain spanned the chest pockets of his dazzling brocaded vest. An elegant tall beaver hat hung from a hook on the wall behind his captain's table, which was littered with charts, sextants, and other navigational aids.

Encouraged by Dawn's obvious interest, Teresa continued. "In rough weather I've seen Grant strap himself into a chair for three days by the helm with icicles forming in his eyelashes and mustache and in his ears, eating hardtack washed down with cold coffee. But early in the voyage, when seas are calm and everything is routine, he designates authority to his mates. In fact, Grant won't interfere with a subordinate's decision unless he believes it to be a critical misjudgment."

Captain Gresham rang for the cabin boy and ordered cakes and tea for the ladies. He said to Dawn: "Mrs Price, as the head representative of the Roberts Lumber Company, perhaps you would care to join the gentlemen and myself at the chart table? I wish to explain to you the sailing track the *Golden Cloud* will follow on our voyage to India."

"I would be delighted." She and Teresa stood up and followed the men to an easel-table at one side of the captain's desk on which was thumbtacked a political map of the world. It was covered with colored crayon tracings, each tracing indicating a nautical route connecting the different continents of the world.

Captain Gresham placed his right index finger on the city of San Francisco. He ran the finger along a red line that arched from the Golden Gate to the island kingdom of Japan.

"Our first port will be Yokohama, Japan, where we will stop only briefly to take on fresh water and supplies. From Yokohama we sail southwest to Canton, China." He looked at Walt Roberts. "You will be happy to hear, sir, that the *Golden Cloud* will be accruing profits to your company even before we load our first shipment of teakwood. At our last port, Seattle, we took on a full lading of seal and otter pelts. The market for furs in the Orient is insatiable. At Canton we will barter our skins for tea and silk. From Canton we sail across the China Sea to Singapore, where we'll stop briefly before sailing through the Strait of Malacca and into the Indian Ocean. After traversing the Indian Ocean, we sail around and up the southwest coast of India—the Malabar Coast——to the port of Mangalore."

"Approximately how much of a distance is it from San Francisco to Mangalore?" Dawn asked.

Gresham smiled. "Somewhat less than fourteen thousand miles."

"By God!" Dennis exclaimed. "That is literally halfway around the world!"

"Indeed it is, sir." The captain nodded. "But I will vouch that it will be a trip you will never forget, and when it is over, you will wish it might have continued much longer. The *Golden Cloud* is a proper queen, and she will accord you all royal treatment. Now, if you will excuse me, I must go up to the bridge. We will be casting off in another hour. I'll have the steward show you to your quarters, Mr. and Mrs. Price. I trust you will find them comfortable." He tugged at a pull cord behind a drapery to summon the steward.

He gave his wife a chaste kiss on the forehead. "I will see you sometime before we dine, my dear. You too, Mr. and Mrs. Price. I hope you will honor Mrs. Gresham and the officers of this ship by dining at our table."

"We would be delighted," Dawn assured him.

Captain Gresham left the room, and Dawn and Dennis said their farewells to her father.

"You will be sorely missed by all of us, dear," he said, somewhat misty-eyed and choked up.

Dawn tried to make light of what, despite the staunch Roberts reserve, was a highly emotional scene for both of them. "I'm sure Peg and Lucy will be dancing with joy now that I am out of their hair."

"Don't you believe it." He stepped forward brusquely and hugged her, pressing his cheek to hers. "Good luck, my darling. Be sure and telegraph us as soon as you and Dennis have safely arrived in Mangalore. And write your mother regularly."

Dawn laughed. "Yes, Daddy, I promise. To hear you talk, one would think I am a hapless child going off to school for the first time."

He kissed her cheek, shook hands with Dennis, and bowed to Mrs. Gresham. "Ma'am, it has been a distinct pleasure meeting you and Captain Gresham. Knowing that he is the skipper of my clipper ship, I'll sleep peacefully at night."

"Thank you." Teresa gave a small curtsy. "And don't worry about your daughter, sir. We'll take good care of her."

After Walt Roberts's departure, Dawn, Dennis, and Mrs. Gresham sat down again, awaiting the arrival of the ship's steward. "Would you care for another tea, Mrs. Price?" Teresa offered.

"No thank you." She hesitated. "Inasmuch as we are going to be together so much during the weeks and months ahead, we should really drop the formalities. I wish you would call me Dawn. Dawn and Dennis."

Teresa nodded enthusiastically. "Oh yes, I do agree. And you must call me Teresa."

There was a rap on the cabin door. "Steward, ma'am."

The steward, like the other crewmen Dawn had seen since she'd been aboard the *Golden Cloud,* was good-looking, well built, and natty in his sharply creased dark trousers and starched white jacket. He informed them that this was a temporary position for him, to enable him to do his apprenticeship at sea.

"Perhaps, by the next voyage, the skipper will be signing on some new hands, and I hope to qualify by then. I *will* qualify!" he said with determination.

"I'll wager you aspire to become the captain of your own clipper one day," Dennis said to him tongue-in-cheek.

The steward was perfectly serious. "Oh yes, sir, that is the ultimate ambition of every man jack who sails the clippers. One day to secure a command, or, at the very least, to obtain mates' papers."

"Highly commendable," Dawn said.

He showed them their cabins with real pride, two roomy compartments with a connecting door. One cabin had been converted into a bedroom that had a double bed with brass corner posts. The cabin adjoining it had been turned into a cozy sitting room with spare but homey appointments.

Dawn clapped her hands in approval. "It's charming! I know we'll be very comfortable and happy in the course of the voyage."

The steward backed out into the corridor. "I'll have your luggage brought down as soon as the baggage coach arrives from the depot," he said, closing the door.

"Well," Dawn said, turning to Dennis, "this is much nicer than I expected." She removed her hat, shawl, and jacket and fluffed up her hair in the mirror above the small dresser. "Is there a bath?"

Dennis shrugged. "Not in here there isn't. Captain Gresham was telling your father and me that we're housed in a section of the ship's quarters reserved for dignitaries." He grinned impishly. "Like the daughter of the ship's owner."

"Don't be a snob, Dennis. Come along. Let's do some

exploring." They left the cabin and walked down the corridor, which was no more than twenty feet long. In all there were four cabins. At the end of the corridor was a single bathroom.

Dawn was pleased. "Since we are the only dignitaries aboard the ship, the entire province is ours. I think I'll bathe before supper. Do you know when that will be?"

Dennis consulted his pocket watch. "Let's see, it's three-thirty now, and we're due to sail at five o'clock. I believe Gresham said something about six bells. Is that six o'clock?"

"No, silly. If you're going to be a seagoing wayfarer you had better learn how to tell ship's time. Six bells is seven o'clock. The day is divided into six sections of four hours each, with each section divided into eight time segments which in turn are marked off by bells sounding the hour and half hour; eight bells comprising one time segment. . . . Now—"

"Never mind," he said, cutting her off. "I'll depend on you to tell the time for both of us."

Back in their bedroom cabin, he watched her undress with the same sense of rising desire he had experienced the first time Dawn had given herself to him at his cottage back in Michigan. She shed her dress, petticoat, shirtwaist, and corselet, then wriggled out of her chemise, coyly turning her back to him. She looked over her shoulder and arched an eyebrow.

"Stop looking at me that way. One would think you had never seen a naked woman before."

"With you it's always the first time." He went to her, putting his arms around her so that his hands fondled her breasts.

Dawn felt the thrust of his rising member against her

bare bottom. "Stop it, Dennis, we really don't have the time. I have to take my bath."

"We can combine the two. I'll bathe along with you."

"You're positively depraved." She turned in his embrace and put her arms around his neck, pressing the length of her sinuous body against him. "But I wouldn't have you any other way." She went to the door, deliberately exaggerating her walk so that her buttocks wriggled and flexed.

"You're not going out in the corridor without a robe, are you?"

Dawn giggled. "I almost forgot where we are." She went to a wardrobe built into the cabin wall. "Teresa said she had put some of her things in here for me to use until our luggage arrives. She's such a sweet girl, don't you think?"

"Indeed I do. And our skipper is quite a fellow himself."

"Yes, but he seems too genial and boyish to be the master of such a ship as this and to command all these rough crewmen."

"Appearances can be deceiving. Speaking for myself, I wouldn't want to serve under Captain Gresham and do anything to incur his wrath."

Teresa Gresham had thoughtfully provided Dawn with a full change of clothing, including shoes, stockings, a robe, and slippers, as well as a sensible plain brown town dress. For Dennis there were freshly pressed seaman's trousers, a work shirt, socks, a robe, and slippers.

She went down the hall to run the tub while he undressed. When he came into the bathroom, she was sitting on the closed commode. "Takes a while for the kerosene heater to warm up the water."

"I know of a splendid way to pass the time."

He took her hands and pulled her to her feet, then slipped her robe off her shoulders and let it billow down around her ankles and feet. His robe followed. They were both eager for consummation when steam began to waft up from the boiler at one end of the tub.

Shaking with desire, Dawn half filled the tub and stepped in. It was a large, cast-iron tub that could have accommodated three people, and Dennis, taking in its size, said flippantly: "If Silver Jack were on board already, we could invite him to join us. There's plenty of room."

Color flamed up in Dawn's face. "What a crude thing to say, Dennis!"

Her reaction took him aback. "I say, darling, where is the famous Roberts sense of humor? Certainly you didn't think I was serious?"

Dawn recovered her aplomb and forced a smile to her lips. "Of course not. And I'm sure Silver Jack would be far more shocked than I am at such a prospect. He's really quite puritanical, in spite of his reputation."

"Yes, I know. All of his breed are like that. There's no limit to what they'll do with whores, but they put their sweethearts, wives, sisters, and mothers on pedestals to be worshiped from afar."

The casual reference jolted Dawn even more than his suggestion that Silver Jack join them in the tub. It was virtually the precise expression that Silver Jack had quoted to her that day at his bungalow: *"I worship you from afar. . . ."*

Dennis was frowning. "What is it, darling? You suddenly look so strange."

"Nothing, nothing important. I was just struck by a terrible thought. Suppose Silver Jack and Pig are lying drunk in some dockside barroom and miss the sailing time?"

His face clouded over. "My God! Don't even think about it. It would be a major disaster if our crew chief didn't show up in India."

She placed a hand on his arm and looked into his eyes. "Would you be terribly disappointed if we just bathed? We can make up for it tonight."

"I agree wholeheartedly. Suddenly I feel very impatient. I'll be tense until everyone is aboard and we've cleared the mouth of San Francisco Harbor."

"My sentiments, too." It was a half-truth. Actually, Dennis's risqué reference to Silver Jack and his uttering nearly the identical words Silver Jack had used to express his deep feelings for Dawn had struck a highly sensitive nerve in her. If she and Dennis pursued their lovemaking, she was in dread that she might be overcome by the same fantasy she had entertained once before: With her eyes closed she had imagined, with shameless lust, that it was not Dennis but Silver Jack McHugh within the bower of her thighs.

# CHAPTER TWO

Dennis and Dawn's apprehensions were allayed when Silver Jack and Pig Iron swaggered up the gangplank fifteen minutes before sailing time with their duffel bags slung across their shoulders. Dawn tried to conceal her irritation with Jack for making the deadline by the skin of his teeth. At least he and Pig were clean-shaven and had fresh haircuts. They were wearing khaki trousers and matching bush coats.

"Hear tell, this is what's in fashion in India," Jack explained self-consciously.

"You'll blend in with the scenery like the British infantrymen," First Officer Delano assured him. "Come along. I'll take you to your quarters. You'll be in officers' digs with the second mate and myself. There's a spare cabin because the third mate came down with dysentery yesterday, so we'll be short one hand."

Dawn and Dennis stayed on deck to watch the *Gold-*

*en Cloud*'s departure from San Francisco. Strutting up and down on the quarterdeck, still in his fancy attire, Captain Gresham took a keen-eyed inventory of the vessel. Satisfied that all was shipshape, he bellowed through a megaphone, "All right, *mister!*"

The first mate, standing amidships, saluted and relayed the order to the crewmen, "Prepare to cast off!"

With the precision of soldiers, the men split into teams to perform their specific tasks. One group worked the windlass that would warp the ship away from the dock, while others hauled in the lines.

As the *Golden Cloud* sailed majestically westward, the setting sun was a dazzling orange sphere balanced on the Pacific horizon and framed in the mouth of the bay.

Dawn shielded her eyes against the glare. "It *is* a golden gate, truly it is."

"Magnificent!" Dennis put an arm about her waist and pulled her tight to him.

A discreet cough behind them alerted them to the presence of Silver Jack. " 'Scuse me, folks. Mind if I join you? God! What a sight! Brings a lump to my throat."

"How are you and Pig coming along? Are you settled into your quarters?" Dawn asked.

"Yes, ma'am, and mighty fine quarters they are, too. Trifle cramped for two men big as Pig and me, but then again, we did our time in the bunkhouse, three men stacked up in a triple bunk. . . . Mr. Price, I want to ask you something."

"Jack," Dawn said in exasperation. "How many times do I have to tell you? We are a partnership in this Indian venture, and formalities are unnecessary. You will call us Dawn and Dennis, is that understood?"

"Yes, ma'am," he replied. "Dennis, Pig and I will be climbing the walls if we have to sit on our duffs for the duration of this voyage. Do you think it would be out of order to volunteer our services to the captain?"

"I think that's an excellent idea, Jack," Dennis said. "As a matter of fact, I thought I'd volunteer my own services to Captain Gresham. You know—keeping ship's books, taking inventory and checking it against the manifest. Tell you what, we'll approach the subject at dinner tonight. You will be eating with us at the captain's table."

Jack was troubled. "No need for that. Pig and I are content to eat with the crew. We'd feel out of place with the captain and the other officers."

Dawn faced him and placed her hands on his arms. "I feel like shaking you, Jack McHugh. If you're to be the field superintendent of the Roberts Lumber Company's Asian branch, you had better start acting like an executive instead of a lackey."

Jack smiled crookedly. "I guess I spent too much time in the swamp as a redshirt. . . . By the way, should we wear jackets and ties at dinner?"

"I think it would be appropriate the first night aboard. It's sort of a celebration," Dawn said.

"Good God!" Dennis slammed a hand to the side of his head. "Pig isn't going to wear that monstrosity he wore at our wedding?"

"Never fear, Dennis. A fellow warned him when he got it, 'Don't get caught in the rain.' Only he did. He gave it to the cook's ten-year-old son. We bought him a blue serge suit in Frisco."

There was an atmosphere of celebration at the captain's table that evening. Wine and champagne flowed like water. There were Gulf Coast prawns served in dill sauce, goose-liver pâté, prime ribs of beef with Yorkshire pudding and rich brown gravy, and plum pudding smothered in lemon hard sauce for dessert.

"This sure beats the grub in the swamp," Pig observed as he washed down his third helping of plum pudding with scalding hot coffee.

"I'm pleased that you are enjoying it, Mr. Malone," said the captain as the steward refilled the champagne goblets.

Teresa Gresham wore a full black taffeta skirt and a smock shirtwaist of white satin to minimize the fullness of her figure. Her hair was done up in an oval barrette wrapped with embroidered silk.

Dawn looked stunning in a bodice of brilliant flowers against a black background skirted in pure silk taffeta of shimmering turquoise. Her long hair, gathered up in a chignon snood of gold thread dotted with small pearls, was alive with quicksilver from the light of the chandelier that swung gently above the table to the roll of the clipper as she ploughed through the dark Pacific.

Over brandy and coffee, Dennis and Jack offered their services to Captain Gresham. The skipper's eyes lit up with amusement, and he stroked his beard.

"In all my years at sea I've never heard a passenger aboard a ship volunteer to stand a seaman's watch. My word, do you hear that, Teresa?"

"I think it is very considerate of Mr. Price and Mr. McHugh to offer. You are short two crewmen and a third mate, Grant." She smiled and winked at Dawn. "And it won't be too long before you lose your trusty assistant." Her hands spanned her swollen belly.

Gresham chuckled and shook his head. "I keep forgetting." For the benefit of the others at the table, he explained: "Since our marriage, Teresa has developed into quite an accomplished navigator. She can use a sextant and make nautical observations every bit as well as I can. She's a wizard at working up time from the chronometer and keeping a reckoning of ship's position on the charts. I've come to depend on her very much. In fact, she is my right-hand man."

Responding to the laughter of Dennis and Jack, he qualified it: "Figuratively speaking." And he joined in the laughter.

Neither Teresa nor Dawn was amused. "I am not your *right-hand man,* Grant Gresham," his wife said hotly. "I am your wife, an equal partner in this marriage, and I will support you whenever I am able and *willing!"*

"Bravo, Teresa!" Dawn applauded.

"It would seem that I have trod on certain feminine toes," the captain said apologetically. "My dear, no offense intended."

"Apology accepted." And Teresa's expression softened. "He really is quite a dear most of the time, Dawn." She sighed. "But he is a man and needs to be reminded on occasion that females are no longer the mere chattels they were a generation ago."

"Amen," said Dawn and cast a wicked look in her direction.

"Well, Captain Gresham, will you have us?" Dennis asked.

Gresham tapped his cigar in an ashtray. "By Jove! If you want to carry your weight aboard the *Golden Cloud,* you shall do so. Mr. Price, I understand you are a bookkeeper and accountant. I think you might spare me an hour's work a day by keeping the ship's log. You'll soon get the hang of it."

"I also did a good deal of sailing with my uncle as

a boy on Lake Michigan," Dennis added. "He's a ferry captain now and has commanded a lake steamer. I know how to use a sextant, work up time, and calculate position on the charts. With a little brushing up under Mrs. Gresham's tutelage, I'll manage very well, thank you."

"Splendid! Now as for you, Mr. McHugh, what can we find for you?"

"You name it, I can do it," Jack said without hesitation. "Scrambling around on your masts and spars is a piece of custard pie compared to the high-rigging we do in the swamp."

"Good man! McHugh, I hereby appoint you as special bosun's mate in charge of anchors, rope, and rigging for the duration of this voyage." He consulted the chronometer on the wall. "Time I made my rounds. Why don't you gentlemen come with me and see what being a sailor is all about?"

They excused themselves to the ladies and walked down the hall to a companionway that led up to the main deck. Brisk, clean salt air stung their faces as they emerged onto the deck. The sky was a black velvet setting for an infinity of dazzling diamonds.

"We'll make a full round of the ship and then we'll visit the helmsman; see if he needs any relief."

After the heavy meal it was a welcome diversion to stroll around the long ship. Here and there groups of sailors were squatting on hatch covers or leaning against the rail, laughing and talking.

"Your crew seems to have good morale," Dennis observed.

They followed the captain up the ladder to the poop deck. The first mate was speaking with the helmsman.

"Everything all right, Mr. Delano?"

"Spanking along, sir."

Captain Gresham squinted up at the sails, taut and full to the inexperienced eyes of Dennis, Jack, and Pig. "But not for long, Mr. Delano. Marley," he ordered the helmsman, "the wind is falling off. Haul three points to the northwest. We'll catch a sidewind."

"Aye, aye, sir."

"And now, gentlemen, I'll bid you all good night and pleasant dreams. We'll discuss your new duties over breakfast."

Dennis went down to the cabin where Dawn awaited him, reclining on the big brass bed. On night tables on either side of the bed there were hurricane lamps. The candles within the globes cast provocative, flickering shadows. Dawn was clad in a sheer satin nightgown trimmed with lace. Her hair fanning out across the pillow had the sheen of burnished copper.

Dennis stood at the foot of the bed, saying nothing, devouring her with his eyes.

She smiled. "Well, what are you waiting for, my darling?"

Without speaking he removed his jacket, unbuttoned his shirt, and cast them over the back of a chair. His socks, shoes, and drawers followed. Naked at last, he stood by the bed, his desire for her evident from his quickened breathing and erect penis.

Dawn sat up and slipped the nightgown up over her head. It fell to the floor at the side of the bed. Dennis gently took her in his arms and kissed her mouth, her eyes, her throat. She threw back her head in uncontrolled pleasure and ran her fingers through the hair on his chest, then caressed the length of his body, across his belly, and finally closing tenderly around his tumescent male organ.

The gentle rolling of the clipper added a new dimension to their lovemaking, and as they reached the height of their passion, Dawn had to bite the pillow to prevent herself from screaming out her indescribable joy. Later, as they lay blissfully in each other's arms, the *Golden Cloud* rocked them to sleep.

When Dawn awoke, the sun was streaming through a porthole, bathing the bed in golden light. She was alone in the cabin. Evidently, Dennis had arisen early to begin his new assignment as surrogate third mate.

Dawn dressed as casually as if she were going riding through the swamp back home. On her honeymoon, she had purchased several pairs of a unique item of female attire called culottes. In fact, the garment was a pair of knee-length trousers with unusually wide legs, but when worn, it gave the appearance of a short dress. This morning she donned a pair made of soft fawn leather chamois with a matching jacket that laced up the front with buckskin thongs. She rolled up her hair in a bun at the back of her neck and fastened it with two pearl combs.

Once on deck she bid a smiling good morning to several seamen who tipped their caps to her as she strolled toward the stern of the ship. The clipper was cruising through the smooth Pacific with all sails set. Because of the tranquil conditions, the first mate had relieved from duty the morning watch, with the exception of the helmsman and the watchman. The helmsman stood relaxed at the wheel, his eyes darting from the compass to the taut sails overhead to the sea beyond the bowsprit and back to the compass.

As Dawn approached the bridge, the watchman said something to the helmsman, who took a small steel hammer and struck a single ring on the bell attached to the binnacle. Up forward, the lookout acknowledged the time reckoning by sounding the big ship's bell once, the flat gong reverberating the length of the clipper.

"Eight-thirty!" Dawn exclaimed. "I had no idea."

First Mate Delano came up behind her. "And a fine morning it is, Mrs. Price. Did you sleep well?"

"Never better in my life." She couldn't help recalling the tempestuous lovemaking that she and Dennis had enjoyed, inspired by the mystic romanticism of the rolling ocean.

"Mrs. Gresham asked me to inform you that she will be honored if you will have breakfast with her in her cabin."

"I'd be delighted. I hope she didn't delay her breakfast on my account. I realize this is a scandalous time to be rising on shipboard."

"Not at all, ma'am. Since she's been in the family way, the captain's wife has been keeping to her bed until late morning."

"Have you seen my husband?"

"Yes, he's down in the forward hold with Captain Gresham checking the cargo against the ship's manifest."

"And Mr. McHugh and Mr. Malone?"

Delano grinned. "Getting their baptism at the stern, helping the bosun and bosun's mate repair the spanker sail. Care to have a look?"

She followed him along the rail past the quarterdeck to a point where there was a clear view of the stern. Wearing only a pair of denim trousers cut off above the knee, Silver Jack McHugh was straddling the boom of the spankermast with the same nonchalance he had exhibited astride tree limbs a hundred feet above the ground. The sunlight reflecting on his glistening, muscular body and tousled hair showed him off at his most striking.

"Handsome figure of a man," Delano murmured. "Looks like a living figurehead."

"Yes," Dawn said in a small voice and turned quickly away from the scene. "I must join Mrs. Gresham."

When she knocked at the cabin door, Teresa called out, "Come in." She and the ship's physician, Dr. Stone, were sitting on the sofa having coffee and biscuits with jam.

"I hope I'm not interrupting," Dawn apologized. "I can come back."

"No, no, Dawn, dear. The doctor has completed his examination and he says that I am in perfect health."

"Absolutely," said the doctor. "Now, if you ladies will excuse me, we have a case of malaria in the crewmen's quarters."

"Malaria?" Dawn was puzzled. "But how—?"

"A chronic case, dating back to the war. It's not contagious, never fear." He donned his officer's cap and left the cabin.

Teresa's smile was radiant. "Oh, you can't imagine what it means to me having you aboard, Dawn. Grant denies me nothing, but the one thing he can't provide is feminine companionship. Do you understand?"

"Of course, I do, and I feel the same way. If you weren't aboard the *Golden Cloud,* I'd feel like a fish out of water." She began to laugh. "That's a bad joke, but it is apt, you must admit."

"What about some breakfast? I'll ring for the steward."

"Don't bother, Teresa. What you have here will do me just fine. I must pay careful attention to my diet during this voyage. I'm unaccustomed to this sort of inactivity. Did you know that I was raised in a lumber camp in Michigan? I had so much physical activity that I could eat pork and beans and slabs of bread covered with molasses three times a day and never gain an ounce."

"What an exciting life you must have led," Teresa said wistfully. "The most exciting thing that has ever happened to me is marrying Grant and going to sea with him. Before that I was a Virginia hothouse flower, as Grant loves to tease me."

"Well, you are making up for it now. It must be very exciting being married to one of the youngest clipper skippers in the service."

"Yes, I love Grant with all my heart. But it does get lonely being the only woman aboard all the long dreary months at sea."

Dawn leaned over and patted her knee. "Once your baby comes along you won't have time to be bored or lonely."

Teresa smiled. "Yes, I can't wait."

"Do you want a boy or a girl?"

"I really don't care, though I guess I hope my first is a boy. I know that's Grant's longing, to have a son to carry on the tradition of the sea. You know, a sea captain is very much like a priest."

Dawn's eyes flashed mischievously. "Not too much though, from the looks of your belly."

The two women giggled merrily. Teresa said, "Dawn, I already think of you as a sister."

"I'm pleased you feel that way. I'd be proud to have

you as a sister. Now, I do believe I'll have myself some biscuits and jam."

"Pull the bell cord behind Grant's desk, and we'll order some fresh coffee. This pot has gotten quite cold."

Below decks, Captain Gresham and Dennis had completed the inventory of the forward hold. "I must say I'm overjoyed that you and your associates volunteered to lend a hand. This task would have taken me twice as long to accomplish alone."

"Glad to be of assistance. I'd like to have a go with the sextant, if it's all right with you."

"By all means, you shall take the noon sight. Let's see how the bosun and McHugh and Malone are faring with that spanker."

They walked aft and found the threesome sitting on a hatch cover smoking gnarled Mexican cigars. The repaired spanker sail was taut and sturdy.

"Good job, Peyton," Gresham complimented the bosun. "How is he treating you lads?" he asked Jack and Pig.

"Like a Dutch uncle," Jack said. He looked at the bosun. "Mike, you said I could take the next lookout watch."

"I dunno," Peyton said doubtfully. "Climbing around a clipper's rigging is a lot different than high-rigging in a forest." He squinted up at the main sky-sail. "That bugger is close to two hundred and fifty feet above the deck, and right now, even in fair weather, it swings in a pendulum arc better'n thirty feet."

Jack laughed. "Tell him, Pig, what it's like topping a Michigan fir tree in a high wind."

Peyton shrugged. "It's the skipper's decision."

Gresham looked at Dennis, who nodded and said, "If he didn't know he could handle it, Jack wouldn't offer."

"Then go to it, Mr. McHugh."

Just before noon, Dennis went up to the quarterdeck with the captain's sextant and shot the sun. At the same time, Jack McHugh was on his way up the mast to the crow's nest. Bosun Peyton and a group of crewmen were craning their necks upward to observe his performance.

"He's nimble as a monkey," someone commented.

Halfway up the mast, Jack took time to put on a show for his audience. With the sure footing of a tightrope artist, he walked out the full length of a spar, turned, and walked back again. The spectators cheered and clapped.

"I'll work in the rigging with Silver Jack any time," a seasoned old salt vowed. "He's a proper clipper rat, he is."

"He ain't got no right taking a risk like that," the bosun said severely.

Pig laughed. "Risk? You got to be kidding. His right hand was no more than six inches away from a sheet anytime. Jack wasn't risking his neck, take my word for it. He don't do nothing without insurance."

Dawn and Teresa were also witnesses to Jack's feat. When he finally climbed into the lookout's tower, Dawn exhaled in relief.

Teresa contemplated her shrewdly. "Why, my dear, you are as white as a sheet. Mr. McHugh means a good deal to you, doesn't he?"

Dawn, momentarily flustered, recovered her aplomb. "Indeed he does. Silver Jack McHugh is one of the company's key personnel. He's virtually irreplaceable. I don't know what Dennis and I would do without him in India."

"Yes, of course," Teresa agreed.

But there was a certain quality in her voice and in the steady gaze of her eyes that Dawn found highly unsettling.

# CHAPTER THREE

For the first four weeks at sea, conditions were ideal. Captain Gresham took advantage of the excellent weather and strong tail winds to push the *Golden Cloud* westward at record speed.

Morale was excellent among the crew. High spirits overshadowed the fact that the fresh rations had given way to commonplace seafare. The crew had achieved a degree of teamwork, swarming aloft and managing canvas, that enabled them to function like a precision machine.

Crossing the international date line was an occasion for celebration aboard the *Golden Cloud,* as it had been for generations of seamen before them. A canvas sail was rigged up on deck so that it resembled a large saucer. Then seawater was pumped into it, forming a shallow pool.

"You'd best put on your oldest and cheapest

clothes," Teresa advised Dawn, grinning broadly. "You are about to be baptized into a new world."

All of the crewmen were congregated on deck, attentive to Captain Gresham as he made repeated sightings from the quarterdeck. At last he put down the sextant and addressed the assembly: "Avast, me hearties, this is it. We've crossed the line."

A tumultuous roar went up from the crew, and a score of hands seized upon Dennis, Dawn, Silver Jack, Pig, and several other greenhorns who were making the symbolic crossing for the first time. One by one they were tossed into the canvas pool to commemorate the historic moment.

Later, Gresham cautioned Dennis: "Remember, in crossing the international date line, we have lost a full calendar day out of our lives. A half hour ago it was two P.M. Wednesday. Now it is two-thirty P.M. Thursday. You must make that notation on the charts."

The nights were balmy and tropical now. Dennis liked the midnight-to-four-A.M. watch. There was little to do but keep track of the time so that he could wake up the next watch and gossip with the helmsman. Pacing the deck, he had to pick his way among the shadowy huddled figures who preferred to sleep topside, lulled by sweet gentle breezes and the rocking-cradle motion of the ship. One night he came upon Silver Jack leaning on the rail at the stern, mesmerized by the phosphorescent wake of the fast-moving clipper.

"Looks like a mess of stars," he observed to Dennis.

"Yes, not unlike our Milky Way." He searched the sky for confirmation. "Having trouble sleeping, Jack?"

"No, I just hate to waste a gorgeous night like this."

"Bosun Peyton treating you and Pig all right?"

"Yeah, Mike is a nice guy, but every day gets more

monotonous than the one before. How much farther you reckon we got to go?"

"Captain says three weeks to a month."

Jack sighed and threw his cigar butt into the sea. "Well, I made it this far. I guess I'll hold out for another month."

On the bridge, the helmsman struck the binnacle bell twice, and from the lookout there sounded a matching response from the ship's big bell.

"I'd better go on making my rounds," Dennis said. "I'll see you in the morning, Jack."

The next few weeks dragged agonizingly for everyone except Captain Gresham. "Stop thinking about the end of the journey," he would say. "Like a pot watched too attentively, it will never come to a boil. Or at least it seems that way."

The good weather and winds held, and the *Golden Cloud* voraciously devoured the nautical miles. On the big map tacked to the wall in the captain's cabin, a new pin was added each morning after the previous day's travel distance had been computed. And each pin brought ship and crew closer to Japan.

One night Teresa did not appear in the lounge for dinner. Gresham looked calm but grave. "I have a notion it will not be too long before Teresa goes into labor," he announced.

Jack and Pig pretended to be engrossed in their food. Having babies was strictly women's business, and they were indignant that anyone would try to foist such a delicate matter upon them.

Dawn put down her knife and fork and started to rise. "I must go to her at once. I'll take her a pot of tea."

"No, no, don't concern yourself, my dear. Finish

your meal. When I left the cabin she was sleeping peacefully," the captain assured her.

Nevertheless, Dawn passed up coffee and dessert and ordered the steward to fetch a pot of tea and sweet biscuits to the captain's quarters. Teresa was sitting up in bed, propped up on pillows, reading a book by the bright illumination of a large kerosene lamp suspended from a swag chain. She was obviously pleased to see Dawn.

Dawn sat down on the side of the bed and patted the other woman's swollen belly. "I give you one more day, two at most."

"I hope you're right. He or she is getting highly impatient to escape into the real world. I can't sleep at night for all the kicking."

"Bear with it, dear." She picked up the book Teresa was reading. *"Stormy Destiny,"* she read the title. "What's it about?"

Teresa laughed. "About a ship's captain back in 1812 who brings his new bride to sea with him. Did you know that until fairly recently it was considered bad luck to have a woman aboard a merchant ship? We were put in the same category as black cats and fleeting rats."

Dawn laughed. "What ridiculous rubbish the male animal invents to maintain his so-called superiority and ascendancy over the female. Never mind, this crew owes you and me a debt of gratitude for the splendid sailing conditions that have prevailed all through this voyage. We women are the harbingers of good fortune."

"Amen," Teresa concluded, and the two women shook hands solemnly.

Teresa still had not gone into labor as the *Golden*

*Cloud* raced across the China Sea heading for Canton. On a sultry Sunday afternoon Dawn and Teresa were lounging on the deck when the lookout sang out, "Canton Bay, dead ahead!"

"All hands on deck! All hands on deck!"

The call was passed on from First Officer Delano, down through the ranks, to the men off duty in the hold. Captain Gresham took his place on the quarterdeck and peered through a spyglass, turning to the second mate from time to time to relay an order.

Jack and Pig were two of the first crewmen aloft, clambering around the rigging like monkeys. The sleek clipper sailed gracefully into Canton Harbor, breasting the sagging tide. One by one, her studding sails crumpled as the light canvas was taken in and furled. The *Golden Cloud* proceeded cautiously and slowly through the crowded harbor. As far as the eye could see, they were surrounded by sailing craft of every nationality, design, and size. Naval vessels represented every major power in the world. And scurrying about the larger ships like water beetles were Chinese junks, sampans, and the houseboats of the water people.

"Did you know that there are children aboard some of those boats who have never set foot on dry land?" Teresa said to Dawn.

"How terrible for them. Teresa, why do some of those Chinese boats have eyes painted on their bows?"

"To keep them on a true course and to alert them to the presence of the devils of the sea."

Little boats with bamboo decks and festooned with flowers pulled alongside the clipper. Women waved and screamed: "You buy fresh flowers?" "You wanna washee clothes?"

Dawn stood up, shading her eyes with her hands.

On the mainland, rice paddies teemed with workers, mostly women. Beyond the paddies, green and verdant hinterland stretched away to rolling foothills, pale with mist. The Pearl River emptied into the bay, twisting upstream to the city of Canton.

The clipper was abreast of the narrow island of Lintin when Teresa doubled over, clutching at her belly.

"It's coming, Dawn! My water just broke."

"Come along, I'll help you down to the cabin and then summon Dr. Stone."

Captain Gresham was so absorbed with bringing his ship into the anchorage that he was oblivious of what was taking place below the quarterdeck. A tug pulled alongside the *Golden Cloud* and put aboard a pilot who wore a richly brocaded robe emblazoned with dragons and a black skullcap. His beard was gray and stringy, and his elegant queue hung halfway down his back. He saluted the captain and took up position behind the helmsman, issuing a series of commands in a soft but authoritative voice in passable English.

Gresham monitored the helmsman's every move, and when at last the *Golden Cloud* slid into her berth with the smoothness of a knife gliding into its sheath, the skipper straightened up, wearing a broad grin, and shouted through cupped hands to First Mate Delano, "Let down the anchor, Mr. Delano!"

There was the harsh clatter of the heavy iron anchor chain feeding through the scupper, and a waterspout geysered deck high as the iron monster struck the surface of the bay and submerged.

Captain Gresham received the shock of his life when he burst into his cabin some time later. His wife was writhing and moaning on the big bed as Dr. Stone and Dawn Price hovered over her. Dr. Stone said something to Dawn, who came over to the pale and stricken captain.

"Is—is she all right?" he asked.

Dawn smiled reassuringly. "She is perfectly fine, Grant. I think it would be better if you waited outside."

From the bedside, Dr. Stone called out, "Go down to the galley and have yourself a cup of coffee laced with rum."

"I think I'll do just that." He turned and fled the delivery room gratefully.

Word spread quickly that the skipper's wife was giving birth, and as Gresham strode along the deck, the crewmen pressed around him, offering congratulations and patting him on the back.

"Don't you fret, skipper. Mrs. Gresham will pull it off as slick as you brung the *Cloud* into her berth!"

In the officers' mess, Gresham collapsed in a chair and, abiding by the physician's prescription, told the steward to bring coffee and rum. He was shortly joined by the first and second mates and Dennis Price. They all shook his hand, and when the coffee and rum were served, Dennis lifted his cup in a toast.

"I'd like to drink to your firstborn. Be it boy or girl, may it not be your last, sir."

"Thank you." Gresham looked self-conscious as the other men drank in silence.

They were on their third drink when Dawn burst into the room, her face radiant with excitement: "Captain Gresham, I am proud to announce that you are the father of a bouncing baby son. He's healthy as a horse, the doctor says, and from the deafening volume of his voice, I'd say he's born to be a clipper master."

Gresham sat immobile in his chair, his mouth agape and his eyes glazed.

"He's in state of shock!" Dennis said.

"Skipper! Skipper! Didn't you hear what Mrs. Price told you?" Delano shouted. "You're the father of a baby boy!"

Second Mate Lassiter pounded Gresham on the back. "Congratulations, Captain Gresham. What a banner day for you. First you bring the *Golden Cloud* into Canton in near record time, and then you become a father the same day. What are you going to call him, by the way?"

The captain was striving to recover his composure. He swallowed hard and then spoke in a hoarse voice. "Teresa and I had planned to call a boy Walter Gresham, after my father. Of course his middle name will be Lintin."

Delano and Lassiter smiled. "Not bad, sir. It could have been bloody worse, say, Hong Kong or Macao."

Dennis and Dawn were perplexed. "Whatever are you talking about?" Dawn asked.

"Old clipper custom, Mrs. Price," Delano informed her. "When a child is born at sea, it's considered good luck to add a middle name to celebrate where the birth took place. In this case, Mrs. Gresham went into labor when the ship was passing the island of Lintin."

"How quaint," Dawn said. "It does have rather a nice ring to it. Walter Lintin Gresham. And now, sir, why don't you visit your wife and son in your cabin? Teresa can't wait to show him off to you."

"Yes, yes, by all means." He stood up and raised his cup, toasting the mates and Dennis and Dawn. "Mr. Delano, Mr. Lassiter, Mr. and Mrs. Price, my eternal gratitude to all of you for being so supportive of me and Teresa in our exciting but intimidating endeavor." He smiled wryly.

"Hear! Hear!" Dawn was handed a cup, and they all drank to their present good fortune and their high expectations for the future.

They continued to sit around the table after Gresham departed.

"Well, we've completed the first leg of our long pilgrimage," Dawn said. "I'm so impatient to get to India and commence our teak lumberjacking."

"Patience is our foremost virtue," Dennis reminded her. "We are quite literally building this business from the ground up."

"Not quite, darling. You forget that Daddy arranged with the British authorities to build living quarters and office space even before we embarked."

"It's still a long, tough road to hoe," Dennis said. "We have options on a score of land tracts in the Malabar mountain ranges. It will take us at least six months to select a half dozen sites we want to purchase. Then Jack and Pig are going to have their hands full training a native labor force to work the tracts. For that matter, Jack and Pig are going to have to reeducate themselves. Felling teak trees is quite another proposition than felling the firs back in the swamp."

"I have every confidence in Silver Jack McHugh."

"And so do I."

"Well, my heart will be with you, I can tell you," the first mate offered. "If your Indian operation is a great success, the skipper says the Roberts Lumber Company will be buying two more clippers, and that he'll put me up for master of one of them."

"Yes, and I'll replace Delano as first officer," Lassiter added.

"Splendid," Dennis said. "Then all of us have a

stake in the outcome. Gentlemen, and you my love, I want to propose a toast: To the future. To the future realization of all of our aspirations."

*"And that includes you, Silver Jack,"* Dawn thought to herself.

# CHAPTER FOUR

That afternoon the American consul at Canton visited the *Golden Cloud*. Roland Dreyfuss was a short, stocky man with curly red hair and weak blue eyes that squinted from behind blue-tinted spectacles.

"Captain Gresham, your fame precedes you," he said to the master of the clipper. "Mrs. Dreyfuss and I would be honored if you and your wife and passengers would join us for dinner this evening."

"It is we who are honored by your generous invitation," Gresham replied. "But I am afraid that Mrs. Gresham is presently incapacitated."

"I am indeed sorry to hear that, sir. I hope it is nothing serious."

"Quite serious," Gresham said with a straight face. "I can think of nothing more sobering than becoming the mother of an infant son—except, perhaps, becoming the father."

"You mean—?" The consul burst out laughing. "I say, that is an occasion for celebration."

"I think I had better do my celebrating aboard with Mrs. Gresham. However, I am sure Mr. and Mrs. Price would be delighted to attend your dinner."

Dawn echoed that sentiment. "Indeed we would, Mr. Dreyfuss, but I do hope it is not a formal dinner."

"No, not at all formal, just a simple dinner party. Come as you please. I will have a carriage dockside at six o'clock. Perhaps we will have time to give you an abbreviated tour of our city."

"That would be delightful," Dawn said. "We will be at the top of the gangplank awaiting your arrival."

Dreyfuss tipped his hat and departed, and Dennis and Dawn went back to their quarters to bathe and dress.

"I propose we bathe together to save time and water," Dennis suggested.

Dawn slapped his face playfully. "I've heard that story before. Save time, is that your thinking? You know as well as I do that such a proposition would entail twice as much time than if we bathe separately."

"You do have a point," he admitted with a smile.

After bathing and washing her hair, Dawn put on a terry-cloth robe and wrapped her head in a voluminous towel. When she returned to the bedroom, Dennis commented, "You look like an Indian princess with that turban."

"Maybe a rajah from Bombay will ask me to join his harem," Dawn jested.

"His purdah, you mean. That's what it's called in India."

"Whatever. Imagine having twenty or more women at your beck and call!"

"I have all I can handle with one woman." He went down the corridor to the bathroom, and Dawn began dressing. She put on a pink teddy undergarment with a snap crotch and thin whalebones built into the bodice to support her breasts. Over that went a lace shirtwaist worn with a starched petticoat. Her gown was of silk crepe georgette with a long, brightly banded broomstick skirt in blue, yellow, red, and green.

Dennis returned from his own bath. "You look beautiful. What should I wear?"

"Dreyfuss said it would be informal. Why don't you wear your blue blazer and white flannel trousers?"

"Yes, I've heard that white linen suits and matching hats are worn like uniforms in this part of the world."

"Maybe we can do some shopping in Canton or Macao before we set sail again. In my opinion, oriental and Indian garb are far more exotic and alluring than our so-called civilized attire."

"I agree," Dennis said. "You'd look ravishing in a sari or a Japanese kimono."

"Than I shall buy some. I want you to always think of me as exotic." She pulled off the towel he had tied about his hips and contemplated his erect phallus. "Well, that answers my question. You do find me alluring. I only wish there were something I could do to alleviate your condition, but I'm afraid it will have to keep for tonight."

"You vixen. I have half a mind to rape you, party dress and fancy hairdo be damned."

She kissed him and said, "I'm going up to visit with Teresa and the baby until Dreyfuss gets here."

Roland Dreyfuss's carriage arrived on the quay at five minutes before six o'clock. He had changed his white linen suit for a black swallowtail jacket and gray trousers and a beaver hat. A coachman assisted Dawn and Dennis into the carriage.

"You're very punctual, Mr. Dreyfuss," Dawn said as she settled herself on the soft velvet seat.

"Part of the foreign-service training, Mrs. Price. May I say that you look very lovely."

"Thank you. You did say something about a brief tour before we go to dinner."

"Yes, indeed. I think you will find it very informative and possibly instructive inasmuch as you and Mr. Price are going to settle in India. The Indians and Chinese, all Asians, have many things in common. For one, they fear and distrust Occidentals."

"And for good reason, from what I've read," Dennis said.

"That may be, sir, but it is a distinct disadvantage that we who live and work in Asia must contend with on a daily basis. Before the first Opium War, which ended in 1842, China was shut off from the rest of the world. The emperor, an absolute despot, had decreed that no foreign devils, as Westerners were called, should ever set foot on the mainland of China. However, out of deference to the wealthy Chinese nobility—the mandarins, roughly the equivalent of English dukes and earls—who stood to make fortunes out of healthy trade with the West, he permitted Western traders to occupy a narrow strip of land along the Pearl River on the outskirts of Canton where they could build offices, warehouses, and other functional dwellings. The warehouses were full of steel, iron, tin, other valuable metals, tools and equipment, animal pelts—all sorts of items from the industrial West. They were traded for, among other things, tea, silks, jade, and various oriental spices.

"The Cohong, or 'officially authorized firms,' held a monopoly on trade with the West and served as middlemen between the white traders from England, America, Holland, and France and the inscrutable Chinese government. They were among the richest men in the world.

"This comfortable and mutually profitable arrangement was disrupted when the British began to smuggle opium into China on a large scale. The opium headquarters was situated on the island of Lintin, a heavily guarded fortress. In 1839 the emperor lost patience with the foreigners who were turning his people into drug addicts and launched a military operation against Lintin. The British were driven off the island and fled to Macao, and the emperor's troops dumped six million dollars' worth of opium into the river.

"In retaliation, the British navy shelled the Chinese forts at the mouth of the Pearl River, and British marines marched inland, killing and pillaging along the way, to the city of Canton.

"Three years later the emperor sued for peace, but it was obtained at a high cost. The British were given the island of Hong Kong, and five coastal ports were declared open treaty ports, were Westerners of all nations were permitted to set up shop and conduct unrestricted trade with the Chinese mainland."

"And of course the opium trade was resumed without restriction, as well," Dawn observed. "Small wonder the Chinese fear and mistrust the foreign devils."

They passed through the sector where commerce had formerly been conducted from the warehouses, now rickety, decaying artifacts of a bygone era.

The consul lived in an American settlement on the outskirts of Canton. It might have been a New England village with its white colonial homes surrounded by picket fences and privet hedges in a setting of trees, colorful flower gardens, and terraced lawns. There was even a prosperous-looking Christian church on a high hill overlooking the town.

Roland Dreyfuss and his family occupied the largest and most impressive dwelling in the occidental community, actually a lavish estate set in the middle of a four-acre tract of land surrounded by a wrought-iron fence. A Chinese gate guard opened the magnificent portal, and the carriage passed through and traveled along a winding road that displayed exquisite scenic wonders. A bamboo bridge crossed an artificial pond highlighted by a waterfall whose spume was a source of refreshment for swans and ducks. A dazzling peacock preened and strutted atop a marble pagoda across the pond. The landscaped lawns and gardens were a potpourri of rainbow colors.

The house was as spectacular as the grounds around it. The entry hall, where Mrs. Dreyfuss greeted them, was a gallery with a high fluted ceiling. The marble floors were covered with silken oriental rugs, and the furnishings tended to a Far Eastern motif, delicately structured and inlaid with teak or japanned wood. The wall draperies, the bronze and china figurines, the porcelains, the oil paintings—all were magnificent.

"It quite takes my breath away," Dawn confessed. "What if you ever return to the United States? How will you survive giving up all this?"

Mrs. Dreyfuss, a short, chubby woman with tightly curled hair very similar to her husband's, had a cherubic smile. "I refuse to part with any of it, Mrs. Price. I have extracted a vow from Roland that if we are transferred back home, he will dismantle the house stone by stone and reconstruct it in Vermont along with all of the appointments."

"And that will be a tall order," her husband added.

"Do come out on the patio and meet our other guests," Mrs. Dreyfuss said. "And please call me Mae, dear."

"Mae and Rolly," her husband said, echoing the sentiment.

"And Dawn and Dennis," Dawn returned.

"Good, we're all very informal and clannish here in the American sector."

The house swarmed with Chinese servants all clad in native garb. The men were distinguished by their queues and skullcaps. A dozen or so guests, mostly yankee traders and their wives, were gathered on a flagstone terrace at the back of the house. The women wore plain, outdated dresses, and Dawn felt rather flashy and self-conscious in her stylish gown.

"I'll bet they're all wearing white cotton bloomers," she whispered to Dennis.

"I have no wish to find out," was his retort.

One of the guests was a mandarin, a small, bald-headed old man clad in an ornate silk robe embroidered with an exotic design in gold thread. Around his neck were strands of pearls, gold chains, and precious gems. The ruby button on his black skullcap was the symbol of his rank. He spoke perfect English with a marked Oxford accent; he revealed to Dennis and Dawn that he had attended the university in England for four years.

"The Phoenicians invented commerce," he discoursed, "and the English turned it into a fine science. Do you know what enabled England to outstrip the French, the Spanish, all of the aspiring sea powers in

Europe? A small but significant thing. The English were the first to develop a foolproof method of curing pork and beef. Up until that pivotal discovery, both warships and merchant ships of all nations had to transport their fresh food with them to carry them over the long months at sea. Can you imagine, a merchant vessel or a man-o'-war teeming with pigs, chickens, cows, goats—all variety of livestock? Think of the valuable space these creatures occupied that could have been employed to better advantage filled with salable cargo. Not to mention the insidious effect it had on the crew's morale to be confined aboard a floating barnyard. Yes, England certainly earned its reputation as queen of the seas."

"What a fascinating concept," Dawn declared. "Mr—? I do beg your pardon. My tongue is unaccustomed to dealing with oriental names. I'm afraid I don't have your remarkable talent for languages."

The ancient, wizened face expanded in a hundred smile creases. "And I find you to be a most fascinating woman Mrs. Price. As for the name think nothing of it. My name is Wu Ping-ch'ien, but you may address me as Houqua. In the early days when China was first opening up to Western trade, an illustrious relative of mine was without a doubt the most famous member of the Cohong, a group of merchants who were instrumental in persuading the emperor to let them do business with the foreigners. He was known as Houqua."

"Why was that?" Dawn asked.

The old mandarin sighed. "You see, at that time it was considered quite unseemly for noblemen to barter and bargain in the public marketplace. Therefore, they used assumed names so as not to reflect disgrace on their families." He reached out and put a delicate hand on her arm. "Today there is no longer any such stigma, but I have a fond affection for the name and what it represents. So, Mrs. Price, I will be honored if you count me one of your friends and call me Houqua."

"I would be delighted, Houqua."

He insisted on escorting Dawn in to dinner and sat at her right hand. On the other side, Dennis whispered to her, "It seems you have made a conquest."

The mandarin bent forward and glanced across Dawn at her husband. "I heard that, Mr. Price. My esteemed wife claims I can hear the rice shoots growing in the paddies. And 'conquest' is an abominable understatement. I am totally enamored of the glorious creature. Tell me, how long will your ship remain in Canton?"

"Not for any longer than it takes to dispose of our cargo and take on Chinese cargo to be transported back to the United States," Dennis told him. "Three or four days at most."

"That is regrettable, indeed. I was hoping you would spend a day with my family at our humble estate near the Ts'ung Hua hot springs. Hua is reputed to be the site of the mythical Fountain of Youth sought by the explorer Ponce de Leon."

"He certainly was a long way off course," Dawn jested. "We are grateful for the invitation, Houqua, but I'm afraid we just won't have time. It is imperative that we reach our destination, Mangalore, on the Indian Malabar Coast, as soon as possible."

"Yes, Mr. Dreyfuss had apprised me of your most ambitious undertaking. I have never understood why the British have neglected such a promising enterprise, the potentially flourishing trade to be gained from teakwood."

"Possibly lumberjacking is not indigenous to the nature of the British," Dawn said, "just as trading and bartering were anathema to your mandarin princes. You said yourself the English are sailors and traders. On the other hand, since the first boatload of Pilgrims set foot on the American continent, they have fashioned a culture with their bare hands, working the fertile fields and the virgin forests. We're builders and growers, we Americans."

"And we've learned a bit about seamanship and trading from our British cousins," Dennis reminded them.

Conversation was less animated as the servants began to serve the most sumptuous and exotic meal that Dawn and Dennis had ever tasted. It was far more than an appeal to the taste buds. The table was a work of art and beauty.

The meal consisted of twenty-five courses. Among the delicacies served were broiled sharks' fins, Peking and mandarin duck, jellied octopus, plovers' eggs, giant prawns, lobster, roast suckling pig—the list was endless.

The food was served on exquisite porcelain platters flanked by solid silver cutlery, and the wines were poured into fragile silver cups.

"A far cry from the pork and beans that was common fare back in the logging camps of Michigan," Dawn told the assembly.

Captain Gresham was a topic of conversation in his absence. The almost godlike men who skippered the big clipper ships, many of them legends in their own time, were held in high esteem by the China trading community.

Houqua lifted his goblet and proposed a toast: "To

the lovely ladies assembled here tonight." His gallantry in including all of the women was apparent, for he never once removed his steady gaze from Dawn Price.

A merchant from Hong Kong with a heavy Dutch accent offered a more somber toast: "I would like to drink to the demise of the noble clipper ships." Digesting the murmur of dissent and indignation that passed around the table, he amended his words. "It saddens my heart, as well as your own, but we must face reality. The transatlantic ship of the future is the steamship. Already, merchant steamers propelled by engines that turn propellers at the stern have bettered the best records set by sailing ships."

"Bah, humbug!" growled an Englishman at the table. "The steamship is a flash in the pan. Unreliable, I say. They are constantly breaking down."

"Only because they are in their infancy," rejoined the Dutchman. "Within ten years the steamship will have entirely replaced the sailing ship as the commercial ocean carrier. What is your opinion, Mr. and Mrs. Price? You are Americans, the most inventive and visionary people on earth."

Dawn looked at Dennis, and Dennis cleared his throat. "I regret to say that my wife and I must agree with Mr. van Dyke. The steam engine is to our modern society what the wheel was to our ancestors—a major breakthrough in technology. In time it will revolutionize every conceivable aspect of world affairs. Shipping, industry, transportation, even warfare. Just before we left America for China, a New York manufacturing company was trying to convince my father-in-law to invest in the development of a saw that is driven by an engine. He claims it will do the work of an entire crew of loggers."

"Preposterous!" the Englishman puffed.

The mandarin eyed him shrewdly. "You really believe that, Colonel?"

"I most certainly do!"

"You are, no doubt, familiar with the renowned artist and scientist Leonardo da Vinci?"

The English colonel wrinkled up his long nose and said archly, "Italian chap, I do believe."

The mandarin smiled. "Italian, yes, he was. You really should read his notebooks dealing with hydraulics, mechanics, physics. Da Vinci predicted that one day there would be sailing craft that would operate beneath the seas and still other vehicles that would sail through the air above land and water."

The colonel's eyes popped, reflecting absolute incredulity. "By Jove, now I *have* heard everything." He winked at his host. "Then again, what can you expect from an Italian? They're all mad."

Dreyfuss saved the awkward moment. "I think it time that the gentlemen retire to the study for brandy and cigars while the ladies take some after-dinner sherry in the music room."

There was a scuffling of chairs and feet as the assembly rose and separated into two groups.

"This archaic custom annoys me beyond all patience." Dawn commented to some of the women as they walked toward the music room. "Why should we be relegated to a portion of the house far removed from the gallant gentleman with their brandy and cigars? It's as if we were children."

The other women looked at her as if she were a creature from another planet. One of them overcame her shock and found her voice. "Surely, my dear, you would not care to be present in a smoke-filled room listening to men's raucous laughter and bawdy jokes? What *lady* would subject herself to such an indignity?"

There was the germ of a revelation in what the woman had said. Dawn pursued it. "In other words, madam, you feel that the male of the species is not on the same civilized level as we females are?"

The woman laughed at her. "My dear girl, how naive can one be? Of course, you are a newlywed and we must make allowances for your inexperience with the married state. We all went through it at one time."

"Went through what?"

"The realization of the true nature of man. Men are motivated by greed, lust, avarice. They revel in witnessing contests of bestiality and in killing other living creatures."

"All men are beasts," Dawn repeated mechanically.

"Certainly. Come along, we're dawdling."

It was a rude awakening for Dawn Roberts Price. Up until this moment she had held the male animal strictly accountable for the birth and development of the myth of male superiority and for its unabated perpetuation century after century. It struck her now with a jolt that there was another side to the issue, that both sexes regarded each other as inferior for different reasons.

In the meanwhile, the men were discussing commerce and politics, international banking, war and sports. There was serious talk of the Malayan praus, or pirates.

"Pirates?" Dennis exclaimed. "In this day and age?"

"You had better believe it," Consul Dreyfuss said. "Just last month the buggers ambushed a Dutch merchantman on its way to Singapore. The course that must be taken through the South China Sea is a maze of tropical islands that offer sanctuary for fleets of cutthroats and thieves who prey on the shipping trade.

"Like all of their comrades in infamy, the pirates attacked the Dutchman at dawn. The Dutch crewmen were well armed and drove off the pirates time after time, killing many of them and sinking one of their three brigs with a cannon. But the pirates' superior numbers and firepower eventually prevailed. They boarded the hapless merchantmen and slaughtered all the survivors except for three British women on their way to join their husbands in the colonial service."

"What happened to the women?" Dennis asked tersely.

There was a long silence before the consul answered, "It is something that none of us here in this room cares to contemplate."

"In such cases the phrase 'a fate worse than death' applies only too literally," intoned the Englishman.

"That's abominable!" Dennis said angrily. "Good Lord! The mightiest nations in the world have naval forces here in the area. You mean to say that together their combined fleets can't sweep the China Sea of this scourge on humanity and civilization?"

"Oh, it has been attempted," Houqua interjected. "On countless occasions British, French, German, American, and Dutch naval vessels have scoured the sea for the praus."

"Yes, and they seem to vanish into thin air like will-o'-the-wisps," Consul Dreyfuss said grimly, "only to materialize again when they sight a potential victim."

"It would seem to me," Dennis said, "that the logical answer to the problem is to convoy the merchant ships doing trade in these Asian waters."

"Logic and practicality often do not go hand in hand, Mr. Price," said van Dyke. "The sea lanes between Japan and India comprise some four thousand miles. And the merchant ships trading along those lanes number in the thousands. The combined fleets of all the sea powers of Europe and America could not protect every vessel that traverses the China Sea and the Indian Ocean."

There was a sly tone in the mandarin's voice as he added: "Not to mention the fact that the foreign powers policing the waters off the China coast are loath to disperse their naval power too thinly and too far removed from their primary mission in this remote part of the globe. Although the treaty signed with England and the other foreign powers ceded the free ports to open international trade after the Opium Wars, the emperor has never conceded defeat. There is an ancient saying, 'There is no such thing as defeat; only respectful submission until the next battle.' "

"I fear that Houqua speaks the truth," Dreyfuss conceded. "Right now the foreign nationals in China are sitting on a powder keg that could explode at any minute. Our intelligence agents in China are sending back some very disturbing reports. The Ch'ing emperor, Kuang Hsü, is a moderate leader who has been endeavoring to adopt certain advantages of Western education and administrative techniques into Chinese society and government. But he is vehemently opposed by the conservatives and reactionaries who will settle for nothing less than than total expulsion of the foreign devils This powerful faction supports the dowager empress, the most powerful personality at the royal court. Even now it is claimed that under the empress's auspices a secret revolutionary army called I Ho Ch'uan,

which means Righteous Harmonious Fists, is being
formed." He smiled thinly. "We jokingly refer to them
as the Boxers, but believe me, nobody is laughing at
them."

Dennis addressed the mandarin. "Houqua, as a
Chinese nobleman, a man of education, experience,
and intellect, what is your personal view of the current situation in China and what do you expect to
happen in the future?"

Houqua looked Dennis straight in the eye and smiled
cryptically. "I try to hold myself aloof from politics,
Mr. Price. As an intermediary between East and West,
I must walk a razor-sharp line of neutrality. So, I must
disqualify myself from the present discussion."

Dennis sensed a faint arrogance in his demeanor.

"There is another ancient oriental proverb that
speaks the truth," Houqua continued. " 'One who runs
with the wolves and hunts with the hounds must in-
variably be torn asunder by both adversaries.' " He
rose and bowed first to the consul and then to his
fellow guests. "This has been a most enjoyable and
stimulating evening, but for one of my years it is far
past the time when I ordinarily take to my sleeping
couch. I have arranged for a carriage to pick me up
at midnight, and, as I can see by the clock on the
mantelpiece, that hour is almost upon us. I do not
wish to suffer the fate of the heroine in that charming
fairy tale, Cinderella."

"Well, we can't have you turning into a pumpkin,
my dear friend," Dreyfuss said and put an arm around
the mandarin's thin shoulders. "Come along, and I'll
escort you to the door."

"Thank you, but first I must pay my respects to the
dear ladies."

"To be sure."

Houqua turned at the door and made a low bow to the men in the study. "May good health and good fortune be with you until we meet again And Mr. Price, if you and your exquisite wife change your minds. I'd be delighted to have you visit with me at Ts'ung Hua."

"I am afraid not, sir. and we are terribly disappointed to refuse your hospitality."

Houqua nodded and smiled his inscrutable smile. "There will be another time. Perhaps even sooner than we think."

# CHAPTER FIVE

The *Golden Cloud* sailed out of Canton Bay at dawn on Sunday. When Dennis, yawning and stretching, climbed the companionway to the deck, the island of Macao was no more than a green dot on the horizon. He reached the quarterdeck and joined First Mate Delano, who was speaking with the helmsman.

"Port the helm, Mr. Dana, and hold her steady as she goes. I'll check in with you before you're relieved. Care to join me at breakfast, Mr. Price?"

"Delighted. I don't believe my wife will be at the captain's table this morning. She's dining with Mrs. Gresham in the captain's cabin."

"And how is the skipper's son doing? He's been pretty much confined to the cabin since we docked in Canton."

"Dr. Stone advised that the baby should be isolated from the noxious vapors that permeate the entire harbor area. Canton, Lintin, and Macao are teeming with pestilence. There's dread of a cholera epidemic spreading from the mainland."

"I can tell you that I, for one, am glad to be putting to sea again. We should have an easy run from here to Singapore."

"Barring an attack by pirates," Dennis said, half in jest.

Delano looked grave. "It's no joke. I myself have never encountered any pirates, Malayan or otherwise, in five trips to the Orient, but I know only too well that they exist. One of the most infamous cases was the grisly fate of the crew of the merchantman *Massachusetts*. Chinese pirates murdered a score of 'em. Slit their throats, cut off their genitals, and threw them overboard. It's said the Chinese pirates make the Malayans look like Sunday-school lads.

"The worst tribe of Chinese pirates on record were the Ladrones. They manned fleets estimated to be as large as several hundred ships, and they virtually decimated even heavily armed warships. The emperor dispatched numerous naval expeditions against the Ladrones, but in most of the battles the wily pirates, led by one Ching Yih, put the imperial Navy to rout. Ching Yih arrogantly declared war on China and boasted that he would depose the emperor and declare himself the new emperor of China. Ironically, it was not the emperor's army and navy that destroyed Ching Yih's outlaw regime, but a massive typhoon that wiped out his entire naval empire in minutes."

As Dennis and Delano started to leave the quarterdeck, the helmsman added: "But did you know, Mr. Delano, that it was Ching Yih's widow, Madam Ching, who rebuilt the dynasty and made it as powerful as it had previously been? Some claim she was an even more dynamic leader than her husband." His broad, flat Polynesian face was impassive, but there was a timbre to his voice that perplexed Delano. "It is rumored that the Ladrone organization still flourishes today, but on a subversive level."

"Is that so, Dana?" the first officer said. "You seem to be well versed on the history of piracy."

The helmsman allowed himself a thin, enigmatic smile. "We learned many things at the mission school on Maui, sir."

As they proceeded to the dining saloon, Dennis said, "I don't recall seeing that Dana chap before today."

"You didn't. He's an extra hand the skipper signed on at Canton. Originally from Hawaii, a mix-breed— Chinese, Polynesian. Has excellent credentials, and as you heard, he has a head on his shoulders."

The captain was alone at his table when Dennis and the first officer took their places for breakfast.

"How are Mrs. Gresham and little Walter Lintin this fine morning?" Dennis inquired.

"They're both first-class seamen. I can tell the lad can hardly wait to stand on a quarterdeck with the salt spume brushing his face."

Dennis and Delano exchanged surreptitious smiles of amusement. "I expect he'll have to be patient for a few more years before he's up to that, sir," Delano offered mildly.

The skipper pretended to glower. "Oh, don't think the two of you are pulling the wool over my eyes. I know what you're thinking: There's no fool like a new father. Well, you are absolutely right. I'm proud as a peacock to have fathered such an exceptional child, and I don't care who knows it. Do you know what the little tyke did this morning? He reached out and grasped my finger. He actually grasped my finger in his little hand and squeezed it! And let me tell you, he's got an iron grip!"

That was too much for Dennis, who doubled over with his napkin stuffed into his mouth to muffle his mirth. Delano was made of sterner stuff and stared straight ahead with his lips compressed in a fine white line, holding his breath to prevent himself from exploding into a guffaw.

"All right, Mr. Price," Gresham said in good humor. "That outburst demeaning the exceptional qualities of my son will cost you double duty this afternoon. And I will appreciate it if you take some sightings as soon as you are through with your breakfast."

Dennis snapped to attention. "Aye, aye, sir. And begging your pardon, sir, for the affront, though I assure you it was not intended."

Gresham laughed and leaned over to slap Dennis on the shoulder. "You are pardoned, sir. I am in such ebullient spirits this morning, I would pardon Blackbeard the pirate if he were in my brig!"

The passage through the China Sea was the most picturesque stretch of the long voyage so far. They sailed past a myriad of islands, large and small, dazzling green with tropical foliage vividly silhouetted against the azure sky and the pale blue-green water. In the hinterlands of the islands, stark mountain ridges were haloed in violet mist.

Dawn and Teresa and her baby spent long hours lounging on the deck above the cabin. The warm air caressed their skin and tantalized their nostrils with the aromatic scent of sandalwood, spices, bananas, pineapples, and melons. The *Golden Cloud* made good time even with her skysails and royals furled.

On the third day out, while Dennis was taking the noon sighting, the lookout bawled, "Jackass barque and schooner brig on the horizon to the west!"

On the quarterdeck, Captain Gresham swept the horizon with his spyglass. "Can't spot them yet from down here. . . . What flag are they flying?" he hollered up to the lookout.

"No sign of a flag, sir."

"What is their course? Can you make it out?"

"Appears to me they're sailing directly parallel to our ship."

"All right, keep a sharp lookout and let me know if they close the distance between us."

"Aye, aye, sir."

Dennis approached the captain. "You look concerned, skipper. Any problems?"

"Not likely, but one cannot be too cautious in this part of the world."

"Pirates?"

"There's always that possibility." He called to the second mate down on the main deck. "Mr. Lassiter, is Seaman Hiram Dana off duty?"

"Yes, sir, he's below decks sleeping. Should I rouse him?"

Gresham hesitated, then said, "No, it's nothing so urgent that it won't keep until he has his next turn at the wheel." He explained to Dennis, "Dana is undoubtedly the most experienced hand aboard when it comes to the China Sea."

"So I gathered the other day when Mr. Delano and I were discussing piracy. He's really quite well informed. Wherever did he get a name like Hiram Dana?"

"He hails from the Hawaiian Islands. Hiram is an extremely popular name there, given to children in honor of the beloved missionary and humanitarian Hiram Bingham, who was one of the few so-called reformers and educators who did not rob the natives blind. Obviously, his father was a seaman. Hawaii and the neighboring islands abound with Irish, English, French, and Scandinavian names."

Dennis nodded. "I'm going below to enter my sightings on the charts."

Later on, when Gresham entered the cabin, he found Dennis frowning and chewing on the end of his quill pen.

"Trouble, Mr. Price?"

"With me, evidently. I must be losing my touch. I've calculated latitude and longitude three times, and by my reckoning, we're thirteen degrees off course."

Captain Gresham was not unduly concerned; after all, Price was a beginner. He patted his shoulder and said jovially: "Don't fret over it, we all make mistakes. Come along, we'll go topside and see if we can discover what your error is."

From the quarterdeck, Gresham recorded a series of sextant sightings of the sun; then, followed by Dennis, he went below again and plotted the position of the *Golden Cloud* on the charts based on his own readings. From the deepening gravity of his expression, Dennis sensed that the captain was extremely concerned. He turned in the chair and looked up at Dennis.

"Mr Price, your sightings were letter perfect. We are indeed thirteen degrees off course, and the error is increasing. This could be very serious. We are entering an area, right here"—he described a circle on a chart with the tip of his pen—"an area abounding in barely submerged heads of coral. Come along, quickly."

The captain raced up on deck and summoned his mates. "Mr. Delano, Mr. Lassiter, I want all canvas hauled in at once and a sea anchor put out. The crew will remain aloft and alert until I say otherwise."

"Aye, aye, sir!" they said in unison and dispersed to implement the skipper's orders.

"All hands aloft! All hands aloft!"

"Now about those erroneous readings. Let's have a look at the binnacle compass." Gresham took the ladder up to the bridge two steps at a time.

From the expression on the captain's face, the helmsman knew he was in for a bad go. He straightened up and gave Gresham a smart salute. "Afternoon, sir, Mr. Price. Why are we hauling in, sir? Everything seems shipshape from here."

"Does it, Adams?" There was a sense of foreboding in his voice that intimidated Dennis as well as the helmsman. "Let me see your compass reading." He checked it and pursed his lips.

"Right on course, sir," Adams confirmed in a tremulous voice.

"So it would appear." Gresham took out his pocket compass and checked its reading against the binnacle compass. "Only, first appearances are deceiving. By my reckoning, the ship's compass is almost two points off, south-southwest."

The helmsman swallowed hard. "Isn't it possible that *your* compass is off, sir? I mean, the ship's compass is a highly delicate and reliable instrument."

"We'll see." He walked to the ladder and shouted

down to Bosun Peyton. "Bosun, bring me another compass!"

"Yes, sir!" The rotund Peyton waddled aft as fast as his bowlegs would carry him.

Captain Gresham shouted up to the lookout: "Keep a sharp eye ahead for submerged coral formations! And what is the latest information about those ships on the port horizon?"

The lookout's reply was fraught with anxiety. "They've cleared the horizon, sir, and altered course. In fact, they're on a southeast tack that should intersect our own course within the hour, I'd say."

The bosun returned with the compass, and the new instrument confirmed the reading of the captain's compass and the error of the ship's compass.

"The binnacle compass is definitely two points in error. Mr. Adams, will you and Bosun Peyton please remove the compass from the binnacle?"

Gingerly they lifted the large compass out of its housing. The captain inspected the housing thoroughly. Then he ran his hands around the circumference of the compass itself.

"Nothing here. This is incredible!" He was telling the helmsman and the bosun to replace the compass in its housing when something piqued Dennis's curiosity.

"Excuse me." He knelt down and craned his neck to inspect the underside of the compass. "Well, well. What do you know about this!" He ran his hand along the underside of the casing and stripped away a section of tape affixed to a small rectangle of blue-gray metal that had been attached to the compass.

"What the hell is that?" Peyton demanded.

"If I'm not mistaken . . . Your compass, please, Bosun."

Holding the bosun's compass in the palm of one hand, Dennis passed the sliver of metal back and forth across the top. The compass needle danced and swayed erratically according to the way the metal attracted it.

"A magnet!" Gresham, Peyton, and Adams said in unison.

"Precisely, gentlemen," Dennis said grimly. "And unless I miss my guess, it has something to do with those two ships that are dogging our course."

All eyes turned to the port side of the clipper, which was swaying and bobbing in the gentle swell, her progress hindered by the sea anchor. The jackass barque and schooner brig could be seen clearly, both carrying full sails ballooning in the wind. It was clearly their intention to cut off the *Golden Cloud* in her southwest passage toward Singapore.

In an uncharacteristic display of emotion, Gresham grasped the helmsman by the front of his shirt. "Adams! What do you know about this?" He shoved the magnet under the terrified seaman's nose.

"So help me God, Captain Gresham, I never seen it before!"

"Whom did you relieve, Adams?" Dennis asked.

"Dana, Mr. Price. The one we signed on in Canton."

The captain pounded a fist into his open palm. "Bosun, summon Dana to the quarterdeck on the double. And tell Mr. Delano and Mr. Lassiter to report." He cast still another look in the direction of the unidentified ships.

Suddenly the lookout sang out, "Sir, they're raising their colors now!"

"What flags are they flying?"

"The Jolly Roger, sir. Sure enough, they're pirates!"

"Malayan praus!"

First Mate Delano bounded up the ladder onto the quarterdeck. "What is it, sir?"

"We're about to be ambushed by pirates." He unhooked a ring with an assortment of keys from his belt. "Mr. Delano, here is the key to the weapons locker. Open it and distribute pistols and rifles to as many men as you can. Ammunition, too."

He glanced upward at the crumpled canvas. "The coral will have to be of secondary consideration under the circumstances."

Most of the crewmen were still aloft on alert as previously ordered, straddling the yards and hanging in the rigging. Gresham yelled down to Second Mate Lassiter, "Make sail for a race!"

"Yes, sir!" Lassiter put a megaphone to his mouth and bawled, "All hands aloft!"

The rest of the crew went scampering up the shrouds and masts, and within minutes the *Golden Cloud* was underway, sporting skysails, royals, and topgallants. With a stiff wind aft, the sleek clipper fairly leaped forward in the water and quickly left the pirate marauders floundering in its wake. A mighty cheer went up from the crewmen.

But the jubilation was short-lived. Delano returned to the bridge white-faced and trembling. "Captain Gresham, something's awfully wrong. The weapons locker has been broken into."

Gresham was incredulous. "That's impossible!"

"Come see for yourself."

"It's true, sir." Bosun Peyton joined them on the deck, a man in shock.

"What the devil are you talking about? And where's Dana? I told you I wanted him here at once!"

Peyton threw up his arms helplessly. "That's just it,

skipper. Dana, he's the one ransacked the ship's armory."

"Where is he?"

The fear of God was reflected in the bosun's eyes. "Sir, I—I—"

"Speak up, man!"

"Dana is holed up in your cabin with your wife and baby and Mrs. Price."

"Filthy swine!" Dennis made for the ladder leading down to the main deck. "I'll tear out his heart!"

"I'd be careful, Mr. Price. Dana says that if anyone tries to break in, he'll kill the two ladies and the baby."

Captain Gresham might have collapsed if Delano and Adams hadn't moved quickly to his side. "My God! What kind of devil is this man Dana? What does he hope to accomplish?"

Peyton turned and pointed to the pirate vessels falling far behind the racing clipper. "He's one of them. A spy put aboard to help them capture the *Golden Cloud*."

Dennis came back and confronted the captain, who had regained his composure. "What happens now, Captain?"

Gresham's voice was sharp with restrained fury. "It would appear that we do not have a choice, Mr. Price. That is, if you value your lovely wife as much as I value my beloved Teresa and my son. All right, let's go below and see what bargain we can strike with the blackguard."

Hiram Dana had planned his coup well, and he executed it with flair and finesse. He waited patiently at the top of the companionway leading down to the crew's quarters until Dennis and the ship's officers were preoccupied with the threat of the pirate vessels hovering nearby and the erratic compass. Then, at his leisure, he jimmied the lock on the weapons locker in a small chart room that Captain Gresham used at night when his wife was sleeping. He selected two Colt revolvers and a sixteen-shot Spencer rifle for himself and stuffed his pockets with ammunition. Disregarding the other weapons in the locker, he loaded all the available ammunition into a gunny sack and dumped it out an open port into the sea. Purposefully he headed for the captain's quarters, where he knew Mrs. Price was visiting the new mother and her child.

He paused at the cabin door and knocked softly.

"Yes?" Dawn opened the door a fraction and peered out into the corridor.

Dana took off his seaman's cap and smiled. "My apologies for disturbing you, but it's skipper's orders. He wants me to stand guard here until the crisis passes."

"Crisis?" Dawn eyed with alarm the brace of pistols in his waistband and the rifle slung over his shoulder. "What's wrong, Mr.—?"

"Seaman First Class Dana, ma'am. Nothing to alarm you too greatly, but it seems that we have a saboteur aboard the *Golden Cloud*."

"What do you mean?"

"It seems that someone has tampered with the compass to steer the ship off course."

She was reminded then that Dennis had mentioned a new hand who had signed on in Canton. He had remarked that the man had a good head on his shoulders.

Dana's eyes were flint hard in his expressionless face. "May I come in, ma'am?"

"I think the captain would prefer that you do your

guarding outside the door. Mrs. Gresham is nursing her baby at the moment."

"But I would prefer otherwise." He hit the door hard with the heel of one hand and sent Dawn careening across the cabin. Quickly, he stepped inside the room, closed the door, and bolted it.

Smiling boldly, he surveyed the interior of the captain's cabin. "Very nice, very nice indeed." Teresa Gresham, clasping her baby to her bosom, cringed as he strutted toward the bed.

"So this is the heir apparent, eh?" he said with open sarcasm. He bent over the bed and extended a hand to tickle the wide-eyed child underneath the chin. "Cute little tyke."

"Don't you dare touch my child!" Despite her brave words, Teresa wore the look of a terrified doe.

"Afraid he'll be contaminated by bilge scum like me?"

Out of the corners of his eyes he was dimly aware of a flurry of motion. He whirled around just as Dawn pounced on him, arms and legs flailing like the limbs of a wildcat. Her nails raked red welts down both cheeks. One pointed shoe caught him flush in the groin.

Dana gasped and half doubled over. With a lightning motion, Dawn seized one of the pistols from his belt and sprang back, leveling the muzzle at his gut.

"Stay where you are, or I'll blow you in half!" she warned.

A smile of unadulterated malice spread over his broad, flat face. "You are one hellion, I'll say that for you. If I had the time, I'd tame you, Mrs. Fancy Pants." One eyebrow lifted insolently. "And I'll bet you do wear very fancy pants, just like them French whores they imported to Hawaii." Deliberately he drew the other pistol and thumbed back the hammer. "So you're not so smart after all, lady. You forgot to cock the damned thing." As her thumb moved, he snapped, "Don't be a fool. It's too late now. You'll be a dead woman before you get the hammer back. Now throw it down!"

Full of despair Dawn dropped the Colt.

"Now get over to the bed and sit down by the little mother."

As Dawn obeyed, she heard the sound of running footsteps in the corridor, followed by an urgent banging on the door. Captain Gresham's voice boomed through the heavy portal. "Open this door instantly, Dana! If you've harmed a hair on the head of either one of those women or my son, I'll have you keelhauled and chopped up into mulch for the sharks."

Dana chuckled. "Relax, Captain Gresham," he said loudly enough to be heard on the other side of the door. "No one is going to get harmed in any way if you do what you're told."

"Do as I'm told! You arrogant snake! I happen to be in charge of this ship, and I'll do as I please."

Dana sighed and spoke very calmly. "As long as I have your wife and son and Mrs. Price hostage, you will do as I please. And at the moment, it is my pleasure that you furl all sails and sit still in the water until my compatriots board the Golden Cloud."

"Never! I'll die first!"

"Not true, Captain. It is your wife and child who will die first." He aimed the gun at the infant squirming in his mother's desperate grasp.

"Grant!" Teresa screamed. "Please do as he says, if you love us and value our lives!"

"All right, Dana," Gresham capitulated. "I see I have no choice."

Teresa began to weep, and Dawn buried her face in her hands in defeat. Dana, wearing a victor's smile, relaxed and shoved the pistol back into his waistband. Again he addressed himself to the captain.

"When my comrades board your ship, you will have your crew confined to quarters, except for the officers and your passengers. If any crewman so much as shows his face on deck, he will be summarily executed. Is that understood?"

"Yes." Gresham was striving desperately to pull himself together. "You may take any of the cargo you wish. Just don't harm anyone. My wife—"

"I guarantee that no one will set foot in this cabin to frighten your wife or your son so long as you obey my orders to the letter."

"You have my word."

"Then return topside and prepare to receive the boarding party."

Dawn regarded Dana disdainfully through narrowed eyes. "I thought you were something more than an ordinary seaman. Your choice of words—it's obvious you have been educated."

"I am flattered by your perspicuity, madam. I confess to attending college, and I speak French and Spanish as well as English and my native tongues, Chinese and Polynesian."

"Remarkable, Mr. Dana. One thing puzzles me, however. Why do you attack the *Golden Cloud* at this juncture? The cargo we unloaded at Canton—pelts, machinery, the produce of the industrial West that is of so much value to the Orient—it would have made sense had you stolen such valuable booty. But what we took aboard in exchange—tea, spices, silk—your people have that in abundance. I don't understand, Mr. Dana."

He did not reply immediately but merely regarded Dawn with a crass smile. She squirmed under his scrutiny.

"Perhaps there is cargo aboard whose worth you have no concept of. Cargo far more priceless than the mundane articles you mentioned."

"Do you mean smuggled goods?" She had an inspiration. "I think I know what it is! There is opium aboard the *Golden Cloud!* That's it, isn't it?"

Dana threw back his head and laughed so heartily that the reverberations rattled the delicate tea service on the sideboard.

The pirate brig pulled alongside the *Golden Cloud* on the port side; the larger barque held to the starboard side. Grappling irons were cast over the clipper's rails, securing her fast to her captors.

Even if the crew of the *Golden Cloud* had had access to weapons, it would have been no contest. The pirate ships had two cannons apiece, fore and aft, trained on their prize. True to his word, Gresham had ordered his crew below decks. Only Silver Jack and Pig remained aloft, balanced casually on a spar halfway up the mizzenmast. On deck, Captain Gresham, his two mates, and Dennis Price waited to confront the boarding pirates.

They were a malevolent-looking lot clad in loose baggy trousers and tight shirts that displayed powerful muscles. Their beards and mustaches were scraggly and untrimmed. Around their heads they wore colorful bandannas. Pistols and knives bristled in their wide leather belts, and some of them wore bandoliers of cartridges crisscrossed over their chests.

They were a mixed bag of nationalities: French, Portuguese, Irish, Scandinavian, Chinese—mongrels for the most part, with the dominating characteristics Chinese or Malayan. One thing they all had in common —they were cutthroats to a man.

The leader of the boarding party was a massive, shirtless man with a shaved head. His torso was a patchwork quilt of scars from sabers, knives, and bullets. He stared intently at Captain Gresham before sweeping his gaze over the clipper from fore to aft and upward to the masts. He scowled at the sight of Silver Jack and Pig swaying on a spar, each with an arm wrapped loosely around the mast.

"Your orders were to send all your crewmen below," he said in a guttural voice flavored with a mixture of French and Portuguese.

"My crewmen are all below decks," replied Gresham. "The men up there, as well as Mr. Price here, are passengers."

"Yes, Mr. Price. And where is Mrs. Price?" he asked Dennis.

"She is below in the captain's cabin, attending to his wife and their newborn child under the guard of one of your ruffians," Dennis said angrily.

The pirate looked him up and down scornfully. "One of our *what?*" was the ominously quiet query.

Dennis, a head shorter than the pirate and forty pounds lighter, confronted him bravely. "You heard me. You are a band of ruthless ruffians and cowards!"

The pirate's thick right arm was a blur of motion like the strike of a cobra. The back of his hand caught Dennis across the side of the head and knocked him to the deck. He lay there stunned, blood pouring from his nose and mouth.

The leader turned and spoke to his henchmen in Chinese. Two of them nodded and walked away.

"Where are they going?" Gresham demanded, as Delano and Lassiter stooped to assist Dennis.

The pirate's smile was a wicked scimitar. "To your cabin, Captain Gresham."

"No!" Gresham started after them, but the giant barred his way with an arm. "Your cohort, Dana, gave me his word that my wife and child would not be harmed or disturbed."

"Nor shall they. I want Mrs. Price brought on deck."

Gresham was mystified. "You seem to know a good deal about my ship—my name, the names and identities of my passengers."

"You're damned right he does," Dennis said, getting painfully to his feet. "This is no chance ambush, Captain. It has all the earmarks of a carefully planned coup, a naval operation."

The pirate chieftain laughed, showing four gold teeth in front. "Let's face it, Mr. Price, we have been at war with the foreign devils for generations."

"What do you want from us?" Gresham asked. "Take whatever you please and leave us alone; just be quick about it. I'll even have my men assist you in transferring the cargo from the holds to your own vessels."

"Very obliging, Captain, but that will not be necessary." His gaze cut to the side, where the two men he had dispatched were leading Dawn between them. She was cursing at them and struggling in their grasp.

"Get your filthy hands off me, you swine!" She spat at one of them. He turned red with anger and lifted a hand as if to strike her. A sharp reprimand from his leader stopped him.

"You know what the royal master has decreed. If one hair of that woman's head is harmed, the one responsible will hang by his thumbs in a dungeon for two weeks."

"The royal master?" Dennis was alarmed by this unexpected turn of events. "What has my wife got to do with your act of piracy? Take your filthy spoils and get off this ship and leave us alone."

The pirate's eyes glittered like obsidian. "Your wish is our command, sir," he said disdainfully. "We have our booty and now we will depart."

The officers of the *Golden Cloud* and Dennis Price were utterly bewildered.

"What the devil are you talking about?" Gresham demanded.

"Why, Mrs. Price, naturally," was the arrogant reply. "Take her aboard the *Dragon*," he ordered the men who had dragged Dawn from the cabin.

Dawn screamed and redoubled her efforts to escape, but to no avail. Leaping forward to help her, Dennis and Gresham were deterred by the sharp points of sabers digging into their bellies. They were held at bay as two of the pirates dragged Dawn across the plank to their brig.

Suddenly, Silver Jack and Pig, each still holding onto the mast with one hand, let go the belaying pins each had jammed into the waistband of his trousers. One of the pirates was struck on the side of his skull and killed instantly. The second missile broke the sword arm of the other brigand. Dennis and Gresham sprang to retrieve their fallen weapons and advanced on the pirate chieftain and the men struggling with Dawn.

An instant later, Silver Jack came sliding down a sheet, swinging back and forth in an ever increasing arc. Timing his move perfectly, he let go and crashed into Dawn and her captors, now halfway across the plank. The impact sent the four of them hurtling into space and down into the sea between the two ships.

Dawn and Jack surfaced first. "You swim around to the starboard side of the *Cloud*," he gasped. "I'll take care of these water rats."

When the two pirates came up, Jack's huge hands closed around their throats like twin vises. Then, with a mighty heave of his powerful shoulders, he slammed their heads together. Jack shoved them aside, and without a word or motion the unconscious men sank like stones, leaving a trail of bubbles in their wake.

On deck, Dennis and Gresham were locked in combat with the burly pirate leader. The other pirate lay on the deck, moaning and writhing and holding an obviously broken arm. Dennis was flung aside by the pirate and sent crashing into the ship's railing. Choking Gresham with one hand, the man pushed him down on a hatch cover and drew a dagger from his belt. The captain grabbed his wrist and tried desperately to ward off the fatal blow, but his strength was no match for the muscular buccaneer. The point of the dagger was within inches of his jugular when Pig Iron Sam Malone dropped off a spar onto the pirate's back. With a deft motion, perfected from long practice, Pig slipped his arms under his foe's armpits and bent his forearms up and back so that he could lock his hands together at the nape of the pirate's thick neck.

The pirate bucked and tried to hurl Pig over his shoulders, but the logger was as immovable as a sturdy oak. A bloodcurdling scream that reverberated the length of the ship signaled the conclusion of the combat. Pig released his grip and the pirate slid lifeless to the deck, his head twisted grotesquely on his broken neck.

Aboard the pirate ship, the second-in-command dispassionately witnessed his comrades' deaths. Life was cheap in his profession, and one had to be prepared to pay dearly for ill-gotten treasures.

"Cast off the grappling chains!" he barked and knocked away the boarding plank with a savage kick. "Haul up all sails and let's get underway!"

"What about the woman?" another pirate asked.

"They'll pick her up on the starboard side." He unslung a rifle from one shoulder and began to fire at Captain Gresham, Dennis, and Pig, who hastily sought cover behind a hatch.

At the sound of the gunfire, the crewmen of the *Golden Cloud,* despite the captain's firm command that they remain below, poured out of the hold onto the deck. They were greeted by a hail of pistol and rifle fire that felled several of them before they could retreat to safety.

Hiram Dana, who had remained in the captain's cabin to guard Teresa, was growing increasingly apprehensive at all the shooting and commotion topside. Evidently the well-laid plans of his masters were not proceeding as smoothly as had been anticipated. Muttering and cursing, he kept pacing, pausing every few minutes to open the cabin door and peering up and down the corridor.

Taking advantage of his inattention, Teresa calmly placed her baby on the bed beside her and steathily opened the top drawer of the small night table alongside the bed. In her frothy bed jacket, Teresa was the epitome of femininity and gentleness. But the captain's lady had a backbone as hard and implacable as the clipper's keel. From the drawer she removed a derringer pistol that Grant had presented her with on their maiden voyage together.

*"Never point it at anything or anyone unless you truly intend to fire it,"* he had cautioned her.

Now there was no uncertainty at all in the woman's mind. Quietly, she drew back the hammer and draped a shawl over her gun hand.

"Mr. Dana," she said in a normal voice. "Would you please fetch me a glass of water from the desk?"

Grumbling, he shut the door and bolted it. "Is that all you can think of at a time like this? I have half a mind to get the hell out of here and see what's going on on deck." Nevertheless he filled a glass with water from a flagon and carried it over to the bed.

Smiling sweetly, Teresa pulled the shawl aside and took dead aim at a spot in the center of his breastbone. "Thank you kindly, Mr. Dana. And good-bye."

For the first time since he had come aboard the *Golden Cloud,* Hiram Dana's face registered emotion. His slanted eyes were disbelieving; his jaw sagged. He fumbled clumsily for the pistol in his belt, but even as his fingers touched the butt, two shots rang out and two bright splotches of blood welled up through his shirt. He gazed down at the spreading crimson stains in astonishment and clasped his hands over them as if to staunch the flow. Then his eyes glazed over and he slumped to the floor, quite dead.

In the water at the stern of the clipper, Jack made the turn and reached the starboard side just in time to see Dawn engulfed by a fishing net flung down from the other pirate craft.

He swam desperately to her, only to find himself enmeshed as inextricably as she was. They were hauled aboard the four-masted barque by a group of jeering, laughing pirates.

"The catch of the day!" said an enormous, fat Mongolian whose bare chest, belly, and back were covered with thick glossy hair so that he resembled a grizzly bear.

While they took their time releasing Dawn and Jack, the brig and the barque were fast putting distance between them and the clipper, which was still sitting dead in the water.

"North by northwest!" an officer shouted to the helmsman. And peering down into an open hold, he issued another order. "Prepare to start the auxiliary engine!" He gave his attention to Dawn and Jack, who were surrounded by armed pirates. "Take these two below and lock 'em up until we receive further orders from His Highness."

Dawn and Jack were herded down a companionway and along a narrow, dark hall that stank of fish and human waste. At the end of the corridor they were shoved into a small, windowless room scarcely bigger than Dawn's clothes closet on the *Golden Cloud*.

"I'm frightened, Jack," she whispered when they were alone.

"You got company, lady."

"It's my fault you're here, Jack. If you hadn't tried to save me, you'd be safe aboard the *Golden Cloud*."

"From the sound of all that gunfire, that is highly debatable. Just how safe is anyone aboard the *Cloud* right now?"

"It isn't just being a captive of these praus that scares me. It's the why of it that terrifies me."

"The why of what?"

"You heard what that cutthroat said when he ordered his men to take me on board their ship: 'We have our booty.' Don't you see, Jack? They had no intention of stealing the *Golden Cloud*'s cargo. They were after me all along!"

Jack shook his head in befuddlement. "After you? You mean to say they'd stage a dangerous raid just to capture one woman? I mean no offense, Dawn, but to risk life and limb for *one* woman? Who would conceive of such a hazardous escapade?"

"My guess is that it must be the one they refer to as His Highness."

# CHAPTER SIX

Dawn was napping, curled up in a corner of the cramped cubicle, when a loud voice disrupted her slumber.

"On your feet, and be quick about it!"

She opened her eyes and saw the fat, hairy pirate filling the doorway of the room. He held a pistol in one hand and a scimitar in the other. Behind him two other pirates stood silently.

"No funny business!" The Mongolian growled and waved the pistol under Jack's nose.

"Relax, friend," Jack said. "One lesson I've learned is never start a fight you've got no chance of winning." He and Dawn went out into the corridor and were herded up a companionway to the deck.

After being cooped up in the dark cell, the brilliant sunlight blinded Dawn and Jack. Shading their eyes against the glare with their hands, the prisoners were taken to the stern and prodded up still another companionway to the poop deck.

"Who is in charge of this vessel?" Dawn asked. "I demand to speak with him at once."

The pirates laughed and the Mongolian said: "Your wish is our command. You are about to have an audience with our exalted leader."

He knocked softly on a cabin door. "The prisoners are here to see you."

"Bring them in" was the reply muffled by the thick oak door.

The Mongolian opened the door and motioned for Dawn and Jack to enter the cabin. The room was exquisitely furnished, its walls covered with tapestries woven of gold and silver thread. The scenes were of ancient warriors doing battle, an armored knight spiking his lance into a fire-breathing dragon, fairy-tale panoramas of landscapes, oriental gardens ablaze with multicolored blossoms, a magnificent snowcapped mountain peak. Elaborately hand-carved chairs inlaid with ivory and jade were adorned with silken pillows. Most of the exquisite ornaments on the shelves and tables were fashioned of jade.

At the far end of the cabin was a large marble-topped table-desk strewn with papers. Behind it, sitting in a high, brocaded wing chair, was the "exalted leader"— and to Dawn and Jack's amazement, it was a woman! She was handsome and no more than in her mid-thirties, with almond eyes and skin the color of saffron porcelain. Her mouth was large and sensuous, as were her flaring nostrils. Her raven hair was set in an elaborate pompadour and held in place by gold combs inlaid with jewels. She was wearing a robe of crimson silk richly embroidered in silver and gold.

"You may leave now, Chou," she said to the Mongolian in a clear voice that rang with authority.

He frowned disapprovingly. "One of us should remain here to subdue the prisoners should they become unruly."

"They will not be unruly, I assure you. Now leave me alone with my"—a hesitation—"with my guests."

"As you wish." Chou and his cohorts bowed and backed out of the cabin.

"I am Madam Ching," she said to Dawn and Jack. "Welcome to my flagship, the *A-Ma*. I regret the inconvenience you have suffered, and during your stay aboard my humble vessel we will do our best to make amends and make you as comfortable as possible."

When she had recovered from the shock of finding out that the pirate leader was a woman, Dawn gave vent to her anger and indignation.

"You regret our *inconvenience?* You ravage our ship, inflict bodily harm on our crewmen, kidnap me and Mr. McHugh and almost drown us in the process, and you call such infamy *inconvenience?* I call it a capital crime, and the courts in every civilized nation in the world would concur."

Madam Ching smiled indulgently. "Inasmuch as you have no access to a so-called civilized court in this region of the world, your viewpoint is irrelevant." Her pencil-thin eyebrows arched. "The so-called civilized courts condoned the acts of the Western smugglers who were and are still bent on turning the Chinese people into helpless drug addicts so that they can be manipulated into cheap slave labor; the same courts gave control of Hong Kong to the British and opened the five free ports to the ruthless and unconscionable foreign-devil carpetbaggers. You were saying, Mrs. Price?"

Dawn felt herself flushing. "Neither Mr. McHugh nor myself condone the injustices and indignities inflicted on your people, but their conduct scarcely justifies your conduct in abducting us. It is plain that you know a good deal about me and that your sole objective in attacking the *Golden Cloud* was to kidnap me. I've heard about you praus. You kidnap wealthy people and hold them for ransom. Let me assure you, just name a price and my father will be only too willing to pay you to secure our release."

Madame Ching smiled and rose from behind the desk. She indicated two chairs at the side of the desk. "Please sit down. I'll have a pot of tea and some refreshments sent in."

"Not on our account," Dawn declined stiffly. "Madam Ching, I suggest we skip the niceties and get to the point. How much ransom will you accept for our release?"

Madam Ching leaned back against her desk. "There will be no ransom," she said quietly. "Taking you off the *Golden Cloud* was a business transaction. And, I might add, a highly profitable transaction at that."

"Business transaction?" Dawn was bewildered. "I don't understand."

"Our organization was employed for the express purpose of abducting you and delivering you safe and unharmed into our employer's hands."

Dawn put a hand to her head and swayed unsteadily. Jack stepped forward and grasped her elbow firmly.

"And just who is your employer?" he demanded.

Madam Ching smiled. "I am not at liberty at present to divulge that information. You will have all your questions answered and your doubts resolved at the appropriate time. Now, why don't you sit Mrs. Price down while I have some tea served. It would appear that she is in need of a settling stimulant." She walked to the door and, opening it, issued an order in Chinese to someone outside.

Then she returned to the love seat where Dawn was sitting, still deep in shock. Madam Ching patted her shoulder.

"Please, Mrs. Price, let's have no more talk of ransom. You are bought and paid for." Her dispassionate laughter hardly reassured Dawn.

Dawn shook her head. "I have never heard of a woman pirate."

"She's not the first," Jack said. "There was Mary Read and Ann Bonney."

Madam Ching smiled again. "Crass amateurs compared to my illustrious ancestors. Our people, the Ladrones, comprised a dynasty that would have overthrown the effete, decadent government of the emperor. My grandfather, Ching Yih, commanded a prau fleet of a thousand ships, six squadrons, each led by an admiral who had been trained in the royal academy."

She laughed. "Every time the Imperial Navy attacked the Ladrones they were sent fleeing with their tails between their legs." Her smile became a bitter, twisted grimace. "But just when complete victory was in Ching Yih's grasp, the gods betrayed us. The Ladrone fleet was destroyed in one of the worst typhoons to sweep the Sea of China. Ching Yih himself was one of the casualties.

"But even as the admirals were panicking and making plans to seek asylum in India or Borneo, Ching's widow was the pillar of strength that held the decimated pirate empire together—the keystone of a mighty arch that reconstructed the Ladrone forces. Like the legendary phoenix, we were resurrected out of our own ashes. And Madam Ching," she smiled with pride, "was our rock, our refuge, our rescue."

"Madam Ching?" Dawn said. "Then I assume that you are—"

"I am her granddaughter. Oh, I do not have illusions of grandeur, of rebuilding the Ladrone empire. Even Madam Ching foresaw that with the growth of Western influence in the Far East, and with modern fleets dominating our seas, the age of buccaneering on a large, profitable scale was fast approaching the twilight of its glory. The Ladrones made peace with the Manchu government in a historic meeting at Canton. Some of the fleets refused to surrender, and they were overwhelmingly defeated in a bloody sea battle near Manila."

"But your brand of piracy is evidently still flourishing," Dawn observed.

"On a small and discreet scale, yes. The government leaves us alone for the most part. You see, the name Ching still commands a good deal of respect and fear in high government places. After her retirement, my illustrious grandmother married the governor of Canton, a favorite mandarin of the emperor."

"Where are you taking us? To China?"

"No, not for the time being at least. When it is learned that you have been abducted, the entire China coast will be swarming with warships and patrol boats. Our present destination is a place that has provided sanctuary for the Ladrones for generations. It is aptly called Pirates' Cove." There was a knock on the cabin door. "Come in."

A young boy entered, bearing a tray with an exquisite silver tea service. "Put it down on the table and pour three cups." She glanced at Silver Jack. "Or perhaps the gentleman would prefer a stronger beverage? Gin? Scotch whiskey? Cuban rum? In our peregrinations we have acquired a quantity of liquors and wines."

Dawn glanced at the fragile silver cup the lad placed before her on a filigreed saucer. "Among other treasures," she said archly.

"We make a respectable profit. And why shouldn't we? Your people have skimmed all the heavy cream off the cup of the Orient. It is only fair that we Chinese, those of us who are enterprising, should partake of the lighter cream."

"But piracy! It's barbaric!"

The women shrugged. "A matter of definition. Take your original destination, for example—India. There are members of the Islamic faith who believe zealously that white men who eat the flesh of pigs are the most loathsome of barbarians. No matter, I prefer not to discuss controversial subjects with my guests. Mr. Mc-Hugh, whiskey?"

"Thank you, ma'am, I could do with a tot of rum if you please."

"Papu, fetch the gentleman a flask of the best rum and a tumbler worthy to serve it in," she told the boy, who fled the cabin as if the devil were a step behind him.

"The boy appears to be terrified," Dawn said.

"He will overcome his fear in time. He was a cabin boy aboard the last prize we took. Several of our worthy crewmen were recruited from vessels we detained. It is an ancient Ladrone tradition to encourage recruits to our cause. Our men fare far better than the average merchant seaman. They get better food and drink, and every man aboard receives a share of the booty when it is disposed of." She appraised Silver Jack thoughtfully. "You are a fine specimen of a man, and I understand you are the devil incarnate in a battle." And so casually that Dawn was shocked, she added, "Did you know that you killed three of my Ladrones before you were overcome?" Her slanted cat's eyes fixed him coldly. "If the *A-Ma*—that means goddess of the sea—abided by the laws of Mrs. Price's so-called civilized naval codes, you would have been tried on the spot for murder, summarily convicted, and by now you would be swinging from a yardarm at the end of a hangman's noose. No, we Ladrones are not handicapped by Western bigotry, biblical pomposity, and such petty emotions as lust for revenge. We are pragmatists, realists. You killed three men; they would have done the same to you. I entertain no grief over their deaths except that the ship is now short three good seamen. Mr. McHugh, I am offering to cancel the debt if you will agree to sign on the *A-Ma* as an able seaman. You will be reimbursed with a full crewman's share of our profits—including the sizable purse we are to receive for Mrs. Price."

Jack could only stare at her with mounting hatred. "I can't believe what you are saying. You expect me to turn traitor to Mrs. Price and her father—the two people who gave me a chance to make something of my life, to educate myself, to secure a good job?"

At that moment the boy returned with a bottle of dark rum and a burnished pewter mug on a silver tray. He placed the tray on a table by Jack's side, poured the mug half full, and withdrew.

"Certainly you owed Mrs. Price and her father your loyalty," Madam Ching continued. "You proved that deep loyalty when you killed three men in her defense. But the conditions of life are mercurial, Mr. McHugh. We are in a constant state of flux. So long as you were the master of your own destiny, you were obligated to acknowledge the debt you owed them. But that obligation was terminated as soon as you were both brought aboard the *A-Ma* as captives. Now your debt has been transferred to me. You owe me your allegiance for dispatching my three crewmen."

Jack gulped down the rum in a single swallow and refilled the mug from the bottle the boy had left on the table. "Madam Ching, I have never met a woman like you in all of my life. You are—are—"

"Outrageous," interjected Dawn.

"Yes, outrageous. I've done some things in life I'm not too proud of, but I'd rather slit my throat before I'd betray Mrs. Price and her father."

Madam Ching said calmly, "Sadly, that is your only alternative. Be reasonable, Mr. McHugh. My sole objective in ambushing the *Golden Cloud* was to obtain possession of Mrs. Price. Your presence aboard the *A-Ma* is strictly a matter of your own doing. Quite frankly, unless you join our family and contribute to the common Ladrone cause, you are quite expendable —mere excess baggage to be disposed of along with the rest of the garbage we feed the sharks."

Silver Jack leaped out of his chair, his face flaming with fury. "I'd sooner feed myself to the sharks than join your slimy pirate crew!"

Unfazed by his tirade, Madam Ching sighed. "As you wish, but it would be a pity to destroy a man like you. Perhaps you will change your mind before we reach our destination." She smiled at Dawn. "Mrs. Price, maybe you can persuade him. My instincts tell me that you exert a good deal of influence over Mr. McHugh."

Silver Jack did not deny it. "If it weren't for Mrs. Price I'd still be a stupid river hog back in the swamp."

Madam Ching was mystified. "River hog? Swamp?"

"The parlance of the lumber camps," Dawn explained. "Now, with your permission I would like to get out of these filthy clothes and have a bath."

Madam Ching laughed. "This is not exactly a luxury liner, my dear, but we will do the best we can for you."

She opened the cabin door and issued an order to one of the pirates. "Tell Monique to heat some water and fill a tub for our guest. She'll be housed in the small cabin amidships for the remainder of our voyage."

"I wish you would not refer to me as your guest. I am your prisoner, Madam Ching."

Madam Ching summoned the fat, hairy pirate into the cabin. "Chou, the safety and well-being of Mrs. Price will be your responsibility."

Chou bowed. "Yes, madam, as you say."

"You may escort her to her quarters now and tell Monique to keep a civil tongue in her head or I shall have it torn out by the roots."

At the door, Dawn hesitated. "What about Mr. McHugh?"

"He will share quarters with my first lieutenant. Right now I wish to detain him for a few more minutes." Smiling, she walked over to Dawn and gripped her arm. "I will see you later, Mrs. Price. Enjoy your bath." She propelled the girl out of the cabin and shut the door. Turning to face Silver Jack, she leaned back against the portal with her arms folded underneath her breasts.

"Now, what are we to do about you, Mr. McHugh? You have flatly rejected my generous offer to have you join our crew."

"I'll do a day's work to earn my keep, but I won't consort with thugs and murderers."

"Hmmmmm . . . I wonder. What other qualifications do you possess?" She sidled over to him, her smile wanton and inviting. She trailed her fingers slowly over his broad shoulders and down the length of his powerful arms, and then suddenly hit his midriff with the back of one hand. "You're made of solid steel! I'll wager you have pleased many women in bed in your time, Mr. McHugh."

Jack remained silent, his lips tightly compressed.

"I have pleased many men in my boudoir. Do you find me attractive, Mr. McHugh?"

"You are a very beautiful woman," he conceded.

Casually she unfastened the sash of her ornate robe and parted the front. She was completely nude. Although unusually tall for an oriental woman, Madam Ching had small but perfect breasts that thrust out high and firm. There was a graceful fluidity to her body. Madam Ching was a sleek, female animal, as svelte as a panther.

He stepped back as she took one of his hands and placed it on her breast. "Do you like the feel of me, Jack? I think it is time we dispensed with the formalities. You may call me Lai."

"This isn't right," he protested, but he did not remove his hand. It had been a long time since Jack had caressed the warm, velvet flesh of a woman. And what a woman she was, pirate chieftain or not!

She let the robe billow to the floor and put her arms

around his neck, kissing him passionately, teasing the underside of his tongue with the tip of her tongue.

All sense of propriety, all of his willpower and good resolves abandoned him. He stripped off his shirt and trousers and she gaped with awe and ravenous hunger at his rampant manhood, held in check for so many months.

She pulled him down onto the thick silk carpet in front of her desk, wrapping her legs around his waist, digging her heels into the small of his back.

"Now! Do it now!" Her juices were flowing copiously, but when he began to penetrate her, she gasped.

"Ah," she groaned in a frenzy of pleasure and pain caused by the size of his throbbing member, and soon she felt herself soaring to pinnacles of ecstasy. One, two, three orgasms, and then a fourth; never once did Silver Jack falter.

When at last she was sated, she stretched out luxuriantly on the rug, held tightly in the circle of his arms.

"Well, at least we have one problem resolved."

"What's that?" Jack said.

"How to use your talents and energy to contribute to the noble Ladrone cause. Yes, my darling, your contributions aboard my flagship will prove to be invaluable."

He was silent and pensive.

"What's wrong? Don't pretend you didn't enjoy it as much as I did."

"Yes, I did."

She studied him thoughtfully, her intuition suddenly understanding his remoteness. "Do you feel guilty?"

He snorted. "Guilty? That's crazy!"

"Is it? You feel that you have betrayed Mrs. Price."

He was shocked. "Betrayed Mrs. Price! She happens

to be another man's wife, and I can bed any woman I feel the urge to have!"

"Oh, I agree with you completely. But the fact that she is a married woman can't prevent you from feeling what you do."

"And what am I supposed to be feeling?"

"Why, it's obvious that you are very much in love with the lady, married or not."

# CHAPTER SEVEN

Chou escorted Dawn along the deck to a small cabin beneath the quarterdeck. "This was once the quarters of the third mate, before we captured the ship."

"What happened to him? Never mind, I don't think I care to know," she added quickly.

His moon face cracked in a rare smile. "No, I don't think you do."

"Where does the crew live and sleep?"

"In the hold. All the bulkheads dividing the holds and compartments are torn down when we take a ship over as a prau ship."

Dawn was dismayed. "Do you mean to say that below decks there is just one big communal living space? Is there no privacy at all?"

"Privacy?" He snorted derisively. "The last thing we want is privacy. Our motto is: Never trust another unless you can see what he is doing or listen to what he is saying. He may be plotting your murder. No, too much privacy encourages conspiracy, even mutiny. Madam Ching has had more than one of the crew drawn and quartered."

"A charming woman," Dawn said with ill-concealed sarcasm.

He held open the cabin door for Dawn. "Please enter. If you need anything, do not hesitate to summon me. Ah, your handmaid is already preparing your bath."

It took a while for Dawn's vision to get used to the dim room, a cubicle no more than ten feet square furnished with a cot covered by a straw mat, a single wooden stool, and a washbasin on a stand in one corner. For this special occasion the pirates had hauled a galvanized iron tub into the compartment, and the slave girl Monique was filling it with seawater hauled up through the room's single porthole in a bucket tied to a rope.

"You mean I'm to bathe in filthy seawater?" Dawn exclaimed.

The girl straightened up and brushed a strand of dark, lank hair off her forehead with the back of one hand. "Yes, and since you've already had a plunge in the drink, I can't see why you want to do it again."

At first glance, Dawn thought Monique the most slatternly looking woman she had ever seen. Her torn blouse and long gingham skirt were dirty and disheveled. Her face was streaked with grease and soot, and her hair resembled a tangle of snakes. But, as her eyes became accustomed to the dim light, she was able to see beyond the girl's unkempt facade, and realized that there was more to the poor creature than was at first revealed.

She was really quite attractive, her facial features an exotic blend of European and Asian ancestry. Her figure, beneath the shapeless clothing, was voluptuous —pointed breasts and round, shapely buttocks that molded the seat of her skirt when she bent over the tub.

"Monique, how long have you been held captive by the pirates?"

The girl frowned and shrugged. "Three, four months, I'm not sure. My mother and I were traveling from Singapore to Macao to meet my father, a Portuguese customs agent. The praus captured the boat and took the young girls prisoner. They offered to free me for ransom, but my father judged it was too high and refused."

Dawn regarded her with horror. "Your own father condemned you to a life of slavery for a paltry sum of money?"

"It is far simpler to beget another daughter than to acquire gold and silver."

"How beastly! How savage!"

Monique stood erect and faced Dawn, drying her hands on her skirt. "This is a savage land, madam. Men afford no more quarter to each other, or to their women, than do the marauding tigers in the jungles."

"How many women are there aboard the *A-Ma?*"

"Ten or fifteen."

Dawn cleared her throat. "And what do their duties consist of?"

Monique looked at her in amused disbelief. "Surely you jest, madam? Like women everywhere, we cook, we clean, we provide the men with their physical pleasures, and, when they are drunk and tired of sex, we serve as whipping posts for their despair. Don't be alarmed, madam. You are not slated for such a fate. You are the Chosen One, as Madam Ching calls you."

"The Chosen One? Whatever on earth does that mean? Am I to be sacrificed to some pagan god?"

"Before we attacked your clipper ship, Madam Ching prayed at her private altar to the great god Joss and to A-Ma, the goddess of the sea. However, I think her plans for your future are far more earthly than celestial."

"What do you mean?"

"His Highness commissioned Madam Ching and the Ladrones to abduct you. It is rumored he is paying her a fortune in gold for the pleasure of your company."

"His Highness must be missing a few slates in his roof, as we say back in Michigan. Just who is this person? I certainly don't take any of it seriously. 'His Highness,' indeed!"

"Oh, His Highness is very real, madam, I can assure you of that. In fact, he is said to be one of the most influential men in China today."

"A man of eminence who consorts with pirates and murderers?"

An expression of smugness lightened Monique's grave face. "I have heard that all over Europe and even in your wonderful country there are government officials in high public offices who sell protection to criminals for a slice of their booty. Is that not true?"

Dawn was crestfallen. "Unhappily, it is only too true. My father has dealt with such unscrupulous men."

Monique smiled. "Possibly your father can exert his influence on the pirates in your land and persuade them to bargain with our Ladrones to secure your release."

Dawn gave her a quizzical look, then decided to end the conversation. "I think I will have my bath now."

As Dawn removed her clothing, Monique went to the cot and unwrapped a package. Neatly folded inside was a beautiful robe of white silk with jade buttons down the front.

"A gift from Madam Ching," the girl told her. She smiled. "And an even more precious gift." She brought a bar of green, fragrant soap over to the tub. "I haven't felt soap on my skin in months."

Dawn wrinkled up her nose. "That is all too evident. I tell you what, Monique. After I bathe, you can refill the tub and have a bath yourself. And you can have the clothes I just took off."

The girl's eyes glowed with gratitude. "You are too generous, Mrs. Price. Thank you so much."

"You're welcome." She got into the tub and sat down. Her knees were cramped, but there was ample room for her hips and bottom. Her breasts were buoyant in the salt water.

Monique examined her with admiration. "You have a magnificent body. His Highness is a fortunate man to possess such a woman as you."

Dawn sniffed. "His Highness does not possess me, my dear girl. Nor will he ever. No man will ever own me."

Monique's eyes widened in awe. "But you have a husband. Before you were abducted, you belonged to him, no?"

"No, I did not. In Western society, women were once mere chattels, slaves to every wish and whim of their lords and masters. But that is no longer the case. Especially in England and the United States, women are rebelling against such archaic barbarism."

The girl was shocked. "You could be horsewhipped for speaking such blasphemy!"

"I could, and maybe I will be for defying His Highness, but I will not recant one detail of what I feel and speak, even if I am put to death."

"You are a very special woman, Mrs. Price, and I have much admiration for you. But I also have much fear for your future well-being."

"Never fear, Monique, I can take good care of myself. Has it ever occurred to you that you and your sisters in this part of the world could shed the shackles of your bondage?"

"We do not have your kind of courage, Mrs. Price."

"Then you must cultivate it. And possibly I can be of some help in that endeavor. Now, be a dear and scrub my back."

Her bath completed, Dawn stepped out of the tub. There was no towel, so she had to wipe the excess moisture from her body with the cotton slip she had discarded. Then Monique unfolded the white robe that Madam Ching had provided and held it open for her. She slipped into it, wrapped it around her, and tied the sash.

"I feel like I'm swathed in a froth of meringue," she said, savoring the sensuous feel of the silk on her naked body. "Now for your bath."

Monique emptied the tub with the bucket and then refilled it with fresh seawater. She took off her dirty, threadbare blouse and skirt.

"I think we can dispense with these forever." Squeamishly, Dawn picked up the garments with her fingertips and threw them through the porthole into the sea. She sat down on the cot and watched the girl soap herself. Monique's expression radiated sheer bliss. When she was finished and had stepped out of the tub, Dawn was astonished to note that she was shades lighter than when she had first undressed. It angered Dawn to imagine how many times this young woman had been violated by the gross, insensitive pirates.

Monique clasped the clothing that Dawn had been wearing against her body, looking as happy as if she had been presented with a new ball gown.

"They are so beautiful! I will be the envy of every woman on the ship."

Dawn laughed. "Well, put them on and let's see how you look."

Monique obliged and pirouetted gracefully, drawing Dawn's approval. "A decided improvement over your previous apparel. Now we must see if we can do something about your hair. It looks like a mop, but at least it's clean. I don't suppose there is anything like a comb aboard this awful ship?"

"I will go to Madam Ching and say you have requested one. I know she has several."

"Better still, we'll both pay a visit to the good madam. I assume I am not a prisoner confined to this cabin."

She walked to the door and opened it. A pirate, slouched against the ship's railing, moved toward her alertly.

"You wish something?"

"Yes, I am on my way to see Madam Ching."

"A moment, please." He cupped his hands to his mouth and shouted in Chinese to a group of men gathered around the helm.

Soon after, Chou came waddling down the deck. He nodded at Dawn. "You look much refreshed, Mrs. Price. Can I be of service?"

"Thank you, no. I am on my way to Madam Ching's cabin. Come along, Monique."

Chou stepped in front of her, obviously disconcerted. "I think it would be best if you waited for the
madam to send for you."

Dawn confronted him eye to eye, and it was Chou
who succumbed. "I am not in Madam Ching's employ,
if you please, and I intend to see her now. Please step
aside."

Head bowed and mumbling incomprehensibly, the
man let her and Monique pass, although he followed
close behind the two women.

Monique whispered to her, "I think I am beginning
to understand what you mean about standing up for
one's rights and demanding respect."

"In order to command respect, we must respect
ourselves." Dawn climbed the companionway leading
to Madam Ching's cabin with Monique and Chou at
her heels.

She rapped discreetly on the ornately carved door.

"You may enter," Madam Ching's deep, throaty
voice answered.

Dawn walked to the cabin, while Chou and Monique
remained respectfully outside. Madam Ching was seated
behind her desk, poring over maps and charts spead
out in front of her.

Madam Ching was obviously displeased at the in-
trusion. "I don't recall summoning you, Mrs. Price."

"I tried to prevent her," Chou called from outside,
"but she refused to obey."

Dawn's green eyes flashed like polished jade in
bright sunlight. "I obey no one except when it is dic-
tated by common sense and expedience."

The other woman stood up stiffly, hands flat on the
desk. It was only with great restraint that she controlled
her anger. "And I tolerate disobedience aboard my

ship from no one! I am master of this vessel, and the scales of justice are in my hands. I could have you lashed before the crew or I could have you put in irons on a diet of bread and water for the duration of this voyage."

Dawn threw back her head and laughed, disdainful of the other woman's threats. "If what you say is the truth, about the high price on my head, I do not believe His Highness would appreciate any damage inflicted on such costly merchandise as you claim I represent."

She observed with a smug smile that her counter-thrust had obviously reminded Madam Ching of her mission.

"All right, Mrs. Price," she said more reasonably. "Just what is it I can do for you? You must understand that for the next few days I will be overwhelmed with responsibilities and the *A-Ma* will be in constant jeopardy. Every naval vessel in the China Sea will be on the alert once your abduction has been announced. We will have to deal with enemy sailors in order to insure the success of this mission."

"Then I assure you that I will try not to compound your burden. Just a few simple requests will suffice."

Madam Ching shrugged and sat down again. "Please state them briefly."

"First the girl, Monique." She glanced over her shoulder at Monique, who was chewing her lip and twisting her hands together nervously. "She pleases me as a companion and a maid. I will be most appreciative if you would see fit to assign her to me while I am aboard."

"Granted," Madam Ching said without hesitation. "In fact, I bequeath her to you as your personal slave girl, and she may accompany you when you leave the *A-Ma*. Anything else?"

"Yes, I am deeply concerned about the future of my friend and business associate, Mr. McHugh. If any harm were to come to him . . ."

Before she could continue, Madam Ching held up one hand, and an inscrutable smile crossed her features. "Save your breath, Mrs. Price. Mr. McHugh and I had a lengthy discussion after you left, and we have achieved a reasonable compromise that is mutually satisfying. There are important duties aboard ship that are highly compatible with Mr. McHugh's considerable abilities. You need not fear for his safety, I can promise you."

"But after we reach our destination, what then? What will happen to him then?"

"Mrs. Price, though it may come as a shock to you, there is a code of honor among thieves, especially the Ladrone clan." For some reason Dawn found Madam Ching's smile maddeningly condescending. "And so, Mrs. Price, at some future date, when Mr. McHugh has fulfilled all his obligations to me, I think it only fitting that we release him at a neutral port of call so that he can resume his life and career. Now, if you will excuse me."

"Thank you, Madam Ching, but just one more thing. I assume I have total freedom so long as I am your captive aboard this ship? I mean, I can hardly escape."

"That is so. And, yes, you may have the run of the ship." She added with obvious amusement, "At your own risk, of course. As Monique can tell you, the lechery of our Ladrones is notorious."

"I can deal with lechery whether it comes from a

gentleman in a drawing room or a pirate aboard the *A-Ma*." She nodded curtly. "Good day, Madam Ching."

She left the cabin and closed the door behind her. "Well, Chou," she addressed the enormous pirate. "You heard Madam Ching. You no longer have to follow me around like a watchdog."

"I will do my best not to get in your way, Mrs. Price, but I prefer to keep an eye on you, if you don't mind. I know you are a very special woman—one who dares to stand up to Madam Ching the way you did. I admire and respect you, and I intend to see that no harm befalls you. After all, there are many cutthroats among us."

"Oh, I have no doubt of that in the least." Dawn was amused and a little touched by his efforts to establish for her benefit that he was a man of higher caliber than his compatriots. "I like you too, Chou, and I appreciate your intention to safeguard my well-being. Thank you. Now, Monique, let's return to the cabin and I'll do something about your hair, as well as my own."

The girl clapped a hand to her mouth. "The comb! We forgot to ask Madam Ching for a comb!"

Dawn held up a long ivory comb inlaid with jade. "I didn't forget."

"Where did you get it?"

"I picked it up from the floor in front of her desk."

"Did she see you take it?"

"Yes, but she ignored it. She merely smiled. I find Madam Ching's smile to be very infuriating at times." She paused thoughtfully. "Strange, there were two more combs lying on the couch. She seems like such an immaculate and fastidious woman, not the type to leave her toilet articles about like that."

To Dawn's surprise, Monique covered her mouth

with her hands to stifle her giggling. "Now what on earth brought that on?" Dawn demanded. "Monique, stop this silliness at once and tell me what is so funny."

"I am sorry, Mrs. Price, but it is not like you, a woman of the world, to be so innocent about a fact that appears so plain to a stupid girl like myself."

"What on earth are you talking about?"

"The compromise that Madam Ching has reached with your friend, Mr. McHugh. The 'important duties' he has agreed to perform. The 'considerable abilities' she speaks of, and her promise to free Mr. McHugh after he has 'fulfilled all his obligations.' Oh, Mrs. Price, don't you see? Do you know what her Ladrones say about Madam Ching behind her back? That she has a tigress's appetite for men. The Man-eater of Malaya, they call her."

Dawn stopped, transfixed as if nailed fast to the deck by the girl's horrendous insinuations. "Are you saying that Jack McHugh and Madam Ching . . . ?" She could not bring herself to say it.

Monique laughed. "I saw your friend when he was first brought aboard. He is a magnificent man, just the sort of man to inflame Madam Ching's insatiable desires. Why else would she grant him amnesty? I think we can be certain that Mr. McHugh—judging from Madam Ching's present appearance—has already commenced fulfilling his obligations to her."

Dawn was too shocked and angry to speak. She nodded curtly at the girl and resumed walking along the deck to her cabin.

When they were inside, Monique asked with concern, "Mrs. Price, why are you so silent? Are you angry with me for what I said about Madam Ching and Mr. McHugh? Have I offended you?"

"Not in the least, Monique. I am merely surprised that Mr. McHugh would allow himself to be intimidated by Madam Ching. I thought he had more character."

"Why, Mr. McHugh is a virile man, a man who surely has strong sexual appetites. And it cannot be denied that Madam Ching is a highly desirable woman. In my humble opinion, they decided they were ideally suited to satisfy each other's physical needs. As for Mr. McHugh, a man's true character has little to do with his sexual appetites. There is an ancient Chinese proverb . . . how can I translate it? 'There is a certain part of a man, and when it is hard, it has no conscience whatsoever.' Do I make myself clear?"

"Perfectly clear," Dawn snapped. "Now sit down in that chair and let me do your hair."

The girl obeyed, and Dawn drew the comb through her matted hair with hard, impatient strokes. Monique howled like a cat whose tail has been trod upon: "Owwwww! You're hurting me!"

"I'm sorry," Dawn apologized. "My mind was on something else. I didn't realize. . . . There, there, I won't hurt you anymore." She resumed her combing, paying careful attention to the snags and tangles that plagued Monique's long, dark hair.

But her mind was still far away. She recalled the moment when she had left Madam Ching's cabin. She imagined the woman murmuring lusty enticements and invitations to Jack. All too clearly she could see Madam Ching caressing his hard male body, coaxing his manhood to assert itself. Jack's eager hands exploring Madam Ching's exotic body, her flesh the color of honey and just as sweet to his taste. The two of them, panting like beasts on the silk carpet. Silver Jack McHugh mounting Madam Ching.

She could not suppress an outcry of anguish.

Monique leaped up from her chair, her face contorted with fear. "Mrs. Price, what is wrong? Are you in pain? Are you ill? Can I do something? Shall I call for help?"

Dawn put her arms around the trembling girl, hugging her close. "No, no, calm down. I am perfectly well. And I feel like a silly ass frightening you this way. It's just that . . . that . . ." She struggled for the right words. "All the pain of what has befallen me in this one day, torn from my husband and friends, manhandled by this pirate crew! Suddenly, just now, the full weight of it came toppling down on me."

Monique pressed her cheek to Dawn's, and Dawn felt the wetness of her tears. "I do understand, Mrs. Price," she whispered in a small, quavery voice. "I too had a similar experience when first I was abducted and thrown down into the hold like a soup bone to a pack of mad, hungry dogs. I wanted to die, to kill myself. I prayed to the Almighty for his compassion, begging him to let me vanish into the oblivion of the hereafter. You are far more fortunate than I was. You have a friend by your side to watch over you."

"A friend? And who might that friend be?"

"Why, Mr. McHugh! He will always watch over you."

Dawn shut her eyes to hold back the tears.

# CHAPTER EIGHT

On her third morning aboard the pirate ship, Dawn was awakened by sunlight streaming through the open port at the head of her cot. She looked around for Monique, who had been granted permission to sleep in Dawn's cabin, and saw that her straw bedroll was rolled up neatly against one wall.

"Lazybones," she chided herself and stood up, naked, to peer out the port. She was greeted by lush tropical splendor such as she had never seen before. The *A-Ma* was surrounded by heavily wooded islands, the foliage vivid jade green. The beaches were brilliant white, and beyond them, dazzling multicolored blossoms splashed across the mountain slopes like the colors on an artist's palette. The headlands of the steeper islands were shrouded in purple mist.

"A veritable Garden of Eden," Dawn mused. She took her silk robe from the chair and put it on. As she was tying the sash, the door opened and Monique entered, bearing a tray containing a teapot, cups and saucers, and biscuits and jelly.

"Good morning, madam," she said cheerfully.

"I'd prefer you not to call me madam. There is only one 'madam' aboard this ship, and I do not wish to be connected with her in any fashion."

Monique grinned. "Okay, boss lady."

"Don't be flip with me, young lady," Dawn teased.

" 'Young lady,' " the girl repeated airily. "I am not much younger than you are, and I know more about life than you do."

"Yes, in worldly experience you are a very jaded woman. Hmmm . . . that tea smells delicious. It has the aroma of cinnamon, orange, and lemon. I have never tasted such a variety of teas as you have here in the Far East."

They sat cross-legged on Dawn's cot, facing each other across the tray. Monique served the tea while Dawn put jam on a biscuit.

"From what I can see, we are getting closer to our secret destination. What did Madam Ching call it? Pirates' Cove? So many lovely islands."

"This region of the China Sea is called the Land of a Thousand Jade Islands. I have never been so far from the mainland before."

"It must require an exceptional navigator to steer a course through this labyrinth."

"Yes, and that is why the Ladrones have made it their homeland. They have been playing hide-and-seek with the imperial fleet for years, and seldom have any of them been captured."

They had just finished eating breakfast when there

erupted throughout the ship a cacophony of loud, excited voices, running feet, and lurid expletives.

"Come on," Dawn exclaimed. "Let's see what's going on." She ran to the door and opened it. The pirates were running back and forth, their waistbands bristling with pistols, daggers, and wicked-looking short swords with curved blades. Chou came lumbering up to them breathing heavily.

"Madam Ching says you are to remain in your cabin until the danger is past."

"Madam Ching gave me free run of the ship, and I intend to indulge the liberty. What danger are we in?"

The immense pirate shrugged. He had learned the futility of arguing with this stubborn spitfire with a temperament to match the color of her hair.

"Enemy junks lie in wait for us around the point of that island off the starboard bow."

"How do you know?"

He pointed to the island in question. On the sandy beach at the edge of the jungle, Dawn saw a continuous succession of bright flashes.

"It looks as if there's someone with a mirror flashing signals."

"That's exactly what they're doing. The Ladrone beach watchers. A primitive form of semaphore communication. They're warning us that lying in wait in a cove on the other side of the island are three junks, disguised as fishing boats, manned by Imperial Marines."

"So now we turn about and sail off in another direction?"

Silver Jack had unexpectedly come up behind her. "I think not," he said grimly as Chou hurried off. "I believe that Madam Ching has more aggressive plans."

"You seem to know a good deal about Madam Ching's plans," she said tartly.

He ignored the barb. "We're going to put into the beach on this side and put Ladrone troops ashore. They'll cross the island through the jungle and take up positions around the small cove where the junks are anchored."

"Then what?"

He looked at her sternly. "I don't think you would care to hear about it. Certainly not to witness it. Better go back into your cabin."

Dawn slammed her hands down on her hips and stamped a foot. "Silver Jack McHugh! I don't take orders from anyone. Not Madam Ching. And definitely not from *you!*" She turned away from him and strode toward the bow with Monique running after her. As they approached the prow of the barque she was startled to see Madam Ching standing on a raised platform built out over the bowsprit—a startlingly different Madam Ching than the scarlet-empress role she played in her private quarters. Her long dark hair was banded tightly around her head and tied with a red bandanna. She was wearing baggy sailors' trousers tucked into black leather boots and a white cotton blouse that billowed in the wind. A wide leather belt about her waist contained two pistols and a scimitar.

She looked around and frowned at Dawn and Monique. "I thought I gave orders that you be confined in your cabin."

"And I thought I told you that I do not obey orders."

Madam Ching laughed harshly. "Suit yourself, my lady. Though I can guarantee that you will regret your obstinacy."

She flung out an arm and shouted an order in Chinese. With military precision the crewmen leaped to their assigned tasks. One unit posted itself at the capstan; another scrambled up the ratlines into the rigging.

The *A-Ma* veered sharply to starboard and put in for the island. Two hundred yards offshore, Madam Ching ordered the sails furled and the anchor dropped.

Two longboats were brought up from a hold and lowered over the side. Each carried a light cannon in addition to twenty men armed with short swords worn in special scabbards strapped just beneath their armpits.

Madam Ching left her post on the bowsprit to review the details of their hazardous assignment. Monique translated for Dawn:

"When they reach the far side of the island, they will set up the cannons, but they will not reveal their presence until they get the signal from Madam Ching. The *A-Ma* will be used as a decoy to divert the enemy's attention from the beach. It will proceed around the head of the island and sail directly past the junks, inviting them to ambush our ship. However, they will be in for a shocking surprise."

As soon as the longboats were beached, Madam Ching ordered the sails set again and the anchor weighed. She resumed her place high in the prow of the barque while Dawn and Monique took up posts at the starboard rail.

Once again, Chou cautioned them, "There will be shooting, and you will make fine targets on this side of the ship."

His reasoning made sense to Dawn, and she and Monique retired to the port side, where the cabins and hatches provided a certain measure of cover.

As the *A-Ma* came abreast of the point, rats began

to scurry out of the dark holds and onto the deck. The ship was infested with rodents, which provided one of the main protein staples in the pirates' diet, along with the caterpillars and maggots that made their homes in the flour and grain barrels. The emergence of the creatures into the open was a bad omen for the renegade seamen.

"The rats always know when the ship is in peril," Monique explained. "If we start to sink, they will be the first ones overboard." Like an army, hordes of them scampered up the masts and spread out across the spars.

Balancing her spyglass on one forearm, Madam Ching scanned the island and the ocean around it as the ship crossed the headland. The junks waiting inside the cove came into view. The crewmen who had remained aboard were all at their stations on the starboard side, crouched low out of sight below the rail. Three cannons had been set up on the starboard side, well concealed underneath bamboo and canvas trappings.

The *A-Ma* was pursuing a course that would take it across the mouth of the little harbor, no more than two hundred yards from the disguised naval vessels at the closest point. Madam Ching ordered two crewmen to run up bogus colors—in this instance the flag of Siam.

The junks did not identify themselves until the *A-Ma* was almost even with them. Then, at last, they ran up their colors. Exploding into the wind, the billowing silk flags bore the emblem of the Imperial Marines. There was a flurry of activity aboard the junks as the marines flung off their coolie hats and bandannas and removed the camouflage from their cannons.

The small vessels were so overcrowded with troops that they kept getting in one another's way. Madam Ching smiled and nodded with satisfaction. Her battle strategy had been conceived on the premise that excess can only contribute to inefficiency. She put down the spyglass and said to Jack, who had joined her on the platform: "How is it you Americans say? It will be like shooting fish in a rain barrel."

Although the range was still too long for effective use of the primitive cannons, she ordered one of them fired as a signal to the Ladrones on shore behind the unsuspecting Marines. As the vessels closed, the junks' cannon went into action. The first volley fell far short, but their second barrage was far more effective: It tore a hole in the *A-Ma*'s bow above the waterline and shattered the top portion of the mizzenmast. Shards of wood, canvas, and scores of rats splashed into the sea around the ship.

The tide of battle was abruptly reversed as the Ladrone batteries onshore went into action at point-blank range against the junks. And it was just as Madam Ching had predicted: In short order, the marines were totally demoralized as shells rained down on the overloaded vessels. There was no place to hide. They were blown into the water in lots of fives, tens, and twenties, and Madam Ching swiftly moved her barque in close for the kill. Soon they were close enough to pepper the frenzied marines with rifle and pistol fire.

The battle was lost, but the troops were too realistic to entertain the idea of formal capitulation. In the frequent battles between Chinese government forces and the Ladrones, it was acknowledged by both sides that no quarter would be accorded to a single defeated foe.

Abandoning their junks, the surviving marines leaped overboard and, along with hundreds of rats from the *A-Ma*, swam for the island. They would have done better to remain aboard the doomed junks and die a quick death, for now the pirates emerged from the forest and ran down the beach to the water's edge. Unsheathing their short swords, they waded out into the surf to greet the approaching swimmers. Spurred on by blood-lust, the Ladrones swung their swords with lethal precision. Grinning from ear to ear, they lopped off hands, arms, legs, and heads. Soon they were standing waist-deep in a sea of blood. Not a marine reached the beach.

Mission accomplished, they trekked back across the island to the longboats, singing lusty sea chanteys at the top of their lungs:

> *"A mandarin late of Hong Kong*
> *was blessed with a three-headed prong,*
> *a small one for sucking,*
> *a large one for fucking,*
> *and a monster to beat on a gong!"*

Meanwhile, the Ladrones on the *A-Ma* finished off the job, sinking the junks with volley after volley of cannon fire and sniping at the survivors struggling and screaming for mercy in the water.

White as her silk robe, Dawn mumbled to Monique: "I believe I will go inside and lie down. I feel positively ill."

But before she could enter her cabin, Madam Ching came loping down the deck from the prow, her face flushed with victory. "Mrs. Price, not so fast! I want to speak with you."

Dawn turned to her and said with loathing: "But I do not wish to speak with you. Ever again, Madam Ching. I could never have imagined in my wildest fantasies that human beings could be capable of inflicting such ruthless, outrageous carnage. Of course, you are not human beings, not in the real meaning of the word!"

Madam Ching laughed, and her voice was heavy with sarcasm. "You were advised to remain in your cabin, Mrs. Price, so that your tender sensibilities would not be offended. But no, you are the lady who takes orders from no one. Ha! Yes, you are correct, we Ladrones are not human beings in your conventional definition of the term. We are the tigers of the human race, and we live by the law of the jungle: 'Eat or be eaten!' And now, if you will pardon me, I will retire to my cabin to bathe and refresh myself."

She called to Chou, who was mopping his face, sweaty and black with caked gunpowder. "Chou, tell Mr. McHugh I will see him in my quarters immediately." She fairly devastated Dawn with a scornful smile. "To the victors go the spoils. Is that not so, Mrs. Price?"

Dawn rushed into her cabin and slammed the door as hard as she could. She flung herself facedown on the cot and dissolved in a flood of agonized tears.

# CHAPTER NINE

On the following afternoon, the *A-Ma* approached the largest and highest island Dawn had seen since the ship had entered the intricate archipelago. From a distance it appeared as an awesome monolith that had been carved out of a gigantic block of rock in tribute to some god. From the high bluffs that distinguished it on all sides, precipitous walls of stone plunged to narrow, rocky beaches that were eerily uninviting to seafarers. A broad mesa, overgrown with lush vegetation, constituted the summit of the island.

"I wonder why we are heading for that island?" Dawn mused as she and Monique watched it looming up at the prow rail.

"From what the pirates are saying, I believe it is our destination," the girl told her.

After the barque had made a full circle of the island, Dawn demurred: "You must have misunderstood. This place is absolutely inaccessible."

The foreboding cliffs were rugged and uneven, so that their rock faces were mottled in everchanging shadows as the sun's rays played across them from different angles as the day wore on.

When the *A-Ma* had completed its circuit of the island, the ship veered abruptly toward a point where the rock wall gave off a venetian-blind effect with alternate stripes of chalk-white and onyx-black stone running from the top of the bluff down to the sea.

A hundred yards from the beach, Madam Ching came forward to her command post at the prow. She was wearing black silk mandarin pajamas, and her hair was done up in a white silk turban.

"You appear worried, Mrs. Price," she said, mounting the platform.

"It would seem you are about to scuttle your ship," Dawn opined.

Madam Ching laughed, her perfect white teeth gleaming in the sunlight. "You are the victim of an optical illusion, as you will shortly realize. We Chinese are masters of the art of illusion and are therefore far more able to distinguish between that which seems to be and that which constitutes reality. Now watch closely as we draw nearer."

The *A-Ma* proceeded at a snail's pace on minimal canvas, and when the distance had been reduced to some forty yards, the slatted texture of the rock wall assumed an altogether different aspect. What had appeared from a distance to be a narrow niche running back a short way into the rock began to emerge as a far broader passage, more than capable of accommodating a vessel of the barque's proportions. And with each yard they covered, the realization was confirmed.

"The Strait of Ladrone," Madam Ching advised her. "It was discovered by our forefathers generations back. It would never attract the attention of a Western seaman, nor even of a captain of the Imperial Navy, whose native instincts and intuition have been dulled by Westernization. A classic illusion, I must confess, and a natural phenomenon, possibly conjured up by some playful deity."

The *A-Ma* nosed smoothly into the passage while Madam Ching shouted calm orders to the helmsman and called for all sail to be furled. Now the momentum of the ship was provided by a strong current. They were propelled along a gently curving course with sheer walls towering over the ship on either side.

"It's as though we are traveling down into the bowels of the earth," Dawn observed.

"In a sense you are correct," Madam Ching said. "This is not a conventional island. Hundreds of years ago, it was a mighty volcano, spewing lava and dust across the China Sea. Then there was one last eruption so powerful that it lit up the sky above the Imperial City at midnight and rattled the crystal chandeliers at the royal palace. For six days and nights the volcano shook the earth in its final death throes, and then, on the seventh day, it was still. In time, the interior of the caldera, or crater, cooled, the sides began to shrink, and rifts like this one appeared, allowing the sea to flow into the empty caldera. The sea tides and the winds deposited layer upon layer of sand and soil, rich in volcanic ash, within the pit and on its slopes. The trade winds carried pollen from the mainland and from the surrounding islands and impregnated the barren soil.

A new world was born, waiting for the Ladrones to discover it. Soon you will have your first glimpse of Pirates' Cove, and I think you will not be disappointed."

The journey through the Strait of Ladrone lasted twenty minutes. It was an unnerving experience for Dawn, and even more so for Monique, who clasped her hands and began silently to pray. The deeper into the gorge the ship plunged, the darker it got. Overhead, the strip of blue sky visible between the sides of the bluffs at the top grew narrower and narrower, until only a hairline of daylight remained. Premature twilight closed over the *A-Ma*. And then, unexpectedly, the ship broke out of the canyon into dazzling sunlight.

It was several moments before Dawn could open her eyes against the glare. When she was able to, a wondrous sight greeted her. The ship was gliding through a blue lagoon more than a mile in diameter. From its shoreline, the landscape resembled the interior of a bowl with gently sloping sides that angled up sharply a few miles inland. The scenery was a kaleidoscope of spectacular colors—blossoms, stunted trees, ferns against a background of strangely beautiful silvery grass. Lava formations of all sizes and shapes, ethereal and grotesque, geometric and without recognizable form, intertwined coils of lava rope that reminded Dawn of snakes, and wide rippling tapestries of lava, some of them translucent, were draped from the soaring crags that surrounded the little community.

For Pirates' Cove was a community in every respect. The lagoon was an anchorage for numerous Ladrone sailing vessels—barques and brigs and luggers. At a sizable dock, four ships were being unloaded. In the

small village dominating the north side of the crater
there were neat rows of thatched cottages; bamboo
frames were draped with layers of long, silvery grass
bound together with vines that gave the sides a furry
appearance, and the thatched roofs were high and
steep. Beyond the village, high on the slope, was what
to Dawn's astonished view appeared to be a small
palace.

Madam Ching ordered the anchor dropped about a
hundred yards off the dock and came down off her
platform. "Mrs. Price, if you will come with me, I will
provide you with attire more befitting this auspicious
occasion."

"What occasion would that be?"

"Why, your presentation to the royal mansion this
afternoon."

Dawn and Monique followed Madam Ching to a
cabin next to the one where she had originally received
Dawn and Silver Jack. Almost an entire wall of the
room was occupied by a long closet with sliding doors
that contained Madam Ching's extensive wardrobe.
Dawn was surprised to see several elegant Western
gowns amid the collection. When she mentioned it,
Madam Ching remarked casually, "Oh, yes, they are
Paris originals."

On her bed she laid out a diaphanous undergarment
of white silk trimmed with lace that bore a strong resemblance to a Western chemise. The outergarment
she chose for Dawn was a long, voluminous robe of
black silk lined with white satin. The collar and both
sides of the robe from neck to hemline were trimmed
with a glossy fur that Madam Ching identified as white
mink.

"Why don't you try it on?"

Dawn obliged and examined herself in Madam Ching's full-length mirror. "It's positively gorgeous." It fell free-floating from her shoulders and billowed around her to the floor. Attached to it was a short train that extended behind her.

"You may remove it for the present so that I can do your hair," Madam Ching said.

Dawn's eyes widened. *"You* do *my* hair? Madam Ching actually stoops to perform such a menial task?"

Monique was flabbergasted, but Madam Ching dismissed the barb with an airy chuckle as Dawn changed into a simple robe. "Madam Ching has scrubbed floors, scraped decks, and washed pots and pans in the galley. Ladrone women begin training for their future missions from earliest childhood, and their education is lengthy and grueling. Only the strongest and most intelligent and persevering attain rank equal to my own. Please sit down."

Dawn sat down in a straight-backed chair and Madam Ching, with Monique assisting her, went to work on her subject's hair. She worked quickly and deftly, using comb and brush, ribbons, pins, nets of silver and gold thread, all frosted with fresh flowers and sprayed with a fragrant lacquer. When she was satisfied, she stepped in front of Dawn and appraised her accomplishment.

*"Magnifique!"* she exclaimed. "What do you think, Monique?"

"I am at a loss for words to describe the beauty of it," the girl said with one hand clutched to her throat, hardly able to contain her emotion.

"I must have a look." Dawn rose and went to the

mirror. Mouth agape with wonder, she regarded herself. It was as if she were looking at a stranger on the
other side of the glass, a mythical fairy-tale princess of
some exotic land.

"Do you know, you almost look oriental? Sit down
again while I experiment with something."

The female in Dawn was beginning to enjoy this
highly unusual experience; she was reminded of her
girlhood days back in Michigan when, on cold wintry
days, she and her sisters would play in the attic decked
out in discarded clothing of their mother and assorted
aunts, reveling in their make-believe world.

Madam Ching powdered Dawn's face with a large
pom-pom, then, with a dark pencil, she traced Dawn's
eyebrows, elongating them past the outer corners of
her eyes. As a final touch, she darkened and exagger-
ated her eyelashes with a small brush dipped in a black,
viscous substance.

She smiled in approval. "Now look at yourself."

Dawn returned to the mirror and, in truth, she could
not believe her eyes. The transformation was complete.
She *was* an oriental princess. Madam Ching's skillful
use of powder, pencil, and paint had superimposed an
oriental mark on her occidental features. The naturally
almond shape of her eyes was amplified, and they stood
out like brilliant emeralds against the white powder.

"I think I can say with assurance that your patron
will be overwhelmed when he first sets eyes on you
again." It was as near as she had ventured to define
the nebulous force behind Dawn's abduction. One word
in particular echoed through the corridors of her mind.

*"Again."*

*"Again."*

Haltingly she asked, "Then—then he has met me before?"

Madam Ching's face was inscrutable. "I didn't say that."

"You said, 'When he first sets eyes on you *again.*' That implies that we have met on an earlier occasion."

Madam Ching sidestepped the query. "Come, come, enough chatter. We are wasting time. Take your garments back to your cabin and dress. I must do the same." She picked up several bottles and tubes from her vanity table and handed them to Monique. "Anoint her body from head to foot with these balms and unguents and oils. Within the hour we will go ashore."

On their way along the deck to Dawn's cabin, Monique directed her gaze at the large dwelling in the distance. "Your patron must be a rich and important Ladrone to live in such a fine house."

"My patron?" Dawn laughed harshly. "Why do you call him that?"

"Because it is obvious. Ladrone chieftains have many concubines. And now you are to be installed as his number one wife, without a doubt. He must have taken quite a fancy to you the last time he saw you."

"You heard her say it too? That this person and I have met before?"

"Of course. Why else would he have gone to all this trouble to capture you and bring you here if he had not gazed upon your beauteous countenance?"

"It's too absurd. I mean, if I had met a Ladrone chieftain, I certainly would remember him. The only people I have met since we docked at Canton were American and Chinese dignitaries. Well, we shall find out the answer to the riddle very shortly."

Back in her cabin, Dawn removed her robe and prepared to don the formal robe that Madam Ching had given her.

"First you must be anointed," the girl reminded her.

"Nonsense! I just bathed this morning, and I have no intention of turning myself into a greased pig."

"But there will be no grease. These are magic unguents that have been used in this part of the world for centuries. Natural food for the human skin. Your body will absorb them, and your flesh will be as smooth as satin. Please, let me massage you. You will not be disappointed."

"If it will make you happy." She lay facedown on the cot, resting her chin on her folded hands. "Be careful not to disturb my hairdo."

Monique spread oil and salve along the hollow of her spine from shoulders to buttocks. She spanned her two hands flat on Dawn's shoulder blades and commenced massaging. Her hands moved in circular motions, gently kneading the pliant flesh, up and down, side to side, employing her knuckles from time to time in a more vigorous and stimulating method. Dawn had to admit to herself that it was a pleasing and relaxing experience. She could truly feel the potions sinking deep into her flesh. The sensation was tingling, cooling, and vaguely sensual. She shivered as the girl's long fingers caressed the mounds of her buttocks, stroked her thighs, working down her legs to her feet. She started and yelped as Monique mischievously tickled the soles of her feet.

"Stop that, you little minx. I can't stand being tickled. Especially my feet."

Monique giggled. "Did you know that the soles of the feet are one of a woman's love spots?"

"Love spots? What on earth are love spots?"

The girl blushed. "You know, the places where a man touches you when he makes love to you." She touched her breasts and her mons veneris.

Dawn sniffed. "Well, no man has ever tickled my feet, and no one had better try," she said, sitting up.

Monique pushed her down on her back. "Lie still while I do your front."

Dawn closed her eyes, savoring the motion of Monique's hands and fingers as they massaged the oils and ointments deep into the flesh of her upper chest and her breasts. Self-conscious about her hardening nipples, she urged the girl to complete the treatment with more dispatch.

"We don't have all day, you know."

Her stomach muscles tightened and her legs stiffened as Monique's soft, slippery hands stroked her belly and down her thighs. Then the caressing fingers insinuated themselves between her thighs. Dawn bolted upright as if struck by lightning. It had come as a distinct shock to her to recognize the tide of urgent desire that the girl's ministrations were stirring up inside her body.

"That will be enough, thank you." She swung her legs off the bed to the floor and stood up.

"Why are you trembling so?" Monique inquired in a sly voice. "And look at the gooseflesh all over you."

"It's nothing. It must be the stimulants in those potions." She dared not meet the girl's eyes for fear that she would betray the chaotic emotions churning within her. Dawn was badly shaken, and this episode would disturb her for a long time to come. She had been aware from puberty that there were certain girls who would rather be touched and kissed by another girl than by a boy. But such abnormalities beset remote strangers, not one's friends or family. Certainly not one's self!

She put on the black silk robe with the white mink trim over the wispy undergarment and fastened the jade buttons that held it together down the front.

"You look like a goddess," Monique told her. "Here, one of the combs is loose in your hair. Let me fix it." She moved close to Dawn and reached up to adjust the errant comb. Dawn was all too aware of the girl's upthrust breasts brushing against her own breasts.

"There, that's better." Monique lowered her hands, and for an instant their eyes met and held unblinkingly. In a gentle, understanding voice, Monique said: "I know what is troubling you, and you shouldn't concern yourself that you felt pleasure when I touched you. It is the missionaries you listen to who preach of fire and brimstone and sin." She smiled. "To hear them talk, everything that gives one pleasure in life is sinful."

Dawn laughed, and the tension was broken. "You are so right. We Westerners are far too prudish and puritanical, so filled with self-righteousness and the concept of original sin."

"So you see, what is the sin of giving and receiving love and physical fulfillment as well as spiritual fulfillment in the relationship of a man and a woman, or a man and a man, or a woman and another woman? We should all love one another, and then the world would be a happy place."

"You are a sweet girl," Dawn said, and tears blurred her vision.

Monique cupped Dawn's face in her hands and told

her unashamedly, "I love you, beautiful lady." And she kissed her tenderly on the lips.

Dawn hugged her and then stepped back. "It is a great comfort to have you for a companion and a dear friend. Now it must be time for us to go ashore."

# CHAPTER TEN

When Dawn and Monique went out on deck, Chou informed them that Madam Ching was waiting for them in "Cleopatra's barge." He smiled at Dawn's perplexed expression. "Come with me, please."

He led them around the cabin to the starboard side of the barque. Amidships alongside the *A-Ma* there was a barge. A silk canopy was suspended from four corner poles, shielding the deck entirely from the sun. It did, indeed, remind Dawn of pictures she had seen in history books depicting the royal barge of Cleopatra, queen of Egypt. There were deck chairs, tables, and a refreshment buffet. On either side of the craft there were troughs, near water level, manned by oarsmen. Dawn observed immediately that the oarsmen and two other personages, apparently servants, bore little resemblance to the dirty, unshaven, unkept Ladrone pirates. They all wore white linen trousers, black jackets, and bamboo sandals. Skullcaps perched squarely on their heads and neatly braided queues hung down their backs. Indeed, the uniforms were very similar to those worn by Consul Dreyfuss's household staff in Canton.

Chou escorted Dawn very carefully down the steep gangway that descended to the barge's deck, with Monique trailing behind. At the foot were two servants, who bowed as she came aboard. Lounging in an easy chair under the canopy was Madam Ching, resplendent in a golden silk brocade gown ornamented with green dragons, blue and crimson flowers, and other designs worked in a multitude of colors. Her hair was a dark beehive framed by a sunburst headpiece of pure gold festooned with precious gems.

Sitting across a lacquered, inlaid table from Madam Ching was Silver Jack McHugh in a white linen suit, a white dress shirt, and a black string tie. He was clean-shaven, and his hair was cropped short. He rose to greet Dawn.

"Madam Ching did her best to prepare me for your appearance, but mere words are inadequate. You look like a heavenly princess. No, a queen."

Dawn flashed him a haughty smile. "And you look like a missionary. Where on earth did you get that outfit?"

Jack laughed. "Madam Ching is a conjurer. You name it, and she can make it materialize."

"You look positively ethereal," Madam Ching said. "Please sit down." She clapped her hands at the oarsmen. "Make for shore."

The servants served tea in small, dainty china cups adorned by scenes of pagodas, bridges, and placid ponds.

"I must say you really travel in style, Madam Ching," Dawn told her.

Madam Ching smiled thinly. "This is hardly the style we Ladrones are accustomed to. It smacks more of the royal court in the Imperial City."

They disembarked at a small quay and walked to the shore, where two sedan chairs awaited them.

"You and the girl will ride in one, and Jack and I will share the other," Madam Ching informed Dawn with ill-concealed, malicious relish.

"So, now it's 'Jack,' is it?" Dawn seized the chance to fence with her. "As long as we're getting so informal, you may call me Dawn and I'll call you—" She paused and glared at Jack. "What do you call Madam Ching, Jack?"

"Lai Cho," Madam Ching answered for the tongue-tied logger. "That is what my given name is. And if you choose, please feel free to address me informally. Come along, Jack."

When the four of them were seated in the sedan chairs, four bearers at the corners of each chair stooped and gripped the hand poles. They wore the same neat, clean uniforms as the servants on the barge.

As they were borne along the village's main thoroughfare, curious residents lined both sides of the street to stare at the procession.

They left the village behind and followed a dirt road through verdant forest. Overhead the thick, intertwined tree branches formed a natural arched roof. On both sides of the road there abounded bushes covered with red berries.

Madam Ching reached out a hand and gathered a clump of the ripe fruit. She called back to Dawn:

"These berries are a delicacy and considered sacred by many. Try them."

Dawn grabbed a handful and stuffed them into her mouth. They were sweet and juicy, with a distinctive tang that she could not associate with any other fruit she had ever tasted.

The foliage thinned out as they came upon the lava bed of the dormant crater, a black, gleaming, petrified jungle inhabited by inhuman creations, both beautiful and grotesque.

Then, as they approached the foothills ascending to the caldera's summit rim, there was more greenery, sparser than what they had left behind, and most of the trees were stunted. On the top of the hill, looming up before them ever larger and in more distinct detail, was the "royal mansion," as Madam Ching had cryptically described it.

It was a long building built of natural wood that had been lacquered to bring out the beauty of the grain. Its slanted roof was covered with tiles. The lawn and gardens around the mansion were on three tiers and separated from the dwelling by a low, white-washed stone wall. Two fish ponds were situated at either end of the second terrace. The gateway in the wall was flanked by two altars. As they approached, Madam Ching explained, "They are the altars of Heaven and Earth."

The sedan chairs were carried up three flights of white marble stairs and through the gate. A curving path of mosaic tiles led up to the entrance. The four passengers disembarked and mounted a flight of three steps. Obviously their arrival had been witnessed surreptitiously, for no sooner had Madam Ching set foot on the top step than the door was opened by a servant attired identically to the oarsmen and the porters. He bowed low, and they exchanged words in Chinese.

"Come along. His Highness awaits us eagerly." They followed her into an enormous high-domed foyer mirrored on all four sides. The servant led them down a short hall and into an exotically beautiful living room, reminiscent of the home of Consul Dreyfuss in Canton. There were exquisite tapestries on the walls, a silk rug, furniture of teak or japanned wood decorated with intricate carving, and elaborate china figurines and porcelains. From this area they passed through an archway into a circular room whose windows were covered with elaborately painted oiled silk that was translucent, so that the daylight passing through created breathtaking designs on the white marble floor. The servant opened a sliding door.

"His Highness awaits you on the terrace."

The terrace was of the same mosaic tiles as the path. On the far side of the terrace there was a table laden with food, wines, and liquors. To one side of the table there was an arrangement of chairs around a smaller, round table. Their host sat in a high-backed wing chair facing away from them as they emerged from the house. He did not reveal himself until the servant announced them in Chinese. Slowly he stood up and turned around. The shock of recognition caused Dawn's knees to tremble, and she grasped at Monique for support. It was the genial, aged mandarin they had met at the Dreyfuss reception, Wu Ping-ch'ien, the elder known as Houqua.

He smiled and bowed. "Welcome to my humble abode, Mrs. Price, Madam Ching. And you, sir, must be the Mr. McHugh about whom Mrs. Price spoke so highly the last time we met in Canton."

He dismissed the servant in Chinese and indicated to Monique that she was to follow him. Then resuming his English, he explained to Dawn: "Your handmaiden will retire to the company of the other servants. She will be well treated and well fed."

Dawn was still too astonished and bewildered to take note of Monique's departure. She could only stare at the mandarin in utter disbelief.

His silk robe was trimmed with the same white fur as Dawn's gown. His arms were folded across his middle, hands tucked into the gown's full sleeves. The ruby on top of his black skullcap glittered in the sun's slanting rays. He admired Dawn, tilting his head from side to side, his face and smile radiating pure adoration.

"Without a doubt you are the most beautiful woman on this earth. You could only have been sent to me by the grace of our most benevolent gods in Heaven."

"By the gods in Heaven, my foot!" Dawn snapped, finally finding her voice. "I was forcefully abducted by this woman's cutthroats and literally dragged up here at your direction. Houqua, I demand an explanation!"

"My dear lady, you have every right to one. But first, why don't we retire to the refreshment table and partake of some food and drink?"

"I will tolerate no further procrastination, Houqua. I demand to know why I was brought here and what you intend to do with me now that I am here."

The mandarin sighed and clasped his hands together. He indicated the small circular table. "Please sit down and I will begin. But why don't you have some cool wine? It is quite delicious, I assure you." He snapped his fingers and another servant appeared as if out of thin air. Among the mandarin's extensive staff there was always one servant waiting unobtrusively within earshot to heed his call promptly.

"Before you begin, Houqua, there is one thing that shocks me. How is it that a man of your reputation, character, and high office has an alliance with these notorious and infamous pirates, who are outlaws and murderers with a price on their heads, self-proclaimed enemies of the great state you represent?"

Houqua smiled and nodded his head. "My dear lady, as any student of political science will attest, the basic tenet in the eternal quest for power is that the end always justifies the means. Every nation has understood it since the beginning of time. World leaders, politicians pay lip service to the noble qualities of honor, sincerity, honesty, and fair play, but there isn't one of them who would not make a pact with the devil if it would further his personal ambitions. Madam Ching, you understand that better than any of the others present."

Madam Ching smiled and sipped her wine. "It is a fact of life, Your Highness."

"Why do you address him as 'Your Highness'?" Dawn asked.

"Because Wu Ping-ch'ien is a Manchu prince—a distant cousin to the emperor and to the dowager empress."

"To finish answering your question, Mrs. Price," the mandarin went on, "there has been a tacit understanding between the Manchu dynasty"—he paused and smiled superciliously—"and the Ladrone dynasty for generations. In the course of events, there will arise occasions when it will be mutually advantageous to engage in cooperation. Your own case is an excellent example. If your abduction had been effected with the consent, in fact under the auspices, of the Chinese government, at the direction of Wu Ping-ch'ien, friend and confidant to foreign businessmen and colonial servants living in China, chief liaison between them and the imperial palace, can you imagine the crisis it would have precipitated? Possibly outright war between China and the United States; certainly it would provide the foreign devils with an excuse to make still deeper incursions into our territory. The preferred alternative was to strike a bargain with the Ladrones. If they could successfully abduct you from the *Golden Cloud* after it sailed from Canton and place you safely into my hands, then, in return, I would insure the release of a score of prisoners, some of them high-ranking Ladrones, from the government prison where they are presently incarcerated." He nodded to Madam Ching. "You have fulfilled your part of the bargain, madam, and you have my word that, within the week, those hostages shall be released into your hands."

Madam Ching acknowledged his pledge with a smile and a deferential nod of her head.

Dawn was thoroughly exasperated. "But, *why,* Houqua? Why do you want *me,* a very ordinary American woman? Of what possible value can I be to you or to the government of China?"

He shook a finger at her. "No, no, Mrs. Price, you are anything but ordinary. *Extra*ordinary is the proper term. Mrs. Price, as the great English poet Shakespeare wrote, 'There are more things in Heaven and Earth, Horatio, than are dreamt of in your philosophy.' We Chinese take our religion, our gods, extremely seriously. We regard them and respect them, just as we revere our sage elders. When you walked onto the terrace that day at the American consulate, I knew at once you had been sent by the god Tsao Wang."

"This is insane!" Dawn clapped a hand to her forehead.

Houqua did not hear her. His vision, his hearing were attuned to a time past. He went on speaking in a dreamy, hypnotic voice: "It was at the time of the New Year, the twenty-third day of the twelfth moon. It is the time that the god Tsao Wang returns to Heaven. All year his picture had been fixed to a shrine above the kitchen stove, stamped in vivid colors on rice paper. As the eldest of our family, I offered a feast to him—cakes, honey, candied fruits. I smeared the honey on Tsao Wang's lips so that he would speak sweet things about you when he arrived in Heaven. Then I bowed before the picture and removed it from the shrine. I handed it to my youngest grandson, and he carried it out into the yard and placed it on a small stone altar. I followed him and gave him a handful of grain, which he put on the altar for the steeds who would transport Tsao Wang up to Heaven. My grandson set fire to the picture, and as the paper and the grain burned, Tsao Wang was carried upward in the smoke and flames."

He paused and leaned over and placed a hand on Dawn's arm. "Mrs. Price, that very night Tsao Wang spoke to me in my dreams. He told me that within not too many moons he would send to me a priceless gift, a woman who would become the true spiritual consort of the young Emperor Kuàng Hsü. And even as he was speaking, an iridescent image began to materialize in the darkness above my bed. A face—the face of a woman more beautiful than any human countenance I have ever beheld."

Even before he said it, Dawn felt the fine hairs at the base of her neck bristle in frightening precognition.

"Mrs. Price, it was your face that Tsao Wang painted for me on the canvas of my unconsciousness. Even before you were born on the other side of the world, Mrs. Price, it was decreed in Heaven that one day you would be the one true and only acceptable consort of the emperor of China."

Jack bolted out of his chair, fists clenched, and hovered over the frail mandarin. "That's the craziest thing I ever heard in my life! Mrs. Price is a married woman!"

"Our religion does not recognize Christian marriage."

Jack seized the old man by the throat and lifted him out of the chair. "I ought to wring your scrawny neck, you old tyrant!"

"Jack, no!" Dawn shouted. "Don't hurt him!"

At that instant two huge, brawny men came charging around a corner of the house and leaped onto the terrace.

"Look out!" Dawn warned him.

Jack shoved Houqua back down in the chair and whirled around to confront his new antagonists. From the scowls on their faces, it appeared that they had deadly business on their minds.

The mandarin spoke to them angrily in Chinese.

Madam Ching stood up, a stricken expression on her face. "No, Your Highness, you can't have him killed! I promised him freedom!"

Houqua looked at her and cackled. "You promised a prisoner freedom, against the creed of the Ladrones? You know that unless a prisoner joins the cult and takes a vow of blood he must be eliminated."

"I had my reasons." She averted her eyes.

"And I can guess what they were, Madam Ching. Your predilection for virile males is legendary. No matter, I care not for Ladrone custom. This man must die because he has violated my royal and holy person!"

"Says who?" Jack snarled. He moved forward, frowning uncertainly at the curious style of fighting his foes adopted. Their hands were held chest high and slightly to the sides, their feet spread wide apart with the knees bent. The closest man leaped at him, chopping at Jack's neck, using his hand like a hatchet, but Jack had lost none of the speed, strength, and reflexes that had made him a living legend back in the Michigan swamp. He caught his attacker's wrist and it stopped dead as if it had run into a stone wall. He wrenched the man's forearm hard to one side and heard the wristbone snap. Even before the agonized scream could escape his lips, the man was dragged forward, and Jack bludgeoned him with an overhand right that almost tore off his head. He went flying off the terrace into a clump of bushes, stone-cold unconscious.

The second guard literally threw himself at Jack through the air, feet first. Bewildered by the unorthodox tactic, Jack was caught off guard. A brutal kick caught him flush in the chest and sent him toppling backward across the banquet table. Platters of food, bottles, glassware, and decorative flower bowls crashed onto the patio tiles. It was a blow that would have killed a normal man; certainly it would have rendered even the strongest unconscious. But Silver Jack McHugh was in a class by himself. Battling extreme weakness and instability, he got to his hands and knees, shaking his head like a wounded bull. His opponent skirted the table and the debris to finish the job. His advancing blow was a blur to Jack's giddy vision, but instinct motivated his defense. Mustering all of his remaining strength, he launched himself from all fours in a flying tackle at the man. His right shoulder caught the Chinaman just above the knees and sent him sprawling on his back.

Jack knew that he could not survive another blow of such magnitude in his reduced condition. So, employing the free-for-all style developed in the logging camp brawls, he threw himself on top of the man. They wrestled around on the tile floor, rolling over and over.

Jack drove a knee into the fellow's groin, doubling him up, then turned him onto his back and straddled his chest. In a blur of fists so rapid that the human eye could not follow them, he struck him on the sides of his face, using the man's head like a punching bag. He only ceased when he felt his foe shudder and go limp. Breathing hard, he stood up and faced Houqua.

"Well, I suppose it's your whole army now. Your people sure can't whip me in a fair fight."

As if on cue, a phalanx of six fresh combatants came out of the house and advanced on him. To Jack's surprise, Houqua spoke to them rapidly in Chinese and they stopped. The old man snapped his fingers and made a gesture with one hand. Obediently, the formation did an about-face and retreated back into the house.

"What was that all about?" Jack demanded.

The mandarin smiled. "You dismantled two of my most formidable bodyguards as if they were children. Such astonishing physical prowess must be admired. And rewarded. Mr. McHugh, I am offering you the opportunity to accept employment with me." He glanced disdainfully at the two that Jack had dispatched, still unconscious. "I suspect that those two unfortunates will not be capable of resuming their duties for some time. However, one of *you* more than compensates for both of *them*. Well, Mr. McHugh?"

Jack studied Houqua quizzically through narrowed, calculating eyes. He glanced at Dawn, then back at the mandarin. A precarious plan was taking shape in his mind. At last he answered: "I say, I don't believe I have much choice. And stay alive, that is."

Houqua laughed. "You speak the truth, Mr. Mc-Hugh. Then it is settled."

Madam Ching was distraught. "But Your Highness, this man is my prisoner. He is valuable to the Ladrones."

Houqua regarded her with bland amusement. "Valuable to you, Madam Ching. Yes, indeed. Well, to compensate you for your great loss, I will add a reasonable stipend to the amount we agreed upon when you delivered Mrs. Price. Will that be satisfactory?"

Madam Ching knew that in dealing with a powerful figure like Wu Ping-ch'ien she had no choice.

"As you say, sir," she consented.

Houqua eyed the scattered remains of the refreshments strewn all over the terrace and grimaced. "I suggest we retire into the house and have the servants tidy up this mess." He rose, moved closer to Dawn, and offered her his arm. "Allow me, Mrs. Price."

"You can't actually be serious, Houqua, about my becoming a consort of the emperor. After all, I am a Westerner, an American."

"To be sure. The thing is that it is not an infallible

rule. Some years ago the king of Siam wished to take as his wife the English governess of his children, but the lady declined his offer."

"As I am declining your offer to become wife to the emperor of China." She rested her hand lightly in the crook of his elbow, and they walked into the house with Madam Ching and Jack bringing up the rear.

Houqua sighed. "The situation is somewhat different in this case. The whole world knew the whereabouts of the English governess. No one knows where you are, nor will anyone discover that you are residing in the imperial palace. Except for the free ports, China is shrouded from the rest of the world."

Houqua led them down a marble corridor that reminded Dawn of a Byzantine temple. Scarlet pillars held up the ceiling, which was covered with golden tiles. The beams and eaves were ornately carved and painted. At the end of the corridor there was a flight of marble steps flanked by lions carved out of alabaster. They mounted the steps and passed through an archway into a pentagonal room whose walls were covered in crimson satin. At one side of the room there was an altar where candles kept vigil, and the swirling smoke of burning incense permeated the room. At the other side of the room was a small sitting-room area overlooked by a huge stained-glass window.

Houqua escorted Dawn over to a settee and told her, "You must excuse me for a short time. Madam Ching and I have to finalize our business arrangement. So if you and Mr. McHugh will take seats, I will have the servants bring you some refreshments." He bowed to Dawn.

Madam Ching was ill at ease. She addressed Dawn. "It is unlikely that we will see each other again, Mrs.

Price. I won't be a hypocrite and say that I am sorry for having been the instrument of your present predicament. It is a condition of my occupation one becomes inured to. The Ladrone livelihood is derived from the misfortunes and deprivations of others. So I will merely say good-bye and good luck."

"I can do without your good wishes, Madam Ching. Good-bye and"—her eyes flashed—"the very worst luck to you."

Madam Ching flushed and turned to Silver Jack. "I am truly sorry to lose you to His Highness. You would have been an invaluable crewman for the *A-Ma*. Good-bye, Jack."

"Good-bye, Madam Ching."

Madam Ching followed Houqua through the archway and down the marble steps. Dawn was silent until the echo of their footsteps on the marble floor faded.

"What happens now, Jack? To put it bluntly, I will kill myself before I am installed in the imperial palace as the emperor's number-one whore."

Jack's smile was grim. "Let's hope that won't be necessary. There are a lot of miles and obstacles standing between Pirates' Cove and Peking, China."

"Yes, we have to cross the China Sea to the mainland, and the ship could be intercepted by naval patrols. I'm certain that Dennis and my father are raising all kinds of holy hell with the American consulate and the Chinese government. The brash kidnapping of an American citizen by a pack of Chinese pirates could be blown up into an international incident."

"It's an attractive possibility, but I'm sure that it has occurred to Houqua and his henchmen as well. Damned clever, these Chinese, as Consul Dreyfuss says. They'll hide you in some secret compartment of the ship so that even if it is stopped and searched, you won't be detected. And remember, this Houqua is one of the most powerful princes in China and a dignitary well liked and respected by the American community. I am certain that all of the officials in China—Americans, British, French—consider Houqua above suspicion. His personal yacht probably would not even be searched."

"His personal yacht?"

"Yes, I saw it earlier, soon after we arrived here. White, sleek-looking craft, flying the flag of the Chinese government along with a half-dozen other pennants attesting to the high rank and titles of its owner. No, we can't count on your being rescued on our way to the mainland. We have to have some contingency plan."

"Do you have anything specific in mind?"

"I have the germ of an idea. You know, a good many of the crewmen aboard the *A-Ma* are not pirates by preference. They served aboard ships that were captured by the Ladrones and were impressed into service under threat of death. I got to know the crew pretty well on the voyage over, and I sense a strong undercurrent of discontent among them. It's my conviction that if the circumstances were favorable for success, they could be persuaded to join in a mutiny."

"Mutiny!" Dawn was enthralled by the bold plan. "Oh, Jack, do you really think it could work?"

"If I have anything to say, it *will* work."

Dawn walked to him and put her hands on his shoulders. "As Madam Ching says, Jack, you are a special kind of a man."

"Do I detect a note of sarcasm in your statement?"

"Decidedly."

He placed his hands on her waist, and his eyes were fastened on her eyes. "And maybe a hint of jealousy?"

"Jealousy?" Dawn felt her cheeks flaming. "Me jealous of Madam Ching? That's absurd!"

"Is it?" He pulled her against him and bent his face to her face. Stunned, Dawn offered no resistance.

Jack's mouth closed over hers tenderly. She shut her eyes and stood limp in his embrace at first. Then, as the ardor of the kiss heightened, and the blood pumped faster in her veins, throbbing with increasing vigor in her temples and in the pulse at the side of her throat, Dawn stirred to life. She pressed her body against Jack, thrilling to the dynamic surging of his manhood against her quivering loins. A spark glowed at the very core of her being. His hands caressing her back and her buttocks fanned the spark into bright flame. The fire spread with the fierce urgency of that memorable holocaust in the swamp. Desire obliterated all sense of conscience or commitment to her husband; all of her inhibitions went up in a flash fire of lust.

They separated then, and Jack held her at arm's length. "All the rules have changed out here, Dawn. Back in the civilized world we were snatched from, I would have cut off my hand before I touched you, even though I'd been aching for you since the first day I saw you. Remember how you dumped me in the drink?"

They laughed in sweet nostalgic reminiscence.

"This is a different world," he continued. "And you and I are different from who we were before this happened."

"You're right. At this place and at this time, all I can think of is that I want you, Silver Jack." Her eyes misted as she recalled the lusty fantasies she'd had when she and Dennis were making love. "Maybe I always did want you, Jack," she admitted candidly.

"Well, I've always wanted you too, my darling. God! You don't know how wonderful it feels to be free to say it to you. My darling. My one and only darling. I love you, Dawn, and I don't care if I'm damned for it!"

"Dearest!" She stroked the back of his neck and kissed his cheek. "Love, I don't really know. I think I love Dennis—at least I thought I loved him all along. But now I'm confused. Please don't ask me to make such a serious commitment before I can put my confused thoughts and feelings in order."

"Take all the time you want to make up your mind. It isn't important." His voice was determined now. "But the other part, the physical need I have for you. I don't want to wait any longer for that, darling. I want you *now!*"

She smiled. "And I want *you* now; at the earliest opportunity, that is. We can't very well make love here on Houqua's floor. Tonight. We'll find a way to be together tonight."

They stepped away from each other at the sound of footsteps approaching along the marble corridor.

# CHAPTER ELEVEN

Like everything else in the mandarin's mansion, the dining hall was worthy of a king's palace—it reeked of royal splendor. The domed ceiling was as dark a blue as the night sky and festooned with tiny crystal prisms through which sunlight filtered, creating a realistic illusion of stars. The banquet table could comfortably accommodate twenty diners, and the walls around it were covered with tapestries depicting sumptuous feasts—tables laden with all kinds of food and drink.

When Dawn commented on it, Houqua laughed. "It is consistent with the workings of the oriental mind. Let me demonstrate." From a pocket of his robe he produced a little round box about four inches in diameter. While Dawn and Jack looked on, he removed the cover, revealing another box, slightly smaller, nesting within the first box. Chuckling, he removed the cover of the second box; again there was another box nesting within the second box. He repeated the procedure ten times; the last box was no more than a half inch in diameter.

"How quaint," Dawn murmured.

Now Houqua stacked the covers together neatly and, with a deft motion, replaced them on top of the original box. He shuffled the box about on the table a few seconds, allowing all of the enclosed covers to fall into place. Passing on the box to Dawn to inspect, he explained: "We Chinese believe that life itself is a series of concentric circles, one circle lying within a larger circle and expanding into infinity like the universe itself. We sit here within the confines of this room. The room is enclosed within the walls of the house, which is inclosed by the outer wall. And all of it is confined within the crater which is surrounded by the sea. Do you follow my logic?"

Dawn nodded as she opened the cover of the first box.

"Our capital city, Peking, is built on the same principle. There is the outer walled city; within it lies the Imperial City, separated by another wall; and within the Imperial City lies the Forbidden City, where the emperor resides."

With irony, Dawn observed: "The emperor sealed off from his nation and his people, and all of China penned in behind a wall of isolation. Has it occurred to you, Houqua, that the very principle you advocate" —she upturned the box, and the other nine smaller boxes tumbled onto the table—"is directly responsible for China's vulnerability in the face of the Western world? The fatal weakness of isolation; a vast nation feeding upon itself, as it were."

The mandarin stroked his sparse beard and contemplated her pensively. "There is much wisdom in what you say, but it is inaccurate to claim that *I* advocate the principle. Yes, my dear lady, you will make a fine consort for the emperor."

Reminded of what lay ahead for her, Dawn remained silent while the servants served the meal: pressed duck, roast pheasant, enormous prawns, squid, and varieties of exotic food that were unrecognizable to Dawn. She was particularly intrigued by a dish, served on a canapé tray, that resembled hard-boiled eggs.

"One of the rarest delicacies in the Orient, indeed in the whole world," Houqua told her. "Thousand-year-old eggs. You must try them."

Dawn regarded them with distaste. "They really aren't a thousand years old, are they?"

"They are very ancient, I assure you," Houqua said with a twinkle in his eye.

"I do believe I will pass up the eggs," she said and handed the tray to Jack.

"So will I. No offense intended, sir."

"To return to the subject of China. For centuries, the rulers and their ministers have been living behind walls, surrounded by archaic ceremony. All they have known about conditions in China is what their mandarins chose to tell them. It is my fervent hope that the present emperor, Kuang Hsü, will effect changes that will modernize China." He sighed sadly. "His course will not be easy. When the old emperor died, over twenty years ago, his wife, the dowager empress, who by law can select a successor to the throne, chose her nephew, a young boy. A self-indulgent, selfish, power-hungry woman without any concern about anything that happens outside the Forbidden City, she picked the child so that she could rule in his place until he attained maturity.

"A studious, brilliant lad with an inquiring mind, he unfortunately lacked both physical and moral strength. And by the time he assumed the throne, he was under the total domination of his tyrannical aunt. His advisers persuaded Kuang Hsü to pledge a large sum of money to bring China's naval forces up to par with the Western fleets so that the nation could defend itself against a repetition of the Opium Wars. The dowager empress vetoed the grant and used the money to build herself still another grandiose palace to indulge her fancies for extravagant recreation.

"So you see, Mrs. Price, what is required in the Forbidden and Imperial cities is a force to counteract the power that the empress wields over Kuang Hsü. And you are that woman, Mrs. Price. Tsao Wang has decreed it, and, with your love, support, and guidance, the Emperor Kuang Hsü will overcome all obstacles."

Dawn looked helplessly at Silver Jack, who merely shrugged. It was inconceivable to Dawn that anyone of such high intellect, education, and wisdom could be so devoted and faithful to supernatural beliefs handed down from pagan ancestors thousands of years back.

After a dessert of a rich, flavorful pudding that Dawn could not identify, Houqua suggested they retire to his study for brandy and coffee. When they were settled there, sitting in a circle around a jade-topped coffee table, Dawn queried their host about his unusual lifestyle.

"Is this your permanent home, here inside Pirates' Cove?"

"No, this mansion was built by the famous Ladrone chieftain Ching Yih, one of Madam Ching's ancestors.

He considered himself a prince of sorts, and I suppose he was. Long after his death, I was approached by an emissary of the pirate clan regarding some kind of a compromise that would benefit both the Ladrones and the government. An agreement was reached, and that is why, for a price, Madam Ching abducted you and brought you to Pirates' Cove. My first visit here was as the representative of the government of China, empowered to seal the official bargain. Since then I have returned many times for rest and recreation. I find its isolation from the outside world extremely tranquil."

"That's a fine yacht you have," Jack commented.

"Thank you. I purchased it from a British duke. It's fully motor-powered, and can outdistance any sailing vessel in the China Sea."

"How interesting," Jack said and looked at Dawn meaningfully.

Dawn yawned. "Excuse me, Houqua, but it has been a hectic day. May I go to my quarters now?"

"Why, of course. I will have your handmaiden draw you a bath and turn down your bed." He rose, walked to a window, and pulled a bell cord concealed behind the drapery.

A servant appeared promptly. Houqua gave him instructions in Chinese, and he bowed and departed. "It will be only a few minutes, my dear," he told Dawn.

"Thank you. You know, Houqua, I am constantly amazed by how many Chinese speak English."

He smiled. "And French and Spanish and Dutch. It is the natural outcome of Western snobbery. They, particularly the English and Americans, would not stop to master a foreign tongue like Chinese. We are more realistic. So it was the Chinese who undertook to establish communication with the foreign devils—I use the words in jest—in order to facilitate trade."

"You seem to be a roving ambassador, Houqua," Jack said.

"Well put, Mr. McHugh. I am chief liaison officer between the government and the demimonde typified by the Ladrones—those elements of Eastern society who lurk on the fringes of respectability."

The servant reappeared and said something to Houqua. "Kim says it would give him pleasure to escort you to your quarters. Good night, Mrs. Price, and sweet dreams."

"I am not so sure about the sweet dreams, but I will sleep well, I can promise you. Incidentally, this charade that was the inspiration of Madam Ching— the royal robe, the makeup—I have no intention of making it a daily habit."

"To be sure. As long as we remain here at Pirates' Cove, you may choose your own attire, and you and Mr. McHugh will have the free run of the island. There is a circuitous route that leads to the upper rim of the crater. The view from the top is magnificent."

"Aren't you afraid we'll try to escape?" Dawn chided.

Houqua laughed heartily. "Escape from here? No, indeed. Did you observe those bluffs on your way here? The rock walls are vertical. No, the only way down from the summit is to jump."

Houqua and Jack rose as the servant led Dawn out of the room. Then they sat down.

"More brandy, Mr. McHugh?"

"I believe I will, thank you." He helped himself from a crystal decanter on the table. "Just how long are we to remain here in Pirates' Cove?" Jack asked.

"A month at least. Until the excitement over Mrs.

Price's abduction has subsided among the Western community. Until her family resigns itself to the inevitability of her death or the certainty that she will never return to them. I won't be here with you, though. I have other business in Malaya. By the time I return, it will be propitious to spirit Mrs. Price to the mainland and from there to Peking."

"How do I fit into your plans?" Jack inquired, swirling the brandy around in his glass.

"As I said earlier, you will replace the two indisposed guards. Whenever I leave this dwelling, you will be at my side, along with other guards, but you will be the one I place the greatest faith in."

"Does that mean I'll be going with you to Malaya?"

Houqua shook his head. "I think not. At this point you are as notorious as Mrs. Price. But soon they will forget you both. That is the way of the world. Out of sight, out of mind."

Jack finished his brandy and stood up. "It's been a long day for me too. I think I'll turn in. Where are my quarters?"

Houqua's smile was cryptic. "Why, directly across from Mrs. Price's quarters. I will have Kim show you the way when he returns."

Jack was struck dumb. Directly across from Dawn! He couldn't believe it. He tried in vain to penetrate the old mandarin's inscrutable countenance. He felt sure that Houqua, crafty old man that he was, had to have some ulterior motive for giving him a room in such close proximity to Dawn's.

All of the sleeping quarters in the mansion were in a wing of the dwelling to which there was a single access, a marble archway guarded by two armed sentinels. Dawn's bedroom was as luxurious as everything else in the house. The furnishings were an interesting and artistic blend of East and West: Both the vanity table and the four-poster bed were French, and the silk canopy over the bed was in the shape of a pagoda.

"You must see the bathroom, Mrs. Price," Monique said in awe. It is truly fit for a princess or a queen." She curtsied. "And you are to be a queen, no?"

"It is common knowledge among the servants that His Highness is taking you to the Imperial City to be installed as consort of the emperor."

"And how would the servants know a thing like that?"

The girl giggled. "In any well-run household, the servants are always the first to know the most intimate secrets of all the family members. Shall I address you as Your Majesty?"

Dawn feigned a threat, lifting her hand as if to strike Monique. "You call me Your Majesty and you'll get a taste of the same medicine Jack dealt out to Houqua's bodyguards."

Monique's eyes widened. "Yes, it caused quite a stir throughout the household. He is a very powerful and courageous man, Mr. McHugh."

"Yes. . . . Now where is the bathroom? I can't wait to get out of this carnival costume and wash off this makeup."

Monique took Dawn by the hand and led her through a short corridor at one side of the room that joined the bedroom with the bath. Dawn stood in the doorway, gaping like a child viewing a Christmas tree for the first time.

"It looks like something out of the *Arabian Nights*," she exclaimed. The tile floor and walls were inlaid with forms of birds and animals and flowers. The large bathroom was dominated by a sunken tub large enough to accommodate at least six people comfortably. Steaming water was gushing into it from a solid gold spout fed by solid gold faucets shaped like coiled cobras.

Dawn shed her clothing, which Monique carried back into the bedroom to be hung carefully on teakwood hangers. When she returned, Dawn was lying on her back in the warm water.

"This is pure heaven," she murmured. "I could almost fall asleep and drown."

Monique, who had changed from the long white robe into a knee-length silken garment belted at the waist with a sash, sat down on the top step of the huge tub and clasped her arms around her updrawn knees. There was a mischievous glint in her eyes.

"The servant, Kim, tells me that Mr. McHugh has the room across from yours."

Dawn refused to acknowledge the innuendo. "Yes, I imagine they want to keep all of the prisoners in the same area. You did observe the guards at the end of the hall?"

"You could climb out a window."

"There are guards patrolling the perimeter of the property all night. Hand me that washcloth and soap, please."

It took her fifteen minutes to scrub away all vestiges of the powder and paint that Madam Ching had applied to her face, and another fifteen to wash the lacquer out of her auburn hair. At last she felt cleansed and climbed out of the tub. Monique helped her into a white silk nightdress with a pleated skirt comprised of yards of the gauzy material.

"If only the emperor could see you now," Monique teased.

"He'd see more of me than he is ever likely to." She looked at herself in the full-length mirror on one wall. The silk was so fine it was practically transparent. Her body was provocatively silhouetted, and her breasts and pubic triangle were clearly visible in detail.

"Do you wish anything else from me before you go to bed?"

"No thank you, Monique. You may go now. Where do you sleep, by the way?"

"In the servants' quarters. They are very elegant compared to the poor living conditions I have been accustomed to most of my life. Good night, Mrs. Price, and sleep well."

"Good night, Monique. And I've told you before, you may call me Dawn."

"I cannot bring myself to be so bold," the girl said seriously. "It is not proper for a handmaiden to be so informal with a future queen." With an outburst of mirth she bolted for the bedroom door as Dawn threw a hairbrush after her.

"Insolent girl! I shall have you whipped tomorrow."

After Monique departed, Dawn blew out the oil lamps on the vanity, dresser, and night table; there were two candles burning in wall sconces on either side of the doorway which she left untouched. She opened her door a few inches so that the candlelight would be visible in the hallway and went back to the bed and lay down. It was as heavenly soft as the goose-down feather beds she had luxuriated in on bitter winter nights back in Michigan. The humid tropic air, fragrant with the scent of exotic flowers, affected her with its aphrodisiac properties. She stirred restlessly, impatient for Jack's arrival. He did not disappoint her.

Her body tensed as the door opened slowly and Jack slipped into the room, closing the door quietly behind him. He was wearing a short robe, belted at the waist. He advanced toward the bed, a dark, broad, masculine silhouette against the candlelight at his back that took her breath away.

"I wanted to bathe before I visited you," he said, sitting down on the side of the bed. His eyes devoured her. "You are even lovelier undressed than you are dressed up like a fancy lady. In my wildest dreams I never hoped to gaze upon you like this. No, that's a lie. In my dreams I imagined all kinds of abandoned acts with you, my darling."

She held out her arms to him. "Well, you're not dreaming now. Come to me, and we'll do them together in the flesh." She sat up and drew her nightgown over her head. Jack removed his robe somewhat self-consciously, baring the eloquent evidence of his flaming desire for her.

Dawn reached out and took him in her hand; he was too large for her fingers to encircle. Inside, she was quivering like a bowl of jelly. He covered her breasts with his huge hands, and the calluses on his palms teased her taut nipples. She took one of his hands and guided it down her body, across her belly and into the soft, moist nest between her thighs. On all of the occasions that she had slept with her husband, her desire had never been so intense; she lusted for this male with every nerve-ending in her aching body. She trembled as he put his arms around her and pushed her back gently on the soft bed. She opened her thighs to him, and he lowered himself against her. She was thrilled by the way the muscles of his powerful shoulders, chest, and belly rippled across her body like the dash of waves against a sandy beach. When he entered her she gasped in pain; she felt as if she were a virgin again.

"I'm sorry," he whispered and lay still upon her until Dawn ground her pelvis against him.

"It's all right. Please don't stop now." She clenched her sphincter muscle so hard that it was his turn to wince in pain. He resumed his rhythmic thrusting, and Dawn matched his pace with her own undulations. Faster, faster, ever faster in their frenzy to scale the heights. They climaxed in unison, and both cried out in pure enchantment as if it were the first time for each of them.

Much later, they collapsed in sheer exhaustion, the passion that had gone unrequited for so many years satisfied at last.

# BOOK THREE

# CHAPTER ONE

Sara Teasdale was the niece of Harvey Teasdale, the representative of Britain's Cunard shipping line at the seaport of Mangalore on India's Malabar Coast. Sara was slender, with smoldering dark eyes, long raven hair that she wore in a sinuous coil atop her head like a coiled cobra, and olive skin. When she wore the native sari, as she often did, she was indistinguishable from the other young women of high Indian caste who were her principal companions; most of the English women in Mangalore and its environs were her Aunt Sophie's age.

She met Dennis Price at a reception in his honor at the home of Kent Mulvane, the British resident in Mangalore, shortly after the *Golden Cloud* arrived there. The establishment of the Roberts Lumber Company's logging enterprise was a much welcome boom to the district's economy in that it would provide employment for many of the impoverished natives, and Mulvane had been instrumental in securing the landsite options for the Roberts Lumber Company on the seaward slopes of the Western Ghats mountain range. Favored by heavy rainfall the year round, the mountains abounded with lush tropic vegetation and thick hardwood forests.

"How long will it be before your operation is off the ground?" Mulvane inquired of Dennis.

"It's hard to say," he replied. "The loss of my wife and my foreman, Jack McHugh, has dealt our plans a severe setback."

"Yes, terrible business, your wife being kidnapped by the Ladrones, but I would not abandon hope, Mr. Price. If the pirates run true to form, they have kidnapped Mrs. Price in order to hold her for ransom. I am confident they have not harmed her, and will not."

"Yes, I keep hoping that is the case, and that soon they will contact me and declare their terms for her release. As I was saying, Mrs. Price knows more about the logging business than I do. She and Mr. McHugh were the cornerstones of our team. In all truth, they are indispensable. Until my father-in-law, Walter Roberts, sends someone to replace them, Mr. Malone, my assistant foreman, and I will have to fend as best as we can. I imagine I can find among the local foreign residents a party competent to handle my secretarial chores and do bookkeeping under my tutelage?"

"I'll look into it first thing in the morning," Mulvane assured him.

"No need, the job has already been taken," Sara Teasdale chimed in.

Her Uncle Harvey's eyebrows lifted. "I say, my dear, what do you mean?"

Sara turned a radiant smile on Dennis. "Just that I am offering my services to Mr. Price. I am as literate as anyone to be found on the Malabar Coast, and I am a wizard with figures."

Teasdale was badly flustered. "I am sure Mr. Price is grateful to you for your offer, but I am afraid that it is out of the question."

"But why, Uncle?"

He reddened and stumbled all over himself verbally. "Well, that is—I mean—well, it's just not done, a young woman of your social standing and breeding performing menial labor."

"To be sure," she mimicked him sarcastically. "Proper young ladies are put on earth to sit atop pedestals inside glass boxes like dolls to be admired and pampered and gradually die from softening of the brain. Well, I say to the Devil with that kind of existence! I am dying of boredom and mental stagnation, and if Mr. Price will have me, I will be most grateful to accept his offer of a position."

Dennis was tongue-tied, and a stunned, awkward silence descended over the company. Harvey Teasdale was stricken with embarrassment. In the background, the older women exchanged uncomplimentary remarks sotto voce about this brash young lady: Sara Teasdale used shocking language in public; she defied her guardian; and she had earned herself an incorrigible reputation in the two years since she had arrived in Mangalore after the death of her parents in a boating accident on the Thames. To add insult to injury, and to compound her defiance, Sara casually removed a silver cigarette case from her lamé purse and extracted a cigarette from it. Walking to a nearby table, and swinging her buttocks saucily as she moved, she bent over and lit it from a candelabrum.

To the astonishment of the shocked assembly, Dennis began to laugh.

"Mr. Price, I fail to grasp the humor of my niece's unforgivable behavior," Teasdale said stiffly.

"I am sorry. Please accept my apologies. My reaction was spontaneous. You see, sir, your lovely niece, Miss Teadale, reminds me a good deal of my wife, Dawn. They share the same propensity toward independent thinking and action." He glanced at Sara, who was regarding him with amused appreciation. "They both like to tread on the tails of sacred cows, as it were."

Now it was Dennis's turn to be the object of their cold, disapproving stares.

After dinner, Dennis and Sara took a stroll around the broad veranda that flanked the government house on three sides. They stood by the porch rail admiring the small fountain that nestled like a jewel in the middle of the front lawn. Water shot up from the mouth of a marble dolphin and fell back on all sides into the basin in thin streams that glittered like silvery chains in the light of the full moon.

"It's beautiful, isn't it?" she said.

"Hypnotic."

She turned to face him. "Did you mean what you said before, that I reminded you of your wife?"

"Yes, although not in appearance. Dawn is auburn-haired and light of complexion, with jade-green eyes. You are both very beautiful women. But you are definitely sisters under the skin. I admire spunk in a woman."

"I'm pleased to hear it, and I think your wife and I would get along very well indeed." Wistfully she added: "I'd like to have a woman friend. It's so lonely for me here, you can't imagine. I can't endure those horrible old colonial wives. They are such biddies."

Dennis chuckled. "I hope that in the very near future you will meet Dawn. The prevailing opinion is that she'll be ransomed off by the Ladrones at the proper time."

"I truly hope so, Dennis. I can imagine how lonely you must be without her."

"It's as though a part of my body, an arm or a leg, were missing."

Her eyes glistened in the half-light. "You must love her very, very much."

"Infinitely."

She took one of his hands in her two small, soft hands. "She'll return to you, I know she will. Just keep hoping and praying."

"I thank you, Sara." He cleared his throat and changed the subject to one less painful. "You are serious about coming to work for the Roberts Lumber Company?"

"Most assuredly. I hope you were serious about the offer."

"The position is yours."

"You'll probably be ostracized by the colonial community for abetting my insurgency."

"I may be stretching a point, but our foreman, Silver Jack McHugh, had a saying: 'Hell! I've been thrown out of better barrooms than this!' Well, that's how I feel about your stuffy colonial community."

Sara laughed. "Bully for you! When do I start work?"

"I can't say for sure. Tomorrow, Pig Iron Sam Malone and I will set out to look over the company offices on the eastern slopes of the Ghats. Kent Mulvane told me the buildings were completed just last week."

"Yes, there were prolonged delays occasioned by the monsoon season. Say, wouldn't it be jolly if I could accompany you and Mr. Malone up there? I could take notes, cook your meals, be your all-around girl Friday."

Dennis laughed. "That is a highly tempting proposition, Sara, but I am going to back away from it. I've made enough enemies tonight, encouraging your un- orthodox behavior. Don't be impatient. As soon as I am confident that everything at the camp is running smoothly and that our quarters are habitable, I'll send for you. Now I think we had better go inside and join the others before your uncle comes looking for you."

The reception broke up early, and Pig Iron Sam and Dennis returned to their quarters in Mangalore, an old inn run by a retired British army sergeant and his wife.

In the carriage on the way to the inn Pig couldn't wait to tear off his tie and jacket. "One more minute in this monkey suit, I'd have strangled to death," he grunted.

"You're really becoming quite the fashion plate," Dennis needled him. "And you cut quite a figure on the dance floor showing the ladies how to do the buck- and-wing American style."

Pig winced. "It was all that bubbly water they kept forcing on me."

Dennis snorted. "Force indeed!"

When the carriage dropped them off at the John Peel Inn, Dennis suggested, "What do you say we have a nightcap at the bar before turning in?"

"I'm all for it," Pig said. "What I need to wash

away the taste of all that wine is a belt of good old-fashioned whiskey."

Next morning they rose at dawn. Downstairs, waiting in the inn's sitting room, was Basil North, a British government botanist who had been assigned to them as a guide and adviser. North was a slender, wiry man with thin graying hair and steel-rimmed spectacles. He wore a bush jacket, riding breeches, boots, and a pith helmet.

He frowned disapprovingly at the white linen suits worn by Dennis and Pig. "I do believe, before we start, that we should make a stop at a local shop so that you gentlemen can purchase more suitable attire. We're heading into some very rugged country."

The shop he took them to was a saddlery and army-surplus establishment whose principal clients were the British soldiers stationed at a nearby garrison. In short order Dennis and Pig were outfitted with khaki attire similar to the clothing that North was wearing. Dennis and Pig also each purchased a rucksack to carry their toilet articles and other necessities.

Then they walked to the local railroad station and boarded an antiquated train consisting of a single coach and three cattle cars drawn by a steam locomotive.

"The foothills are as far as it will take us," North advised them. "I've arranged for three horses to be at the receiving depot when we arrive. I hope you ride?"

"We've done our share of it, Mr. North," Dennis assured him.

"Please call me Basil."

The train ride on the Pride of India, as the line was facetiously named, seemed endless. The narrow-gauge track was uneven and bumpy, which compounded the punishment inflicted on the passengers' rumps by the hard, splintery wooden seats. When they disembarked at the terminal at the foothills of the Western Ghats, Dennis and Pig hobbled about like old men, massaging their buttocks and the backs of their thighs.

North grinned at their discomfort. "Never mind, old cocks, it takes a little getting used to, but you'll work out the kinks in time."

As North had promised, there were three horses, saddled and ready to go; a young Indian lad held their tethers. North gave him a coin and said to him, "Tell the Sahib Wilson we send many thanks and that I will visit him upon our return from the mountains."

He explained to Dennis and Pig: "Local farmer, another army dropout. It's a strange thing, a lot of chaps who have spent nearly their whole service lives in India come to think of it as home. I think they're afraid to return to the helter-skelter civilization of England and civilian life. They buy small plots of land, and with their army pensions they barely make do."

They mounted their horses, and North led the way to the southeast along a winding road that became increasingly narrower as they rode higher and higher into the rain forests on the slopes of the Ghats.

Dennis and Pig Malone were awed at the first sighting of a teak forest.

"Gawd!" Pig exclaimed. "Some of them buggers must stand bigger'n two hundred feet!"

"Actually, there are no teak forests per se. Teak grows in clusters in the midst of other forests. We'll be approaching the Roberts preserve shortly."

Where the trail ran through the teak trees, the sky was literally eclipsed.

"Never saw nothin' like this back in the swamp," Pig observed. He reached out and picked up a fallen leaf that lay on top of some underbrush. It was larger than any leaf Pig or Dennis had ever seen before and was an exotic purple color. He placed a huge hand across the teak leaf but could not span it either lengthwise or widthwise.

"Some of the leaves run close to two feet in length," North said. "This is *Tectona grandis,* Indian teak. It's a bigger tree and superior to the teak grown in Africa. Incidentally, the leaves are a by-product for your company, Dennis. They produce a special type of dye that is in great demand in the Western world. The wood, as you know, is the finest in the world. Termite resistant, impervious to dry rot and fungus, tough as steel, yet easily worked."

"Say, these trees are all girdled!" Pig said. It was true. At a height of about six feet off the ground a strip of bark six inches wide had been cut around the circumference of the trunks. "That'll kill 'em for certain."

"Precisely," North said. "You see, teak trees must be killed and seasoned for two years before being felled."

Dennis frowned. "That's a disadvantage I hadn't counted on. It will hold up production a devilish long time."

"Not as long as you think. These trees were stripped under government supervision thirteen months ago. By the time you get organized here and whip your logging crew into shape, the current batch will almost be ready for felling."

"Yes, and we'll want to go on stripping at a faster pace than before. Our estimated output of lumber will be ten times the yardage produced under government supervision."

North smiled. "We are counting on it, old man. Frankly, the business has been a white elephant for the Crown, and we're looking forward to increased revenues."

The headquarters of the Roberts Lumber Company was situated on the eastern slopes of the Western Ghats, which, by a quirk of meteorology, were dry and barren. The camp was very much like the logging camp back in Michigan: two barracks to house the workers, a cookhouse, and an office building all built of teak with thatched roofs.

A group of laborers were busy unloading a wagon filled with supplies and logging equipment. North, Dennis, and Pig dismounted, and North called over one of the workers to take care of the horses.

They climbed the steps of the office building and entered. A thin, swarthy young man with slick black hair was poring over a ledger at one of the four desks in the main room. He stood up and bowed to the new arrivals.

"It is good to see you, Sahib North," he said in excellent English. "Did you have a pleasant journey?"

"Tolerable. This is your employer, Mr. Dennis Price, and his assistant, Mr. Malone. Gentlemen, Pa-pu, your gang foreman."

The amenities concluded, the four men sat down and discussed business.

"What about living quarters?" Dennis asked Pa-pu.

"They were built away from the camp, over the ridge to the east where there is a natural spring. I think you and the Memsahib Price will be pleased with your bungalow."

"Memsahib Price will not be residing here for the present," North said quickly.

Thinking of Sara Teasdale, Dennis inquired, "Are there any other living quarters at the camp?"

"No, sir. Sousa, my assistant and your interpreter in the field, and I live with the workers."

"There may be a slight problem when my secretary, Miss Teasdale, arrives."

North's eyebrows lifted, but he did not comment.

Pa-pu grinned, showing the whitest teeth Dennis had ever seen. 'No problem, sahib. There is an extra bedroom in your bungalow."

Dennis felt himself flushing. "Well, we'll deal with that matter when we have to. Where is the supply room?"

"It's at the rear of the cookhouse."

"Let's have a look. By the way, Pa-pu, we must have filing cabinets."

"They just arrived by wagon but are not unloaded as yet."

He led them to the supply room, which was built onto the rear of the cookhouse. A crew was arranging equipment under the direction of an enormous man who weighed at least four hundred pounds. He was wearing Turkish trousers and a red fez. His waxed mustache curled up at the corners like a scimitar.

"That is Sousa. He's a mixed breed," Pa-pu told them. "His father was a Turkish revolutionary who fled here one step ahead of the hangman." He introduced his assistant.

Sousa spoke good English but with a thick accent, not the clipped British English that Pa-pu spoke. Rummaging around the supply room, Pig held up a peavey hook.

"Who the hell sent these buggers?" he asked, laughing. "Fat lot of good they're gonna do. There ain't no river for miles around."

"Oh, but you are wrong, sahib. Across the summit on the western slopes there are raging torrents throughout the forest during and just after the rainy season. In fact, the Western Ghats are the watershed for many rivers, east as well as west."

"I know," Dennis said. "There'd be no point in having a logging camp at a site without rivers to transport the logs to a shipping port."

Pig picked up a new ax with a gleaming blade and swung it around in the air. "I'm hankering to take a cut at one of them teak trees."

North winked at Dennis. "And you shall have the opportunity this afternoon, Mr. Malone. . . . He's in for a surprise," he whispered to Dennis. "Now, let's go back to the office and Sahib Price will outline a projection for his future plans and what role you two men will play in their execution," he told Pa-pu and Sousa.

"Have we signed on a full crew yet?" Dennis asked Pa-pu.

"No more than half, sahib. "I have been very selective in my choices. The workers we have to date have all had some forestry experience working in the government camps."

"Then you should have no trouble filling the quota here."

Pa-pu grimaced. "It is not that simple. In the government projects supervision is lax, and many of the workers are lazy or unqualified. But do not fret, Sahib Price. We will have a full complement by next month at the latest."

After a long and exhausting session the meeting

adjourned for lunch. "We're going to have our hands full," Dennis confided to Pig. "You especially, working out in the field and instructing these novices, working through the interpreter no less."

Pig shrugged philosophically. "One way or the other, things will work out. But I sure wish Silver Jack were here."

"Amen," Dennis said soberly, thinking that if Silver Jack McHugh were here, then his beloved Dawn would also be at his side.

After lunch, North and Dennis and Pig rode over the summit to what Pig christened the "Indian swamp." Pig dismounted and unsheathed his ax from the saddle boot. Twirling it around his head to limber up his muscles, he approached a large teak tree. "Now, let's have a go at this big bugger."

Cocking the ax high behind his right shoulder, he braced his legs, knees slightly bent, and took his famous cut at the bole. The blade of the ax struck the tree with all the power his mighty shoulder muscles and biceps could muster. The repercussions were instantaneous: the backlash shot back up the ax handle, causing it to vibrate like a tuning fork, all of it transmitted through Pig's hands and up his arms. He felt as though he had been struck by lightning. The ax flew out of his grasp and he staggered backward, eyes bulging.

"Je-*sus* Christ!" he gasped. "That was like swinging at an iron pole. Thought you said this wood was easy to work, Mr. North."

"It is, once it's seasoned, but even so, felling teak is quite a different proposition from felling fir trees. The ax must take a back seat to the saw."

Dennis stroked his chin thoughtfully. "I must remind Captain Gresham before he sails for home to ask my father-in-law to look into those newfangled motor-driven saws they've been experimenting with back in the States. We could use a lot of them out here when we start cutting."

Dennis was silent on the ride back to camp. He could not help but consider how uncomfortable it would be to live in the bungalow built for him and Dawn with a house guest as desirable as Sara Teasdale.

# CHAPTER TWO

The next two months flew by for Dennis Price. One day, aboard the *Golden Cloud,* he bid his farewells to Captain and Mrs. Gresham and little Walter Lintin. He gave the captain a letter for Walt Roberts in which he divulged the unhappy news of Dawn's abduction.

*"I held back as long as I could, in the hopes that any day we'd be contacted by her kidnappers, but . . ."* The sentence trailed off on a hopeless note.

Tears welling in her eyes, Teresa laid a hand on his arm. "Oh, Dennis, don't give up. In my heart I know that Dawn will come back to you."

He smiled sadly. "I live on hope, Teresa, but every day that passes without word from the pirates, the hope grows dimmer. Thank God for the hard work that confronts me each day. Except for that, I think I'd go mad."

He shook hands with Captain Gresham and kissed

Teresa on the cheek. "God be with you. Next time you dock in Mangalore, Grant, we'll have a shipment of teak for you."

"Good luck, Dennis."

They walked with him to the gangplank and watched him descend and head despondently up the quay.

Dennis, true to his vow, did immerse himself in organizing the logging camp. Orders for the precious teak were coming in from all over the Western world, forwarded from the Roberts Lumber Company's main office back in Michigan. In the second month, he sent for Sara Teasdale.

She arrived on a Sunday morning on horseback; tied behind her mount was a small burro laden with her luggage. She looked marvelous in a natty riding habit with black and white checks and a red peaked cap, the kind worn on fox hunts.

Dennis eyed her baggage and laughed. "I fear you've overdone it a bit. This is no place for pretty frocks and other frou-frou attire."

Sara was unfazed. "It's an old British tradition. Dress for dinner every night, even at the most remote colonial outpost. It's good for the morale and keeps one civilized."

"You may have a point," he conceded. "I'll have one of the men take care of your luggage and the horses and burro." He ruffled the little beast's long ears.

"Where do I bunk?" she inquired.

Dennis felt his face heat up. "Well, your being the sole woman at this camp poses a small problem. I hope you can accommodate the inconvenience."

"What inconvenience?"

He massaged the back of his neck self-consciously.

"The original plan was for Dawn and me to live in a small bungalow on the campsite. That's about it, the bungalow. What I mean is, you will have to occupy the second bedroom in the bungalow."

His obvious embarrassment titillated the girl. Her dark eyes lit up. "You mean I will have to *live* with you?"

"Yes, but if you have any serious objections we can work out—"

"Don't be silly," she said, cutting him off. "Why should I have any objections to living with you?"

"Come along, then, and I'll show you your quarters."

Sara was satisfied with the bungalow, except that the only furnishings consisted of a bed and dresser in each bedroom and two chairs in the living room. Dennis apologized for the sparseness of the rooms. "I'm having a couch and a few tables sent up from the coast."

"And you'll need curtains and pictures and some ornaments. What about cups and saucers and cutlery?"

"We have some," he answered defensively.

Sara faced him with her legs spread and her hands on her hips. "Yes, indeed, this place sorely needs a woman's touch. Is there a bath?"

"I'm afraid our bathroom facilities are primitive. There's an outhouse at the back. And there's a storeroom in here that I've converted to a bath. There's a tub and an oil heater to heat up the water, although the water here is tepid enough to bathe in as is."

"Then I shall have myself a bath at once."

He showed her to the makeshift bathroom and filled the tub with a bucket from the tank at the back door. He made a hasty departure as she began to unfasten the buttons of her blouse.

While Sara was bathing, two workers brought over her luggage, and Dennis went into the small kitchen to brew a pot of tea on the oil stove. The walls were paper thin, and he could clearly hear her splashing about in the tub, singing as she bathed:

*"Around the corner and under a tree,*
*a handsome laddy made love to me.*
*He kissed me once, he kissed me twice.*
*It wasn't just the thing to do,*
*But, oh, it was so nice."*

All in all it was very distracting. He was mortified, yet unable to prevent his imagination from fantasizing about Sara in the tub. Sara soaping her pear-shaped breasts. Sara standing upright to rinse off the creamy suds, ladling clear water over her sleek body.

"Damn!" he howled as he scalded a hand with hot water from the kettle. "Serves you right, you lewd bastard," he muttered.

The worst was yet to come. She came out of the bathroom with a full-length robe wrapped around her and toweling her long black hair.

"Oh, tea! I'm yearning for a cup." Seeing him wringing his hand, she frowned. "Did you burn yourself?"

"Yes, and it stings like the devil. Never mind, let's have our tea." He carried the tray into the living room and set it down on a crate that served as a table. "I have some sweet biscuits that I've been saving for a special occasion."

Sara smiled. "How nice of you to think of me as a special occasion."

He mumbled something unintelligible and fetched two chairs over to the makeshift table.

"Isn't this domestic and cozy!" she said.

Damn! She certainly had the knack of unnerving him!

She sat down, crossing her legs, and the robe parted briefly, affording Dennis a glimpse of a shapely leg clear up to mid-thigh. He was helpless against her desirability. Deploring the weakness of his flesh, he felt sexual desire kindling in his loins. He had been celibate for months, but he was resolute: Whatever longings he might feel toward Sara Teasdale, he would contain them.

In the weeks that followed, Sara Teasdale proved that she was considerably more than an ornament to decorate the offices of the Roberts Lumber Company. She was a crack secretary and bookkeeper; her shorthand and typing skills matched Dawn's efficiency. And when the occasion demanded, she served as a courier between Dennis and Pig, Pa-pu, and Sousa in the field.

During office hours she dressed in the informal fashion of the men—shirt, trousers, and boots—and wore her hair in a ponytail tied with a ribbon. After work she would retire to the bungalow, bathe, and dress as formally as she had back in Mangalore. In the evenings she and Dennis would read. Occasionally, Pig Malone and Pa-pu would visit, and Sara was a perfect hostess, serving coffee or tea, cakes, and ale.

"It's almost like you was married," Pig observed privately to Dennis.

"Yes . . ." He did not meet Pig's gaze. "And I don't feel comfortable with the situation."

"I can guess why. Living with a sexy girl like her, sleeping in the next room, man has got to be wearing the horn a good deal of the time."

Dennis blushed. "I don't allow myself to think of Sara in that way," he lied.

"Listen, Dennis, if you get too horny, you might want to come with me and Pa-pu some Saturday night. There's a little village across the mountain where there's some real friendly gals. Cheap and clean, too."

"I appreciate that, Pig," Dennis said wearily. "I'll think about it."

One afternoon Sara came into Dennis's office and announced: "There's a Chinese gentleman who wants to see you. He says his name is Houqua."

Dennis stared at her blankly. "Houqua? The name sounds familiar, but I can't place him. Please bring him in." He stood up when Sara escorted the old mandarin into the office.

Dennis recognized him immediately; the sharp, bright eyes, the scrawny beard, the ruby on top of his skullcap. It was the mandarin he and Dawn had met at the consul's house in Canton.

"Houqua, what a pleasant surprise!" He came around the desk to shake hands with the old man. "What on earth are you doing here?"

Houqua was exceedingly grave. "Mr. Price, my dear friend, I regret to say that my presence here is anything but a 'pleasant surprise.' This is not a social visit. I am here as an emissary of the Chinese government."

A heavy weight of dread settled over Dennis's chest. He took a deep breath. "An emissary of what?"

"Bad news, Mr. Price. The very worst news. Perhaps you had better sit down."

Dennis sat on a corner of the desk. His heart was hammering against his breastbone. "It's about Dawn?"

"I am afraid so." He removed a kerchief from the

sleeve of his jacket and wiped his eyes. "She was such a beautiful woman. Another Helen of Troy."

"Was?"

"Mr. Price, your wife is dead."

Dennis went numb. "I don't believe it. How can you know that?"

"Because the emperor's naval forces sank the two pirate vessels that abducted her from the *Golden Cloud*."

"How could they be certain they were the same pirates?"

"Survivors were picked up. They told of a beautiful Caucasian woman and a giant white man who were being held for ransom. They were in chains down in the hold when the ship went down."

Dennis covered his face with both hands and rocked back and forth in silent grief.

"You have my personal sympathy, Mr. Price, as well as the official regret and sympathy of the Chinese government. The emperor feels responsible for sinking the pirate ships, but how could our captains have known that your wife was aboard one of the pirate vessels? We have been waging war against the Ladrones for more than a hundred years."

Dennis pulled himself together with great effort. "I appreciate that you have made the long and arduous journey up here to tell me this, Houqua."

"It is the least I could do to honor the memory of a woman for whom I had unbounded admiration and respect."

Sara was standing in the doorway; she was as white as chalk. "I didn't intend to eavesdrop, but I couldn't help hearing. Oh, Dennis, how horrible for you." She began to cry softly. "And for poor Dawn."

Dennis cleared his throat. "Houqua, will you do me the honor of visiting with me in my home for a while? Sara will make us tea, or there's wine and brandy if you prefer."

The mandarin bowed. "It will be my honor." He glanced at Sara and smiled. "It would appear that you are surrounded by beautiful women."

"Forgive me, Houqua. This is my secretary and assistant, Miss Sara Teasdale."

Houqua took one of her hands, bowed over it, and touched his lips to her fingers. "I am charmed, Miss Teasdale."

The exchange made Dennis uncomfortable. "Well, let's be off to the bungalow. It's extremely humble, Houqua, but life out here doesn't allow for many luxuries."

"It is not the size or the content of an abode that is the measure of a home. It is the quality of those who inhabit it."

Since Sara's arrival, the bungalow had gradually begun taking on the guise of a home rather than merely a place to hang one's hat. Two tables had replaced the packing crate. There were two easy chairs in addition to a settee. Lace curtains adorned the windows, and pictures brightened up the drab walls. Sara brewed tea and served it in graceful, translucent china cups.

The mandarin smacked his lips. "Delicious, Miss Teasdale. Souchong with a hint of cinnamon and lemon peel."

"You certainly know tea, sir," she said and passed a platter of jam tarts to him.

The conversation was steered away from the loss of Dawn and Jack to mundane topics such as Houqua's official duties as representative of the emperor and the progress of the Roberts Lumber Company's new venture.

"We'll be felling teak before the year is out," Dennis said. "And we'll be driving the logs down to the coast after the rivers swell from the monsoon rains."

Houqua visited for nearly an hour, then he announced that he must be on his way. Jack and Dawn accompanied him to a waiting sedan chair carried by four bearers. He shook hands with Dennis.

"Once again I want to express my personal regret and sympathy, as well as the official tidings of the emperor, for your enormous loss. Farewell, Mr. Price. And farewell to you, beautiful lady." He bowed low to Sara.

They watched the chair descend the rugged forest trail and disappear. Slowly they walked back to the bungalow. Inside, Sara put her arms around him as a mother would comfort a hurt child.

"I know what you must be enduring, and I share your pain."

"I don't think I could bear it here alone. You are a source of endless comfort to me, Sara." He hugged her and stepped back. "I think I'll go back to the office and clear up the letters and contracts on my desk. Work helps me forget."

"Will you be needing me anymore today? I'd like to cook us a nice supper."

"You do that." He smiled wanly and left the house.

Leaning against the doorjamb, Sara looked after him thoughtfully. She repeated the precious words he had spoken to her: *"You are a source of endless comfort to me, Sara."*

"I could be a source of even more comfort to you, Dennis," she mused aloud. "But not so soon."

Another month slipped past, and still Dennis could not rid himself of the vision of Dawn's face hovering over his lonely bed each night as he tossed and turned restlessly in the dark.

One night as he was sitting on the edge of his bed, smoking a cigarette and staring out the window at the moonlit compound, there came a tapping at his door.

"May I come in?" Sara called to him softly.

"Just a moment," he said. He slept in the raw, but kept a pair of pajama trousers on the chair beside the bed for occasions when he had to leave his room and risk being seen by Sara. Quickly he put on the trousers. "Come in."

The door opened and she entered—a pale, luminous wraith in the darkness with the moonbeams shimmering on her white nightdress. "I heard you pacing about. Are you all right?"

"Just not sleepy." He flinched as she laid a hand on his bare arm.

"You're as tense as a bowstring," she said.

"I've been drinking too much before going to bed. Alcohol is supposed to relax one, but it has just the opposite effect on me."

"Dennis, we both know what the real problem is. The time for mourning over Dawn is past. You've loved her and you've lost her. It's over."

"I will always love her."

"Of course. The memory of the love and happiness you knew together should be cherished. But you must go on living. And loving. After all, you are a young, virile, attractive man. How long do you intend to perpetuate this monastic existence?"

Her frankness disconcerted Dennis. "I'm perfectly satisfied with my way of life."

"Satisfied? Stop deluding yourself, Dennis. You have repressed your emotions so far, but one day they will burst loose like water gushing over a dam." She moved closer to him and grasped both his arms, looking up into his face. "Do you think I am a desirable woman?"

"It's not my place to think of you in such terms," he said stiffly.

"Don't be so stuffy. I don't mind telling you that I think of you as a highly desirable man."

"Don't talk like that!" he protested hoarsely. He tried to back off, but she held fast and pressed her body against his.

Dennis gasped at the sensation of her ripe, firm breasts flattened against his chest. Through the thin fabric of her gown, her nipples stood taut and erect. He was powerless to resist her. She ground her loins against his and thrilled to the response of his manhood.

"I know you want me, Dennis, just as I want you." She stepped back and bent to grasp the hem of her nightdress. Dennis looked on with rising passion as she drew the gown over her head and tossed it aside. Naked, she stood before him, looking like a white marble statue of Aphrodite in the moonlight. She walked to him and untied the cord of his pajama trousers. They tumbled about his ankles and his swollen lance reached up to touch her navel. Shivering with delight, she drew him down on the bed beside her and caressed him.

With trembling hands Dennis stroked her shoulders, her breasts, her flanks. He almost cried out in joy as her warm, velvet thighs clasped his hand, encouraging him to indulge in further intimacies. She moaned when his fingers found her cleft. It had been so long since he had been with a woman that he felt like an inept schoolboy experiencing sex for the first time.

She opened her arms and her thighs to him and Dennis descended on her slowly and gingerly, and she guided his way with sure hands. He did not believe she was a virgin, and it didn't matter. His easy penetration of her citadel confirmed the assumption. Up and down he moved, with a smooth, even rhythm; but then his strokes began to grow ever faster and more frantic. Her spasms commenced an instant after his own, and seemed to go on gloriously forever. Then Sara uttered one last gasp of fulfillment and collapsed. Equally spent, Dennis rolled off to one side and lay motionless in limp, absolute lassitude and contentment.

Her teeth gleamed in the moonlight. "That was the best ever. How about you?"

He hesitated, feeling unfaithful to the memory of his wife, but it is true that in the pursuit of pleasure, it is the moment at hand that counts the most. Making love to Dawn had been the most rewarding experience of his life, but Dawn was lost to him forever, and the pleasures her body had blessed him with were gone with her. Sara was here beside him—warm, wanton flesh with the hot blood of desire pumping through her veins.

He answered her at last. "The very best."

To his surprise she began to cry. "I am so very grateful to you for saying that. All too often, the second woman is at a hopeless disadvantage, competing with a dead love. I love you so very much, Dennis. I think I have loved you since the day we met."

"And I love you, Sara, my darling." And miraculously and with boundless relief, the albatross of guilt and betrayal that he had borne so long was lifted from his shoulders. He was free of the past!

Tenderly he bent over Sara and kissed her on the lips.

# CHAPTER THREE

Dawn and Silver Jack were at Pirates' Cove for three months. Although they were prisoners, in one sense it was an idyllic existence. As Dawn expressed it: "We are no longer in control of our own lives. We are not responsible for being here, and, consequently, we are not responsible for what is happening to us; what we do or do not do. Everything has been prearranged by some higher power, just as the gods in the ancient myths manipulated mere mortals the way one would pieces on a chessboard. Win or lose, the result is out of our hands. You and I are no more guilty of adulterous behavior than Oedipus was of fornicating with his own mother. Here in Pirates' Cove, time is standing still for us, Jack."

"But not forever," he said with regret. "Houqua will return and take you to China—or try to, at any rate. But not if I have anything to say about it."

Meanwhile, they lived every day to the hilt. As Houqua had promised, they had free run of the community within the crater—the entire island, for that matter. One of their favorite diversions was to climb the circuitous and difficult trail up the interior wall of the caldera to the rim of the extinct volcano. From the rim to the outer bluffs overlooking the China Sea there was a half-mile swath of vegetation around the circumference of the volcano: trees, shrubs, exotic flowers. It was lush, verdant, fragrant—a veritable Garden of Eden.

Usually they would take with them a hamper filled with delicacies and wine from the mandarin's well-stocked larder. At one side of the island there bubbled up an underground spring that fed sparkling cold water over a miniature waterfall into a small lagoon, which in turn flowed down the side of the crater in a tumbling freshet that provided fresh water for the inhabitants below.

Dawn and Jack would undress and frolic like unspoiled children in the refreshing pond. In this paradise, their lovemaking took on an added dimension apart from physical desire and fulfillment.

"I feel as if we are performing a spiritual act at a sacred shrine," Dawn said one afternoon as they engaged in unhurried foreplay on the warm volcanic sand beside the still pool. She knelt beside him and took his engorged phallus tenderly in her hands, bending her parted lips to it. It was an act of pure adoration; pure in the literal sense. Purity was at the core of every act of their love.

Sated, he would stretch Dawn out spread-eagled on the soft sand and adore her body—every finger, every toe, every portion of her satiny flesh tanned bronze from the tropic sun.

At sunset they would dress and descend into the crater, where cook fires were already being ignited in the village in preparation for the evening meal. Often they would stop in for a drink at the little tavern frequented by the Ladrone men and women. By now Dawn and Jack had been thoroughly accepted by the pirates as two of their own.

One evening when they entered the Peg Leg, as the tavern was colorfully named—after its one-legged proprietor—they met Monique and Spinoza, her Ladrone lover, a crossbreed offspring of a Chinese mother and a Spanish sailor.

Spinoza was a large, formidable man with a wild head of black hair, brooding deep-set eyes, and a drooping mustache. His wicked countenance was accented by the slant of his eyes. In reality he was a good-natured, kindly man and seemed to have genuine affection for Monique.

Monique called to Dawn, "Come and join us."

She and Jack walked through the close-packed rustic tables to a corner of the room where Spinoza and Monique were drinking rum and a concoction of tropical fruit juices out of tumblers fashioned from coconut shells.

Monique was flushed from the alcohol and from an afternoon of lovemaking in Spinoza's shack. Her eyes danced. "Where did you two come from? As if we didn't know."

"We took our daily constitutional up to the top of the crater. You two should try it; you could use the exercise."

The girl giggled and nudged Spinoza. "We would,

only we wouldn't want to spy on you in your private Garden of Eden. Adam and Eve and the forbidden apple. Did you partake of the fruit today?"

Dawn pretended to be angry. "You insolent wench. One more of your affronts and I'll have you tossed into the mandarin's dungeon." The truth was that formality between the two women had all but dissipated, and they had become close and confidential friends—as had Jack and Spinoza.

Glancing around furtively to insure that none of the other revelers were eavesdropping, Jack and Spinoza put their heads close together and spoke in low, conspiratorial tones. Dawn and Monique, on cue, began chattering like magpies and laughed louder and more frequently than they would have normally, as a buffer against the men's conversation.

"Word has it that the old mandarin will return to Pirates' Cove either tomorrow or the next day," Spinoza said.

"And the chances are he won't be tarrying here for long. My guess is we'll be on our way to China by the end of the week."

Spinoza smiled and lit a black, twisted cheroot. "China? Not if our plans go well."

"I'm confident that they will go exactly as we want them to. We'll have ten of our allies working on the dock and performing chores aboard the mandarin's yacht before it sails again. Painting, cleaning, polishing, mending sails. His own servants don't sully their hands with menial work like that. Besides, Houqua told me that in his opinion the most able seamen in the world are the Ladrones."

"He's right. Most of them are born to the sea, not reluctant conscripts like you and me."

"Anyway, I don't see any real opposition standing in our way. When we make our move, we'll overpower Houqua's crew without too much of a fight. Then it's through the Strait of Ladrone to freedom."

"We'll be pursued, no doubt of that."

"Houqua told me that his motorized yacht can outsail any ship in the China Sea."

"I think it's time we got back to the house," Dawn said. "Houqua's chief houseman has been keeping tabs on our comings and goings."

"Right you are." Jack downed his mug of ale and stood up. "Keep your fingers crossed, Spinoza."

Monique accompanied Dawn and Jack back to the house. Cheng, the major domo, opened the front door even before they had reached the steps. He bowed and smiled.

"Did Madam have a pleasant excursion?" He spoke English almost as well as the mandarin.

"Very, thank you. I'm starved. What's for supper, Cheng?"

"Bird's-nest soup, poached salmon, and pressed duck."

"Sounds wonderful. I want to take a quick bath before I eat."

"As you say, madam. Oh, it might interest you to know that His Highness will be coming home soon."

"I heard some talk of it in the village. His journey has taken longer than expected."

She and Monique went up to Dawn's room, and the handmaiden drew a tepid bath for her. Watching Dawn step into the tub, she said casually: "You look very relaxed and radiant. Mr. McHugh is a good lover, isn't he?"

Dawn blushed. "Don't be impudent, wench! It's none of your business."

Monique giggled. "Why not? I don't mind telling you that Spinoza is a bull in bed."

"I'm not interested."

"Maybe one day we can trade partners and decide which one is best." She whooped and darted out of the bathroom as Dawn heaved a bar of soap after her.

For the most part, Dawn found oriental attire more comfortable than Western garb. In the daytime she wore a loose silk jacket over mandarin trousers. In the evening she chose a long billowing robe of pongee silk that was softer than ordinary silk.

For variety she would come down to dinner wearing a calico frock sprinkled with tiny blossoms and trimmed with lace and colored ribbons. Underneath she wore a silk or satin teddy or French panties. The storehouse in Pirates' Cove held an abundance of clothing, both male and female, from all parts of the world, booty culled from ships they had victimized.

She and Jack retired early that night, and Dawn slept like the dead until the sun was high in the morning sky. She was awakened in the most pleasant fashion: Jack was kissing her breasts.

"No wonder I was having such a lascivious dream," she said, wriggling languidly under his ministrations.

"Was I making love to you?"

"No, I was copulating with the old mandarin."

Jack laughed. "It's been a long time since he's been up to that sort of mischief."

"Don't be too sure. Monique says Chinese men can perform well into their nineties. They take an aphrodisiac; it's called ginseng." She felt for his crotch. "Well, it's obvious you don't require ginseng. Not yet, at any rate. Let's get on with it, darling. You've brought me this far—now do something about it."

He laughed and stood up to remove his trousers.

That afternoon Houqua's yacht steamed into the harbor. It was a small fore-and-aft schooner with an auxiliary engine; her two stumpy smokestacks looked incongruous amid her masts and spars. She was painted snow white, and her rails and her abundant hardware were of solid brass that set her aglitter in the sunlight. There was a golden aura about her that fit the name embossed on her prow in Chinese characters that, translated into English, meant "golden dragon."

Dawn and Jack watched from the quay as the barge that had transported them to shore from Madam Ching's pirate ship was rowed out to the yacht to pick up His Highness.

Houqua beamed when he saw Dawn and Jack waiting for him. He embraced Dawn and shook hands with Jack. "My dear friends, what a delight to see you again. How do you Americans say it? You are a 'sight for sore eyes.' I can't tell you how happy I am that this long mission has been accomplished and now I can devote myself to self-indulgence and relaxation until we arrive at the Forbidden City."

A servant helped him into a waiting sedan chair and he waved to them. "I will see you later back at the house."

As he was carried off, Spinoza and Monique strolled along the beach to where Jack and Dawn were contemplating the anchored yacht.

Spinoza tugged at the swirling ends of his mustache. "It has been arranged. Six of our men have been assigned to the work crew that will refurbish the *Golden*

*Dragon* for the voyage to China. Three more will be painting the brig twenty-five yards aft of the yacht. At my signal they will leap overboard and swim to join us."

"What about the yacht's crewmen?"

"All but a skeleton crew will be ashore, resting up for the next sailing. They won't pose much of a problem, I assure you. Now it's up to you two to find out exactly what Houqua's plans are and relay them to us as soon as possible."

"Right, and the sooner the better." He took Dawn's arm. "Come on, let's go up to the mansion and welcome our host home."

They bid good-bye to Monique and Spinoza and set off for the big house on the hill.

After dinner that evening, as had been the custom before Houqua's departure from Pirates' Cove, the three of them retired to his library for coffee and brandy.

The mandarin rolled the crystal snifter around in his palms to warm the elixir and inhaled it with deep satisfaction. "Yes, tea is my favorite beverage, but somehow it does not do justice to fine French brandy."

"Tell us about your trip," Dawn urged.

"It was an extensive voyage. Singapore, Borneo, Java." He paused and fixed her with a sly smile. "Oh, yes, and we put in at Mangalore on India's Malabar Coast."

The declaration so startled Dawn that she slopped coffee over the rim of her cup into the saucer. "Mangalore? Why, that was the destination of the *Golden Cloud,* where my father's teak plantation is located."

"Yes, I know," he said blandly, sipping his brandy.

Jack leaned forward, bracing his elbows on his knees. "What was your business in India?"

"Actually, it was not business, not in the same sense as my other ports of call. I paid a visit inland to the Roberts Lumber Company's Indian offices. Remarkable tract of teak forest you possess; it should prove to be extremely lucrative when it is in full production."

Dawn could not believe her ears. "It's incredible! Why would you do a thing like that?"

"I wanted to have a chat with your husband. Incidentally, he appears to be in excellent health."

"My husband? What cheek! What did you tell him?"

Without blinking, he met her gaze and smiled. "I felt it was unfair to keep him in a state of chronic uncertainty as to your fate. Better the matter be resolved once and for all. Mrs. Price, I told your husband that you were dead; that you perished along with Mr. McHugh when the Chinese navy sank the Ladrone ship on which you were being held prisoner."

Dawn flew out of her chair, upsetting her coffee cup. Tears of fury welled up in her eyes. "You didn't! You couldn't! As unspeakable as you are, there has to be a trace of decency somewhere within you!"

Houqua was impassive. "I told you I did it as an act of mercy."

"You cur!" She started toward him, hands extended like cat's claws, obsessed with one idea, that of killing him.

Jack leaped up and grabbed her from behind. He spun her around and warned her, "No, Dawn, anger and violence will accomplish nothing."

"Mr. McHugh is correct. Please calm yourself, my dear Mrs. Price."

She read something else in Jack's eyes: *"For God's*

*sake, don't spoil everything we've been planning. We've got to play along with the old bastard in order to get our big chance to escape."*

She relaxed, and he let go of her. Dawn touched her hand to her flaming forehead. "I don't know what came over me. The shock. The terrible shock of hearing that Dennis believes I'm dead. I think I had best go to bed."

"A good idea," Jack said pointedly. "Undoubtedly you'll be facing a strenuous day tomorrow. Right, Houqua?"

"You mean our departure on the *Golden Dragon?* No, our sailing time will be sometime after noon the day after tomorrow. The pirate work crews have quite a bit of labor to perform before we sail."

"Do you hear that, Dawn?" Jack asked.

"Yes. Well, good night then."

She went directly to her bedroom, where Monique was turning down the coverlet. "Your bath water is drawn," the girl told her.

"Never mind the bath water. I want you to get word to Spinoza as soon as possible. We leave the day after tomorrow—Thursday afternoon."

"I will see him first thing in the morning." She looked at Dawn anxiously. "Do you really think we have a chance? It's such a dangerous undertaking. If we fail, it means death to all of us."

"It may at that," Dawn said dourly. "But even death is preferable to becoming the emperor's concubine."

That night Jack came to her just as she was beginning to fall asleep.

"My darling," she said, "I'm too tense to make love. I can't help thinking about Thursday. And that awful business about Dennis."

He sat down on the side of the bed. "I didn't come to make love. I came to tell you something more about Dennis."

She sat up abruptly, wide awake. "Dennis? He's all right, isn't he? Houqua said he was in excellent health."

"Yes, he's fine." He massaged the back of his neck, a sure sign that something was troubling him. "After you left, Houqua told me more about his visit to the teak camp. There's a woman up there at the camp. Her name is Sara Teasdale."

"Whatever is she doing there?"

"She's an office worker, the niece of a British mucky-muck at Mangalore."

"Well what about her?"

He took a deep breath. "She and Dennis are living together."

She stared at him in bewilderment. "Living together? Sleeping together, is that what you're saying?"

"It would appear so. They share a bungalow on the premises. Houqua says she's a fine hostess and a good housekeeper."

"Houqua is lying, just another of his foxy tricks to unsettle me."

"I don't think so, Dawn."

"It's unthinkable. I mean, how could Dennis take up with another woman when there still was a good chance that I was alive?"

Jack laid a hand on her bare shoulder. "These things happen. After all, let's face it, darling, you and I have been living together as husband and wife for three months. And all the while we've *known* that Dennis is alive."

Dawn was struck speechless. "I—I—" She swallowed a lump in her throat and cleared it. "I never thought of it that way. Of course, you're right, Jack. What right do I have to play the self-righteous wife? He's no more to blame than I am. What we were talking about at the pond—that we are all mere mortals manipulated by a higher power like pieces on a chessboard." She flung herself into his arms. "Poor Dennis. Poor me. Poor Jack. Oh, my darling, hold me tight. I'm suddenly terribly frightened."

He stretched out beside her and cradled her in his arms as if she were a child. He kissed and caressed her chastely until she fell asleep.

Jack lay awake a long time, his mind in chaos. If they succeeded in escaping from Houqua's clutches, and Dennis and Dawn were reunited, what would the outcome be? The answer to that question filled him with far more apprehension than the showdown with the pirates on Thursday afternoon.

Too restless to sleep, he rose and went back to his own room. He stood by a window chain-smoking and staring out across the exotic garden where Houqua's guards patrolled vigilantly with rifles slung over their shoulders. Far down the slope in the harbor, the fleet of pirate ships drifted at anchor like ghosts in the luminous moonlight. And Houqua's white yacht stood out from the rest—the most phantasmagoric of them all.

# CHAPTER FOUR

Thursday dawned ominously. Uncharacteristically, a dark cloud ceiling obscured the sun, and although the air was still in the bowels of the caldera, the trees on the summit rim were lashed by wind. The water in the cove was choppy, indicating uncommon turbulence in the sea around the island.

While they were at breakfast, the captain of Houqua's yacht paid a visit to the mandarin's mansion. After conferring with him in the study, Houqua came back to the breakfast table. He appeared concerned.

"Captain Luan informs me that a storm is brewing to the northwest. He thinks it might be advisable for us to delay our departure until we are better informed as to the severity of the disturbance."

Dawn and Jack looked at each other with distress.

Regardless of whether or not the *Golden Dragon*

sailed on schedule this afternoon, the work aboard her would nevertheless be completed, and there would be no further opportunity for Spinoza and the other conspirators to board her a second time. All of their plans would have to be scuttled.

"It might clear up by noon. After all it's only ten o'clock," Dawn said lamely.

Her hopes did not materialize, but at least there was no intensification of the inclement weather. By noon, in fact, the haze hovering over the volcano had brightened discernibly. Houqua made his decision. "We will sail on schedule."

Up in Dawn's room, she and Monique hugged each other. "The gods are with us," the girl said. "Soon we will be free!"

"There's an old American saying," Dawn cautioned her, " 'Don't count your chickens before they're hatched.' " She and Monique began to pack a sea chest provided by Houqua with the variety of wearing apparel she had acquired while at Pirates' Cove.

Downstairs, Houqua summoned Jack to his study. "I have certain reservations about having you accompany me on this voyage."

Jack was thunderstruck. "But why, Houqua? How can I serve you in my capacity as bodyguard if I am stuck here in Pirates' Cove with hundreds of miles of sea between us? I mean, if your purpose in sparing my life was to let me stagnate here, you should have let your guards kill me that first day. I am not geared to an idle existence."

The mandarin began to pace, stroking his beard. "Yes, yes, I understand that. It is just that you could become a problem if we are stopped by foreign naval forces."

"I don't see why. I must assume you do not trust me, and I can understand that. But obviously you have contingency plans as to how to deal with Mrs. Price in the event the yacht is stopped and searched. Those same plans can apply to me as well."

The mandarin nodded. "There is a false bulkhead at the prow of the vessel that conceals a compartment for smuggling contraband. It should be large enough for two. Yes, Mr. McHugh, your point is well taken. What good are you to me back here in Pirates' Cove? All right, you will sail with us."

"I am grateful, Your Highness," Jack said with affected obsequiousness.

The real drama was unfolding aboard the *Golden Dragon,* where Spinoza and nine other Ladrone workmen were putting the final touches on the mandarin's yacht. The brass gleamed, and the deck had been freshly varnished. The yacht's hull bore no reminders of the months she had spent at sea. Of the nine workers, six were in on the plot; Spinoza could only guess as to the disposition of the other three. No matter. If they opposed the takeover, they would be overpowered and thrown overboard or killed.

The moment arrived when Captain Luan and the six crewmen of the yacht who had remained aboard while the work was in progress appeared on deck. He made an announcement to the workers: "The crewmen who are ashore will shortly be returning to the *Golden Dragon,* and you men can return in the same boats that transport them. You have done a commendable job and done it rapidly. His Highness will be most gratified."

A subordinate spoke to him rapidly in Chinese. The captain frowned and looked toward shore. Spinoza followed his gaze and his heart leaped. The royal barge, carrying the mandarin, Dawn Price, Silver Jack McHugh, and a coterie of servants, was drawing away from the quay on its way to the yacht.

Captain Luan was displeased. "His Highness was not due to board for another hour. This is highly embarrasing. Meanwhile, most of my crew are still ashore, sitting in the Peg Leg tavern or consorting with whores. Lieutenant Mushima, launch the small boat and go ashore and collect our crew."

The lieutenant chose two seamen and they ran to the stern, where a small boat lay nestled beneath a tarpaulin. Spinoza could not believe their good fortune. Now there would only be Captain Luan and three crewmen to contend with, plus the unknown factor of the three uncommitted Ladrones.

The small boat was launched and was halfway to the beach when the royal barge drew alongside the yacht and a gangplank was put over to her. The honor of boarding first was accorded to Dawn, along with her handmaiden, Monique. The mandarin went up next, with Jack close behind him.

Spinoza and his conspirators had casually moved to the rear of the group milling around the deck at the top of the gangplank. Captain Luan and his three crewmen stood at attention, and bowed low as Houqua set foot on deck. The moment was at hand. Spinoza's gang quickly drew pistols and knives from beneath their shirts. Spinoza whistled and tossed a pistol to Jack across the heads of the astonished spectators. Jack grabbed it deftly and spun around to confront the other members of Houqua's party as they prepared to board the yacht.

"The first man sets foot on this gangplank will get a bullet in his belly," he warned.

"The rest of you down on the deck on your bellies," Spinoza ordered. "Be quick about it!"

The mandarin was shaking with anger and outrage. His voice was high-pitched and tremulous. "What is the meaning of this? I swear, you will all hang before this day is over!"

Spinoza fired a shot into the deck between his feet. "Down, I say! The next one will be higher."

Houqua appealed to Jack. "Jack . . . Mr. McHugh, my good friend. You have sworn to protect me."

Jack laughed harshly. "Consider that a little white lie, mandarin. Better do as he says."

There were no heroes among the crew of the *Golden Dragon*. The captain and his three crewmen complied wtih alacrity, throwing themselves down on the deck with their arms and legs spread wide.

Spinoza was carefully observing the three outsiders among the work crew. Plainly, they were bewildered and at a loss to cope with this dramatic and startling occurrence.

"Well, what is it going to be?" Spinoza addressed them. "Are you with us or against us? Either way, make up your minds quickly." He trained two pistols on them.

Houqua assailed these three vehemently. "You call yourselves Ladrones, yet you permit these scoundrels to intimidate you! Attack at once, I am ordering you!" When they continued to procrastinate, he frothed at the mouth. Hopping up and down in his frenzy, he screeched: "Scum! Scum! You are lower than the slugs who cling to the bottom of rocks on the shore." He spat at them.

A subtle change of expression was evidenced on the faces of the undecided three. They looked at each other and spoke in undertones. Then a spokesman hooked his thumbs inside his belt and swaggered over to the mandarin.

"Scum are we? Slugs? Well, let me tell you, for a long time now we Ladrones have had it up to here with your high and mighty manners, *Your Highness,*" he said with sharp sarcasm. He drew a finger across his throat. "We know you value our lives less than you do the cats who rub against your legs and share your bed. You tolerate us only because you can use us to your own advantage. Well, here are three Ladrones who are finished doing business with you and your lackeys and your puppet government." And he spit directly into the mandarin's face.

Spinoza and the original six mutineers let go with an encouraging cheer. "Good for you, my friend," Spinoza said. "Now, no more dallying. Houqua, you and your people return to the barge."

Seized with an apoplectic fit, Houqua collapsed on the deck and began to kick and thrash about. It required the remaining three of the yacht's crewmen to carry him off the ship.

The gangplank was withdrawn, and Jack waved to the spellbound guards and servants gaping at them from the barge. "Now get back to shore, and don't try anything funny. First man makes a false move will be gunned down." Cowed, the barge's rowers bent to their oars with gusto, and soon the craft was putting distance between it and the yacht at a spanking rate.

Jack turned to Spinoza. "How did you make out with the engineer?"

Spinoza grinned. "A man of immense ego, he was

an easy mark. He devoured flattery greedily. He talked endlessly about his marvelous ship and extraordinary engine. I have a thorough grasp of the rudiments of how to start it and run it properly."

"Then get busy." He finally got around to Dawn and Monique, who had drawn back to the shadow of the cabin while the issue was still uncertain. "See how easy it was." He took Dawn into his arms and kissed her on the mouth.

Monique and Spinoza were embracing too.

"All right, you lovebirds," one of the mutineers called out cheerfully. "Break it up and let's get out of here before they come after us."

"He's right," Spinoza said and went below to start the engine. Moments later, it roared into action, just as the three remaining defectors, who had been working on the nearby brig, clambered over the rail, dripping wet.

"What took you so long?" Jack jested. "We were just about to leave without you." As the *Golden Dragon* came to life, the skilled Ladrone seamen scurried around the deck to their respective chores, weighing the anchor and climbing the masts to insure that all the sails were securely furled, since the ship was being driven by engine power. A giant of a Chinaman named Fong, one of the finest helmsman in the Ladrone fleet, was at the wheel.

"Full speed ahead!" Jack sang out. "Fong, head for the passage out of this cul-de-sac."

"Jack!" Dawn grabbed his arm. "Look! There's a ship trying to cut us off!"

It was true. One of the Ladrone ships in the harbor, an armed brigantine, had been alerted to what was happening and was attempting to intercept the yacht before it could reach the mouth of the Strait of Ladrone.

"They're manning a cannon!" Spinoza shouted.

"Damn!" Jack cursed. "We've got to prevent the gun crew from becoming operational!"

"There's a gun rack in the captain's cabin. Brand-new shiny American high-power cavalry rifles," Spinoza said.

"Let's get 'em fast!"

Jack and Spinoza dashed into the cabin and collected the weapons from the rack—six in all—along with boxes of rifle ammunition.

On deck, he passed out ammo and rifles to Spinoza, himself, and four of their crewmen. They loaded hastily.

"Pick off those bastards manning the cannon," Jack ordered. "Fire at will!"

Even as he spoke, a cannon shell sent a geyser of water high into the air off the port bow.

The mutineers knelt at the railing, shoulder to shoulder, and began to fire at the Ladrone gun crew. The first volley felled the gunner and one of the loaders. Another pirate picked up a shell and tried to jam it into the breech. A bullet struck him in the chest and he toppled backward. The shell went rolling across the deck.

It was apparent that the motorized yacht was going to win the race to the mouth of the strait, if the pirates didn't score a hit with their cannon. They managed to get off one more round that went whistling harmlessly through the bare rigging. Than the riflemen felled every gunner who tried to get off a third. A mighty cheer went up as they cleared the mouth of the strait and plunged into the canyon that led out of the cove. The tide was coming in, and the engine was taxed to its fullest to make headway, but it proved equal to the task. There was no chance of a sailing ship bucking the powerful current, so they would be safe from pursuit until the next outgoing tide.

"By the time the Ladrones can put a ship to sea, we'll be leagues away," Jack said jubilantly.

Monique and Dawn hugged each other and then hugged their lovers.

"Free at last!" Monique exulted. "Doesn't it feel wonderful?"

Spinoza was full of plans. "We'll go to Macao. I have an uncle there who owns an export business. He'll give me a job, and we can get married."

Everyone aboard the *Golden Dragon* was full of excitement and expectations for the future except for Dawn and Jack. He put an arm about her waist and led her to the prow of the ship, where they stood at the rail watching the sleek ship cleave through the foaming waters.

"What happens now?" she asked dully.

He shrugged. "That depends on you, my sweet. You are a married woman, and when Dennis finds out you're alive . . ." He did not complete the thought.

"There is Miss Teasdale," she suggested. "Maybe he won't want me back."

"No doubt she's a handy sex partner, but you're his wife and his business partner as well."

She buried her face against his chest. "Oh, Jack, whatever shall we do?"

He smiled wryly. "Remember, the decision is out of our hands. The gods will decide our destinies."

That night Jack and Dawn occupied the captain's cabin. For more than an hour they lay naked together on the narrow bunk, pressed breast to bosom, belly to belly, loin to loin, doing absolutely nothing, saying very little, each lost in his and her private thoughts. At last Dawn sighed and caressed Jack's flaccid member.

"What's this?" she joked. "It doesn't speak very well for my desirability."

"Do you know something, my darling?" he said in all seriousness. "If I could be with you forever at the price of losing my potency, I would accept the bargain. Just being together would be enough."

"What a sweet thing to say, love." She kissed his cheek and caressed him encouragingly. Soon the desired effect was achieved and he mounted and gently entered her.

"My Garden of Eden," he whispered, and they became one.

# CHAPTER FIVE

Four days later they were sighted by a British naval cruiser flying the Union Jack. She signaled the *Golden Dragon* to heave-to. As the warship approached them, a squad of British marines armed with rifles took up positions at the starboard rail. When they were within hailing distance, an officer put a megaphone to his mouth and called to them, "Identify yourself and state your destination and point of embarkation!"

Jack cupped his hands to his mouth and shouted back: "We're escapees from a pirate penal colony! Can we come aboard?"

Fifteen minutes later Jack and Dawn were seated in the captain's wardroom narrating the account of their incredible adventure while Captain Evans and his executive officer listened with mounting incredulity. When they concluded, Evans said to Dawn: "For almost two months you were the object of a widespread search that encompassed the boundaries of the China Sea and beyond. Then you were reported to be dead, and all hope was abandoned. Mrs. Price, this is the nearest thing to a miracle I have ever seen. I can't tell you how honored and pleased I am that H.M.S. *Good Hope* has been the instrument of your salvation. We will head for Canton immediately and put you in the hands of the American consul there."

"What about our other friends?" Jack demanded.

"I am afraid that under the circumstances it will be necessary to confiscate the mandarin's yacht. His conduct will elicit a very serious protest to the Chinese government filed jointly by the United Kingdom, the United States, and their allies here in Asia. However, we will put a salvage crew aboard the *Golden Dragon* and they will deposit your fellow escapees at a destination of their choice."

This procedure was promptly acted on, and before the yacht and the cruiser went their separate ways, Dawn and Jack said their good-byes to Spinoza and Monique. Monique embraced Dawn and began to cry. "I would dearly like to stay with you and be your handmaiden forever, but I must go with Spinoza," Monique said through her tears.

"Of course you must go with the man you love and whom you will soon marry. Besides, American women don't own slaves—not anymore, at least."

They returned to the *Good Hope* and waved as the *Golden Dragon* pulled away. As it faded out of sight over the horizon, Jack mused, "And now to Canton."

Dawn looked wan. "And then I must reckon with my husband."

The arrival of a British cruiser in the harbor at Whampoa was a cause for excited speculation among the crewmen on the other ships anchored in the big port at Canton. Roland Dreyfuss and his wife, Mae, were eating lunch on their spacious patio, and from the high point on which the house stood they could observe the approach of the *Good Hope* on its way upriver.

"Hasn't been a warship put in here since the search for Dawn Price was abandoned," the consul mused. "I wonder what's up."

They shrugged off the incident and turned their attention back to their lunch. No more than an hour later, while Dreyfuss was working in his office, he heard a loud commotion from the front hall. Moments later Mae came bursting into the office bubbling over with excitement, her face radiant.

"Roland! Roland! You won't believe it. I've seen her and I still don't believe it! She's come back from the dead!"

Somewhat disconcerted, Dreyfuss got up and came around the desk. He took his wife by the arms. "What on earth are you babbling about, my dear? Calm down or you'll have a stroke. Now, who is it that has come back from the dead?"

"I have, Mr. Dreyfuss," Dawn said from the shadow of the hall.

He saw her then, and his eyes bulged in utter stupefaction. There stood Dawn Price, looking as cool and beautiful as she had the first time he had met her, in a plaid flannel dress of fawn cotton with a shirred shoulder yoke and pearl buttons running down the frill-top blouse from throat to waist. Beside her was a giant of a man whom he vaguely recognized.

She smiled and came into the room, holding out her

hand. "Don't look so shocked, Mr. Dreyfuss. I am not a ghost. Here, feel me." She grasped his hand.

Dreyfuss touched his free hand to his forehead and shook his head. "Forgive me, I'm in a daze. We were certain you were dead. Words cannot describe my feelings right now."

"I understand." She looked back at Jack McHugh. "I believe you and Jack met briefly the last time we were in Canton."

"Yes, of course, the chap who was kidnapped along with you by the pirates." He shook Jack's hand warmly. "Do come in and sit down. Mae, have one of the boys bring in some refreshments. Cool wine. No, make it champagne, the best. This is indeed an occasion for celebration." He escorted Dawn to an easy chair near his desk, and Jack sat down in a wing chair off to the side.

"Don't keep us in suspense, Mrs. Price. It would appear that you have dropped out of the sky."

"Not quite, Mr. Dreyfuss, although there is a quality of unreality about the whole affair—indeed, about everything that has transpired since Mr. McHugh and I were abducted by the Ladrone pirates. A fanciful adventure one reads about in a work of fiction." She recited in as much detail as she could recall all that had happened in the months she and Jack had been held captive.

Dreyfuss and his wife were incredulous and horrified. "Imagine that old scoundrel, Houqua, basking in our hospitality for years—the hospitality of the United States government, for that matter—and all the while he has been double-dealing with the Ladrones. If I have my way, he'll swing from the yardarm of that warship in the harbor."

"I seriously doubt you will ever see or hear about our mandarin friend again," Dawn said.

"You're probably right. Now that he's been exposed as the fraud he is, he has lost all value to the Chinese government. Not only will he lose face among his peers, he may lose his head as well for permitting you two to escape. Exile to Manchuria is about the best he can hope for."

The champagne was served, and Dreyfuss offered the first toast: "To your safe return, the both of you, and to a long and happy life in the future."

After she had sipped the sparkling wine, Dawn looked at the consul and said with deep concern: "Yes, the future, Consul Dreyfuss. We cannot avoid what lies ahead of us in the future. What have you heard recently about the Roberts Lumber Company in India? My husband, Dennis?"

Silence descended over the assembly. Dreyfuss and his wife exchanged glances, and neither of them could meet Dawn's gaze.

"What is it?" Dawn asked with rising anxiety. "The last we heard of him was from Houqua, who said that he had visited the company camp and lied to Dennis about my alleged death. Houqua said he was in excellent health."

"Yes, indeed, excellent health." Staring at the tops of his white shoes, the consul sat forward in his chair with his hands resting on his stout thighs. He exhaled loudly, rubbed a hand across his jaw, then scratched his ear.

"Consul Dreyfuss . . ."

Dreyfuss braced himself and finally was able to say it. "Mrs. Price, your husband believed the story the mandarin told him—that you had perished in the sinking of a Ladrone pirate ship. At first he was inconsolable, stricken with grief. But eventually he had to accept the hard reality of it. No amount of grieving, no amount of dwelling on the tragedy would bring you back—or so he believed. He did his best to dismiss what had happened and immersed himself in the considerable work and responsibilities that confronted him in your company's logging enterprise." He cleared his throat nervously. "His recuperation from the shock of your loss was due largely to the support and solace tended him by his assistant, a Miss Sara Teasdale." He took a white handkerchief from his breast pocket and mopped his brow. "Mrs. Price, this is extremely difficult for me."

"I have heard about Miss Teasdale," Dawn said levelly. "From Houqua. I know everything."

"Everything?" Dreyfuss and his wife regarded Dawn curiously. "I don't think—"

"Houqua told me that she and my husband were sharing a dwelling together."

"Oh, dear me!" Mae Dreyfuss commenced to fan herself with her handkerchief.

Dreyfuss coughed into his clenched fist. "Mrs. Price, there is a recent development that you cannot be aware of. Two weeks ago your husband married Miss Teasdale, and they are presently honeymooning in Japan." He massaged his eyelids with his fingertips, and his voice was weary. "They are expected to visit Canton on their way home to India."

Dawn was momentarily struck dumb. She could only stare at the consul in disbelief. Finally, she managed to get out: "Married? But that's absurd!"

Jack cursed under his breath.

Dawn stood up and walked to the window. "Isn't

there some statute that prohibits that kind of thing? I mean, I've only been reported dead for a short time."

"Back in England or the States, yes," he informed her. "But in this part of the world, a person is declared legally dead if two or more witnesses testify to the fact. At least four pirates took an oath that you were killed in the wreck of the pirate ship."

"The word of pirates is accepted by civilized authorities? Absurdity piled upon absurdity." She clasped her hands in front of her and turned to Dreyfuss. "Consul, we would appreciate it, Mr. McHugh and I, if you could provide us with living accommodations until this matter has been resolved. You say that Dennis and his new bride will be returning to Canton soon?"

"Yes," he said, removing his steel-rimmed spectacles and wiping his watery eyes. "And, of course, we will be happy to accommodate you and Mr. McHugh here at the embassy until this matter has been resolved."

"Thank you, Mr. and Mrs. Dreyfuss. We will have our belongings sent up from the *Good Hope*."

"Excellent. I will attend to it. Also, I think it only proper to hold a small reception for Captain Evans and his officers to show the gratitude of the United States government for effecting your rescue and return to Canton."

Later in the day, Jack and Dawn were strolling in the consulate's gardens. "I think it would be wise if we restrained ourselves during our stay here," Dawn observed.

"I wouldn't have it any other way," he agreed. "God! What a bloody mess! Wait until Dennis walks in and sets eyes on you!"

"Not to mention dear Miss Teasdale's reaction." She

smiled with a tinge of malice. "Even though she has no inkling of it, she still *is* Miss Teasdale."

Jack grinned. "Do I detect a note of jealousy?"

"Jealousy?" She thought about it. "No, not exactly jealousy. I can't fault the girl for sleeping with Dennis. I'm too much of a realist. No, you and I and Dennis and Miss Teasdale, we're all young, vigorous animals with red blood and a hunger in the flesh. I felt an urgent physical deprivation while I was in captivity, far away from husband and marital intimacy. Yes, I lusted for you, Jack McHugh. I'm not ashamed of it, and I have no regrets. And I'm sure that Dennis and Miss Teasdale—"

"Except that you wish all of it hadn't happened in the first place," he interrupted. "If the Ladrones hadn't come along, you and Dennis would be playing house on your teak plantation, and Pig and I would be playing cribbage and slugging Indian hootch in our bunkhouse."

"You're probably right," she conceded. "But I'm not all that certain that I wish it hadn't happened. There have been times when I've wondered whether or not I made the right decision in marrying Dennis. Oh, you know how those things go with young girls. He was my first lover, and I had stars in my eyes."

He put his hands on her shoulders then, and looked deep into her enormous green eyes. "Your first lover? Damn! Would you believe it? I'm jealous thinking about it, you and him in bed. I wish I had been your first lover!"

Dawn's merry laughter pealed through the gardens. "Just like a man! You want to be the first with me, but it doesn't matter a damn to you that there were scores of girls before me in your wild life. I've heard all the stories about your exploits immortalized in story and song throughout the swamp. Silver Jack McHugh, the Bull of the Woods! Ha!"

Jack's face reddened, and he dropped his eyes. "Aw, come on, Dawn! There never was a woman in my life before you. Saginaw whores don't count."

"Like hell they don't!" She laughed and took his arm, and they resumed walking. "The point is, it's all water under the bridge. As Matthew says in the New Testament, 'Which man can add an ell to his height by troubling over it?' That's how I feel. To get back to what I was trying to tell you, I'm not certain that I regret being abducted and being thrown together with you. I've been strongly attracted to you since the first day we met."

He put an arm about her waist and pulled her against him. "I keep telling you that I've loved you from that first moment."

"I think it's possible that I've loved you from the first as well. But Dennis was in the way, and he interfered with my true and clear perspective of you, Jack."

"In a way, then, this relationship between Dennis and Sara Teasdale could work in our favor."

She looked up into his ruggedly handsome face and smiled. "It's in the hands of the gods now, darling. It will be interesting to note how they move the pieces about at this stage of the game."

"Let's see," he mused. "What are the options? First of all, Dennis and you could resume life as husband and wife, and Sara and I would be removed from the board. Secondly, the four of us could live together as one big happy family."

Dawn laughed. "Frankly, I can't see myself playing musical beds."

"And last but not least, you could divorce Dennis and then he could make Sara his legal wife."

"And you could make me your legal wife. Yes, I rather like the last option." She put her arms around his neck. "I don't give a damn if Rolly and Mae are watching. I'm going to kiss you as you've never been kissed before."

He glanced back at the sprawling mansion. "That could lead to consequences right here on the lawn that would shock the pants off Mae and Rolly."

"It would do them both good to get out of their pants once in a while and frolic about."

"You are a hussy."

"And you are my stud. My exclusive stud from now on, and we'll forget about the Saginaw whores."

# CHAPTER SIX

The time spent at the consulate during the weeks that
followed was a pleasant interlude for Dawn. The true
extent of the mental and physical ordeal she had suffered as a prisoner of the Ladrone pirates only became
apparent to her now that she and Jack were free. In the
mornings she slept late. The afternoons were given over
to pure self-indulgence: She lounged on the sunbaked
terrace, strolled in the cool and fragrant gardens, and
served as co-hostess at the cocktail parties that the
Dreyfusses had three or four times a week for fellow
diplomats and the Western commercial community. In
the evenings Dawn and Jack would lie on the terrace,
staring at the diamond-studded navy blue sky. Some
nights they could observe a myriad of shooting stars.

"The Saginaw Indians say that a shooting star is the
soul of someone who has just died on its way to
heaven," Dawn said.

"A safe bet," Jack said cynically. "There's someone dying every second somewhere in the world."

"Then again, my mother used to tell us when we were children to make a wish when we saw a shooting star. I'm making one right now."

"What is it?"

"I wish Dennis and his bride would return so that we can get this mess over with."

"Amen."

The next afternoon Dreyfuss drove up from the waterfront in his buggy at top speed. He burst into the dining room, where his wife and Dawn and Jack were having tea.

"It's arrived!" he announced breathlessly. "The *Indian Princess* just sailed into the harbor!"

"What about it?" Jack asked.

"It's the ship Dennis Price and his wife"—he cut himself short and glanced nervously at Dawn—"that is, Miss Teasdale and he are traveling aboard the *Indian Princess.*"

Dawn went pale, and her heart beat quickly. "Well, my wish came true overnight. I'm glad." She reached for Jack's hand and squeezed it. "And I'm scared, as well."

"Everything will work out. Don't fret over it, my dear," Mae Dreyfuss said in an attempt to comfort her.

"Will they be coming straight up to the consulate?" Dawn wanted to know.

The consul wiped his head with a handkerchief. "I expect so. I left word at customs that Mr. Price should report to the American consulate as soon as was convenient."

"Now all we can do is wait," Dawn said.

And wait they did. The minutes dragged slowly into

hours, until at last it seemed to Dawn that time stood
still. She paced up and down the terrace, her eyes
constantly searching the harbor and dock area below for
some sign that the confrontation with her husband was
imminent. At last her vigil was rewarded. A small surrey with a red fringe on its canopy left the dock area
and proceeded up the winding road that led to the consulate. Dreyfuss came out of the house with a spyglass
and trained it on the horse-drawn vehicle.

"It is Price and Miss Teasdale," he confirmed.

The skin drew taut across Dawn's high cheekbones,
and her lips were compressed and bloodless. Jack put
an arm about her waist. "Relax, darling."

Dreyfuss had a suggestion. "I think it might be wise
if you and Mr. McHugh retired into the house, my
dear. I feel that Mr. Price deserves the consideration
of receiving some forewarning that you are alive and
here in the consulate. It is bound to come as a shock
to him, but it will be easier if I break the news to him
privately before he meets you."

"I agree. Come along, Jack." She took his hand and
led him through the French doors into the house.

A few minutes later the surrey pulled up before the
consulate. Dreyfuss came down the marble steps to
greet the arrivals.

"Mr. Price . . ." He compromised by nodding at
Sara. "Good to see you two again. Was your holiday
pleasant?"

"Very pleasant, thank you," Sara answered.

Dennis looked tense and grim. "I received your
message. What is the urgent matter you have to discuss
with me? Is it about Dawn?"

"Yes, it is."

"Have they recovered her body?"

"Mrs. Price has been recovered," Dreyfuss said, and corrected his blunder hastily. "That is, *not* her body. . . . She herself has been recovered—no, not recovered, but rescued."

"Get on with it, man," Dennis said irritably. "What do you mean, rescued?"

"Just that, sir. Your wife is not dead, as was erroneously reported. She is very much alive. In fact, she has been living here with Mrs. Dreyfuss and myself at the consulate for some time now."

Dennis turned ashen and clutched at the side of the surrey for support. Sara wore the blank expression of a mannequin. The startling declaration was beyond her comprehension. To accept that Dawn was alive was unthinkable; it threatened to undermine the very cornerstone of her existence.

"That's impossible," Dennis said in a hoarse whisper. "I don't believe it."

"Come inside and see for yourself. Both Dawn and I decided it was better if I broke the news to you first."

Like sleepwalkers, Dennis and Sara got down from the surrey and followed the consul up the steps and into the house. The confrontation took place in the study. Face to face at last: Dennis and Sara and Dawn and Jack. There was a long awkward silence before Dawn took the initiative. She walked forward and stood before Dennis.

"Dennis . . . I realize what a shock this is to you."

"Dawn . . . shock is an understatement. It's like seeing a ghost." He made the noble gesture. "Dawn, I can't tell you how marvelous it is to see you alive and well." Mechanically he lifted his arms and embraced her. They touched cheeks, but did not kiss.

"Dennis, Dennis, this is as bewildering to me as it

is to you. So much has happened." She looked at Sara Teasdale.

"Yes, indeed it has." He coughed nervously. "Dawn, this is Sara Teasdale, my—" There was no way to describe the woman who, until they had entered this room, had been his wife.

Dawn disengaged herself from Dennis and approached Sara, who involuntarily backed away from Dawn, wearing the expression of a frightened doe at bay.

"Sara," Dawn said gently. "It's all right. I know this is as much of a trial to you as it is to me and Dennis. Perhaps even more of an ordeal for you, dear." She smiled reassuringly and held out her hand in a symbol of friendship.

Gingerly, Sara accepted the overture and touched her fingers to Dawn's. Her voice was soft, almost childlike. "You mustn't think that I am distressed because you are alive. Quite the contrary. When I first met Dennis, he was obsessed with worry for you. He talked about you constantly. I came to know you even though we had never met, and I came to share his grief. What a joyous occasion this could have been if only . . ." She could not complete the sentence, but Dawn comprehended her meaning.

"We are all victims of fickle destiny, Sara," Dawn said consolingly. "I bear no ill will toward you for marrying Dennis. You thought I was dead. You had every right to do what you did, you and Dennis, to start a new life together." Her smile was rueful. "It's funny, I'm beginning to feel like the guilty party, ruining everything for you like this."

Dreyfuss intervened. "I believe Mae and I will withdraw and let you two work things out between you."

"Yes, the two of us, Dawn and I," Dennis said. He

looked at Sara and Jack. "Would you mind leaving Dawn and me alone for a while, Sara . . . Jack. It would be easier with just the two of us."

"By all means," Sara agreed, and Jack added his consent. They and the Dreyfusses left the room.

Dawn walked to a serving cabinet against one wall. "Would you care for a drink?"

"I could use one very badly, thank you."

She poured two scotches and added carbonated water from a siphon bottle. She served Dennis, and he fingered his highball glass nervously before speaking.

"I'd like to propose a toast, Dawn." He lifted the glass. "To your safe return to the world of the living. And I mean it sincerely. Those of us who love you"— he paused, and their eyes met—"yes, it's true, Dawn. I have never stopped loving you."

She placed a hand on his arm. "I know, Dennis. Just as I have never stopped loving you, but when you accepted that I was gone forever, you transferred a very special and complex emotion to Sara. I'm saying this badly, Dennis. Look, neither of us is naive enough to believe that adolescent fantasy that there is one and only one man and woman made just for each other. There are scores of women in this world to whom you could be happily married. And the same goes for me. You and I, we happened to come together at the right time and the right place, when we were both ripe for mating."

"I suppose you're right, darling."

The endearment twisted a knife in her heart. "You mustn't call me that any longer, Dennis. Sara is the one now."

"Must you be so damned civilized?" he said impatiently. "Dawn, no matter how you rationalize it, we're all mired in a nasty mess, you and I and poor Sara. I am still legally married and bound to you."

"I'll give you a divorce and you can marry Sara and make her your official wife this time."

"You'd do that for me?"

She regarded him steadily. "I'm not being all that altruistic, Dennis. Since we've been apart, my life has altered too."

Intuitively he grasped it. "Do you mean what I think you mean? You and Jack McHugh?"

"That's right," she admitted candidly. "Jack and I have been having an affair. When you and I were together, I would have cut off my arm rather than be unfaithful to you."

"And I to you."

"Then our life together was disrupted by a cataclysmic upheaval. We have emerged from that harrowing experience two different people. Dennis, you will always occupy a very special place in my heart, but the truth is, I don't want to give up Jack and try to resume where we left off. Be honest, Dennis. Do you want to give up Sara?"

He hung his head and shook it slowly. "No, I love her too dearly now."

"And I feel the same way about Jack. So there is only one reasonable and civilized thing to do. I will return to the States with Jack and file a petition for divorce as soon as I can."

He came to her and clasped her arms. Tenderly he bent and kissed her cheek. "You are a very special woman, darl—I mean, my dear. That's acceptable, isn't it?"

She smiled. "My dear . . . yes, I hope I will always

remain dear to you. Now, let's speak with Jack and Sara and tell them our plans."

Both Sara and Jack accepted Dawn and Dennis's decision in a reserved fashion; neither of them wanted to sully the delicate moment by displaying outright joy.

"Mr. Dreyfuss, when does the next ship bound for the United States sail from Canton?" Dawn asked the consul.

"Let me see, there's a clipper putting to sea next Monday. Do you want to book passage on her?"

"By all means." Dawn took Jack's arm possessively and said to Sara and Dennis, "Come along, you newly-weds, Jack and I will show you the consul's beautiful gardens."

As they were leaving the house, Mae Dreyfuss put a question to Dennis. "Will you be staying with us, Mr. Price, or aboard your ship?" Her manner was most agitated.

"Well, our ship will be in port for two more days. What do you think, Sara? The accommodations aboard ship are rather cramped."

"We'd be delighted to accept your hospitality, Mrs. Dreyfuss," Sara told the older woman.

Mae's face was beet red, and she twisted her lace handkerchief in her fingers. It took all of her courage to muster the nerve to ask, "Will you be wanting separate rooms now that you're not—"

"Mae!" Dreyfuss exclaimed, shocked and embarrassed at the indiscretion.

The four young people thought it was highly amusing and could not stifle their laughter. When she could speak, Dawn went to the poor, dismayed woman and hugged her.

"Dear Mrs. Dreyfuss, you are truly precious. I can

appreciate that this may come as an affront to your tender sensibilities, but there's no sense locking the barn door after the horse has been stolen. And believe me, dear, in this instance the horse has most definitely been stolen."

"Yes, Mrs. Dreyfuss," Dennis said solemnly. "If it will not distress you too much, Sara and I will continue to share the same bedroom. Thank you for your consideration."

Arm in arm, the four of them went striding jauntily out onto the terrace and into the gardens.

# CHAPTER SEVEN

*Dear Dennis and Sara:*
    *Your letter was received with much joy and some sadness as well, because Jack and I could not be present for the christening of your new son. Our heartiest congratulations to you, and all of our love as well. Jack says he's sure you're thrilled that you finally got the boy you wanted so badly after two wonderful girls. My father, God rest his soul, never did have the son he wanted, but just before he passed on he told me that, in retrospect, he would not have traded me for ten sons. It was comforting to hear. In case you have lost track, our son, Peter, is ten years old, and he's well on his way to becoming another Bull of the Woods. He works with the high riggers and can limb and buck with the best of the redshirts. And the scarf of his undercut is almost as smooth as his father's.*

It's a pity that such skills are no longer essential in the modern logging industry. As my father and Jack predicted long ago, the day of the redshirt and river hog is in its twilight and fading fast. The slide rule, the gasoline engine-powered saw, and the turbine have truly revolutionized the industry.

And they have brought a new breed of man into the swamp. His face is clean-shaven. After the working day, he bathes and changes into store-bought suits, wears a white shirt, and has his trousers pressed by the camp tailor. The bunkhouse has been replaced by neat frame cottages with picket fences, lawns, and sidewalks, where he lives with his wife and family. He can't roll a cigarette to save his life. And when he goes to church on Sunday, he cannot be distinguished from the local banker, storekeeper, or schoolteacher. In the swamp, the whinny of the horse and the mule has been replaced by the roar of the tractor, and the rhythmic chunk of the ax is rapidly being supplanted by the whine of the buzz saw. And birling is a disappearing art, although Jack insists that any man he hires must acquire a degree of proficiency at the sport.

Speaking of birling, I must tell you of a memorable experience that took place when Jack and I went East to attend the wedding of my sister Lucille to John Eastwick III, a member of the Harriman clan. It was a lavish ceremony attended by almost all of the Hudson River aristocrats. The reception was held in the grand ballroom of the Plaza Hotel. Later in the afternoon, the groom's parents took Jack and me on a tour of

*New York City, the highlight of which was a carriage ride through Central Park, a unique expanse of rustic wilderness in the midst of all the ugly concrete and steel that comprises the nation's largest city. In the inner recesses of the park one might almost be back in the Michigan woods. In any case, Central Park was the scene of a most unusual adventure. The four of us were still clad in the formal attire of the wedding, Mary Eastwick and I in our ballroom gowns and Jack and John Eastwick, Jr., looking swank in their swallow-tailed coats, striped morning trousers, and high silk hats. Our carriage was circling the park's picturesque pond when we chanced upon a group of picnickers who . . .*

Jack grasped Dawn's arm and said in an excited voice. "Am I hallucinating or do you see what I see out there on the pond?"

Dawn's eyes widened in astonishment at the sight of two men balanced on either end of a floating log. They wore red shirts, work trousers, and hobnailed boots, and there was no doubt at all about what they were doing.

"Birling in Central Park, in the heart of New York City!" she exclaimed. "I don't believe it!"

The Eastwicks were mystified. "Whatever on earth is birling?" asked John Eastwick.

"That's birling!" Jack exulted as one of the men went flying off the spinning log into the drink. "An ancient custom of the lumberjacks going back as far as anyone can remember. The object is for one birler to upset his opponent. Driver, will you please stop here for a while? I want to find out what this is all about." When the carriage stopped, he leaped out and approached a group of the revelers.

"Excuse me," he asked a stout fellow wearing the shirt and boots that were the loggers' trademark. "Where are you people from?"

The man eyed Jack in his fancy clothes with distrust. "We're from Maine. Having a convention for Maine loggers here in New York," he replied in a Down Eastern twang.

Jack held out his hand. "It's a pleasure to meet you. Makes me feel more at home. I'm Jack McHugh, from Saginaw, Michigan. Do a bit of logging myself."

The other members of the group gathered around, appraising Jack's clothes and his clean, manicured fingernails. "Sure, we can see that!" someone said with sarcasm, and the other men laughed.

Jack joined in the laughter. "Hey, I don't look like this all the time. Just came from a wedding."

The beefy man nudged the man beside him. "So, you're a logging man, eh? Ever do any birling?"

"Are you kidding? You mean to say you never heard of Silver Jack McHugh up in Maine?"

The boast evoked more hilarious laughter. "Silver Jack McHugh, is that what you call yourself?" another logger said.

Jack's keen ears detected a murmured aside from the rear of the group. "He must be stewed from all the bubbly water they serve at them fancy weddings."

Now here was a challenge that could not be ignored. The smile vanished from Jack's face. "I sure would appreciate it if you gentlemen would do me the honor of birling with me."

Catcalls and whistles filled the summer air.

"He's not only drunk, he's crazy!"

"Hey, mister, the fun and games is over. Now go back to your fancy friends."

"No, wait a minute. Let's give the dude a chance to prove himself."

"Yeah, what the hell. Every circus has to have at least one clown."

"All right, Mr. McHugh," the beefy man conceded. "It's your funeral. You aim to birl in them duds?"

Jack winked. "Don't see why not. I don't have any intention of getting wet."

"Ya-hoo!" An old man began to jump up and down, slapping his hands against his thighs. "We got us a live one, boys!"

"I'll have to borrow a pair of boots, though." He lifted one of his patent-leather shoes. "These aren't exactly made for birling."

"No more than you are, mister. Okay, Sam, your dogs are about the same size as his. Give the man your boots."

Grumbling, a big redhead, almost as big as Jack, unlaced his boots and removed them. Jack carried them back to the carriage, where Mr. and Mrs. Eastwick, no less flabbergasted than the picnickers by Jack's erratic behavior, gaped at him in wonder.

Jack grinned and removed his high hat and swallow-tailed wedding coat. "This shouldn't take too long," he assured them as he rolled up the sleeves of his ruffled dress shirt and took off his bow tie. He sat down on the step of the carriage and slipped off his shoes, replacing them with the heavy, steel-caulked loggers' boots.

"What on earth are you going to do, Mr. McHugh?" asked John Eastwick.

"Going to give these Maine lads a lesson in Michigan birling."

The Eastwicks looked at each other in consternation. "Has he had too much to drink, do you think?" Mrs. Eastwick whispered to Dawn.

Dawn laughed heartily. "Maybe a little, but that's not what put him up to this. My husband still has a streak of Peck's bad boy in his nature, and you know something? I wouldn't change him one iota. Come along and watch the fun close up." She hiked up her long skirt and hopped out of the carriage. Thoroughly befuddled, the Eastwicks followed her and Jack down to the water's edge.

The Maine lumberjacks lost some of their cockiness when they saw Jack without his coat and with his sleeves rolled up—the way his shirt spanned his thick bull chest when he moved, the girth of his forearms and biceps.

"He just might be a logger at that," one commented.

"All right, who's about to take me on?" Jack issued a challenge. "Put up your best man."

"That would be Tug Fisher," the beefy man he had first addressed said. "Get over here, Tug."

Tug Fisher reminded Jack of Pig. He was shorter than Jack, with a flat face and steel-wool hair, powerful through the shoulders and chest.

"Pleased to meet you, Tug," Jack said, offering his hand. Tug flashed a snaggle-toothed smile and extended his own enormous paw. Jack sensed that Tug's aim was to apply a bone crusher, and he was ready for him. Tug strained until the veins stood out in his temples, but the smile never left Jack's face.

"Come on, get on with it," several men urged. "We ain't got all day. There's a cold barrel of beer waiting for us over at the ball field."

Jack and Tug were carried out to the floating log in

a rowboat, Jack studied the log; it was a fast-rolling pine job about two feet in diameter. He and Tug took their places at either end of the log and waited for the referee's signal.

"Now *birl!*" came the command.

It had been a long time since Jack had done any birling, so he let his adversary take the initiative. Tug started spinning the log, jogging slowly at first and building up speed until his moving feet were a blur. Jack kept up with him easily, with his thumbs hooked under his suspender straps.

The Maine men gave credit where credit was due:

"Not bad for a New York dandy."

"He wasn't lying. He's been on a log before, that's for sure."

When Tug braked the log abruptly to a dead stop with his spikes and Jack hung on effortlessly, a cheer went up.

"You done bit off a large hunk of trouble, Tug!" someone shouted. "He's a human fly!"

Scowling and fighting hard to keep his temper under control, Tug Fisher began to jump up and down on the log, pounding it with all of his weight so that it rode up and down like a seagoing seesaw. Knees flexing loosely, Jack rode out the storm with bland unconcern. Puffing like a steam engine, Tug abandoned that strategy.

"You about finished, son?" Jack called to him.

"Like hell!" Tug jammed his cleats into the log on either side, feet spread apart, and commenced pumping as if he were riding a bicycle—left, right, left, right. The log lurched violently from side to side. It was one of the most effective tactics in birling, and it required all of Jack's river savvy to weather the storm.

The Maine men were shouting encouragement to their gladiator, clapping and cheering.

"Gotta give the dandy credit, Tug!" one of them yelled.

Tug gnashed his teeth and redoubled his efforts. He was sure he had his opponent close to defeat, and it kindled within him a fatal degree of overconfidence. When, without warning, Jack made his move, poor Tug was totally unprepared.

As Tug slammed his right foot down hard and sent the log rolling in that direction, Jack brought down his left boot simultaneously, adding momentum to the roll. Tug went flying into the lake with a loud splash. When he surfaced, he was greeted by the boos and jeers of those he had let down.

Jack hopped lightly into the nearby rowboat and stood in the bow wringing his hands over his head in a symbol of victory. When he stepped ashore, he was mobbed by the Maine loggers, gracious and good-natured in defeat.

"Never forget this day long as I live."

"Imagine, Tug gettin' whupped by a city slicker!"

"Wait until the rest of the gang back in Maine hears about it!"

"They won't believe us!"

Jack shook many hands and started back to the waiting carriage, with Dawn hanging proudly onto his arm. Bringing up the rear were the Eastwicks, stupefied by the wild contest they had just witnessed.

"Are you very wet?" Dawn asked.

"Scarcely a drop got on me." He put on his coat and tie and hat and shoes. A young boy came over to retrieve the logging boots. Then the Eastwicks and the McHughs got back into the carriage and the ride resumed.

Later that night, lying in bed in their hotel suite, Jack observed, "You know something, darling, what happened today taught me a lesson."

"What's that?"

"The board of directors has been pushing to transfer our main office to New York City, and I've been giving serious consideration to the suggestion. After all, it's the business hub of the world. Besides, I thought it might be an advantage for young Peter and Lucy to be reared in a cosmopolitan environment rather than in the sticks, as we were. I even discussed it with John Eastwick. His company has a new building under construction."

Dawn propped herself up in bed on an elbow and looked at him curiously. "How did today change your mind?"

"Because I realized that today was probably the first and last time that New York City will ever be the site of a birling match. Living here, we'd be giving up a very important part of our lives—the smell of the cook fire before dawn wafting in the bedroom window, the music of the gut hammer and the cookie shouting: 'Beans are on the table; daylight's in the swamp. You lazy lumberjacks, ain't you ever gettin' up?' Listening to the thunder of the spring drive. Hell! Those Maine boys called me a dandy today. If we were to live in New York, it wouldn't be too long before I'd become one. I don't want that for me, and I don't want it for my son. I was born a woodsman and I'll die one. What do you think?"

Dawn bent over and kissed him. "I think you are my most favorite feller in the whole world. And now

I'd like a little demonstration of the prowess that earned you the sobriquet Bull of the Woods."

"Sobriquet? Damn! As many words as I learn, you always come up with another to stump me. As for the bull part, here's how it goes." He took her in his arms and kissed her; meanwhile his hands worked the nightgown down over her shoulders, baring her breasts. She clasped her hands behind his head and pulled his face down into her cleavage.

*"All this and heaven too,"* she thought as her desire soared.

> *. . . And so, Sara and Dennis, here we are back in the swamp where we belong, living the good life. Mechanization and the new industrial revolution have changed the lumberjacks, but they haven't changed us. As Jack says, you can take the boy out of the woods, but you can't take the woods out of the boy. The hobnailed boots no longer swing from the tree limbs along the banks of the Saginaw after the spring drive, but there are old-timers who claim that on certain nights, when the full moon is bright on the river and the freshet is running wild, you can see the ghosts of the river hogs who gave their lives to bring the logs downriver riding the milltail as they did in the old days. And now I must end this missive, dear Dennis and Sara. Love to all of yours from all of ours.*
>
> > *Affectionately,*
> > *Dawn*

As she sealed the envelope, Jack and Peter came back from the compound and stopped to look in on Lucy, who was practicing the piano in the music room.

"What's that you're playing, darling?"

"Mozart. Do you like it, Daddy?"

"It's very nice, but Pete here and I lean more to less fancy music. Right, Son?"

"Right, Dad. What do you say, Luce?"

Dawn smiled as her daughter switched without a pause from Mozart to honky-tonk every bit as down and dirty as could be heard in a Saginaw saloon, and her voice, clear as a bell, belted out her father's favorite song:

> *"I see that you're a logger,*
> *And not just a common bum,*
> *Because nobody but a logger*
> *Stirs coffee with his thumb."*